$1.00

BY TADEUSZ KONWICKI

A *Dreambook for Our Time*
Anthropos–Specter–Beast
The Polish Complex
A Minor Apocalypse
Moonrise, Moonset

MOONRISE,

MOONSET

TADEUSZ KONWICKI

TRANSLATED BY RICHARD LOURIE

MOONRISE, MOONSET

FARRAR·STRAUS·GIROUX·NEW YORK

MOONRISE, MOONSET

1

I am being rejected. I am being rejected from literature. With the force of a jet engine I am being ejected from fiction. To maintain your prestige you must produce a novel every so often. It's high time I stammered out another work of prose. But I can't. But I can't.

My vicious memory obligingly reminds me of the book I wrote seven years ago. Seven years already. Something like a diary, a pseudo-memoir, autobiographical apocrypha. A real-life novel but in fact a novella—a stretch of life in calendar time. To wit, my book *The Calendar and the Hourglass*. A pleasure to write, easy, not forced labor. Not a matter of ambition. In judging prose, critics and authors place a higher value on what comes from the head—meaning, out of nothing—than on what comes from life, the biography. And so it's a serious dilemma. Write easily and without ambition, or labor away but hitting the high notes.

Easy is better, better to catch it on the wing, better the garbage of life. Or rather, the novel as a chunk of life. Let's pretend that I am a well-written hero in a novel and that in 1981 I'm experiencing an avalanche of extraordinary adventures, a cascade of amazing conflicts and a few, not too many, a few major catastrophes in my love life.

. . .

Back then I had impregnated my colleagues. *The Calendar and the Hourglass* was followed by an outpouring of calendars and diaries. Someone might well have asked: Writing diaries, that's supposed to be something new? It's true, there's nothing new about writing diaries. But diaries that are filled with the terrible longueurs of an entire life are one thing, and a literary work in the form of a journal is something else again. It's one thing to drum out the weeks and months as they go by, and something else to create a year from juicy life and unfettered fantasy. And so, all the same, I did invent something. It might not have been on a European scale, or even a national one, but still I did invent a little something.

I also know it's bad to brag. Especially just as I'm beginning this strenuous marathon. But, you'll pardon me, I can put an evil eye on this simplified plan of mine. And so let this be the simplified made difficult.

And now suddenly I feel an urge to burst into song. With the help of adjectives, pronouns, and periods, with the help of epic material, to burst into song without a moment's notice, to draw the reader by his ear toward heaven, which shall figure often in this my own personal patented 1981.

Perhaps I'm mistaken but I hear certain seductive remnants of melody and graceful scraps of rhythm in the limping tap of my prose. Maybe in the years I wasn't writing, part of my brain turned into a portable musical instrument. Perhaps there's an ocarina, or at least a whistle, in my head accompanying me as I make my way through the world.

It's shameful to say this, but for a while I've been suffering from the writer's professional disease without being a professional writer. And so I panic and seize on all sorts of projects so as not to go out of circulation. I've started on various books more than once, I've sketched out films that struck even me as bizarre. But I've known the hysteria of impotence for a long time now. I've observed it in others and could divine it in my own masochistic inclinations.

I know I'm still not getting on with it, that I'm wasting time on the digressions, which I am using to fuel the vehicle of my prose. But, you'll excuse me, I have to warm up, stretch my muscles, get the rhythm if I'm going to go the whole distance. And worse, I have to hear myself, recollect the sound of my inner tuning fork, which will lead me on in this new adventure.

I still can't hear it. I'm groping in the dark. I don't know when it will happen. Maybe on the next page or maybe only on page 44. I mention precisely that page to help advertise my fellow Lithuanian from outside Nowogrodek. *

---

* Adam Mickiewicz (1798–1855), Poland's national poet. Author of Pan Tadeusz, a novel in verse, whose place in Polish literature is comparable to that of Pushkin's Eugene Onegin in Russian literature [Trans.].

2

1981. I look at that date with the eyes of a man from the unknown future. What will that date mean, bring to mind; what psychological aura will it pass on to posterity? 1980 and 1981, years of yet another uprising. A Polish invention—bloodless uprisings. Or rather, nearly bloodless. Psychological uprisings. Insurrections in the realm of consciousness. Revolts in the nerve paths of libido. 1956, 1968, 1970, 1976, and 1980.

Did we win or did we lose? No one knows. Neither Brezhnev nor the Pope. I say to someone: "I held your place in the line for pianos." And in reality a line had formed in front of the music store on Aleje Ujazdowskie because an enormous trailer truck had arrived with Calisia uprights and grand pianos. A half hour before this I had seen a long line in front of the Soviet store Natasha. Why were the descendants of Hetman Zolkiewski and General Dowbor-Musnicki standing in front of that lousy store on a freezing cold day? Perhaps some Soviet gold rings had been "thrown" on the market. In despair I invented a few cheap gags in my books, cheap gags which my fellow countrymen have put into practice with sullen obstinacy. A year ago my films were shown at the Health Theater in Warsaw, whose marquee advertised *Lenin in Warsaw*. Today *Workers '80*, a documentary film made in August of last year, is showing at a few theaters whose marquees read PRIVATE SCREENING. In my novel A *Minor Apoc-alypse* I had joked that the Volga Theater, formerly the Escarpment Theater, was showing a Polish film of moral anxiety, *Transfusion*, while the marquee advertised a Soviet musical comedy, *The Radiant Future*.

Food stores with vinegar and fermented compote, clothing stores with clothes for cripples, shoe stores without shoes, appliance stores plastered with messages and appeals from citizens' queue committees offering to purchase vacuum cleaners or refrigerators by the subscription or lottery system. On one store's door there is a sign: STAFF CLOSED DUE TO ILLNESS OF STORE.

A few hundred, or perhaps a few thousand, copies of the newspaper *Solidarity*. But they exist, they fall each day from the sky instead of snow this snowless winter. They write about everything that had not been written about for thirty-five years. They write about things people were afraid to think during the sleepless nights of the last four decades.

Our beloved Party, the Party which fought against God, who had drawn its admirers away, the Party which had combated destiny as an arrogant rival, the Party which had begun to think that it created the universe at one of its plenums—our fussy, pampered, self-adoring Party had fallen face-first in the mud and for six months now has been weltering in humiliation, utter ruin, total collapse. And it is not the vultures of imperialism that drag and tear at the Party's body but the infuriated Party rank and file, proletarians, representatives of the people. And, torn to pieces, kicked around, violated, the Party only squeals softly about its leading role.

In a few weeks' time, Polish society divided into two biological substances. The great mass of the nation and a minute bacterial strain of a foreign agency. Some twenty-odd thousand of those foreign agents are attempting to rule a nation of thirty-six million people. It's a bit reminiscent of the mouse who tried to copulate with an elephant.

.   .   .

The Lord God had begun to look kindly on the Poles. No one knows why all of a sudden at the end of the twentieth century my countrymen were dealt that card.

Even that winter, the winter of 1980–81, seemed to tiptoe delicately in, with no hostility or brutal pranks. Weakened, the regime would have gladly frozen the impudent Poles, and, here and there, was even holding back coal deliveries to the heat and power plants, but Providence was watching over us and did not allow the mercury to fall below zero. That winter I might have worn my old sheepskin coat from Sokolow Podlaski two or three times, that sheepskin that was the precursor of today's Eastern European fashion.

A few snow flurries, a few warm breezes from the hard-currency countries, a bit of mist and drizzle, and we're on our way toward spring. People suffer breakdowns and sudden anxiety attacks by night, but life goes on one way or the other by day. From one line to another. A quarter kilo of butter here, a kilo of flour there, and elsewhere two meters of lining material and other "inside stuff."

And all this attends, cooperates, and rhymes with my own fate. Last year an operation for throat cancer, a little of everything this year, ten different diseases. I could say they're from getting old but no, no such luck. This isn't old age. That's just starting. For now at least, these are punishments for my sins. But what sins? Who did the sinning, and when? Me? Us? Them? Everyone. We all have sinned, are sinning, or will sin.

I fall asleep at midnight and sleep for two or three hours. Then I lie in bed, dozing off from time to time, staunching some viscous inner pain—bad presentiments, bad experiences, bad angers. Something is eating away at me. But it's got a long way to go. And there's no consolation.

Our unstrung building buzzes with its night buzz. The building where I've been living twenty-five years, a quarter of a century. A building with cracked windows, broken locks, crumbling pipes. A person should rejoice in every hour, in the gift of each day. Who said that? Some ass. Some satisfied ass or philosopher.

You must get out of bed and rejoice in life.

It's a strange thing. Never before had society obtained so much under this system. But no cries of joy, no glimmer of enthusiasm, no moments of euphoria. Why is that, and what does it mean?

Six months of extorting the basic democratic freedoms, or at least their ersatz equivalents, from the regime, in an atmosphere of pessimism, melancholy, touching wood in superstition, a lack of faith, gloom.

And the Party's in the dumps too, very bitter, slightly masochistic. Muttering sternly, it reveals that it stole, appropriated, usurped.

The collaborators' behavior makes no sense. In the past, when the regime was in crisis, they always threw themselves into the arms of the opposition, desperately seeking alibis. They renounced their past, beat their breasts, promised to change. Many of them elbowed their way to the front of the Renewal procession.

But not this time. This year they turned arrogant. But not all at once. First they came rushing to the presiding officers of Solidarity, and had just opened their mouths to shout something against the regime when suddenly their mouths closed and they slipped away from the den of revolt. A few weeks later and there they are sneering at Solidarity, ten million strong. They jeer at society's aspiration to self-rule. And they provoke the awakened nation with sacrilege.

What happened, why aren't they trembling in their boots the way they always trembled in similar situations before? What do they know that we don't? What do they see looking over our heads that we don't see?

We visited Marysia, my older daughter, in October of last year. Faithful to ancient ritual, we visited her in distant, legendary America. With bundles and bags, packed in a jumbo jet as if in steerage, we crossed the great water, the Atlantic. I assumed the demeanor of a worthy old man dispatched by some higher order on this ritual pilgrimage. With the dignity of a simple man I crouched on a plastic seat in the belly of a flying whale. It is easy for me to attain that sense of inward simplicity when I am flying to a country whose language I have not mastered as well as I should.

How quickly the last trip vanished in memory. The two preceding American peregrinations are inscribed in my memory. And no doubt they have played some role in my mind's electrochemical processes. They certainly gave it something, and took something else away. Those two trips formed entire archipelagoes of anecdotes, stories, bon mots. Like true works of art those trips had elegant form and vivid colors. But the last one—nothing. Like a passing moment. Like a road through a plowed field. Like an intention unfulfilled.

But that was a good trip. Maybe even the best of them. We spent five weeks of family vacation with Marysia in the very heart of Manhattan. Long walks up or down the island, a lot of television-watching on edge, a little reading in Russian, and the nights with their stealthy advance of fears, a new batch of which I acquired in the hospital during my two, actually three, operations. Those fears would come to me toward daybreak, when I'd begun to suffocate from the lack of air. In laborious convulsions, I would gasp for air until morning, until breakfast, even though I was perfectly well aware that this was usually hysteria, because now, after the operation, my windpipe is much larger than a normal mortal's.

The small bedroom where I resided had a large window, like a painting by an unknown Swiss artist from the end of the nineteenth century. At the bottom of this painting in its unadorned white frame was a mass of plane trees, gray, gone slightly gray, and from that fading greenery, as from an undergrowth of dwarf mountain pine, the Alps' skyscraper peaks shot upward, and in the midst of them was the great, majestic, sun-struck mass of Mont Blanc. All this was set against an intense, banal-and-proud-of-it, light-blue sky at the end of Indian summer.

Of course, this alpine landscape was formed of skyscrapers, the largest of which, bone-white, touched the vault of the sky and was suffused with dense autumn sunlight. Among the plane trees a type of nut I didn't recognize shone red, while from the sides of the frame shrill white clouds would enter from time to time and affix themselves to the peak of Mont Blanc; a few times, in the alpine valley passes, the letters of advertising slogans would erupt from the blue of the sky, trailing from planes, to swell and then dissolve.

I grew attached to that picture; it was my own, personal, super-realist landscape unseen by anyone else. That colorful picture actually still exists to this day and is easy to recall when I close my eyes. Who knows, it might be the most valuable trophy I ever brought back from a distant journey.

But that's not what I started to say. I had intended to speak of Poland, ours, mine, yours, which was reflected in short bursts of tragic light here in strange, ancient-modern-nouveau-riche America. Maybe that light isn't tragic, but at least it's somber, very dark. And in anthill New York, Poland has blossomed luxuriantly out of those brief, inanimate flashes of unhealthy light. Poland at every step, popping up everywhere, and speaking cautiously, one might say that Poland has run rampant. For the first time in this century we have crossed a certain essential boundary: intelligent attention paid to a cause, a problem, has begun to turn into sympathy for a certain geographic area and for a certain people.

For the first time in this century we have ceased to irritate the all-too-wise Western powers with our presence, our very existence. For the first time it turns out that our life is the origin of their life, our fate the basis of theirs.

I've skipped ahead a bit. Things may be that good at some future date. But at least they've stopped pretending not to understand us. They've stopped dismissing us. Stopped shrugging their shoulders with impatience. They've stopped changing the subject. Their little love affair with the Russians is over. I'm overdoing it again. Maybe the affair isn't over, but at least they've stopped thinking about having a child.

It surprises everyone, us included: under one and the same system the Czechs live so-so, the East Germans not bad, the

Hungarians are almost affluent, and the Poles have hit bottom. For example, in Prague the shelves in the butcher shops buckle with meat, while in Warsaw the cupboard is bare. In East Germany the trains are three-quarters of an hour late, here, six hours; in Hungary you wait ten years for an apartment, here you wait your whole life.

The explanation that comes immediately to mind is that Poles have no head for economics, are undisciplined and chaotic. But here I would modestly like to point out that before the war those same Poles produced excellent sewing machines, first-rate bicycles; Gerlach manufactured splendid iron goods, we made the longest-lasting cars in Europe—the Fiat Polski—renowned wool cloth, and the best airplanes in their class. No one in Poland chased after imported goods, which is to say, I am not very convinced by the notion that we lack economic sense, though it is hallowed by long tradition. Somehow I think that there's something else at work here.

The Poles are the most seasoned slaves in Europe. For two hundred years now they've had to contend with a great variety of invasions, partitions, occupations. Perhaps the nation's body has already reached a critical threshold and can no longer bear any further deprivation of its freedom. Certain animals cannot live in zoos. They cannot be kept in captivity. Perhaps our unconscious alarm systems for self-protection and self-regulation are commanding us to commit political and economic suicide. Poles do not want to live under these social and political conditions. Like whales, the Poles are beaching themselves on the shore of nonexistence. The Poles are committing collective self-immolation.

Or perhaps it is our destiny to destroy Communism. Perhaps this terrible variation of totalitarianism has to perish at the hands of these unruly veterans of slavery. The Poles are not trying to tame the monster, to paint a human face on it, to humanize the furious beast. The Poles want to blow it up along with themselves. Or drag it to the bottom like a millstone.

.   .   .

A café politician. I am a café politician. Professional politicians nod with pity. They know better, they know everything. They can see ahead. Politics is the gift of foresight.

The gift of foresight? All the gallows in the world groan with the weight of politicians who boasted of their foresight. All the government old-age homes are packed with farsighted political men. All of history is nothing but the lack of foresight.

It's only us amateurs, us café connoisseurs, who are able to understand and foresee. Because we issue our prophecies disinterestedly, in a miraculous state of naïve grace, like poets.

And that's why you should listen to me. Take off your hats grimy from constant, obsequious doffing, and listen to my feverish delirium, which contains an infinitude of accurate diagnoses and wonder-working prescriptions.

My blood boils when I recall a certain professor. He had read my book A *Minor Apocalypse* and said: "You see our entire nation as one big dung heap. Well, maybe it is."

Gray-haired, dignified, he had studied everything, knew everything. He is a scholar. What a lovely, delicious sound it has when they say it—I am a scholar. Their erudition is the height, the Himalayas of conceit. They are more conceited than certain writers, perhaps even more than certain actresses.

He is a scholar but he does not see what's right there on the page or why it's there. He does not even see me, shy and bow-legged, as I sidle onto the pyre with my hero. He does not understand that if I thought nothing of this nation, I wouldn't have struggled as best I could decade after decade for that nation. He doesn't grasp that I am a little sick of that nation.

Of course, one could also remark that this professor, though he has certainly read ten thousand books, knows nothing about literature, its laws, duties, customs, aesthetics, experience, perversities, psychology, perceptions, its sinfulness and holiness, its greatness and pettiness, its mysteries, which every lonely old lady, every clerk with a grievance, and every sensitive, pimply high-school student is able to imagine.

As bad luck would have it, this century's philosophers were high-school teachers, educators of the young. And that led to— Boy Scout campfires, campouts, sheaves of sparks, the rustle of the forest, serene nights, and long talks. What is happiness? What is love? What is patriotism?

3

I was a different man thirty years ago. An entirely different person. I was a complete stranger to the person I am today, the person, or, if you will, the prey I am now.

What I'm saying here is not mere fashionable talk, I'm not musing on the passage of time or admiring evolution. I am talking about two totally different people—Konwicki in 1950 and Konwicki in 1981. The dates are, of course, arbitrary.

Last year, just before spring, I struck on the none-too-ingenious idea of getting an old novel, written in 1948 or 1949, out of my desk, a book never published and, with the possible exception of the censor, never read, and to weave a contemporary plot or commentary into that novel, thereby producing a layer cake of sorts, an essay with layers of plot. I dragged out the bluish corpse from the cobwebs, blue because that was the color of its cardboard folder. But its very title, in ink now faded, made me die a little. For that title, remaining unchanged in its cursed keeping place, was—*The New Days*. *The New Days*, an odoriferous turn of phrase. It stinks of dead bodies, reeks of cesspools, poison, venom.

I traveled outside Warsaw where no one could see me and I began to read it alone. Not because the book is stupid and untruthful. It's just that the person who put it on paper is a complete stranger to me, and has no meaning for me. Patiently I sought signs of our having something in common, some symbol of our mental and biological unity, some family traits, some shared identity. Unfortunately, from those yellow pages there stared some guy for whom I cared nothing and to whom I was bound by neither casual affection nor even ordinary human solidarity.

But for a long time now I've been experiencing this sort of startling encounter with this complete stranger, this oddly alien person who bore my name, looked like me, had the same shoe size, even lived in the same houses I had, and, if that weren't enough, had been in love with the same girls I had.

I encountered that ill-fated Konwicki only through other people, people we knew in common. We were unable to encounter each other in any written text because I had never before looked into any book marked with our name. And thus our confrontations came through people who had known him at one point and who now associated with me. They say: Do you remember saying this or doing that? And I listen, astonished, to some nonsense about a person with a completely different psychology, sense of humor, and perhaps even morality. I don't know how to put it, I can't describe it, but believe me—I beseech you, believe me— that was another person. And it's not a question of my not wishing to take responsibility for him, not at all; I can take the responsibility for all of you. The point is that he frightens me. My life is made up of two Konwickis. And I no longer know where one ends and the other begins. And I no longer know which one was good and which bad. And I no longer know which one I'd like to be now.

Listen, listen, we used to run into each other in the past and we still do every so often. I haven't changed, I'm not one iota different. It's just that I'm someone else.

My cat Ivan, who graced *The Calendar and the Hourglass* with his presence, is sitting on the windowsill and looking out at Gorska Street, which is packed with cars. He looks out at the hopeless traffic of tin cans that poison us with exhaust, he looks and says nothing. Only his ears revolve, each on its own axis, when he hears our voices from the depths of the apartment.

"Vanya," I say. "Vanya, there's nothing to eat. The canned

food is gone, there's no fish in the stores. Do you hear me?"
Ivan turns his shaggy ear so as not to miss a word of mine, but he does not turn his head. Cats have their honor too. First and foremost, cats have their honor.

"Vanya, we're going to have to put you to sleep. The veterinarian is coming . . ."
Ivan's ear resumes its former position. The cat has no desire to hear such utterly stupid jokes. He's fond of observing the snowflakes, which are few and far between. In real life, people are given ration cards for meat, but what about Ivan the cat, who means so much to us; Ivan, that extraterrestrial dressed in a costly striped coat? No one thought about Ivan the cat. It goes without saying that I give him my rations. Ivan, however, prefers Bobo-brand chicken pie. But where can I get any for him? How can I explain to him that it's pointless to be fussy, that if beef neck's available, beef neck's what you eat? How can I make him fathom that there's not much else but vinegar in the stores?
Oh, Ivan, Ivan, we've grown old.

The Defense Committee for Prisoners of Conscience, to which I have the honor to belong, presented the State Council and the Parliament with a letter demanding the release of a dozen or so people arrested in the fall of 1980.
I recently received the following form letter:

In reference to your letter of 1/30/81, which was passed on to the Attorney General's office by the speaker of the Parliament of the PPR, a letter written by citizens of whom you were one, I respectfully inform you that the persons mentioned in the letter are under arrest for the present, charged with committing specific crimes, in Ziembinski's case, those described in Art. 270, para. 1; 273, para. 1; 276, para. 1; and in connection with Art. 10 of the Criminal Code, and the following apply to the other persons—Art. 123 in connection with Art. 128, para. 1; 123, 133, 270, para. 1 and 2; 273, para. 1 and 2; 276, para. 1 and 3; 282 in connection with Art. 10 of the Criminal Code.

Press Spokesman for the Attorney General's Office

Now it's clear, now I understand everything.

18 Bored at a bus stop, I noticed a young woman struggling in a ruin of a phone booth on the other side of the street, a mass of nerves as she dialed, gesturing furiously as she spoke. Finally, she left the booth through the no-longer-existing door and she turned out to be exceptionally comely and good-looking. Tall, well built, with a subtle, charming face and a fine head of ash-blond hair. She was dressed in a stylish sheepskin jacket with excellent accessories that would not disgrace Tiffany's. She began to pace, never going very far from the phone booth, walking nervously back and forth between two second-rate cafés, the sort where people arrange meetings of every type.

My bus hadn't come, and like a young lioness, the girl was pacing between the two cafés, oblivious of the street, the people passing her, and even of her own beauty.

Suddenly she halted, frozen in expectation, inwardly bracing herself. She was looking at a small group of people getting off a bus. Then it was clear that, among the people dispersing in all directions, she had caught sight of a dark young man wearing an American army jacket.

He walked unhurriedly toward her and she, feigning casualness, began moving toward him. They met, spoke, and as always, she gave him her eager lips and for a time they walked united in a kiss. They even walked a surprisingly long time like that— young people usually don't paw each other on the street, engage in mock copulation at bus stops, demonstrate their affection in cafés. It's usually the freaks, the nasty runts with thick, plastered hair, the repellent homunculi who vaunt their shamelessness in public places. They make a show of their popularity for their friends, their right to sex, the fullness of their lives, their superiority to other generations and classes. In a word, they practice the art of love with shameless ostentation, though God knows that, given their nastiness, they shouldn't even reproduce.

But that's not what I meant to say. I've sat in cafés many a time watching wonderful, good-looking girls wait forty minutes without a murmur for their miserable male to arrive. I have also seen young ladies meekly carrying heavy traveling bags for their long-haired, toothless young men. And I have seen them fight tooth and nail to defend the honor of their life's companions, whom they despise.

No, no, I'm not making any point here; God forbid—I have no complaints. I'll be venting no spleen here, as I have in the past. I like the whole thing a lot. In 1946 I traveled from Krakow to Gdynia on the steps of a train to see my girl. For nearly twenty-four hours I hung off the cracked plank, strapped to the railing with my belt. But don't tell me that's how things were then. Things were completely different then, because I was a handsome young man and she was a good-looking, provincial young lady. Goddamnit, what I'm talking about is returning to the normal difference that once divided those two idiotic sexes, male and female.

It's beyond belief that three years have passed since Stash Dygat died. Three years ago, caught in a sudden rush of fear, he wanted to call someone, perhaps his doctor, perhaps me. But I wasn't home. He lifted the receiver, reached out to dial, and fell headfirst onto the table. An hour and a half earlier, he and I had had a long talk about some very intimate problems. But before we could finish that conversation, I left Stash to visit some people for a short time. He was reluctant to let me go, for that was a lonely time for him. His wife, Kalina, was somewhere far, far away earning money to support them, primarily to support their pack of dogs and cats. And so Stash was reluctant to let me go until seven that evening. My wife and I were visiting some people, we may have had some tea, talked about nothing. There was a lot of snow outside, it was a good snowy winter; meanwhile, Stash was breathing his last, surrounded by his animals—his cats and dogs at his side, seeing him off on that final, distant journey.

What a good thing that we had finally reconciled a year before his death. Stash was mortally offended after my *Calendar and the Hourglass* appeared, and he kept me in the penalty box for exactly twelve months.

For years he had instructed me in how to be nonchalant about the writing business; he had spent so much time teaching me to disregard the outward attributes of the trade, had put in so many hours inuring me to the nullity and conventions of the literary world, he had poisoned me for so long with artistic and social nihilism, and then, in the end, he took offense like a child at the part of my book where I portrayed my friend Stanislaw Dygat with love and affection.

And, good God, did he shower me with abuse. I had brought him the confounded book and then forgotten about it. We used to call each other thirty times a day—either about something in the paper or a stupid program on television, a crummy sports match or if one of our colleagues had done something irritating. But then I didn't hear a word from him for three days. And so, suspecting nothing, I gave him a call and met with a furious eruption of anger and hurt feelings. All without any wink of the eye, any distance, any sense of humor. "You'll bitterly regret that book," he repeated. "It's a bad book, terribly written. Tell me, Tadzio, why do you hate me so much?"

The end of the world. He slammed down the phone, leaving me speechless, unable to get a single word out. Later on, I began analyzing the frivolous passages about my mentor to see if they applied to him, the story of his life, and to the past we shared. My dear mentor, Stash, was a great enemy of conceit, or perhaps just of vanity. He lured me into traps, urged me to be sincere, direct, nonchalant, but when I drew his portrait according to his own aesthetic and philosophical principles, he cursed and reviled me.

For a year we kept our distance. Every so often, some furious mutterings would reach my ear; someone even said that Stash was thinking of taking me to court. I was told that evenings had been devoted to tearing me apart. I was very distressed by that and even more so by the emptiness in my phone life. If there was something stupid on television, I would start dialing Stash's number and come to my senses a moment later. Having read an odd interview given by one of our colleagues, I had the receiver in hand and was dialing 39–38, when I recalled it was all over, that he wasn't my friend anymore. A leader would give a speech and my hand would automatically reach out for the phone, only to fall limp and shamed to my side. But for him, for Stash, what had happened between us was constantly confused with his new pose, that of the offended party. My phone was just sitting there. Stash too would dial my number automatically and then, realizing his mistake, would pant in fury at the other end of that ill-fated line.

But the worst thing of all happened a few months later, at the end of the summer or the beginning of the fall. I was in Zoliborz and there was something terribly tempting about passing by Dygat's house. And so I tiptoed very carefully down Kochowski Street, peering guardedly into the windows of his home. Suddenly my eyes went to the garden, and what I saw made me freeze and my hair stand on end. Wearing glasses with dark frames, Stash was sitting in a deck chair under a wild-apple tree, dangling one enormous foot in a way all his own and reading a book. A grim suspicion ran through my heart. Yes, yes, dangling his foot, he was reading *The Calendar and the Hourglass*. Ashamed for him, I fled at a run from Zoliborz.

On the first night after Stash's death, Gucio Gottesman and I were unable to sit still. We knew that Stash was lying alone in his new and now unnecessary house.

We drove north out to Zoliborz. It was below freezing; thin ice crackled underfoot as we walked around the corner to his snowy garden and his house, its windows dark. There was a light only in the basement, where Stash lay, waiting for Kalina and her troupe to complete the plot and epilogue of his play.

"Stash!" I called out. "Stash, don't worry! Gucio and I are here!"

But of course nothing could happen. All I heard was a dog barking. Some animal had called back to us, and now, three years later, I can't be sure which dog was our friend that night. It might have been Zabcia or it might have been Kulka; one of the dogs was lamenting Stash or praying to God to grant resurrection to the dead.

It's shameful to say, but Dygat was killed. At the beginning of the winter of 1977, Stash was simply murdered. And who did it? Scoundrels did it. Certain types that I can't even remember anymore. Murdered by lowlife who have also no doubt forgotten about the murder.

Ewa Kruk made the film *Palace Hotel* based on Stash's book *The Munich Train Station*. To my mind, she made a nice picture, one with a great deal of the charm characteristic of Dygat's prose. But that's beside the point.

Dygat usually grew attached to adaptations of his work, whatever those adaptations happened to be. Loyalty to the adapters certainly played some role here, as well as a sort of childish admiration for the machinery that turned a work of literature into a play or a film. And for that reason too Dygat would follow the adaptation, share in its victories and defeats, always treating it as his own child, even though he never denied his co-creators any credit. But that's not important either.

The film by Dygat and the talented young director Ewa Kruk was first screened for official inspection one December morning (yes, I think it was in the morning) in 1977. There was frost on the ground and it wasn't much warmer in the screening room. The audience of cultural bureaucrats gave our team's product an icy reception. The film played to a hostile silence. It might even be too much to say that it played. It crept and crawled for an hour and a half across the ill-disposed, even hate-filled screening room.

A discussion followed the film. May history consign it to oblivion as quickly as possible. That discussion was a frontal attack on Dygat. He was treated as a scribbler, a villain. Used to hearing abuse and impertinence all his life, he attempted to respond, treating the audience as gentlemen, people of society. But they were apparatchiks—gloomy, anonymous individuals instructed to stick it to a writer who had irritated some high official gone and forgotten today. Dygat was stomped to death. But, as is often the case in disasters like that, Dygat continued to function for a few hours and seemed almost normal. He phoned me, helpless witness to the incident of a few hours before, separated himself from his oppressors with swagger, demonstrating exemplary form with me, making an abnormal situation normal.

But when he called the next day I heard the voice of a dying man. Dygat had lost his will to live, had ceased to defend himself against the force of circumstance, his broken back causing a slow paralysis of his will, his mind, and his hopes.

Stash faded over the next month and a half. He still drank a bottle of vodka on the holidays, still treated his isolation lightly, still flared up in demonic fits of irritation—his specialty—but I felt that life was leaving him faster all the time, and there was nothing anyone could do about it. Stash had been struck a painful blow, one that left him without a hope, shattered in some part of his spiritual identity that is hard to define. Perhaps it is the heart of honor, perhaps the cerebral convolutions of dignity, perhaps the nervous system of belief, order, logic, hierarchy, the god that is the meaning of our existence.

I am not actually accusing anyone here, for no one would feel that my accusation applied to him. Nothing really happened. It's just that a writer with heart disease was smothered in the daily senseless free-for-all of the Polish People's Republic. Nothing really happened. There's plenty of us—as the Russians used to say during the war.

I have a terrible desire to tell a true story here, one that would severely offend Stash again.

One day I was at Stash's when the phone rang. Avid for news and scandal, he snatched up the receiver.

"Hello?"

"May I speak with Miss Kalina Jedrusik?" asked a woman with a charming voice.

"Unfortunately, my wife is away on a concert tour and won't be back for a while."

"That's really a shame. We wanted to invite her here for an evening and a performance. Our House of Culture in Kalisz"— it may have been elsewhere—"has a long tradition of sponsoring such events."

"I'm well aware of that," said Stash gallantly. "I was once your guest there myself."

"And with whom do I have the pleasure of speaking?"

"My last name is Dygat."

"Excuse me for asking, but what is your field?"

Now, a bit irritated, Stash replied: "I'm a chemical engineer."

"Oh, I'm sorry," said the woman with a laugh, "that's not my field. My training is in Polish literature."

4

All day long I kept intending to make a note of something important, and now I've gone and completely forgotten what it was. My memory is lousy, I forget everything right away. I can read the same book again every six months. I don't remember a thing. Everything goes flying out of my head. A memory like a sieve.

Is this an occupational infirmity? Can I remember only what I need for my work? But it's my work where my memory gives me the most problems. It's only years later that someone either reminds me that I'd already used a certain anecdote in a few of my books or that the same incident or landscape appears in other of my novels.

Then I pretend that this is fidelity to my life's story, I do a fairly adroit impersonation of a monothematic writer, just a step away from obsession. This form of etiquette is highly esteemed in the literary world. And so sometimes you can sell that ordinary infirmity, that sclerosis of old age, for decent money.

But, poor me, I'm simply losing my memory. I have to be vigilant; I ought to check every little ingredient before including it in my layer cake. To become an old grandpa who keeps saying the same things over and over—monstrous!

What was I trying to get at? How the thread of human fate or a person's career is woven into history? Or did I want to reflect on the phenomenon of Stefan Bratkowski, a talented journalist and a nice person?

Whatever you might say, it appears that August 1980 took place so that Bratkowski could have an outlet for his logorrhea. Meaning that God, fate, and history, those ultimate forces, played into Bratkowski's hands. This odd occurrence was in the making for quite a while. Bratkowski's books and articles had been growing longer and longer. He needed increasing amounts of words to express his thoughts.

Now he writes about everything—coal mining, agricultural policy, Poland's allies, data processing, economic reform, Saturdays off, the U.S.S.R., drilling for oil, human history, censorship, his colleagues, Poland's repayment of its debts, journalism, sex. No, that's not true, he still hasn't started writing about sex. But he has abundant opinions on the other problems, and from somewhere in the depths of the universe, the Good Lord sends His blessing on Bratkowski's verbal epilepsy.

Let us hope that history will at least demonstrate a little humor and not tear Stefan from us, not elevate him too high, to those regions where the jokes end and the way down begins.

Naturally, I just remembered what I had wanted to say. It was about Stefan, but Stefan Zeromski.

I am reading Zeromski's journals for the second time. I say the second time because it wouldn't be seemly to admit not having read them at the proper time. At one time I read those several volumes, but at intervals. Now, however, I'm devouring the whole thing from beginning to end, even recognizing the fragments I'd read before, which now assume a new position in the context of the whole.

I read with delight and horror. With delight because of his language, marvelous, strange, archaic, ductile, juicy, pulsing with life and truth. And horror because those journals are, excuse me for saying so, are probably—no, I can't get the words out—are, it seems to me, if I'm not mistaken, are simply better—God forgive my impudence—better than any fiction he ever wrote.

Your hair stands on end and you break into a cold sweat at the thought that what survives many writers, the majority of writers, are their journals, those trivial diaries, those scraps of impressions and observations, the waste and trash of their official literary life.

It would have been best not to keep a journal. But I not only keep one, I keep fake journals. And so maybe it's because they're fake that they don't shatter the fragile pyramid of my original work in prose.

I'm scrutinizing the story of Stefan's life. And our venerable bard was indefatigable when it came to the erotic, his persistence touching. Going blind, deaf, his bones rotting, but still going strong as a man, that part of his ill-treated body still full of the desire for life, full of enthusiasm for battle with womankind.

The piercing strength of a pathological existence, the stunning charm of hungry inertia, a furious anthem in honor of—yes, that's just it, in honor of what? In honor of a writer's stubbornness, the raptures of a sensitive soul, faith in the greatness of art's mission?

His violent heart rattled against his tubercular ribs. I can hear his quickened breathing. I can divine the first suicidal impulse. The lamp is smoking in its greenish shade, a blizzard outside the window, hunger rumbling in his stomach. Is that his youth or mine? In the next room Poland weeps. A woman in mourning.

The lines aren't coming to me. I'm encountering problems that I can't surmount. That didn't used to happen before. Three sentences of hulking negativity, with a clumsy rhythm, obviously devoid of any grace. Then suddenly I'll write something that can't be edited into shape, the grammar unable to contain the thought. Something hideous begins to arise as from a box not shut tightly. For the first time it has occurred to me that I won't be able to write anymore. I'm losing my originality, my logic, my grammar.

Perhaps this counterfeit book will be true proof of my incipient mental decline. With all my heart, I dedicate this work to my dear doctors, my dear anesthesiologists.

For better intellectual flow I did something rather provocative in *The Calendar and the Hourglass*. In a special little essay I presented myself as a veteran of the "pimple-faced" movement, a staunch Stalinist from the fifties, someone who took part in the Party's most secret cells. The point was to provoke discussion, a certain state of mind, and a clinical analysis of what had been prettily referred to as the "period of mistakes and distortions."

I expected that this would result in a cornucopia of similar confidences, confessions, intimate revelations, self-exposures, acts of contrition, or an unruly revolt. Meanwhile, I met with a dead silence like that which ensues when an irresponsible guest makes some terrible gaffe at a respectable party. But it wasn't a total silence. Every once in a while someone would suddenly leap up with the euphoria of discovery and unmask me as a former Stalinist. Initially, I found this a cause for consternation and wondered why these discoverers were so late in coming out with their revelations, why only now they hastened to inform and warn their contemporaries.

After long reflection, and after much surprise and astonishment, I realized that the source of their revelations was my heroic and swaggering confession in *The Calendar and the Hourglass*, which was supposed to benefit all of society, but which had only brought poor me shame and disgrace.

Unthinkable before the war, meaning in times of honor. Gentlemen, please, if I have confessed to something publicly, it is unseemly to use that confession to unmask me while taking the credit for yourselves. And if I confessed, you gentlemen should have enough honor to confess to your own rapscalities. Even if you are innocent of them.

For the good of the cause, I made my pimple-faced portrait in *The Calendar and the Hourglass* a bit more demonic than need be. I put a knife between my teeth, I rolled my bloodshot eyes, I emitted horrible death rattles. In order to shock the elegant ladies and the overly intellectual gentlemen.

I may have been afraid, as I was as a child making confession, to forget some of my sins and leave out certain transgressions. I may have feared unconsciously minimizing my guilt, belittling my own role. Or perhaps I simply was ashamed of appearing small-souled.

I was low and rotten, but probably not on such a grand scale that I should now elbow my way to the front. Please remember, my dear unmaskers, that the once proud name of Stalinist, which you now hold in contempt, was something that I could only fantasize about on sleepless nights. As a member of the Home Army I was forbidden any part in the secret assemblies, as one of the impure I was not allowed to approach the Party's altars, as a sinner I had been forever deprived of the pleasure of calling myself by the leader's name.

I had a hand in it, that's a fact. But for the entire time I was on the sidelines, not kosher, with a stain that could not be washed away. I do not say this to excuse myself to you. I say it to explain that I am unable to describe, analyze, reflect on, illuminate, systematize, excavate, compare, or put into epic form that historical period that lasted a few years, a few years.

I took part, but I was on the sidelines. I lived through it, but it is not seared onto my memory. I sinned, but I don't feel like making confession every day of the week.

It is the young writers from the crannies of the opposition who have begun to show the greatest interest in that period. They even took me up, or perhaps I was high on their list of people connected with the crimes of the Stalinist era. I gave them my all, but I couldn't satisfy them. I searched my memory. I lashed my old body. I analyzed my ego to its depths with utter cruelty. I referred them to my disclosures in *The Calendar and the Hourglass* and elsewhere. But it was never enough for them. They rejected my self-diagnoses, and my self-accusations as well. They demanded more.

But what else is there? With a terrible sense of shame, I puzzled over the problem a very long time, until suddenly one sleepless night I understood the secret of the young writers' curiosity.

Their strength depends on their dissatisfaction with me. I writhed in an effort to please them, but they were never pleased. I implored them, saying I no longer recalled the details, but they were ruthless with me because they needed every last one as a warning and a lesson for the future.

And that sleepless night I suddenly saw their curiosity from another angle, a different angle, in a new slant of light. And it seemed to me that their curiosity was a bit indecent, like a taste for pornography. And I was overcome with the suspicion that their curiosity was defective in its one-sidedness.

And then some nasty suspicions crawled out from under the bed. I was frightened by the thought that the younger writers wanted to have their older colleagues—shameful to say—by the balls, trapped, caught in delicate blackmail, under watchful pressure. With our criminal past held constantly up to us by the young, we would be more lenient in negotiating their place in literature with them, the awards, the hierarchy of souls.

Because, my dear colleagues, it is sometimes the case here that grandiloquent gestures, moral severity, and patriotic imponderabilia conceal the usual greed for cash, a laudatory review, and a place on the dais.

I don't do so well with the young. And here I am attacking them again. But unlike other writers, I am not impressed by youth as a category. I was once young myself. And that's why I don't allow myself to be blackmailed by the young people like some witch. I can negotiate with them on an equal footing. Amen.

5

I'll be making a film of *The Issa Valley*. It looks as if I'll be making a film of Czeslaw Milosz's *The Issa Valley*. The project has been in the works for ten or twelve weeks now. I even cooked up a screenplay on the sly. But I hadn't mentioned this venture to a soul because I couldn't be sure of it.

I have never in my life made a film based on someone else's prose. The thought never even entered my head. And then out of the blue one afternoon the laureate's sister-in-law, Grazynka Milosz, called me and proposed this idea, this intrigue, this adventure. She and her friends had come to the conclusion that I was the only one who could make a film out of *The Issa Valley*.

And just imagine, for some reason that risky idea did not surprise me in the least, though I wouldn't have hit on it myself between now and the end of the world. *The Issa Valley*—why not? For a long time now I have been strangely and irresistibly drawn to Milosz, maybe not to the poet himself, whom I met only while in transit, though it was in Berkeley. It was not the man personally but his mentality, his ambiguity of mind, his charisma, his Wilno, Latin, Scandinavian, and Asiatic charisma, his mysterious ethos, that of the pilgrim, the exile, the outcast. And so, to work on his early, one could say youthful, novel seemed an attractive adventure to me, somehow even a respite in my life of silken hard labor, a jolly leap into a simpatico abyss.

But the first problem cropped up right away. Czeslaw displayed no enthusiasm. He covered himself by pointing to the great difficulties an adaptation would encounter. He lingered so long that I grew flustered. But I'm a Cancer like he is. Cancers display great enthusiasm that in the blink of an eye changes into total resistance, a "no." I cooled to the idea and lost all desire in a single moment. The project ceased to exist for me.

Then, suddenly, abruptly, out of the blue, the telephone rings one afternoon and I hear Czeslaw's voice as if he were speaking from the next room. A chaotic conversation on my part. I had a desire to present my objections and fears, but I also wanted to clarify the project and what this commission would mean to me. From Czeslaw there was that Lithuanian-Wilno cool warmth, that not-entirely-friendly friendliness, and that consent which is like a strict injunction. It can't be reproduced. You have to be born on that soil, grow up among dozens of aunts, uncles, and relatives, close and distant, and then go out into the world, your stupid savage European world.

In any case, he said what he said. At a distance of twelve thousand kilometers we made a deal. And constantly unsure of my own situation, at loggerheads, gnawed by vague premonitions, I began making calls around Warsaw to put together a crew of genetic natives from the river basin of the Niemen, the Wilia, and the Niewiaza.

Make a film of *The Issa Valley*, that's easy to say. The quick and eager magic of the Nobel Prize is at work here. A beautiful novel, a wonderful book, a magical world sunk in historical oblivion.

And I'm a pro, an old hand who's written a shelfful of bad, so-so, and pretty good novels. And I've made a few films, had a hand in several, and was literary consultant on dozens of others; I've also done my part in pushing the cart uphill. And so I can't *ooh* and *aah* with delight, because the experiment will put my butt on the line and I'll pay with what's left of my teeth for whatever ends up on that strip of exposed celluloid.

But it's not an easy job. *The Issa Valley* has many charms, but they're submerged in layers of language; it is dramatic in places, but it's the worst sort of drama for a film because it's narrated, because it's part of the author's narration and is not confined to scenes that are played out before the spectator's eyes. A reader is taken by the exotic theme and scenery but what awaits poor me is the treacherous trap of sterile ethnography or the boredom of a cultural museum piece.

And then there's Thomas, the child-hero of the book. Czeslaw exaggerates his role. He thinks that Thomas, like an Atlas, should carry the film's entire intellectual and aesthetic weight on his schoolboy shoulders. In Czeslaw's judgment, the issue of Thomas brings the very filming of the book into question. All in all, Czeslaw makes Thomas into some god of the Wilno life-force.

But for the unfortunate Mr. Konwicki, this Thomas is a puppy who muddles across the screen. There have been millions of films about oversensitive young boys. And there have been tens of thousands of dramatic tricks invented so we see the cruel and magical world of adults through the eyes of a child. These boys who spy on their young aunts in the bath and who weep over the wrong done an animal have been down the pike more times than anyone can count.

Thomas is a stylistic device. Thomas is a formal trick. Thomas is an instrument of the narrative. Thomas can be left out of the film because he does not forward the action, cause conflict, or increase the tension. Thomas only sees or observes or even spies. And those are the camera's functions in a film. The camera ferrets through the world and chooses images, details, or incidents. For that reason Thomas is unnecessary to the film and a tear can be shed while cutting him from the pages of the novel and tossing him in the trash.

But Czeslaw focuses the entire problem of the adaptation on the figure of Thomas. And I'm not altogether sure that the laureate has ever been inside a movie theater. In general, the laureate's literary material is from another parish altogether.

And so, out of love for Czeslaw, I pamper this unnecessary

Thomas, who will place me in the ranks of those kindhearted people who make films for children and young people. And so I will fix that goddamned Thomas on film according to the laureate's thousands of pointers. That Thomas will not be tall but, rather, squarely built, naïve but not stupid, more male than angelic, and so forth and so on. I'll do it all for that persnickety man living by San Francisco Bay, but I will also attend to my own interests, my self-esteem as the adaptor and director. Because I know best what to do with that tangled novel, and how to smelt the noble metal of film from it. But, even while knowing best about everything, I still might make the usual Polish flop. And then woe is me. Then I will bolt to the West, like an outcast, an outlaw.

Yes, my dear future viewers, in the crucible of adaptation, in film, this book must be brought closer to today's audience. Film is not a museum. Beautiful scenery and sentimental characters aren't enough for an hour-and-a-half-long dream in the dark night of the cinema. Old man Konwicki, that wizard from the Rudnicka Wilderness, will have to gather all the strength he'd sucked from Lithuanian oaks in the days just before spring, to remember all the incantations our grandmothers used to soothe the pains of the dying and to halt violent hemorrhages; he will have to soar to the vast sky above Upper and Lower Zmudz in order to imbue that film with the magic of intuition, the menace of memory, and the suffering of divine inertia among you wretched European worms.

Who was Edward Gierek, the head of the Party team, fallen and humiliated at the end of the rainy summer of 1980? Was he a failure, yet another incompetent governor of Poland serving the Russians' will, a genius of destruction to whom Providence assigned the role of destroying Communism, the gravedigger for the latest totalitarianism tormenting weak old Europe?

I don't think this a simple question. And the degree to which Gierek was conscious of his historic role is not important here.

I assume he was not conscious of it, that he had something else in mind, even though it was not what actually happened. And I don't consider it out of the question that some instinct, some impulse, some moral imperative enjoined him to guide Poland's fate in this way and no other.

In my opinion, there is some significance to the fact that Gierek spent a good portion of his life in the West, where he ingested vitamins, read newspapers, and developed habits different from those of the other Polish Communists. He was not a graduate of Soviet schools and academies, was not there during the war or the great purges, and had not become intimate and infatuated with the Russian mentality.

Gierek's career and his fall can be viewed as a period of activity fatal for the country, an epoch of accelerated Russification, the years in which Poland rolled into the abyss of economic disaster. And thus Gierek's tenure in office can be regarded as a sad time of theft, commotion, and the absolute annihilation of our dear fatherland.

But one can also take an entirely different view of Gierek, and that is the experiment I encourage my esteemed reader to make.

Poles have struggled with diabolical Russian imperialism for the longest time. For centuries now, the Poles have been sentenced by Moscow and Orthodoxy to death, the death of the Polish state and nation. And, for Soviet Russia, Poland was their first and tastiest morsel. This time, after the slaughter of the Second World War, it seemed that Poland would be swallowed easily and digested in good order. For this historic mission, this magical mystery play, this divine act fulfilling centuries of longing, Russia changed Poland's social system, changed its skin, changed its religion.

And here the Good Lord allowed a joke, a grimace of irony, a sneer of paradox. Halfway to being swallowed forever, Poland is given a dashing new leader who, bolstered by technocratic ideals, decides to carry out his plans by stifling the country's cultural and spiritual life, to Russify us outwardly, to lick the

Eastern barbarian's feet, and, in exchange, to create a new Poland, one hard to define, where every citizen will have an apartment, an automobile, and meat on the table.

But the unfortunate Gierek was not aware that the system to which he had devoted his life cannot exist without labor camps, prisons, and the daily supervision of informers. Gierek did not suspect that, under that system, democracy is a fatal substance, a breeze of freedom is poison gas, and greater freedom of thought a hideous virus.

Just look at Gierek: he modernized industry, provided salaries that raised people from poverty to sufficiency, established pensions and retirement reminiscent of those customary in democratic countries, and attempted to make the social-service system work. Believing Lenin's deceitful slogans, he dreamed of Europeanizing Communism. And at times he probably felt that he was exploring new territory.

Consumer Communism—work a lot and earn a lot, attend Party meetings and visit your girlfriend in the evening, eat oysters and swap jokes with the maniacal dissidents, grovel in front of the Russians, and love Poland.

God, how Gierek ridiculed, fooled, and abused ominous, bloodthirsty, inhuman Russian Communism. When he revoked price increases the first time and his rotten premier appeared on television whining in a tearful voice about the historic advances made by the government and the Party, when I saw that scandalous spectacle on television, I realized that the great empire of invincible Russia had just cracked in two.

Because no one had ever acted like this before in the shadow of that empire. Tanks should have advanced and leveled those unruly cities and villages, and only then would the good Tsar, meaning the First Secretary, repeal some part of his inhuman ukase on the sly.

Meanwhile, Gierek had revoked the unfortunate decree at the first sign of human dissatisfaction on the part of society. Just as in France or Norway.

For the first time a foolish little smile appeared on the monster's face. A smile we spotted immediately. And we immediately sensed that this smile was the beginning of the final agony, which could last another half century or end in death tomorrow at daybreak.

Gierek had an aversion to blood. But after all, blood is what cements the system's foundation. And, after all, rebellious societies should be bled on a daily basis to weaken them so that they will submissively carry out the ideas of a nineteenth-century maniac.

Hidden somewhere in Gierek was a certain Polish lightness of mind, a complex of impulses, frivolous and unserious, that are characteristic of this community on the Vistula. All told, a terrible mixture of poisons inched its way along fraternal arteries to the heart, lungs, and liver of the Soviet monster.

Dear people, I'll tell you what's going to happen: Gierek has fallen, but his ideas will live forever. Meaning that Gierek has gone off into political nonexistence, but what he did at nearly the very heart of the Communist body will never be undone. Gierek made Communism look ridiculous. Gierek kicked the Party orthodoxy in the stomach. Gierek drove a Polish nail into Communism's Russian coffin.

I am curious how history will judge him.

6

His ordinary summer dream, full of unruly, hysterical desire, suddenly darkened, sank into a murky steep-sided valley, and spoke from a bottomless abyss in plaintive voices of complaint, beseechment, or pain. Men, or maybe boys, were approaching out of the darkness and crying aloud. They walked a terribly long time, endlessly, listlessly calling out in mournful sopranos.

Adam was aware that reality was leaking into the hallucinations of his dream. He wanted to free himself from the malignant fever of the night, concentrated all his strength, grabbed on to one edge of reality, and had already crawled out onto the shore of the dawn when he fell back into the darkness of the dream for a moment.

Grown men were crying, wandering through the night. And their weeping was the weeping of the Last Judgment, and that valley was the Valley of the Last Judgment.

This strange dawn occurred a very long time ago, at the beginning of 1944, when people were fighting all over the world, but at that time the world meant only Europe.

A willow-green dawn diluted the summer night in a sacred spot in old Europe between the Niemen and Dzwina Rivers, where the French writer Romain Gary and the mother of the American journalist David Halberstam were originally from, where Lyonka P., a soldier in Vlasov's army, was born, as were

Czeslaw Milosz, Nobel Prize laureate, and I who am now describing one day in the life of Adam, a boy with transparent blue eyes and halting speech, who is my shadow or, rather, is me from another life—youth, the mortgaged life of time past, past variations on memory, illusion, and longing.

Meanwhile, the moaning or weeping of those sinners from the Valley of Jehoshaphat was rising higher and higher into the black but already lightening sky, losing its plaintive quality and becoming more manly, taking on the power of a curse, and Adam's mind was slowly clearing as he remembered details from his grandparents' house: the black-beetle-gnawed shoulders of the sideboard, a makeshift bed with a straw mattress, and the small window by the kitchen stove, a mysterious aquamarine star in the window.

Then a flurry passed through him, a strong tremor that seemed to arise from his stomach, his empty intestines, his chattering teeth clacking like crockery. Adam put on his clothes, fumbling because of the convulsions that swept him; just then he heard a burst of machine-gun fire, a long chain of insolent shots rousing animal fear, a cascade of lightning bolts, harbingers of death.

Adam fell to the ground, that is, the cherry-wood floor. He was used to those echoes of the Last Judgment. A hoarse-voiced train was piercing the valley crosswise. The men took up their song again, now a deadly cry. A sudden burst of gunfire came crackling through the fence. Adam lifted the window damp with morning mist and jumped down into the cold garden fragrant with the last of the evening stock.

What I care about is the magical moment before the first gleam of day, that moment between the death of sleep and the life of waking, when destiny suddenly emerges from the void. Has anyone besides me experienced that second of infinity, the ardent chill of unearthly presentiment; has anyone besides me remembered it forever? My point is that so many micro-incidents in our lives seem so very resonant in their consequences, so closely connected with the rhythms of nature, so particularly worth remembering forever. There's no point. The point is my useless pain in recalling a July day, a July dawn, during which seven people I knew died, while a bunch of people my age lived through twelve hours of danger, during which five thousand of my countrymen were frozen in sainthood for the rest of their lives, five thousand from the archipelago of the last wildernesses in Europe: the Rudnicka Wilderness, the Nalibocka, the Grodzienska, and others that I no longer remember.

Adam jumped to the garden and then immediately went sprawling onto some unripe tomatoes, because gunfire had broken out at the far end of the orchard; a swarm of fireflies passed by, heading toward the railway station, where they would slant off from the tracks toward the Upper Colony.

"Hurrah! Hurrah!" came shouts from the still-dark gardens.

A shadow tore free of the damp earth, ran a few steps, then fell into the weeds again.

"Hurrah!" yelled Adam in a trembling voice, and dashed to the riverside.

Somewhere nearby, the train was wheezing. Every now and again it would sigh great steam clouds of relief. It wasn't afraid of the cries of the dying or the protracted bursts of automatic-weapons fire. It groaned shamelessly through the end of its black proboscis.

"Hurrah!" someone shouted from the next bush.

"Listen," whispered Adam. "I don't have a gun."

"Me neither," croaked the still-juvenile voice of the shadow in the next bush. "The guns are on the train."

"Which train?"

"The one at the station."

Jesus, but I have no desire to do a battle scene, to describe that attack on an armored train in a little town in the Wilno area which no one has ever heard of. But that toilsome episode of war, similar to all other such descriptions, is necessary to the whole, for it creates the context for the magical incidents, the metaphysical assumptions.

.   .   .

Adam Michnik, that diabolical cherub of the 1980 uprising, once commissioned a piece of prose from me on the Home Army Uprising in the Wilno area in 1944. He gave me a free hand. I could treat the subject in a story, a novel, or an essay. Wishing to unite the pleasant with the useful, I decided on a novel. I thought about it for maybe six months, scribbled a mass of notes, and concocted a special contemporary layer for that historical layer cake. I paced around my desk in a fury, peeked at the scribbled-on cardboard box, nasty womb for a literary-work-to-be, I lay down in my magical den as if on a floor, and, moaning, I feigned the labor pains of a new novel.

But, I'm sorry, there was some sort of block. Nothing was coming alive. Not a single brilliant idea. I can't remember it. I've forgotten it. Some mechanism had ejected from memory that uprising which we called Operation Wilno.

What does that mean? I can't remember the hours when I brushed up against death but can see with thrilling clarity and painful accuracy a day from my childhood when I was four years old. I had been sitting by the window since the morning, waiting for my mother. My mother had gone to work in a factory after my father died. And so I would sit by the window and wait for the factory siren. The beautiful, frightening cry of the siren. A sad and dirty world seen through a dirty window. And in the middle of that dirty world was a dirty three-story building with a flat roof. In the building's low attic there was a mysterious woman in a reclining position, and at a certain moment, she would begin wailing in a piercing voice, which meant that my mother would be home in a while.

That I remember perfectly, and with the right etching tool, and if seized by a mania for artistic perfection, I could engrave that fragment of my life onto infinity. But the day which I should have crammed into my empty head's memory now escapes me completely. I can still catch a feel of the mood, the slight flicker of sunlit images, brief feelings of shame, some vague regrets. I don't even remember the dates. I think that the scattered battle order for the uprising began in Wilno at dawn July 6, 1944, but in someone's memoirs I read that it was July 7. Why has my memory divested itself of that legacy, or is it ballast? Why don't I feel like writing that child's play of a tale? Why don't I feel like winning the gratitude of the combatants, that coveted laurel and bronze?

I wanted to make Adam Michnik the hero of my story about Operation Wilno in 1944. I wanted to shift the Adam of today to that scorching summer and have him experience that chain of episodes in my life and my colleagues' lives, people I knew and people I didn't know, people of whom I'd caught glimpses out of the corner of my eye. I wanted to give Adam a little piece of my youth so that he too would have a war record, for which a certain generation does envy us from time to time. I wanted to make Adam my younger brother, but one already initiated into all the mysteries of Wilno. I wanted to see how he, the darling of salons and temporary arrests, would bear up to that first burst of machine-gun fire, how he would take the sight of blood, and how he would react to the resurrection of freedom wearing the coarse-cloth uniform of slavery.

And so the story would have been a certain little game with Adam, his generation, and today's world racing at breakneck speed into the unknown. And there would have been a variety of charms, various shamanistic devices, various sacrilegious creations. In the contemporary passages I intended to set off on a long voyage to America and prehistoric Wilno simultaneously, I even planned to challenge God and brazenly to cross swords with Him in the name of suffering, unfortunate, trampled humanity.

Yes, yes, that's what I wanted, but I couldn't get it off the ground.

My hero was removing sections of the rail on the Nowa Wilejka–Wilno line to prevent the Germans from escaping when Messerschmitts swooped down from the direction of Porubanek and strafed those daring young men. Adam was hit by an incredible shot. A shell from the plane's machine gun struck him between the tendons at the base of his skull and exited through the front of his cheek, burying itself in the roots of the rye. Adam and his cohorts had taken cover in a field of ripening grain and he was lying with his head pressed to the damp, fragrant earth.

He stood up and, swallowing blood, set off along a wooded hillside in the direction of Wilno, for he had a date that day with a girl he'd been dreaming about since the third grade. He had a date with her because a few days before they had graduated from high school and received their diplomas together in a secret study group, but no one could have foreseen that the uprising, later to be termed Operation Storm by historians, would break out that very day.

And so Adam walked along through that cheerful, sunny landscape, through fields of grain, flowering meadows, cool woodland; he walked all afternoon to meet his girl as the grasshoppers chirped; he walked past weddings of skylarks, through streams of spring-like, even summery aromas; he walked fatally wounded but still alive, glad of his date, and not in the least surprised by the blood gluing his lips together and clogging his larynx, not surprised by the merry roaring in his bullet-pierced head; he was just afraid to be late for the date.

Finally he reached her house. And there, catching sight of nurses, wounded partisans, and a dog wild with emotion, he fell unconscious by the well and only came to late in the afternoon, when the light was already dense and reddish. It was then in the shadowy ravine that Soviet soldiers began appearing one by one, portending yet another end of the world.

But what really happened? Other people can remember. Those for whom this was the most important day in their lives. Those whom those twelve hours of a summer's day entitled to glory, laurels, and a place at the presidium. Those driven by a strange instinct for history who, out of habit and duty, record the scraps of human fate scattered afar, in what now seems another century.

I don't remember a thing. I mean, I can recall the atmosphere, the mood, a few meaningless incidents. For example, I can still see the Wilno Colony or Markucie at the foot of a wooded hillside and, on the other side of the Wilenka, Belmont in a veil of streaky smoke where apparently "Coronation Sword" and his brigade were conducting an artillery duel with German bunkers.

I also knew that the famous partisan whose nom de guerre was "the Father" had lost his life in the gardens of the Wilno Colony. He was a legend to us and meant a great deal to us young people. I set to work writing about him ten times. But this partisan, whom I didn't know and who was called the Father, a twenty-year-old boy from Wilno or Nowa Wilejka, kept receding farther and farther from me, his proportions changing with the new perspectives in my life, my work, my world. The Father diminished, his fate lost substance, his magic dimmed. And in the end I forgot about the Father.

Perhaps only in A Dreambook for Our Time are there any barely visible traces of the Father, who was my Guiding Star during a certain forgotten period of my life.

Still, I do remember, that sixth or seventh of July was a beautiful, sweltering Wilno summer day. I remember the flood of sunlight, alive, unwearied, still full of spring joy.

I recall bits and pieces of the attack on the German armored train that had been halted in the Wilno Colony. It was still night, one second before dawn. I remember the dampness of the late-night dew, the bushes and loose sand where chickens lived, the invisible train belching fire, footsteps, ours, mine, desperately bounding toward the station, the shouts, the sighs of the locomotive, but I don't remember much else. Then we crawled over that captured train, though I don't know how it was captured; then we raced headlong toward Wilenka through Tupaciszki, which had once been a farm. Then the train pulled away, heading toward Wilno, in flight now, for no one had looked into the locomotive, where the German crew had remained untouched.

Later on we returned from above the Wilenka, my brigade, my Eighth Oszmiana Brigade; we sat ourselves down at the edge of a wide valley through which the cool and vigorous Wilenka flowed. And so we settled down on the shore of the valley, and we waited, and waited and waited. And I, an ordinary rank-and-file partisan, still, to this day, do not know what we were waiting for. Overcrowded German transport trains chugged slowly through the valley on tracks fine as guitar strings.

Some of the locals, Staszek D., and maybe Gucio K., and I, reported to command with the suggestion that we remove some of the rails. Our squad was dispatched and with terrible emotion we ran past the Colony toward Nowa Wilejka, past the level grade crossing, where the railroad workers grew vegetables and where I had worked for a few months; then, standing in shallow ditches, we hastily removed some rails, using long iron wrenches. Undermined by hysteria, we did a poor, sloppy job of it. We had pulled up a few sections, when someone shouted to carry them off to the side and throw them down the ditch, but there was no time, because another German train had just emerged from the dark forest that surrounds Nowa Wilejka. It stopped at the edge of the forest, gushing steam to either side, the Germans already jumping down from the high cars.

Shots rang out at once and we leaped into a patch of rye, then ran through a cornfield, shrubs, and a woods, back to our brigade, proud of what we had accomplished. As if from a falcon's nest we looked down at the valley diminished by distance, and at the train, small as a child's toy. After lingering by the dark forest, emitting groans and steam, its wheels rattling on the slippery track, that German transport whistled to bolster its own spirits and began moving toward my, our, little station in the Colony, passing easily over the track we had torn up, and then crept off like a spiny worm toward smoke-covered Wilno.

Our glory faded, dimmed, and shriveled at once. Someone said that we should have taken the rails with us so the Germans couldn't have fitted them back in. We cautiously complained about our leaders, who had let an armored train slip through their hands by not tearing up the rails efficiently.

The Cadre Strike Brigade was right near us. They were Warsaw people of whom we were not overly fond, because each of them, no matter who he was, had been honored with high military rank. Our brigade had ended up being led by a lance corporal, whereas they had a Sergeant Officer in Training peeling potatoes in their mess.

We were attacked a few times by Messerschmitts from the airfield in Porubanek. Many months later, during the winter of '44, in another partisan group, I met Corporal Satyr, who had not been far away from us at the time he was hit by a fighter-plane shell in the back of his head, at the base of his skull, a shell that had exited through his cheek, taking teeth and a piece of his jaw with it. With that wound, Satyr walked five kilometers on that scorching afternoon to a field dressing station, from which he was taken to the hospital.

But he could have been on his way to a date with a girl, and a butterfly had the right to get stuck on a spot where his blood had clotted.

I'm skimming through a solemn essay by some conceited little brat who depicts his conflicts as an artist in a bygone era, meaning before August 1980. There's nothing of interest in that essay apart from the uncanny conceit of that spoiled little mongrel. The conceit, the self-admiration, the total self-absorption of that young man in his thirties—for today even people in their forties are young—and so, that apotheosis, canonization, and Ascension of self attracted me in some unhealthy sort of way. I wanted to toss that dog-eared pamphlet away, but I could not. I continue to slip and slide along those monumental statements. I shudder at the code by which those statements communicate with one another; shuddering as if touched by a queer, and groaning in distress, I read further. That is my duty because of my sinful life, my faithlessness, my endless naïveté and lack of character.

Our spoiled baby continues developing his thoughts with greater depth and greater shallowness, telling how he worked, how he had to work in a bygone era. He had told half-truths because the regime would not allow the whole truth. He could have chosen to pass over the whole truth in silence, to have remained silent in general. Taking into account his talent and the importance of that talent for Polish society, he had decided on taking his place in wretched Polish art at the price of speaking half-truths.

And you're up to your ears in half-truths. You had already forgotten about Walery Lukasinski, a nineteen-year-old officer who had not known it was possible to love and esteem one's own talent, that it was a duty to delight society with one's august presence, that to discover the nation's interest was in one's own interest. You forgot about that naïf who let himself be locked away in Shlisselburg for sixty years. You forgot about that specter of noble intransigence who frightened the Russians for half a century from underground cells in the capital of a barbaric empire.

Once, the stubborn provincial Poles had their heads cut off; today's luxury-loving, European little Poles have allusions snipped from their writings.

Now I know why I'm so fond of that Adam Michnik. Even though from a mile away I can tell he's a tricky devil. Because he's like me and my generation. He could have attended our secret study groups with us—on the condition that he cut his hair a little shorter. Adam would no doubt have been admitted to those elegant wartime soirées centered on a gramophone or piano where, slowly and with great gallantry, we would pick up young ladies, more womanly then than women are now. There surely would have been a place for Adam in the line attacking a machine-gun bunker, and certainly he would have kept his head at those lousy moments when everything collapses and you don't have a prayer and the only thing ahead of you is death, naked and shameless.

Even that deceitfulness of his makes him resemble us, even his straightforward wholesome duplicity is akin to ours, even the ambiguous gleam in his eye was repatriated from the environs of Wilno, from over near Ejszyszki or Molodeczno.

But to hell with Adam Michnik. I have to return to the piece which he commissioned from me.

I'm in despair. Suddenly, at daybreak, before the rest of my fellow Poles have gotten up and gone off to fake a day's work, I, still not fully awake, still wading through swampy dreams, I've fallen apart completely, poor me.

And so, to kill time before breakfast, I turn on the radio. And suddenly I'm hearing my own prose. It makes my heart beat quicker. Out of the blue, on my way through a morning in life, I encounter myself. In a powerful baritone which colors the text, some stranger is reading fragments of *The Calendar and the Hourglass* at daybreak.

My ears prick up like Ivan the cat's. But my pleasure is somehow incomplete, a bit distorted, a little ambiguous. For I also seem to see myself as I was seven years ago and am also surprised at the sight of those seven vanished years. How dense, dramatic, and rich in consequence they were. Just look and listen for a second, just reflect for a moment. Even me. Seven years, and so many changes. But changes for the better. In my frame of mind, my thinking, even my literary tastes.

There is something alien and irritating about that seven-year-old piece of mine. I'm also surprised by its lack of a sense of humor. I mean, I tried to make jokes and be amusing, but what shows through those melancholy efforts is fear, a fear somehow not my own, of going too far, of not going all the way, a fondness for half-jokes, actually for embryonic jokes which only play to and play up to a papered house.

It causes me melancholy now to reexamine myself as I was seven years ago. But that most recent part of my life, those seven lean years, did teach me something. I can no longer treat myself with the same reverence I once did, I no longer cherish such admiration for myself, and I can no longer attain such levels of servility.

Is a text that does not deal with the me frozen in today's time worth reissuing? Is my book *The Calendar and the Hourglass* worth retrieving from lightning-swift oblivion?

At the end of the program, the reader announced that he had been reading fragments of autobiographical prose by one of my more successful colleagues.

And then I saw that the person I was seven years ago is now my literary rival. That he had liked or disliked me for a time and then decided to correct me with his beautiful and intelligent pen.

He had done the job better than I had. To a vulgar joke he had added intellectual depth, a sprinkling of stylistic elegance, and a dash of good taste. And I peeped out of that bath like a poodle from a barrel of hair tonic.

Anyway, I was in despair. How to go on writing. How to continue and expand this epilogue to *The Calendar and the Hourglass* with that mimic's persistent echo in my ears.

What was it like there outside Wilno? When was that? Thirty-seven years ago. I don't remember anymore. That's just what they used to ask old Napoleonic veterans: What was it like outside Moscow in 1812? And they'd say: I don't remember a thing, not a thing. I only remember that it was very hot.

We were lying at the edge of a plateau with the entire Wilenka Valley below us. Actually, it was the serene but deep canyon made by the Wilenka River, my river, the river by which I was born and in which—before I became a complete person or almost complete, in my first incarnation—I used to spend day after day from the end of May to the middle of October. The small Wilenka River was the first I knew of nature.

And so we were lying in the bushes, scrub, the remains of a forest at the edge of a long green bathtub. I don't know what we were doing. Maybe we were out on patrol, maybe we'd run into a little skirmish, or maybe we were just waiting. Airplanes flew over us, evil, fitful; "Coronation Sword's" artillery was firing on the other side of the Wilenka; the Cadre Strike Brigade from Warsaw lay in waiting somewhere on the left bank; the Father,

the famous partisan, was buried somewhere on the right bank;
and we were waiting for something.

And all three of us must have been from the Oszmiana Brigade—Staszek D., Gutek K., and me, Tadzek K. Actually, the
three of us were a detachment of Beaver Scouts in the underground scouts and we were heartily disillusioned. What we had
wanted was weapons, partisan girls, wounds, and victims, and
they had told us we had to graduate from high school first. Even
the underground scouts weren't aware that we had tried to switch
our allegiance elsewhere a few times. We hopped around to other
organizations, but they all wanted to teach us, school us, indoc-
trinate us. We were unarmed, and that was disarming.

No, the uprising in Wilno was not in the least like the one in
Warsaw. It was reminiscent of a school outing, a fresh-air picnic,
a date with girls who don't show up. A beautiful summer day
with unfortunate incidents.

I know that for some people that long July day was the longest
day in their lives. The longest and the most important. The most
important and the most beautiful. A day of manly adventure, an
hour of moral ecstasy, a minute of heroism.

And that's the very day that I forgot, lowlife that I am. And
that's also the reason I've never mentioned it in my writing. From
1929, the year of the crash, when I was three years old, I can
keenly remember a light-blue siphon bottle on the table and the
gramophone playing a hit song of the day, "Hot Rolls"; but I've
forgotten our glorious Home Army Uprising in 1944, the year
my native land was freed of the German occupation.

Why do I have such a dim recollection of that day in particular?
Perhaps because my part in the uprising was a paltry and haphazard one. Perhaps because I did not distinguish myself in any
special way that day. Perhaps because here and there I've already
written something about the fate of our Home Army in the Wilno
area, written it with irony, bias, injustice, and aspersion, which
may have caused me something on the order of psychological
lockjaw.

Or maybe it's simply because late that afternoon, actually just before evening, when our valley was filled with the dense light of a July sunset, there was a sudden stillness at that lovely time of day and, automatically, without orders from anyone, drawn by some fateful premonition, we all turned our heads toward my native Nowa Wilejka, to the northeast, that stretch of land forever magical to me, my friends, and my enemies, and on the cool, shadowy side we saw the slanting slope of our valley and a dark stretch of forest silent before nightfall, and from that dark stretch, that dark blue-green slanted crevice, reddish figures casting long shadows began to creep out, moving in our direction at an un-hurried pace, Pepesha submachine guns extended in front of them like blunt stingers. We froze, then rose from the ground, but not very high, only to our knees, and kneeling at the edge of the valley, literally holding our breath, we looked down at those lazy animalcules slipping down from above but at a slant along the slope. Those were soldiers of the Red Army. That was a new slavery coming to us disguised in the coarse cloth of free-dom.

The Polish earthquake. The end of the world beside the Vistula River. Rummaging through my memories of childhood and youth, I recall friends who have died and are still dying to this day, but outside my window, on Gorska Street and Nowy Swiat, an in-crustation of habits and customs is breaking apart, awakened slaves spurt geysers of fury, the lava of new social structures erupts. What's going to happen? What's going to happen?

I will not attempt to describe those days of March 1981, though I will mutter a little something about them under my breath. To be able to verify it in a few years. To check and see what remains of those emotions, desires, demands, longings, and hopes.

There was a warning strike today. From eight till noon. A general strike next Tuesday. If the authorities don't agree to carry out Solidarity's demands. There's conflict in the Politburo and the Party is divided vertically and horizontally. The Party's lead-ership is cut off from its grass roots, the pro-Soviet gangs are running wild, the regime's flunkies revolt every day, refusing to obey, seceding; nearly the entire country has joined Solidarity now. The Russians emit an occasional threatening groan; the world is rooting for Poland, which it also fears as if it were a madman.

The Western world wants to collaborate. It wants to keep flirting with Russia. Unconsciously, it fantasizes about being raped by the Russians. Please, go right ahead, don't let me stop you.

Today, as soon as the strike was over, I made a mad little voyage. I brought the screenplay for *The Issa Valley* to the film office on Pulawski Street and then went to the Polish TV polyclinic in Woronicz because it has a physical therapist whose services writers are allowed to use. I have a distended synovial cyst on my right ankle and I'd sprained my foot for the third time. The woman doctor prescribed something to ionize the swollen area, that sort of thing.

And so it was a long and dangerous journey through the steppes of Warsaw, the terrible wilderness of our capital city. First, one trolley closed its doors on me as I was getting on, and it did so on purpose, so that I would know in my bones that life is tough. A few times a day the trolley drivers take this form of microvengeance for their dismal lives. And bad luck had delivered me into one such driver's hands. But people helped me. Some young people pried those furious, voracious doors apart and pulled me in.

On the way back from the TV polyclinic I had another run of bad luck with a trolley driver. Trolleys heading back to the barn kept passing me, their cars empty, melancholy. My trolley appeared after half an hour. A crowd descended on the first car, which began to creak and crack. But my shrewd eye saw that the second car was empty. The doors, however, were closed, though one was partway open. So I slid my way in and took a seat, delighted with my good fortune. For a long time the trolley didn't budge. A young man in a nylon raincoat appeared and asked me something through the door I had just entered. I thought he was asking whether it was all right to get on that car. I said that I didn't know, that the door was partway open and so it was worth a try. In an effort to be friendly, I rose from my seat and leaned toward him.

And it was only then that I realized that he was trembling with fury. His eyes were transparent, his face was white as a sheet, and he was frothing at the mouth. It was the driver, in a fit of rage.

Thirty years younger than I, just starting out in his stupid life, at the beginning of his wretched knowledge of our common lot, this raging little shit showered the worst insults on me, and the only reason he did not attack me with his fists was that he was lazy by nature.

And so he went back to his car, where he announced that he would be punishing the other passengers for my escapade. They would all have to get off the trolley car at once, he'd be taking no passengers from that point on.

And he carried out that act of collective responsibility, forcing out the two hundred people packed in the trolley, then drove dashingly off into the mists of Pulawski Street.

And I, the cause of his disfavor, was left face to face with two hundred people dying to get home. When that young man pulled away, I noticed Solidarity posters on the windows of his trolley. Maybe last week at a turnabout the police had beaten him up for those posters and appeals. And so now he had taken his revenge, and the fact that he took it on people who are on his side is another matter entirely.

Universal human rights, socialism with a human face, *raison d'état*, the battle against censorship, the craving for democracy, traditional Polish tolerance, equality and brotherhood, independence and self-rule, love thy neighbor, Holy Communion, Poles let us love one another, the teachings of Marx, chorales and collective tears, but, underneath it all, a return to barbarity, the monstrous heat of animal instinct, the traumatic epilepsy of the victims of a Soviet Russian education.

When will this nation smile with relief, when will it extend its hand in friendship, when will it breathe the relatively pure air of Europe?

Besides, I've reverted to barbarism myself. You cut your coat according to the cloth. And like as not, that's why I'll be untranslatable again. But to hell with you.

7

I wanted to mention Zbigniew Cybulski. Yes, yes, me too. Everyone has already walked arm in arm with Zbyszek in their memoirs, diaries, essays, poems, fairy tales for children, and tax forms, and so why shouldn't I be able to stroll for a short while toward Wroclaw, that strange city where we lived off and on, as if performing military exercises, enduring exile, serving a sentence. I'm not saying anything against the city. The city's all right. The city has its own power, its own genius loci; it even has a certain charm of its own, though there I'm probably going a little too far.

And so—Zbyszek Cybulski, my fellow citizen of the Polish People's Republic, every guy on the street buddy-buddy with him. Zbyszek, who was so horribly sickened by all those memoirists, diarists, and scribes.

Zbyszek. How old was he when he died? He still must have been under forty. In my day forty-year-olds were worthy elders, fathers of the nation. Zbyszek was the first to launch the era of the youthful old man.

He and I got off to a bad start, we quarreled. At the time, I was the literary director of the Kadr film company; Zbyszek and Kobiela had written a treatment entitled *So Long, See You Tomorrow*. Wilek Mach went to work on the screenplay, but problems cropped up with the two original authors. Zbyszek was being especially aggressive. I came to terms quickly with Kobiela, but my problems with Zbyszek lasted a long time, until I made the film *Salto*.

We didn't like each other. I don't know how he saw me. But I do know how I saw him. Through the prism of *Ashes and Diamonds*, of course, a film in which I had a hand myself, as the company's literary consultant. Maybe it wasn't so much that I had a hand in things as that I was present during the production of the film. Present, with presence of mind.

There's not a lot to be said. That film was never very important to me. And I found Zbyszek especially irritating. No, no, that's sacrilege. In fact, in that film Zbyszek did irritate me for a very long time, but finally I got used to that role, for I had come to know Zbyszek better.

But I didn't like him as Maciek in *Ashes and Diamonds* because he reminded me too much of the American actors in fashion at that time—James Dean, Montgomery Clift. In general, that film reeked of fashionable posing, an odd mode, one not cut to our measure. In a word, I glowered severely at that derivation, that borrowing, that lack of originality draping subject matter that was utterly original.

It's a strange business all around. The film *Ashes and Diamonds* was well received here because it was somehow reminiscent of the Western manner, while in the West it became the number-one Polish film for the same reason—that it was somehow reminiscent of the Western manner. It tamed Communist Poland for the Western viewer, rendering it palatable, acceptable.

But Home Army bumpkin that I am, it stuck in my throat. Yes, we had our fashions, fads, modes. But our fashions did not include blue jeans, sunglasses, excessive drinking, neurotic kicks, hysterical sobbing, and short-term love affairs *à la* Joan Madou and Dr. Ravic.

We were coarse, common, we wore knickers; we were punctual, reliable, restrained, embarrassed, hungry for death, afraid of one another, mistrustful of the elite, and timid in our feelings, gestures, and words. We were simply different, we were simply genuine because we had not yet been reflected in the mirror of art.

The book that served as the basis for the film is the sort of political science fiction that we were writing at the time. It presented reality not as one saw it on the street but as created by an author well disposed to the newly arrived political doctrines and the newly arrived regime. I can say this with no feeling of constraint because I was involved in that process myself.

And so the novel depicted a Poland that was a bit fictitious, an ill-tempered society, politically turbulent, freed of its reactionaries, not shying away from feasting and revelry, precisely like the Roman Empire in the days before the final fall.

But in reality that was a Poland of graves, of Auschwitz, deportation to Siberia, and women partisans slaughtered, a Poland of hunger and orphans, a Poland of torture and prisons, a Poland that had lost the war and lost hope.

No, no, enough. Not another word about that film, the greatest masterpiece of People's Poland. Enough of this querulousness, this mischief, this caviling of an old man, this backbiting with a single loose tooth. I fall on my face before *Ashes and Diamonds*; I value it, respect it, esteem it, admire it, hold it in high regard.

I'd been talking about Zbyszek and the role he played, but I went off on a tangent. What is the truth in a work of art? And who has need of that truth?

I know that I hungrily sought that truth in art. Curious that I would do that, me, the old liar. What is art's truth? Is it the truth of psychology, of historical detail, the truth as something difficult to define, that life-giving vitamin of a likeness to man's fate? What is art's truth and who has need of it?

Me, a liar, I demand the truth. That film became the truth about my generation for the generations that came after it. It has become the truth despite me, one outside my reach; in fact, a truth that goes against me. But it is supported by the mighty hand of the state. The regime used that film to create the Polish ethos after the great earthquake in the middle of our century. It belonged to us, it was our contemporary *Pan Tadeusz*, Chopin's mazurkas for our time.

Jesus, Mary, and Joseph, when will I ever tear free of those three thousand meters of celluloid—after all, I have already humbled and abased myself before that film.

But my point is about Zbyszek, and the first role he played, which now, years later, seems genuine to me, truly as genuinely true as can be. That's how Zbyszek was and how the camera recorded him. Whether or not James Dean was making films at the time. Zbyszek had to play that role that way because he was playing himself, his own melody, his own individual score. And like a reinforced-concrete framework, Zbyszek held the film's structure together, not allowing it to crumble and turn into dust. I guess.

Zbyszek and I didn't like each other. He was haughty and did not seek reconciliation. And later on, we were never too close, even when we were on good terms. I wasn't part of Zbyszek's circle and he didn't fit in with my gang of friends. And consequently, I can write about him without those false, overblown, inauthentic emotions common to those who have deluded themselves that they possess a spiritual and artistic kinship with Zbyszek.

We worked together on *Salto*. I wrote that film with Zbyszek in mind, and had he refused to play in it, I wouldn't have made the film. But Zbyszek didn't refuse.

At that time, the end of 1964, the beginning of '65, in Wroclaw, I had frequent opportunity to observe Zbyszek Cybulski both directly and out of the corner of my eye. Those were not the observations of a director but, rather, those of a writer, an onlooker, a curious passerby. There was some unearthly element in Zbyszek. I've already mentioned that.

Just the way he looked was fascinating. A corpulent young man past his prime, whose charm was something between that of a gypsy and someone from the Caucasus mountains, or perhaps Transylvania. This type can be found in Lvov, and I think that the Cybulski family was originally from Lvov. Everything about him was of a high quality. I mean his swarthy, healthy skin; his thick, intense gypsy hair; his large, strong teeth. Zbyszek had not been done in by time or a frivolous way of life. His characteristic features had been lent him by history, the twisting rules of social systems, the psychological habits and wishes of his audience, which was all of Poland. From Spatif in Warsaw to provincial dives with their cold-food snack bars and organists playing out of sight.

Zbyszek was nonchalant and reckless about his body and his outward appearance. He did not have to take care of his health. That was looked after by forces not of this world. Some Martian slave, some anonymous flunky in the depths of the universe watched over the biological Zbyszek. I tell you, he was sent here from above.

But still, those who sent him to us overdid things a little— they installed a soul that was a bit too Polish in that Lvov-Caucasian or gypsy organism. What I'm thinking of here are certain distinguishing elements like angelicalness, girlishness, infantilism. I'm thinking here of the romantic, messianic, bardlike element. I'm thinking of the inclination, you'll pardon me, to divinity.

Zbyszek was a slightly fleshy neutron bomb of psychological, intellectual, and emotional movement. Zbyszek was human matter condensed to the breaking point in the moment before the great explosion, the colossal detonation. In my life I've had a few encounters with beings sent down to us by someone from the heart of the cosmic labyrinth.

Zbyszek, eternal wanderer, indefatigable boaster, aging child, absentminded sorcerer, fallen saint. Zbyszek, a Pole on an official mission.

Why was he recalled from our world, suddenly and for no reason?

Last year, or maybe two years ago, I read a book by an American historian, or maybe two American historians, on the history of the ancient Persian empire.

Since I have a lousy memory and immediately forget everything, I remembered only two, no, actually three, pages of that book, very strange and thought-provoking pages.

The first concerned the astonishing fate of Alexander the Great. Not his fate so much as him as a historical phenomenon. Maybe not so much as a phenomenon as an edifying example of the meaningless within the meaningful.

According to the American, it was the conquests themselves that were the driving force of Alexander's conquests. Conquest was itself the point of conquest. And the final result of his conquests was the phenomenon of conquest, which disappeared along with Alexander like the first light of dawn.

He did not unite anything, did not lay the foundation for anything, did not create anything. The first pure bandit in history, the first instinctive predator, the first disinterested wreaker of genocide. A sort of horrible sewer pipe. Something went gurgling through it, but nothing remained after. Thin air, empty space, a void.

At that time, or actually a bit before Alexander the Great, a Persian professor arrived in Greece on some sort of scholarly grant. During his trip to the Peloponnesian peninsula, the good professor delivered a few lectures on astronomy and cosmogony.

He said that the earth is spherical in shape and, as part of a system of a dozen or so planets, it revolves around the sun, which is a gigantic incandescent ball of gases and liquid metals. He said that the planets and the sun are part of an unimaginably great collection of other such systems, of which there are billions in the infinity of space, and it all arose from a single explosion that occurred twenty billion years ago.

Those lectures did not cause any special interest in the Greek scientific world of the time. The professor's talks met with a polite reception, though there were no comments and attendance was moderate.

When his stipend ran out, the Persian professor returned to his own country, and that was the last anyone heard of him.

In the remote past the Iranian tribes ate their dead. A particularly disgusting ritual was instituted around that diet. The corpses would be eaten for weeks on end amid a hideous stink accompanied by exceptionally repulsive ceremonies. One time a traveler asked the reason for that state of affairs. The worthy elders smiled craftily and replied: We have this disgusting, filthy, repellent ceremony in order to frighten our neighbors to the north and keep them from invading our country. We try to be so nasty that no one will lust after our land.

Isn't this a forgotten but effective political doctrine?

Winter, ice, barely dawn. We go down to the motor coach to leave for a day's filming. Like the premier of some hated government, accompanied only by Kurt Weber, the cameraman, I slip modestly to a seat at the back of the bus. We wait a long time for the prima donna, the darling. God's gift. He finally appears in the doorway muffled up in a huge sheepskin coat. Now he hurries, accompanied by his retinue—my female assistants, the crew's makeup girls, our script girls. They all belong to him now. They lead him like a turkey cock to the best seat.

But he, our beloved king, has buried himself in his sheepskin collar and does not so much as glance in our, that is, my, direction. I have offended him with the freezing cold weather, his hangover, the early call, and his idiotic role in the film. I stay quiet as a mouse. He murmurs with frightful anger, surrounded by ladies-in-waiting.

The bus pulls away. And then not too loudly I begin speaking with Kurt: "You know what, you know what, it'd be a good idea in that scene when Zbyszek gets up from the floor if he fumbles around with his foot as if he were using it to look for something. That's a tic of his, you see, he always thinks he's lost something."

I say this with my voice lowered and then look up at the pyramid of sheep's wool in front of me. A stir of anxiety. Zbyszek lowers his collar, wriggles, and begins eavesdropping, curious about what we're cooking up.

Kurt says: "That really would be a good idea, pinning that

gesture on him. I'm for it. And you know, I think it would make a good leitmotif. It should be used a few times." Then Kurt asks slyly: "What about in today's scene?"

Now I see Zbyszek's large wonderful red ear come nearer us. Now his hangover's on its way out, as is his discouragement, his anger at us, poor schemers from the Duchy of Warsaw.

And so I strike while the iron is hot: "Kurt, what do you think of this? When Zbyszek gets up from the floor, after the poet shoots, maybe right then, at the most dramatic moment, he could poke around with his foot, what do you think?"

Zbyszek can't take it. He explodes in sudden admiration for my cleverness. He's still not looking at me, but he's admiring me. I still don't acknowledge him, but I've already got him by that gypsy head of hair.

Zbyszek is terribly fond of film "ideas," meaning bits of any sort. Zbyszek loves changes, surprises, the unexpected, the startling, intellectual coups, insane jokes. Zbyszek admires recklessness, sudden inspiration, and a dash of everyday poetry. Any coin of that currency can buy Zbyszek along with his sheepskin coat, and his shoes, the sort called tractors or pioneers.

Another time Zbyszek appears late for the shoot. He's supposedly there, but he's nowhere to be found. The expression on the face of his ladies-in-waiting is mysterious, pained. They run to call him and come back without him. There's some secret here, something like a plot, a totally explicit conspiracy against me.

Finally, the star is brought, sulky and offended at me in advance. The camera rolls. Zbyszek is oafishly clumsy, sits when he should stand, and goes right instead of left. He knows it's all wrong. But honor, aggravated by a few drinks, brooks no compromise, no negotiation, no understanding. And so the entire blame falls on me, along with the unpleasant smell of the vodka. Zbyszek rolls a furious bloodshot eye.

And then suddenly I say: "That's it, we've got the scene. Thanks, everyone. See you tomorrow."

Zbyszek is thunderstruck. He had expected some ceremony,

requests, diplomatic attempts, but after two lousy takes it's see you later.

Then emissaries come running to report that, if need be, God's gift would be able to do one more take, just to be on the safe side. I thank them courteously, but no thanks. I have no desire to work with an actor who's not in good form.

A typhoon suddenly erupts from within the dressing room, his kingdom. I even hear some abuse directed at me. Stern cries, chairs breaking, women weeping and wailing.

Then we go back by bus. I say to Kurt: "Well, if he'd been sober, he wouldn't have forgotten about the bit with his foot fumbling on the ground."

In the rear of the bus Zbyszek freezes and doesn't stir for the rest of the trip.

Then, later, for the entire evening and half the night, emissaries and ambassadors go back and forth between the gypsy lover's castle and my ascetic bunker. What tribute I am offered to shoot the scene again! What apologies are brought me on silken pillows. What prodigious sums are offered our company and Polish film by the actor, sober and in despair, making a guest appearance in the Duchy of Warsaw.

He was surrounded by beautiful women who included—shameful to say—alcoholics, boon companions, erotic hyenas, and stealthy camp followers. The money he earned was scattered along the way, lost in absentminded oblivion; it was dribbled away in loans and gifts to people in trouble. He was adored and, in the blink of an eye, a millisecond, adoration was transformed into a spasm of hatred.

He was always that Zbyszek, our aging Zbyszek, a mysterious transformer of our emotions, our elations, our loves.

What did he transform them into, what form did he lend them, and to what purpose? I don't know. I don't know, though I do think about it frequently. And the more often I think about it, the less often his courtiers do, and those who made money off him.

I have met a few mysterious individuals in my life, beings from other worlds, strangers from outer space, or perhaps from another universe entirely: they were Wilek Mach, Zbyszek Cybulski, and probably Miecio Piotrowski as well.

If you want to know them better, you must rummage through old magazines, yellowed books, forgotten films.

Fine, but what about the uprising in Wilno? What about that commission from Adam Michnik?

That's just it. I have some fear of writing. I am afraid of those people for whom that was a day of Ascension. They've been living off that day for nearly forty years now, telling tales of it over the evening's booze, using that day to instruct their grandchildren in the intricacies of our history. Their scrap of honor is fixed, their particle of human dignity, their grain of earthly sanctity, in the sunlit amber of those twelve or fourteen hours. How to speak of that unsung day here, using the tricks of a rebellious, anarchistic writer from the metropolises of Europe?

But there's no other choice. Others may paint this provincial incident from the last war in epic colors. I'll tell what I saw and haven't yet forgotten.

Soviet soldiers appeared at the slanted edge of the forest followed by evening advancing from the east. The first evening of free slavery or slave freedom. I no longer remember how it happened, but apparently we were given the order to disarm. We (Staszek, Gutek, and I) quickly removed our cartridge belts, laid down our rifles (mine was French and there had been trouble finding ammunition for it), and went home.

I vaguely recall setting off cautiously for home, walking by the woods right by the hillside. My home wasn't far away, and that entire little epic, that microscopic war of mine, had taken place near my home, my courtyard, my little street, and thus had contained a certain element of playing cowboys and Indians, cops and robbers, or just playing war.

And so I went home and went to bed like an ordinary civilian. But the war had not ended that evening. About three days later a

liaison officer arrived and ordered me to rejoin my detachment. I
can recall bits and pieces from the way back. A hot day, dust, ripe
grain along the road. Our platoon leader out in front on horseback. I remember his bulging shoulders and his odd military cap,
an enormous four-cornered cap no doubt made by a village woman.
That cap struck terror in the Soviet detachments that passed us.
They would all stand at attention and give us a long salute.

I also recall that at one point I was issued a rifle, or I may
have come up with it myself, a rifle that had something wrong
with it. I was afraid to shoot it, terrified that it would blow up
in my hands. I feigned stupidity with a senior Soviet non-com.

Making good-natured fun of my youth and my whole little
game of war, he examined the rifle, reloaded it, raised it to his
shoulder, and, aiming at the sky, fired a shot between two exceptionally white clouds.

I recall a Soviet bivouac in the forest. It must have been a field
hospital. Old soldiers, old mustached men, were cooking millet
kasha in an enormous kettle. We were each given a plate full of
that delicacy.

Then the detachment was reorganized; there were meetings,
speeches. Finally, we set off, heading east, perhaps toward Molodeczno. We kept passing Soviet units, kept exchanging greet-
ings, their heartiness forced. To Germany! To Germany! *Kho-
rosho!* Good men!

An American jeep. The letters USA had not been painted over
yet. It must have been new. We went up to the Rooskies and
said: "How come you say those are Soviet-made vehicles but
look, there's Latin letters on them?" And we pointed to USA in
dark green.

The Russians laughed a cunning laugh. "You see, boys," they
said, "when we crossed the old Polish border, we switched to
Latin letters for convenience now that we're here in Europe."

"All right then," said one of the wiseguys, "but what does that
abbreviation USA mean?"

"You mean you don't know," said the Russians in surprise.
"That's simple. Up that Snake Adolf's. USA. Get it?"

At first we marched by day, but later on, only by night. Until, finally, the forest. Day duty in a pine forest. The old veteran partisans whispered that the Germans were deep in the forest waiting for nightfall. They would try to break through to their own lines. The alarm was sounded a few times. We were supposed to go leaping at those Germans. But, in the end, all we did was slurp some lousy soup in an old farmhouse.

Those two weeks were a great philosophical symposium for us freshly baked high-school graduates, us freshly confirmed eighteen-year-olds. We debated day and night. While on the march and when lying in the mud among forget-me-nots, stuffed with mudlike black bread and wildly hungry. We gabbed shamelessly about what the new world should be like, what it would be like, what we would make it. Today people are too ashamed to talk like that. But we were shameless because we had not yet been tainted by sin. We were to be the beginning of a new era, we were discovering a brave new world. And everything around us was so pure, so fresh, so full of color. The sky, the air, and people's merry faces.

Sometimes I remember a little something from those days, like a word that had slipped my mind. But I'm getting to the point, a caricature of a point. Because while we were marching east, led by our circumspect commander, Tur, other brigades of the Wilno Home Army concentrated in the Rudnicka Wilderness had been surrounded by Soviet troops, forced to surrender, and disarmed, then herded into a makeshift POW camp in Miedniki. I was not aware of that. I was also not aware that even earlier, during talks and negotiations, the Russians had arrested the leaders of the Wilno-Nowogrodek Home Army. I was not aware that this was the end of "Storm," one operation in a great war, an operation the world will never hear of and, if it does, will forget immediately.

Talking, talking, day and night. States of ecstasy at the threshold of heaven or hell, at the gate of death's sunny land. Death in the heart of summer, amid unmowed fields, clumps of herbs, forest meadows of blackberry and huckleberry. Patrols, sentry duty, meetings. The baggage of what we had learned in school and the experience of a shepherd boy from some godforsaken provincial hole. Exuberant dreams, absolute impossibility. Rivers flow uphill, smoke stays in the chimney, stars shine in the afternoon. A little hunger, a little fever, a little disenchantment, still unconscious.

Finally, a long march through the forests. Liaison officers on bicycle. Our commander perplexed (did he have his black beard then or did he grow it later, in late '44, early '45?), anxiety, things becoming a bit messy, less military order. Then, finally, a meeting. What kind of forest was that? Pine, alder, or perhaps a mixed copse at the edge of fields? A final speech (it must have been by Tur) and once again we were told to disarm and return home, just a cadre to remain with the commanding officer. Maybe again later, maybe in a while, maybe in the fall. The battle wasn't over yet. Poland had not yet perished . . .

We lay down our arms as if building a fire from resinous pine logs. The clank of metal, a troubled silence, someone muttering under his breath. Then a shortcut back to the road, following the sun toward Wilno. I set off with two other boys, neither of whom I remember. We walked home on small sideroads, through fields. We exchanged our good army trenchcoats for boy's jackets or old-fashioned peasant coats. We still didn't know everything, but we were already aware that we had to be on guard and not let ourselves get caught. A reminder of this came from a Russian plane that caught us in a vast open area, used for threshing, where the grass was sparse. The plane fired a few machine-gun bursts at us, and along with a few other boys we'd met up with, we took cover under a tall black pear tree.

Marching carefully by day, spending the nights on fragrant straw full of prickly weeds and restless beetles. We pretended to be on the way back from helping relatives with the harvest. The peasants were well aware what was up, but were friendly to us.

Then finally it came time to part. We were near Wilno. We could feel the heightened activity of our city. Bye. Bye. Bye. We went off in various directions. I went to the northwest. Through the fields, keeping away from the streets and roads.

The roar of motors. Immense, invisible engines. Hearing that voice which seemed to come from the bowels of the earth, I guessed I was near the military airfield at Porubanek. I'd have to skirt it. But how, which way?

I saw a small solitary hut in a sparse orchard, looking like a boat in a golden ocean of unharvested grain. In the window a teenage boy was looking out at the world and saw me coming home from the war, my eighteen-year-old, high-school-graduate war.

I walked confidently up to the hut and asked the boy the best way to avoid Porubanek. He looked at me with a somewhat stupid expression, then squinted uncertainly into the cool darkness of the hut. Then he looked out at me again, blinking his eyes. I repeated my question in a more confidential tone of voice. The boy did not respond, though he was even more curious than before. Then he vanished, yielding his place to someone else.

A young man hastily putting on a light-blue cap with a rasp-berry-red brim appeared in the window frame as in an old painting. He had a sleek Nagan revolver in his right hand. Now I knew who he was. I knew that breed of Russians who arrived here in 1939 and 1940–41.

And that NKVD man called me over with the barrel of his pistol. So, come in, little man. I went into the hut, which proved to be one large kitchen. There were three of them: him, his wife, and the boy, their son.

Toying with his pistol, the NKVD man began questioning me sternly. Where have you come from? The country. Where are you going? Home. What were you doing in the country? Helping my relatives with the harvest. In what village? Kowaliszki.

They nodded their heads. It was all true, the gospel truth, the young man's telling the truth. Everybody's helping with the harvest now. People need bread.

But by then the NKVD man was playing the role of a good-natured, naïve old uncle, a lazy European. Then his face suddenly contorted, his eyes flashed wildly, and he began roaring so loud the windowpanes rattled. I know you're a Polish partisan, you motherfucker, you Fascist, I'll kill you right here, you bastard, you cocksucker. And so on, and so forth. The upshot was that he would bring me in immediately to the NKVD in Oszmiana or somewhere else nearby, I can't remember now.

I would have been in real trouble if his wife hadn't brought in a few eggs quick as a mouse, cut up some bacon, and started cooking scrambled eggs.

As the smell of the sizzling bacon spread through the air, the NKVD captain began to relent. He was still waving his pistol, but now only to drive away the flies that were gathering over the table. And by the time he uncorked a flask of home brew and the first life-giving drop had flowed down the old Chekist's throat, the situation had turned around.

Still in a bit of a dark mood, the captain shot me a red-eyed glance and muttered, but without anger: Ah, you Polish Fascist.

Then he mixed the eggs in the frying pan with a spoon, gave a somehow moving groan, and set his spoon down. He grabbed hold of a full glass of home brew, shielded his cellophane-covered decorations with his left hand, raised the glass to his mouth with his right, tilted back his head, and began pouring the marvelous fluid into a black maw guarded by a single tooth, but a gold one at that.

He set his glass down. Ah, damnit, he puffed with ceremonial concentration into the sleeve of his uniform. Then he spooned up a bite of egg in whose center was a dark gold square, raised the spoon dripping fat to his lips, and suddenly caught sight of me.

He looked me over for a second—my miserable person was something of an obstacle, somehow out of keeping with that moment of delight, nasty and odious in his eyes. He grimaced, he glowered, and showed me the door with his rapidly cooling spoon.

"You go to hell . . ."

. . .

An unsuccessful operation in Wilno. The luckless partisan campaign of 1944–45. The dispersal of the underground, a good-sized one, after all. Moral decline. The first betrayals and disloyalties. Deportations to Kaluga, and then later to Vorkuta, Kolyma, the Pamir region.

Our first reaction was to accuse ourselves. Seek the sin, the flaw, the evil in ourselves. Irresponsibility, braggadocio, stupidity, parochial nationalism, recklessness, organizational and moral disorder, reactionary leanings, petit-bourgeoisism, smugness, hysteria and cowardice, failure to understand history, obscurantism, et cetera, et cetera. We beat our own breasts, and those of our colleagues, neighbors, commanders, and leaders.

But today we know that, had we been angels, had we soared to the heights of holiness, had Providence endowed us with the political talents of Bismarck and the military genius of Napoleon, we still would have had to lose our war in Wilno and the whole of the Polish Second World War.

We sought the fault in ourselves, we accused each other, we cursed each other, shot at our colleagues, lost friends in the abyss of oblivion; we renounced our young loves, we went mad from moral pain; we hanged each other from dry branches while passing through forests. And none of us knew that this was how the river of history had to flow, that our will was the will of a drop of water dissolved in that river and borne into the unknown, unwanted future. We did not know that the river was guided by the three architects of the mid-twentieth century: Churchill, Roosevelt, and Stalin. The self-admiring Prime Minister who became the unwitting gravedigger of the British Empire, the American cripple who was absolutely infatuated with Stalin, and the tsar of the modern genocides, our own somber, mysterious Joseph Vissarionovich.

8

My schoolmate Karnowski. As far as the quality of the material, the cut, and its accessories are concerned, my high-school uniform was the third worst. My schoolmate U.'s was worse than mine, and it was Karnowski who came in last, the bottom of the barrel. His uniform, I think, was made of cotton. After a few months, it was completely faded and worn to a shine.

My schoolmate Karnowski, my schoolmate of the Jewish faith. I can recall his outward appearance, his uniform, his gravity, but I have forgotten his first name. What was that Karnowski's name? Why pretend, I'll never remember.

My schoolmate Karnowski. That's how he should be spoken of, ceremoniously. We weren't friends, I didn't particularly like him, we didn't do things together. He was just one of the thirty or so students, and there was nothing exotic about him. We also had a Karaite by the name of Mickiewicz; a Russian, Sazonov, who was killed by one of the first bombs that fell in '39; and there was probably a German and definitely a Lithuanian in our class.

But I have never forgotten Karnowski. Actually, I remember them all. But I have made Karnowski into some personal, secret symbol of my own. I constantly scratch his name into stones by the roadside. I inscribe the memory of my schoolmate whom I didn't really know wherever I can. Whenever I can, I commemorate his name in my misshapen prose.

Karnowski and I would talk from time to time. He was dignified, serious, perhaps even a little too serious for his age, intelligent. I suspected he had some ties with the left, perhaps with the Communists. Actually, my acquaintance with Karnowski was limited to those few conversations. Then the war came. Karnowski went off somewhere, disappeared, and I never heard of him again.

I didn't hear a word about him, but he was always on my mind. I swear I have no idea why I think about him. I'm curious about what happened to him. Did he go off to the Soviet Union and stay on there? Did the Germans lock him up in the ghetto and execute him later on in Ponary? Or did he join a Jewish partisan unit or some other sort and then go out into the world after the war, to put distance between himself and that land wet with the blood of his loved ones? Perhaps Karnowski is dead ten times over, or perhaps he's somewhere in America doing research on human genetics. Or is he in heaven, meaning in the bosom of Abraham, or perhaps, under a different name, has he won the Nobel Prize and will he never know that an East European writer painstakingly inscribes his name in his books?

Just between us, Karnowski wasn't a very appetizing sort. A very Semitic appearance; a pale, sickly complexion with traces of dark freckles, sad animal eyes. Karnowski reeked of poverty. Literally. Many of his schoolmates would move discreetly away from him.

Why is it Karnowski whose praises I sing as best I can? That close-mouthed boy whom no one remembers, who disappeared without a trace from our life, and who went unnoticed even by Providence, why do I hold him sacred and make him meager literary offerings, why do I feel the need to save his memory from oblivion?

It was just a few days ago that I was looking through an old film script that I'd done with Kawalerowicz and Stryjkowski based on Stryjkowski's novel *The Inn*. It was written fourteen years ago. At the time political conditions would not permit Kawalerowicz to film the script.

In all these years, that world has receded even further from memory, and yet, strange as it may seem, as it receded, that world also drew abruptly nearer, fusing with the present and increasing in size. And no doubt the same holds true for that stirring novel on which the quite faithful screenplay had been based.

I gazed astounded at those pages, which had yellowed and darkened during those fourteen years, and I thought about that world, great and splendid, majestic and romantic, funny and laughable, moving and tragic, the unforgettable and already forgotten world and universe of the Polish Jews.

A planet died. A globe incinerated by a cosmic disaster. A black hole. Antimatter.

Oh, God, how did it happen? Anti-Semitism, philo-Semitism, Zionism, nationalism, converts and Hasids, hatreds and rivalries, moments of solidarity and community, good days, bad days, humanity, inhumanity, all of it mixed and whirled together in one land, divided and united, two civilizations and two cultures. Then, suddenly, during the brief night of the occupation, something was amputated. Some part of the landscape, the flora, the fauna, the architecture, the sound track was forever severed and borne away into the icy darkness of the universe which is our heaven and our hell.

Yes, a world great as human thought, deep as love, beautiful as longing has turned to ashes. That torments me. That will always torment me.

A breakdown. A terrible breakdown. A cloudy day, a low f-stop, as the photographers say. Darkness outside, darkness between my ribs. In the morning I went to the hospital for television people where they irradiated my foot. They beam radiation through old man Konwicki's foot and false information through the air. But I was ashamed to go there, didn't like telling the cabdriver

the address; it was unpleasant to enter that building's interior
ambiguous with the readiness to strike and the readiness to obey
a boss or foreign powers.

Another breakdown. A terrible breakdown. A horrible feeling
of nothingness. The nothingness that comes from being old. Or
rather, the nothingness that comes *with* being old. Everything
that a person accomplished has crumbled into invisible dust and
ill winds.

Who the hell knows how I got into this profession. It was
because of Krakow in 1945, because of those idiotic Polish studies, because of the poverty of the times, which drove me to seek
work. I was hired as a proofreader by the weekly *Rebirth*. I swore
to myself that I would only correct errors. Fat chance. That was
like a girl swearing to be virtuous when taking a job as a cham-
bermaid in a bordello. I began writing out of my reveries, out of
fascination, foolish ambition, forced into it by what was around
me. God had no desire whatsoever that I be a writer. Providence
was just making up its mind what to do with me. And there's no
luck worse than coming to literature through the rut of time-
serving, years of service at its altar. I knew it would end badly,
but I didn't know how badly.

A terrible breakdown, I never knew the likes of it before. I'm
getting older and my breakdowns are getting older. I have the
head of a mathematician. I can calculate, measure, and predict
everything. It's just that the writing's worse. But writing is what
I chose. Oh, the hell with me and the ink I waste.

I keep beating around the bush because I don't want the most
important thing to escape my lips. The diagnosis of my existential
disease: I am spur-of-the-moment, short-run, temporary. In life
and in my misshapen writing. My books start to die as soon as
the ink dries on the page. I've known that for some time now.
It's shameful to admit, but I've even tried to combat this flaw.
But how?

Play up my personality, make a chess-like calculation of the
consequences of every adjective and predicate, speculate on a

universal stream of consciousness, pump up my soul like an old tire?

No, it's past help. What God creates is not subject to division. Something is either entirely suitable or entirely unsuitable. Nothing can be changed or improved. The only consolation is that it doesn't last long. That this swindle of mine will come to an end. That I have to pretend to be a Warsaw writer less often all the time.

A columnist forced by an unfortunate set of circumstances into becoming a novelist. An ambitious columnist who has to write boring and elevated epics. An old-fashioned Wilnonian with an overblown sense of his own dignity entangled in a situation which even a supermodern New York philosopher would find more than his match. The hell with it.

As through a mist I can see lively movement in the city. The general strike has been called off. Almost a victory for the forces of democracy and sovereignty. But I am deafened by egocentric pain. I grope like a blind man. Hideous. My own hideousness amid beauty.

A gloomy day. The clouds have smothered this sclerotic land until there's no air left to breathe. And it's good that there's no air to breathe. It's no more than I deserve.

I'm listening to the radio. A spring sun outside. My internal chemistry is very sensitive to sunlight. Maybe it is worth staying alive until tomorrow.

The radio speaks of some tectonic movement in Solidarity, among the leaders of our free trade unions. Some people have resigned, others have been dismissed. Personnel problems. Polish personnel problems. The pursuit of personal interests can be suspected here. Positions, pecking order, ambition, early outbreaks of arrogance. But, after all, these first few months of an independent trade-union movement have been a political kindergarten, night-school courses in political science, our first private lessons in political culture.

Political attitudes are clarified in these clashes of views and personalities. Some essential political doctrines are being formulated in those passionate debates. Our future political leaders are being shaped in those workers' symposiums.

Everything is normal, the way it has to be. But my nasty, stubborn, contrary nature enjoins me to be a bit surprised at this phenomenon—that today's likable troublemakers, dynamic, uncompromising, unyielding, were, four years ago, sleeping the sleep of the just. They were deaf to every appeal to their conscience, blind to every ideological or moral crime committed at their doorstep. A few years ago they could not take a pen in hand to sign a humanitarian appeal, but today they want to raise a fist against the regime. It wasn't that long ago that they were afraid to talk on the phone and now they're calling for a war against Communism.

But is Poland's renewal built to scale?

Here, I bow my head sadly and make a proviso—what counts is our intelligence, that leading lady of every season.

A few days later and the view is entirely different, a whole other optics; even my eyes don't seem the same. Once again the entire world is trembling in fear. All governments are losing sleep. Even Reagan, the American President, wounded by an assassin and in the hospital, is running a high fever.

Our entire solar system dreads a Soviet invasion of Poland. Naturally, the term "invasion" is a matter of convention. The Russians do not have to attack our country. They've been here, comfortable and prospering, for thirty-five years. Their garrisons, bases, and fortresses are ingrown; they've settled into the national government, the security system, and into artistic circles as well. I have spotted Russian names even among some of the leaders of secret nationalistic parties.

The world fears a coup d'état and the ultimate Sovietization of Poland. The world still believes that little by little Soviet Communism will be humanized, Europeanized, and will stop at the stage when it has become a gentle, good-natured, exotic clime of bears, blintzes, and caviar. And the bear will dance with the Krakovian, and the Krakovian will nibble on blintzes and caviar and drink the liquid known as Russian vodka.

But poor me, what I see, envision, and ponder is . . . no, no, I'm afraid to write it, afraid to put these sacrilegious thoughts in writing on the back of an old, anonymous typescript; yes, I fear hard proof being found among my papers during the next search of my apartment, which has to happen if I wake tomorrow to the rumble of tanks, the merry sound of accordions playing Russian ditties, and lively cries of Hands up! Hands up!

It's haunting; it haunts me, and despite my fear, I still put in writing these the blasphemous hallucinations of a decadent intellectual who resides by the Vistula River. It will take more than a single episode, an isolated historical incident, an autonomous chance event ever to free Poland from its Soviet cage. Poland will not crawl out from this Slav-Mongol pile in the way that naïve café politicians imagine—one, two, three, and we're suddenly free.

Poland will regain its freedom only when the Soviet empire collapses. That's not all. Poland, among others, will be the cause of that monster's demise.

It's already started. We've already caused a fatal obstruction in that gigantic rhino's innards. It's still bellowing, still pawing the ground in front of it, still on the rampage, making the small and the weak burrow into their little holes. But now it's running a high fever, its blood is having trouble circulating under its iron hide, its excrement has petrified in its large intestine. It won't be long before the monster collapses to the ground. It will still be kicking for another five or six years; it will beat its head against rocks and stones, belch fire and brimstone, while we, the microbes which have fatally infected that dinosaurish organism, will be aware of what these signs mean. And that infernal, death-dealing, gigantic monolith will break into small, healthy, vital pieces—free societies, free nations, independent ethnic groups.

Have patience. Wait for five or ten years. The colossus is in its death throes. And the death throes of a colossus must be colossal. Cities will crumble, islands will sink into the seas. But we shall endure in an air bubble between the monster's buttocks. So let's wait, five years, ten, a hundred at most.

I was setting to work on a novel. The action, set in Wilno, was to provide the objective time element in the story, whereas for the subjective time element I had imagined a special epic layer fashioned from a hypothetical dimension, an invented reality side by side with contemporary reality, today's reality, that would seem taken straight off the street.

And so I saw that portion of my unwritten book, that novel within a novel, as a journey, a twofold, ambiguous expedition to America and the Wilno Colony, both at the same time.

I wanted to make that journey in my imagination or, to be more grandiloquent about it, in my reveries, that half-real trip to New York and that absolutely impossible illegal border crossing into the real Wilno of today. Wilno, where the rest of my relatives, colleagues, and friends are. I wished to interweave those two threads, forming them into one powerful cord with which I could hang myself and be done with it.

My plan was to transfer the people I loved, living and dead, to those two dimensions, America and Wilno. I simply wanted to amuse myself indecorously by braiding different times, mixing reality and imagination, the sad boring truth and the jolly youthful lie.

But, into the middle, the very center of that snarl, that cunning knotted bundle, I would smuggle a certain godless hypothesis on the subject of God. I would coat that private axiom of mine with literature, wallpaper it with stale poetry in order to avoid taking responsibility for my brazen impudence.

And so, a certain unruly and reckless hero of mine who slipped out of my hands and was, in fact, no longer in my control set off into the world, meaning dwarfland. And so, he bestirred himself on those two voyages, one to the New World of America and the other to the Old World of Wilno, and on both peregrinations took along his doubts in the good old Lord God, doubts which spilled like seeds from a sack riddled with holes.

Because the Lord exists, and God exists, but the Lord God does not. Our Lord is no doubt a modest genetic engineer from the downtown area of the universe. A happy-go-lucky scientist instructed by a worthy professor to plant something on the far side of the universe, in the paltry patch of this solar system, something that might come in handy if it grows well. And besides, the professor had pedagogic reasons for giving the young scientist that assignment—so the young man would not be idle, growing lazy and demoralized at the core of the universe. The plantings themselves were of no particular importance to anyone.

And so the young engineer planted some little beings, actually codes for future animalcules, but out of boredom and because he was inclined to pranks, he endowed those beings yet to be with a certain likeness to himself, making them one of trans-universal science's outside hopes.

And here we are, the victims of that prank, proud of our likeness to our Lord, whom we honor all over this insignificant globe and to whom we pray. We have invented a hundred religions to leash our doggish love for our Lord, our snobbery about our Lord, and our faith that our Lord will not toss us into the bucket with all the rest of the failed cells of matter given life.

It is time to revolt against being the playthings of some irre-sponsible individual who multiplies us in accordance with math-ematical game theory, who is doing His assignment none too carefully, and who is not even interested in the results.

I call on you, segmented protoplasm, microbes grazing on a volcano of deadly oxygen, blind deaf stones flying off into the void of nonexistence, I call on you to revolt, to rebel, to offer unruly, stiff, furious resistance. Let us give up kowtowing to our Lord, let us cease praising Him and serving Him faithfully, let us cease rendering Him divine homage. He is not watching over us, He has gone off somewhere and we're lost to His sight; we're of no more importance to Him and it does not matter to Him whether we live on our miserable moral and intellectual heights or whether we die in vileness and sin. Cracking jokes, carefree, He's gone back to the center of the Universe, because it seems He's the same sort of lout we are, His sorry reflection in an old-fashioned, obsolete genetic mirror.

Mammals, amphibians, reptiles, vertebrates, and mollusks, trees and flowers, water and stone, let us unite in anarchy against this unthought-out order. Let us oppose ugly construction with beautiful destruction. Let us love wise death instead of foolish life.

God exists. God lives on the other side of the universe or the Universe of all universes, God is coming in our direction. But He does not know of us yet and we know nothing of Him. He is coming toward us like a sun, a great luminosity, eternal warmth. And finally one day He will enlighten and warm us with a sudden dawn of goodness, beauty, harmony, and logic here in our cadaverous backwater, this dead end, this idiotic cesspool for the alleged universe.

I'll stop here, I'm dashing off to Holy Cross for vespers now.

I'm afraid to write, because I'm obsessed with repeating myself. It's all because of that dwindling memory of mine. Of course, every once in a while I could stop and look through what I'd written during the last few weeks, but some complex or obsession prevents me. I mean, my obsessive dread of what I myself have written, those ill-arranged nouns, verbs, and adjectives extruded and extracted from myself, those false intonations, those rhythms not really mine. I am afraid of repeating myself but am even more afraid of reading my own prose.

Given that, there's no choice but to stumble on ahead blindly, bearing the cursed burden of self-repetition. But perhaps we can make a virtue of that vice, draw some grace and beauty from that deformity, a marvelous, awesome potency from that impotence.

We will repeat ourselves. Because repetition creates rhythm and figures of speech and is the beginning of true art.

Let us repeat ourselves and from those repetitions create something new in literature, some European trick, a worthy experiment for an old day laborer of the pen. By repetition, repetition will repeat the repetitiveness of repetition. Meaning our laborious existence.

Laborious for some, and for others as light as the touch of a butterfly's wing. Bang, bang, you're dead.

The Poles are a wonderful, charming, intelligent nation, but a nation that is infantile, adolescent, arrested at an early stage of development. The splendid Poles, so proud of their Polishness, are childlike.

That is why they have an acute father complex. What the Poles dream of is a normal, mature, responsible man who will assume responsibility for their childish ways. Poles long for a father, a great big man with a mustache, blunt but decisive. Poles love daddies with a leather belt in their hand, wrathful but just, daddies who are respected by all their neighbors. When you're playing in the sandbox it's sometimes nice to remember your daddy, who, when he comes home from work, will give the freckled lout on the next street a good tongue-lashing.

For that reason Poles cannot live without a father of their country. This is the reason that in every micro-epoch Poles use all the resources of their unconscious to give birth to a golden calf, a show-window father figure. And this is the reason that every lowlife in this country dons the garb of the father of his country, that is, the father and sire of immature Poles.

But, at bottom, every nation may suffer from a similar complex. Not an Oedipal complex but a Stash, Zbys, or Wojtek complex.

Wait a minute, when was that? In '45? Yes, in '45, at the end of May or the beginning of June. Right after the war was over. Right after the war we had lost was over.

I had just come out of the forest. I had just come out of the Rudnicka Wilderness in the very beginning of May and begun a march toward the Wilno Colony, where there was nearly no one left. None of the boys and girls I knew. Not one of the guys I'd had a fistfight with, or played mumblety-peg with, or sloshed down my first vodka with. None of the girls I'd fallen in love with a little in grammar school or loved seriously, for real, in high school. No one, an empty landscape. The same small river, the Wilenka, the same meadows, the same woods and mixed forests that seemed of different breeds, but not one person I knew and had grown up with during my eighteen years of life. That's not true, the Blinstrubs, my grandparents, were still there and a few of my other old neighbors, but I didn't see them. I took a nap, then slipped right past them, and then it was on to Wilno, the train station. Leftist papers in the pocket of my partisan jacket. Leftist thoughts in my head. And in my heart, you'll excuse the expression, leftist longings, pain, premonitions.

It was my first time out in the world. I had already had a few close calls with death, but this was my first time out in the world.

And after a few bizarre weeks I found myself on another planet. Meaning in Gliwice, which had just been liberated. I was working in the Provisional National Government. That's right, I remember now, I've already written about that elsewhere.

But I didn't go into the details—that I lived with a friend who was much older than I, in a widow's house on Bahnhofstrasse, that is, Dworcowa Street. One afternoon my friend brought two women home. Actually, a woman and a girl. Both were dark, swarthy, with woolly hair, a bit Negroid, but they were decent-looking, maybe even pretty. Yes, I do remember them. Maybe they were mother and daughter, maybe just cousins. But definitely related, and most likely it was a mother and her seventeen-year-old or maybe eighteen-year-old daughter. I think they were on their way home from Germany, from a concentration camp, I imagine. But they had already been eating regularly, had regained their humanity, and had probably even received some care. The younger one had covered her nakedness with a knit shirt with dark horizontal stripes. Why have I specifically remembered that shirt or blouse? Perhaps because it covered her pert young breasts, which I longed to caress.

Before this time I had spent more than half a year wandering the forest. And so I had seen more rooks, roes, and soldiers of a certain army than young girls. I trembled like an aspen, even though that was the end of May or the beginning of June, and in those days we had proper summers, sweltering, sunny, flowers everywhere.

And so we feasted away the afternoon, stinting on neither our canned food nor our home brew. The slanting late-afternoon sun was glad to warm those enormous German rooms with their high ceilings. Downing vodkas, warmed by the sun and mounting desire, we felt so fine—how fine things used to be sometimes, we had everything ahead of us, the whole great mystery of it, though, goddamnit, we'd lost the war and the Antichrist had passed through our world. Yes, but I was nineteen years old, even though I'd done a bit of killing myself, a young predator. Quick and easy, not giving it much thought.

Then evening came. It turned out that the women were going to spend the night with us. My older friend, who was, as they say, a real womanizer, went to sleep with the mother on the couch, while telling me to lie down with the girl on a mattress on the floor.

I don't know what the older ones did. I think they just lay there quietly, modestly, even though that wasn't the least like my friend. But we did terrible things there on the floor. Our blood gurgled like gas through a large siphon. Our hearts were pounding so hard, they even cracked a plank in the floor. We sucked in all the air in the room.

God, what a night that was. My first time with a woman. For the first time in my life I learned what a woman's body was. The body of a woman my age on her way home from a German concentration camp.

But why go on and on about it. Those were seven or eight hours of terror and sweetness. We hugged each other to death, and it's truly a miracle that we did not die on that German mattress.

A strange and beautiful night of love, but one without physiological fulfillment. An uncanny erotic ecstasy without a conjugal finale. But why didn't we finish it, complete it, come to the point? I don't know, and to this day part of me regrets it a little, and part of me doesn't.

There was something holding me back. Perhaps some fear of the unknown, or of the irrevocable, of that which is over and done with. So, after seven or eight hours we rose from bed covered with sweat, terribly tired, exhausted, ragged, and utterly innocent.

The young girl, she of the woolly black hair and the slightly Negroid lips, was a bit bolder than I and seemed to have learned something about life and copulation in the camp, but she too respected our mutual ignorance, our incomplete ignition on a German mattress in a stranger's apartment on Bahnhofstrasse, our surprise at the wild forces bursting our bodies, our fear of the future and future responsibility.

Then it was morning, again sunny and sweltering, breakfast, her embarrassment, mine, then the tenderness of parting forever.

My friend, who was a pessimist, gave me a close look when we were alone again. I hope you screwed that child good, he said. No, somehow it didn't happen, I groaned with shame. He just made a dismissive gesture and didn't say a word.

For quite a while I've been intending to say a few words about the Czechs or perhaps about Czechoslovakia. I've mentioned Lithuania, paid my respects to Byelorussia, rendered homage to the Ukraine, but somehow there's been nothing about the Czechs. I've been facing east the entire time. I completely forgot about the other parts of the world.

That's not true, I didn't. Stash Dygat and I were loyal supporters of the Czechs. We spread our cult of the Czechs. We taught our colleagues to be humble toward the Czechs.

The fact of the matter is that Poles consider themselves angels, silver-feathered birds, poets, the Christ of Europe and the lands overseas. The Czechs, on the other hand, are dumpling sellers, beer drinkers lacking all flair, bourgeois and philistine, in a word, Germans amid delightful Slavs.

Meanwhile, the Czechs have a literature any nation would be proud of; meanwhile, the Czechs have music which the whole world plays from morning till night; and meanwhile, the Czechs are no slouches at painting either.

Czech film, the Czech film of the sixties. I swear, my heart started hammering and my hair stood on end when I came across those films. No one else made films like those after the Second World War, no other cinema—not the Italian, the Japanese, or even the American—can measure up to those dozen or so films created on the shores of the Vltava in the years between Novotny and Husak, in those few years of freedom never fully savored.

The Czechs received many awards and endless compliments for those films; they accrued a good bit of capital—the respect of the countries they had astounded. But at a certain moment their films seemed to surpass the world's expectations. As if they had overstepped the perceptual limits of the Western middle class and threatened the intellectual existence of twentieth-century philistines. A little more, and the Oscars would have stopped raining down; a little more, and people would have begun to avoid those works in celluloid; another minute, and people would have cursed that art aimed against everything insipid, literal, and petty in human beings.

Yes, I was afraid of those Czech and Slovak filmmakers. Yes, I dreaded their genius. Their genuine, palpable genius, which I could feel in my bones. Think of Herz's *The Cremator*, think of *Closely Watched Trains*, and you must remember at least the beginning of that seemingly flimsy film *Ecce Homo Homolka*. Then came the disastrous year 1968 and that was the end of Czech film. A great shame, and something of a relief. No more of that terrible prodding, that urging, that rival with the steel lungs on the racetrack of world film. A great shame and a great relief. For me, an ambitious, envious man.

One time I was having a chat about Czech art with my father-in-law, Alfred Lenica, a painter. We spoke of music, literature, film, and painting as well. I wanted to know how that small Central European nation, so oppressed by German culture, could generate so much artistic power, such poetic freshness, such intellectual and aesthetic universality. And Alfred replied: "Ooh, Tadzio, they had fantastic surrealists."

I thought that this was just another instance of Alfred playing the crackpot. But now, years later, I see, I hear, I feel some meaning in the old painter's words, one which I didn't catch at the time.

They had surrealists. No, they have always been surrealists. They have no match when it comes to smelting our fate, our daily existence, the human condition into the pure metal of surrealism or, simply put, poetry.

I was on my way back at the beginning of May 1945. I was coming home from the war, home to the Wilno Colony. One more person coming home from a lost war.

Staszek Dygat said that the German occupation was the last period of Poland's independence.

And so I am returning to that return of mine once again. By then the Wilno Colony was empty and Wilno was deserted. Part of the population had been deported to the east, the rest had voluntarily gone west, to a shrunken Poland.

I flitted carefully through the empty Lower Colony and Upper Colony, going through both those colonies as through a vacant apartment. But I still had not realized what had happened and what was happening around me, to those close to me, to my country. There was a certain sadness, a melancholy, a grief for what had passed. But there was also a pleasant anxiety about the future, a shiver of titillation before a great new adventure.

The girls I'd known were gone. They had all gone off into the world. Meaning to distant, unknown Poland, strange now because it had been moved west. Some had gone even farther, overseas, across the ocean. Those girls whom I'd loved fiercely for so many infinitely long years—as the years are only in childhood and early youth.

And some of those girls had even gotten married. Back then, in the autumn of 1944, there were large numbers of various partisans, conspirators, newcomers from distant Europe, many heroes, semi-heroes, and Schweiks from the Home Army hiding out in hospitable Wilno. Legendary in our province, differing from us in their smartness, fashion, and dash, those rats flirted with our girls, turned their heads, and led them to the altar.

By now all those marriages have fallen apart. All those legends and great loves are less than dust today. But, back then, during the first months of autumn, months that were something between stopgap freedom and a new form of slavery, during those warm, sunny months it seemed to everyone that this might be the beginning of an endless holiday, a perpetual Indian summer, a sort of Wilno nirvana.

And so, when I came back, the girls were gone. I know that some gentlemen don't like sentences that begin "and so." To hell with them. They weren't in the Colony in those days; they know little of life, and nothing at all of our life, mine. And so the Colony, my micro-world bereft of girls, seemed an unbearable wasteland to me, a cruel theater without a house to play to, a sunless hole.

My only shock came from the large cemetery on the wooded hill in back of the church in the Upper Colony. There where in the winter the taps on our shoes had made us slip and slide and where in spring or fall we had dashed headlong home to the Lower Colony from school, now, amid ferns, belladonna, pine and spruce, in that sunny jolly woods behind the church, a cemetery for my colleagues and others my age, strangers to me, from Wilno, had erupted from the earth, emerged from the moss, pierced the green. They came from Nowa Wilejka, Oszmiana, Lida, Troki, Worniane, and dozens of other little towns, microscopic urban organisms where the nineteenth century had still been peacefully expiring.

There was a roaring within me like that of an old water mill. Something grand, exalted, very ceremonious. A part of life had come to a close, a new part was opening up.

But still I came close to spending the rest of my life there. Dead or alive. If I'd stayed there alive, I wouldn't have lived this long. And if I'd stayed there dead, no one, not even a demented researcher of the folklore of Wilno, no ant of science, no bookworm, would ever have learned that in the Pavilnys area, formerly known as the Wilno Colony in Polish times, there had once lived a certain Tadzek Konwicki, unlucky in his love for the young ladies, that this Tadzek had dreams and fantasies, was not pushy about getting ahead in life, was attracted to crude provincial metaphysics, and wanted to scratch his initials into the wailing wall we all share.

And that's why I'm writing all this. There's no action here, no plot, no dramatics. Just the somewhat foolish desire to put in writing a certain indefinite state of mind, an unimportant emotion that has kept on gnawing at me until my old age, a minor melancholy that can come back to me at the most unlikely moments, for example, in the middle of Manhattan in a crowd of blacks, terrorists, and gays.

That's why I'm writing all this. To afford myself a skimpy Lenten pleasure of little value.

Today I'd like to write about Mieczyslaw Piotrowski, but here, as if from spite, this form doesn't feel right. Why is this form losing its oomph just when I want to deal with the figure of Mieczyslaw, who called himself Half-Pint Miecio? Why am I falling apart when it comes to Miecio? Why does his memory cause me suddenly to wilt, weaken, and run out of adjectives and punctuation marks?

This is how it was with Miecio. Miecio was the giving sort. People came to Miecio as to a sorcerer or a village medicine man, a folk healer. He was brought their toothaches or the pain of offended pride, suffering livers or itchy egos. Migraines or swellings of conceit. And Miecio would treat the problem. Usually with a half pint of vodka, the source of his nickname.

I too went to see him, for a retreat, confession, absolution. I would try to squirm out of going, to put it off for another week; then suddenly my hat would be on and I'd be on my way, both reluctant and willing. Because I liked going to see Miecio and I didn't like it. Because his very presence, the very sight of him, put me under some obligation. Because Miecio was a reproach of conscience, a reminder incarnate of certain inconvenient moral obligations. When Miecio was dying I grieved terribly, and in what seemed the greatest secrecy, I sighed with relief.

Miecio Piotrowski. Piotrowski, Miecio. A great graphic artist, a great prose writer, a great unknown. The unknown graphic artist, the unknown novelist like the Unknown Soldier. His very name suggests anonymity, the multiplicity of the crowd, something obvious, ready-made. A common name concealing an uncommon man.

I'll put it straight. Miecio was not of this earth. Like Wilek Mach, like Zbyszek Cybulski. His inner workings roused a superstitious dread in me. Physically, he was like everyone else. Nothing special about him, and definitely nothing particularly original. He looked like a civil servant or a high-school teacher or a member of the Democratic Party in one province or another. But beneath all that Piotrowskiness there functioned mysterious, strange, unearthly inner workings of his that caused me metaphysical dread. But how he functioned made no sense; it was somehow backward, wrong side to, against the laws of physics. But he was also brilliantly effective and had a celestial precision and divine disinterestedness about him.

What am I going on about, what am I going on about here? What I wanted was to draw a sharp image of this person whom you disregarded, passing him in this life without paying him any attention, glad to let him slip easily from mind. And that includes me too. Me first of all.

How good were Miecio's drawings? Writing with great conceit in *The Cultural Review*, Julian Przybos stated that, as a graphic artist, Piotrowski was a zero, his drawings worthless, amateurish, hopeless, chicken scratchings. He flayed Miecio with a certain odd ferocity and schoolmasterish arrogance, as if Przybos had never heard any such compliments addressed to himself. I replied to him in *New Culture*, in a note signed with my initials. It was an easy matter for Przybos to guess who the author was and his response was a froth of fury, the last that was said on the subject. Though we met frequently, we never brought it up again. But Przybos could not forget it. He bore his hatred in his heart for a long time and finally let me have it in a review of my novel *Ascension*. But that overdue hatred, like an overdue pregnancy, brought him no joy. His reckless review gave me so much publicity that my book almost became a best-seller.

I mention Przybos here because I thought of him as an authority on the visual arts. I recall his articles on Strzeminski from *Rebirth*, I knew that he considered his own poetry visual, that he considered his work akin to painting, graphic art, architecture. Then suddenly that blitz on Piotrowski, who was pure as the driven snow, a quiet artist, a recluse, operating on a narrow margin by doing illustrations for books and children's magazines. What was there about Miecio's avant-garde art to infuriate the avant-garde poet?

Miecio Piotrowski's art was ascetic. For long years before and after the war it served his asceticism. Other graphic artists moved on from drawing to painting, posters, interior decoration, even to film, but Miecio kept withdrawing from one year to the next, abandoning the richer lines, ornament, the decorative element, and color. He reduced the size of his drawings, slowly giving up everything, even what is commonly known as beauty or loveliness. Had it not been for his premature death, he would have surely ended up with blank paper, which, by the way, is the artistic ideal of our mutual friend, Henryk Tomaszewski, our true friend from before the war.

Piotrowski left an enormous treasure of drawings. Thousands of illustrations, drawings, sketches. All equally meager or spare, equally invisible, and precisely for that reason, gaudy; all uncomely and for that reason beautiful beyond measure.

There is something staggering about Piotrowski's artistic stubbornness, his uncanny monotony, his almost jeweler-like formalism. It can't be that it just happened that way. His obsession must contain some message of importance for us, some very important information must be encoded in those pencil strokes; that nearly imperceptible graphic art should contain, in invisible ink, the point of that artist's Golgotha on this wretched planet.

And what about Miecio's writing? Hm, hm. That's harder, because there's no one to defend Miecio against. Even Przybos left that bizarre preserve alone.

Miecio wrote novels, plays, film scripts, and captions for his drawings, little poetic epigrams. Actually he wrote a great deal. Enough to make a decent bibliography for any venerable Polish author.

You shouldn't think that this is easy for me and that I can comment one two three on his writing and its problems. Or that, like that Wilno know-it-all, I can once again shove my opponents aside and do a nice job of exegesis on a few thousand pages of incomprehensible hieroglyphics.

Like any mortal I suffered with Piotrowski's prose. I know that there exist some more exalted souls who read Miecio at breakfast like a newspaper. For me, he was an effort to read. To pick up something by him was like going out to cut down trees in a labor camp.

I would read him, drop him, return to him, disgusted by his writing's artificiality, its willed quality, and then suddenly would be delighted by a sentence, a word, lose myself in the imbroglio, but then, abruptly entering a stretch of clarity and simplicity, I would begin to doubt and lose desire. Later, for no particular reason, I would be left with a sense of the sublime and want to skip a couple of pages on the sly, but would once again go back and read something for the second time, think of the author with sudden compassion, only to become envious a moment later. When I had thoroughly understood everything about it, I would be stunned with admiration for its mystery a few pages or a page later, I would taste it and think it too thick, indigestible, but at the end, in the final paragraphs of a given portion, everything would begin to seem pure, elevated, soaring, colorful, understood by some finer mind, higher than us in our lowliness, lovelier than our beauty.

The snobs will die off, the mockers will fall away exhausted, and a better human race, the readers of the future, will study Miecio and see in his prose everything that we were blind to. His novels may have contained comfort and cheer for the bad times that befell us, some friendly science of behavior for an age of despair; perhaps those lucid and masterful sentences brought some important tidings to me, to Henryk Tomaszewski, Irena Laskowska, and also to Brezhnev and Pope Paul VI.

Dear people, I wanted to say something about a person whom you did not know, and it's a great pity that your paths crossed but you never met. Still, the more curious and especially inquisitive among you can still trace Miecio Piotrowski down, even though the concentric waves which he emitted have long since been dispersed through the universe. The papillary lines of his talent, the rhythmic breathing of his being, the dissolving outline of his intellectual and artistic identity can be discovered in dusty publication files and in his volumes of prose dozing on library shelves.

His drawings, his books. I had so much to say, to write. But something urges me on and drives me to the point prematurely. I am moved by an unconscious and unhealthy cult of the point. Some disastrous force impels me to abridgment. Things just seem to abridge themselves in my hands, even though that makes me boring from time to time.

And that is why I never succeed in writing what I had intended to. It's like whittling a figure from wood. I sculpt the head, the features, the shoulders, but the rest of the torso, the body is still up for grabs. I barely start before I'm finishing up. That's not good, that's lousy. My condolences.

And so I won't be saying any more here about Miecio. Suddenly I'm high and dry. And I still have a long way to go. Perhaps my appetite for Miecio will return, for Half-Pint Miecio, who never got drunk, never lied, never betrayed anyone. And who may never have even sinned.

I tell you, there was something fishy about Miecio. Someone sent Miecio Piotrowski to us, then later took him back like any normal man, any genuine inhabitant of planet Earth.

Miecio left behind a pile of drawings and a mound of books. Was that a waste of paper, just nouns and adjectives strung together? Or was this yet another fresco capturing our time in an intellectual and aesthetic pattern, another fresco to be discovered by future generations; better, more sensitive, wiser generations?

What a goddamned pity. What a pity that I can't, don't know how, am unable to write the type of prose that I'm spinning and weaving here before you and for you, that I am unable to incise a blank-verse poem on beauty, the miracle of existence, the sublimity of human fate on this finely wrought text which, despite appearances, represents real work; that I cannot all of a sudden paste on a poem here with assonances or real rhymes to demonstrate to you worms that you're not dealing with just any literary rag dealer, any pencil pusher from a Party paper, any grub who writes dissertations on commission. That this Slavic pizza is being cooked for you by a literary gent, an old lion, capable of both rhythmic prose and rhyme, hexameters and Wilno trochees.

Damn it all, I would like to light up your eyes with the beautiful, the sublime. To pique your interest at once, whet your appetite, to spice up this year's worth of work, for which I still haven't found a title.

The title is another problem. I don't feel right about poetic titles like A Hatful of Rain or The Gates of Heaven. I'm also repelled by anything elegantly philosophical, which smacks of the unpleasant pretentiousness of the star pupil, the Wunderkind, or, shameful to admit, ordinary faggotry. A title with a beautiful, grandiloquent ring to it is not suitable either, for we are of another race than those darlings of the salons both here and abroad, those Nobel laureates and those grant recipients of the various literary fraternities, conspiracies, gangs, and brothels.

It behooves us to select a simple and matter-of-fact title, clear but also a bit obscure, unpretentious and almost manly, commonplace and informal, derisive but not repulsive. And so what has to be sought are sets of words that would differ, if only a little, from those by ladies writing from an excess of emotion, men who cultivate the venerable profession of writer, and the shameless old men who have already had their brilliant ideas and now blackmail us with their approaching death.

Here I am, confiding various secrets of the literary trade in detail to my esteemed readers in the hope that one or another of them, coached by me, enlightened by me, and emboldened by their mentor's own low level, will himself take pen in hand and dash off an autobiography that will eclipse me and others by a mile. The age of self-service literature is approaching. People will do their own writing and then read what they've written with delight.

9

The thirteenth. A bad day. Everything bad's happened to me on the thirteenth. Even my cancer of the throat was diagnosed on the thirteenth. The thirteenth is my enemy. On the thirteenth the thing to do is get in bed and stay there. But fate can catch up with me in bed too. Cowering in a mouse hole too.

People would say to me, I heard you were in the hospital. What was wrong? Nothing, I would say. Cancer of the throat. I had an operation. A hint of irritation would cross the face of the person who asked the question. You've always got an answer for everything, he'd mutter with animosity. Had I lied, as sick people are fond of doing, the man would have told the entire town that Tadzio's in bad shape, he's got . . . you know. But since I flaunt that fucking cancer of mine, people in town say Tadzio's being his usual hysterical self, overreacting, overdoing it, looking for pity and attention, hamming it up, exaggerating, putting pepper in a bland soup, overdoing it as always.

Cancer-shmancer, we should all be so healthy, as one old Jew used to say.

Maybe we've already been occupied by the Russians. Maybe Russian blood is already in the circulatory system of our state. Perhaps the plan to enslave Poland by osmosis has already been carried out.

A meeting of Solidarity, the Minister of Foreign Affairs is leaving for Hungary, a Provincial Party Committee Plenum in Pcim, Memorial Day, the restoration of Krakow, Parliament appeals to the newspapers and television not to lie, recruits take their oath, the chairman of the State Council welcomes a guest, a Polish team wins a match in East Germany, Poland's creditors are meeting in Tokyo, the hundredth anniversary of the birth of Wladyslaw Sikorski is approaching, the Easter holidays will be celebrated more modestly this year, the conclusions of the IX Plenum are discussed by the armed forces, the American shuttle is in orbit around earth, Ernest Bryll is feeling good.

But there are Russian tanks in every forest, big and small. Someone was on the way to Rembertow. Tanks in the bushes by the highway. A broken tank was stuck in the mud. Along the highway Poles were doing a brisk business with the Soviet tankmen. They say you can buy a can of gas for a hundred zlotys, can included.

Apparently transportation in Poland is under Soviet supervision. And communications are supposedly already in Russian hands. The latter strikes me as possible. I haven't been able to get Radio Free Europe since yesterday. They haven't jammed like that since Stalin's time. In that din, howl, gurgle, racket, and growl one senses the sweep, abundance, and range of real empire.

Perhaps we in Poland are just playing around, while under our feet, in the depths of the earth, a hundred-story-high Russia has already been built.

I have broken down *The Issa Valley* into its smallest parts, unscrewed the tiniest screws, examined every last little piece, then screwed the whole thing back together in an almost new form, with an almost new function. First I got a screenplay, then, the second time through, in the next phase of reassembling the parts, I came out with a shooting script. The next-to-last phase in the transformation that turns good literature into bad film or so-so prose into splendid cinema.

Now I see a certain striking kinship or resemblance between *The Issa Valley* and the work of Iwaszkiewicz. Twenty years ago Kawalerowicz and I adapted *Mother Joan of the Angels* for the screen. At the time I made a close examination of Iwaszkiewicz's prose, just about breaking it down to its atoms, grinding, mixing, straining it, transplanting it from one flower pot to another, tingeing it with the colors demanded by the cinema, molding it into new forms, drawing new contours. While at the same time trying to respect its autonomy as literature. While at the same time not changing its artistic nature in any way.

Odd convergences between Milosz and Iwaszkiewicz. What does that mean? What's the source of it? Why those affinities?

The thread connecting Father Suryn and Balthazar's fate in *The Issa Valley*. The motifs of crime and the redemption of a mortal sin. Father Suryn runs to see a tsaddik and Balthazar to see a Jewish wonder-worker. Both these characters reflect their authors' pleasure in using a certain moment in the twenty years before World War II to make a fashionable Manichean interpretation of our poor world. This must be the influence of certain French Catholic writers whom they read or what is left of the fascination with Catholic rebirth that seized philosophy in the thirties. I don't know. Poor me; while others were studying, I was either tending geese or running with the partisans, tommy gun in hand.

Actually, there are two threads in *The Issa Valley* that connect with Father Suryn's ethos, that of Balthazar and that of Father Peiksva. Again, Mr. Milosz's character Magdalena is a reflection of folk legend and myth bordering on literature, something like Scandinavian tales, which are so close, after all, to Lithuanian folklore and perhaps even to Byelorussian.

Romuald reminds me of something. My childhood, Wilno's Lithuanian customs, the types of satiric tales told in the Polish borderlands, and perhaps something from Iwaszkiewicz. Though it's shameful to say, Miss Rodziewicz may also be paying her respects here, who knows.

I've also met Thomas's grandmothers somewhere else. The

Polish borderlands teemed with women like that. Both in literature and in life. But most frequently in anecdotes, diaries, memoirs. And so I am at a name-day party in a manor house in the Polish borderlands. But I don't know if the manor house is real, from the real world, or a manor house built by a set designer for the stage. Slanting late-afternoon, honey-gold sun, the lazy buzz of sleepy flies, a shepherd sings in Lithuanian or Byelorussian in the meadow past the unkempt park. The smell of milk, pork, the bitter aroma of herb mead. Young and old are at the table. They're chattering about things they've done or seen, or once read in a newspaper or a book, or were told by a passing traveler. Heavy glasses are raised, telling glances, toasts muttered, exhalations after the drinks are downed, all of a sudden a song, and Thomas's eyes, the eyes of that overly sensitive little boy who for a century now has been woven into all the novels by writers who hark back to their native village or hometown, writers at life's hard moments returning to the paradise lost of childhood, youth, innocence.

A resemblance in the bone structure. A resemblance in the muscular system. A resemblance in the nervous system. A resemblance in the literary prose written by Czeslaw Milosz and Jaroslaw Iwaszkiewicz. In connection with those striking resemblances, I asked a few rhetorical questions worthy of an old hand at comparative literature. I could easily answer those questions, but I don't feel like it. I have more important things to worry about.

I'm weeping and wailing like this about Mr. Milosz's prose because I want to avoid the great variety of dangers that lie in wait for someone doing an adaptation. The worst things are associations with other movies once seen and now forgotten. Remember that there have already been a few thousand films "seen through a child's eyes." This is not the same thing as literature, where that device is transparent, invisible, and just quickens the reader's imagination, rather than obliging or compelling it. But how about the film? What we have in a film is one specific boy, defined once and for all, his age, his crossed eyes, his nose and nervous tic all specific as can be. And whether or not the viewer accepts him, that squirt will continually be thrusting himself on the viewer, attacking the viewer, bombarding the viewer's eye throughout the film. How can repetition, unconscious borrowings, and the stylistic customs of the world's enormous film library be avoided here?

And how about the scene with the tsaddik? For *Mother Joan of the Angels* we hit on the idea of having the same actor play Father Suryn and the tsaddik. The point was to send a coded message to the viewer's unconscious, a message about no-exitness, the universality of human sin, our helplessness against fate, destiny, Providence. To a certain extent, this idea provided the scene with a basis; a scene, had it been played straight, that might have seemed boring in the film.

What am I supposed to do with Balthazar's visit to the rabbi in *The Issa Valley*? How to stage that scene so that it does not repeat motifs of mind and mood already exploited by other filmmakers, myself included, me in *Mother Joan* twenty years ago?

What can be devised so that all those devils, phantoms, and ghosts are not merely hiccups of German Expressionism, the whole flood of Scandinaviana, and the terrible wilderness, bogs, and quagmires of provincial European literature?

You're making a film from Milosz's book? Fantastic! Directing a film based on *The Issa Valley*? Wonderful, marvelous! We're so happy, Tadzio, you've got to do it, it'll really be something!

I am treated to other such compliments. Don't complain, don't grimace, don't be chicken. It has to be a masterpiece, he's a Nobel laureate. Just you try and not make it a masterpiece, the people will tear you limb from limb.

What do you do in a situation like that? All right, I'll make the film if they let me. Something's nudging me to take that terrible risk. Something's drawing me to the brink.

Some sort of old sentiment for that poet, philosopher, and essayist who lives on the shores of San Francisco Bay. Some kinship between us which is my own quite impertinent idea. A desire to go on vacation with someone I feel close to, someone important in my life whom I haven't seen for a long time.

All right, Mr. Milosz, I suggest we get together somewhere near Suwalki, in Punsko or Sejny. Let's meet at midnight in September, when the Jewish New Year approaches from some terrible heaven. All the devils which have inhabited us will be there waiting, we'll be greeted by the corpses and ghosts of friends who betrayed or repudiated us, we will be embraced by the phantom arms of old hatreds and forgotten loves.

Devils tempted me to buy a copy of *The Red Standard*, a Polish-language newspaper published in Wilno. The cheapest thing you can buy in the Polish People's Republic. A copy of that surrealist rag costs only thirty groszy.

I bought two copies, went home, lay down on the couch in my little den, and set to reading every last word in the paper. There's no other way I can read that hideous newspaper. I'm a masochist. I am a demented masochist.

Jesus God, what a read! The language nightmarish, barbaric, completely Russified, and at the same time oddly reminiscent of those Old Slavonic church texts in which even spelling errors could not be corrected. The demented Volapük of an NKVD man who has been ordered to write and publish a newspaper but who does not even know who gave him the order or to what purpose.

Holy Virgin of Ostra Brama, those film listings, those television programs, the richness of kolkhoz life, those news items from timber mills and metal plants, those antiphons of gratitude toward the Soviet authorities, the tapeworms of May Day slogans. One of these days one of those newspapers is going to make me end it all.

And the authors. Russian names, Lithuanian names, and, once in a great while, a Polish name, apparently to add a little seasoning. Russians and Lithuanians write for the paper even though they have periodicals of their own. Then why do they forsake them for a Polish newspaper? Of course, Russians and

Poles write for the Lithuanian press, and Tatars and Koreans, with Russian help, write for the Jewish press. What splendid internationalism. What consistency in extracting the national essence from dying ethnic groups.

In the center of Europe. Before the eyes of the entire world. In the face of the UN, the Pope, and the Lord God. What the Nazis did to prisoners physically is done here to the soul of one little nation or another. Medical and psychological experiments. A vast madhouse for mentally ill peoples. A gigantic prison for insane nations.

I read the four horrendous pages of that Soviet Polish newspaper with a terrible pain near my heart. Wilno is never mentioned in that rag, only Vilnius. And my old Nowa Wilejka is called Nova Vilnya. If that's supposed to sound Lithuanian, then why Nova Vilnya and not Nauja Vilnia, as it should be? Bottle in hand, a drunken Chekist corrects the languages of Central Europe, revising the geography, establishing the human rights. O God! O God! have mercy on us sinners.

Suddenly, among the Polish names twisted to sound Lithuanian or Russian, one last name has a pure ring to it. Why were those names distorted and this one left the way his father had passed it on? His sobriety gone, the policeman plays games with the first names and last names of anonymous slaves. And, in the end, this frivolous game produces useful statistics which gladden the cannibals.

Ex oriente lux. My dear Russian brothers. I will not assure you how much I respect, admire, and love you. You can tell that just by looking. By the way I think, feel, and write.

Nicest of brothers, it's time, it's high time, it's last call. You must become European, meaning human. You must become humanized, which means rejecting our animal nature. To reject our animal nature means to respect God's laws. It's the end of the twentieth century. You've traveled to outer space. You're looking the Lord God in the eye. There can be no whining, weeping, no calling for help from the civilized world. In 1917,

Georgians, Latvians, Jews, and Poles, all your slaves, made a revolution for you and freed you from the tyranny of the tsars. You must make the next revolution yourselves and in one leap catch up with civilized humanity. Our dear twins, lost in the cemetery of Byzantium and Genghis Khan's burial mounds. A dark sun will again rise in the east. One more time. But perhaps the last. *Ex oriente lux.*

That was badly written. No expression, no hierarchy of thought, no grace. The apostrophe was right, but not the form. It happens a lot. The writing convinces no one. Not even me.

But I think about Russia and the Russians often. More often than the Russians think about us, if they think at all, if they aren't satisfied with a knee jerk of irritation or impatience.

My entire education, if it can be called that, is connected with Polish-Russian issues, problems, complications. Russia intrigues me, astounds me, entrances me. Russia draws me deeper and deeper into a whirlpool of complexes, spells, animosity, and violent affection.

A person could, if he so desired, write a library's worth of books on Polish-Russian relations. And I'm trying to do it in a few paragraphs. But I grew angry, I kept flying off the handle. And that's why the writing's clogged, lopsided, slipshod.

O Russia, sweet and ominous. O Russia of the God-Bearers and Azefs. O Russia, in a coarse shirt down to your knees, moving westward on a divine mission, and O Russia flying into space with atomic bombs. O Russia, Russia . . .

Sitting across from me, he was waxy yellow, yellow with that deathbed yellowness which I knew from elsewhere, knew well. Bones large and small jutted against his gray-yellow skin; from time to time a tendon would tremble, cylindrical, not as pointed and sharp-edged as those terrible bones of his. When he spoke the blackened stumps of his teeth were revealed, terrible gaps where teeth had been knocked out. His eyes, yes, his eyes were beautiful. Alive, young, not tortured by prison. Yes, all right, I will praise his eyes because I wanted to praise something about that remnant of a man, that human scrap from which no one could ever reconstruct the marvelous daredevil he'd been in the good old days of the German occupation.

"Excuse me for asking, but how much did you weigh before you went to prison?" I asked.

"A little under two hundred," replied that shriveled chicken of a man.

The sight of him pained my heart, some terrible choking fear seized my throat, my skull rang in horrendous dismay, and I felt like running out of there, but there was no running out. Yes, in some way I was responsible for his fate, I felt guilty that the regime in People's Poland had held him in prison, on death row, for all those months, that Security men had knocked out his teeth and broken his fingers with their heels, that he, a Home Army officer, had waited for death on death row with a Nazi SS general, who had helped slaughter the Warsaw ghetto.

I was sitting across from one of the leaders of the Home Army, one of those people on whom I had turned my childish wrath in '45, the wrath of a generation that had lost the game, a rebellious generation that cursed its own fathers and leaders. Later on, I was to feather my own nest while he was being plucked clean. Still later, I would struggle to lose weight while he struggled with approaching death. Then I . . . then he . . . No, no, he was victorious in the end, no question of that, even though he had lost, even though he had lost a large piece of his life.

"But how could you stand up to prison, torture, death?"

I knew that he knew what I meant. Because both of us already knew the value of heroism and cowardice, the greatness and the poverty of being human. I had already read fragments of his book. He was a fellow Polish writer. With more character than I, a life more worthy of respect.

"You see, they made a certain mistake," he said, speaking unhurriedly. "They wanted to break my spirit and so they told me that my wife and daughter were both dead. Meanwhile, I realized that now I was all alone, no longer responsible for anyone else, I couldn't jeopardize or burden anyone, I was utterly alone and therefore I was a free man. From that moment on, they didn't stand a chance with me. I took it all the best I could. I was able to stand up to everything, but in other psychological circumstances I might not have been able to."

I was grateful to him for that human, wise, and beautiful element in his interpretation of his own vile and inhuman fate. And in his words I could also detect a certain forgiveness for my transgressions, my betrayals, my mortal sins.

On that day, for the first and last time, I met with Kazimierz Moczarski, author of the book *Conversations with a Hangman*.

These are the facts. This is the situation. This has to be made explicit, because facts and situations change every now and again.

When I was a child, Jules Verne's novel *Around the World in 80 Days* was science fiction, or close to it. A hymn to human knowledge, human intelligence, human civilization. The vast, unmapped, endless world encircled in eighty days. A challenge hurled to the laws of physics, God, infinity.

In my childhood there were still blank spots in the atlases from which I learned my geography, spots that were literally blank amid the reddish mountain ranges, green valleys, and light-blue rivers. Every fairy tale began or ended with praise for the world that was without end. All that was beyond measure bespoke the vastness of the world. In fact, our world was the universe, or at least the colossal, boundless, immeasurable heart of the universe.

We didn't used to say the "earth." Because earth is finite, limited, literal. Earth brings us down to earth. We always used to say the "world." And the word "world" meant space, distance, longing, poetry.

Around the world in eighty days. What audacity, what insolence, what arrogance. The boundless circumnavigated in eighty days. Ominous.

And now space vehicles circle the globe in an hour and a half. A slightly pear-shaped globe made of molten metal, covered with a thin, baked layer of crumbled rock, and topped by an armagnac-like sauce of salt water known as H_2O. A few insects on a slimy potato hurtling through cold, dark space.

The greatest dullards are unlearning their stereotyped ideas. The most foolish poets can no longer stretch their imaginations to the back of beyond. And the most undereducated educators no longer try to charm us with statistics demonstrating the greatness of our earth; they no longer flatter our sense of human omnipotence.

Now, toward the end of the twentieth century, in the rubble of the temples of human morality, on the ruins of the crematoria, on the last scrap of our polluted earth, we, oddly stunted and seeming to have reverted to the wild, gaze meekly at the stars above and howl like wolves, the way we howled a million years ago. Voices heard from a distance, images seen from a distance, strength greater than the strength of our muscles, brains swifter than our brains, the rock caves of cities, mechanical horses emitting smoke, it's all nothing compared to what could have been done, to what we cannot imagine and never will be able to.

Now it turns out that Gombrowicz must be taken in dead earnest. Like a professor of sociology, or even economics. I always smile with a bit of amusement at Gombrowicz's idea about the antagonism between the superior and the inferior. It made me laugh, as much fun as the stubbornness of a Wilno type who digs in his heels and, red in the face, repeats the same whim endlessly, ordering everyone around him to submit to his caprice, even though there is a nearly imperceptible, snide snicker, a twitching, an ambiguous Wilno irony directed at himself, vibrating beneath those imperious shouts, swears, and curses.

The struggle of the superior and the inferior, the high and the low. Yet another jolly idea from that old duffer from a philosophical backwater. Yet another bon mot from that pseudo-Lithuanian petty tyrant. The conflict of the superior and the inferior instead of the class struggle.

And now all of a sudden I see that Gombrowicz was right and still is. That's how it is, that's how it was, that's how it will be.

The constant altercation between the superior and the inferior. The engine of progress, the locomotive of history. Not the war of good and evil, not angel versus devil, not the battle of light against darkness. Just an ordinary contest between the superior and the inferior.

In Poland people used to say of someone that he was a real gentleman, a gentleman to the tips of his fingers, with a gentleman's way about him. When saying such things, no one was thinking about Marx or any social or economic categories. To be a gentleman simply meant to be superior to the inferior. The superior and the inferior are psychological or intellectual categories. No, they're racial categories. No, they're not either. They're the materials, the building blocks, the stuff out of which fate, chance, or the Lord God has fashioned man. High and low do not carry a plus or minus sign but are simply the high and the low, like mountain and valley. Gombrowicz of course loved the superior and paid it homage, tried to apotheosize it. But we shall be more restrained. Let's not fall to our knees before the superior. But let us also not deny the superiority of the superior or its superiority to the inferior.

Poor me, for example, I am one of those who bear the mark of superiority. This means that my thoughts, my intentions, my deeds, and my work are superior to similar thoughts, intentions, and deeds on the part of my colleagues who remain in an inferior state. Just as a gentleman differs from his valet, though they may not differ on the face of things, though each of their thoughts, intentions, and deeds may be entirely orderly, proper, regular, and correct. The only thing that differentiates them is the never outwardly revealed difference in their affiliation: to the superior and the inferior.

I, for example, suffer on account of my superiority. It compels me to conduct myself with asceticism, restraint, distance, honor, personal dignity, and fair play, among many other irksome restrictions which rein me in. But my colleagues destined for the inferior state can allow themselves whatever they please. They can lie a bit, cheat a little, and steal now and again. Their inferiority shrinks the mountains in front of them, narrows the rivers, and takes the depth out of the abyss.

Look at the world with different eyes. Look closely now at those closest to you knowing only this much about the sole genuine class struggle, which is the driving force behind everything in this ill-starred solar system of ours. Knowing of the eternal clash between the superior class and the inferior class. The superior eternally brushing up against the inferior. Or vice versa.

Even though Gombrowicz's idea certainly clarifies the greater part of life's mysteries for us, in places it can also be read as a retrograde and reactionary doctrine, even one that smacks of a certain racism of its own. And that is why I divulge this knowledge to you in the strictest confidence, my dear confidants. This knowledge should not be flaunted among the demagogues of our time, but instructional benefits and all other sorts as well should be drawn from it, thus making the world a bit simpler or easier to bear.

I had an itch to give certain people a real thrashing, but I lost the urge. I lost interest quickly.

Renewal, Renewal, a bonny lass. No, Renewal, Renewal, why do all the fine young men run after you? The old bulls of opportunism run after you, the old horses in the flunky professions, the old merchants who traffic in Poland. You can make a killing on Poland's resurrection. But you can do all right on its death throes too.

But let's make ourselves clear, because this text might end up in the hands of extraterrestrials. And so, in a certain Central European country, a rebellious people grabbed a gang of foreign agents by the throat; a gang which, authorized by a neighboring power, rules that unlucky land. And when the rebels' fingers closed around the agents' throats, when those agents' eyes began to bulge out of their sockets, when they were breathing their last, a pack of hyenas and jackals suddenly leaped onto the carcasses of those agents.

But that's just the way it came out in writing. It wasn't actually a pack, it was just the rank and file. And it wasn't hyenas and jackals but moralists, the fathers of the nation, the Michelangelos, the Rejtans, the convicts at hard labor, the prisoners of Shlisselburg, starving specters, poisoned bards, the profaned saints of the nation. And a rainbow began to shine from the Carpathians to the Baltic. Revolving again, the celestial spheres resounded deeply. And once again, the face of God appeared among the crowds on the street.

I am not a moralist. It's all the same to me. All my suffering is that of a provincial tactician. I have no interest in teaching civics. Everything's come to a standstill in this world. Saintliness has come to a standstill and so has sin. A person can sin and ascend to heaven every four or seven years. There is no guilt, no punishment. Just one great hectic mess.

That's not true. Guilt and punishment do exist. For me and for people like me. I see fangs bared on one side and the other. Off you go, on your way, boys, to oblivion, you fucking socialist realists, you Stalinist trash, you traitors to your country.

Two life-giving lights shine over this earth like the sun and the moon—the lust for money and the desire for power over others. But is that true of earth alone? Maybe they shine over every planet. And over the smallest scrap of this strange Earth, Planet of Birth and Death.

There were three of us. Three men in a car. Gustaw Gottesman, then the editor of the weekly *Literature*, Ireneusz Iredynski, a poet, prose writer, and playwright, and the above-mentioned and below-mentioned me. Gustaw and I were supposed to have gone alone, but then Irek joined us. And so there we were, driving across Poland, our fatherland, Gustaw at the wheel, all of us talking away. Actually we weren't so much talking as instructing Irek in how not to express himself. So that at our destination he would not dare use any foul language, especially the word beginning with the letter "f," which he used in place of punctuation. Though an unruly type, Irek swore to obey. We had done him a favor by bringing him along. We were expected in Elblag, he was just along for the ride. Not only that, he had a certain health problem as well and required our good graces.

Reaching Elblag, we drove up the wooded hill where the small monastery, a few utterly secular-looking buildings, was located. We were welcomed by a priest, still a young man; actually, he was a monk, for that was a monastery after all, Franciscan if I'm not mistaken. Or maybe he was both a priest and a monk; in any case, the young Father showed us into the small refectory, where we ate a tasty monastic lunch. Then we were taken to Klimuszko, the clairvoyant, we were taken to Father Klimuszko's cell; that's the name I'll use for him, that's what everybody called him. I don't remember his monastic name, it went in one ear and out the other. I only remember that we all called him Klimuszko the clairvoyant or Klimuszko the priest or, in his presence, Father, because he could have been our spiritual father or our real father.

Father Klimuszko's cell consisted of two comfortable rooms, a sort of living room and a bedroom, two ample rooms furnished modestly but sensibly, not obtrusively devotional. We sat at a large table and a bottle seemed to materialize on the linen tablecloth. It was cognac, a type of brandy nicknamed Medicine, or something like that; some sort of cognac which Father Klimuszko referred to as "papal" and thus it seemed blessed, appropriate to those monastery walls, even prescribed for us worldly sinners.

But we were keeping an eye on Irek to make sure he didn't use the word beginning with "f" that he usually employed without restraint.

The clairvoyant's séance began. Over glasses of papal cognac, Father Klimuszko told us the story of his life. The story of an ordinary priest in the prewar borderlands, in whom the war awoke strange and astonishing powers. His clairvoyance began in a Nazi prison cell and from then on never left Father Klimuszko again. Now, in a sudden visitation of memory, I recall that in the monastery Father Klimuszko was called Father Andrzej.

And so, Father Andrzej, Father Klimuszko, spun out his memories, citing various mysteries and inexplicable incidents from his own life and the lives of people whom he had encountered, while we stealthily took photos from our pockets, photos of our wives, our children, acquaintances, and even ourselves. In some order or other, we pushed those photos over to Father Klimuszko, whose clairvoyance worked only on photographs. In life he couldn't tell the difference between a man's face and a woman's; in life he could not even recognize his own relatives.

The sun set slowly, darkness stole into the room, the level of the tea-colored drink in the cognac bottle kept falling. Now Irek was using that terrible word beginning with "f" more and more often, but fortunately it turned out that he had a way of speaking that made it sound entirely pleasant and tasteful and did not offend the priest's ear. He made it sound like some sailing term— "a forking wave"—or something to do with mining—"a forking vein of coal."

The priest examined the photograph of a young man who was killed in 1939. He said the young man was killed by an artillery shell, described the field of rye stubble at the edge of a forest where it had happened. I pushed a photograph of my daughter Marysia over to him and the priest predicted that she would take a long journey and said what her life's work would be. The first part of his prophecy has already long since come true, but not the second, and no one knows if it ever will. Then Irek, puffing his "f 's," showed the priest a photograph of himself. The priest instantly discovered an inflammation in the poet's body. It was only then that we learned that Irek was scheduled for an operation in a few days' time. But the priest said that the inflammation wasn't serious and could be cured with herbs. He immediately ran to his little desk, which was also a prie-dieu, where, on his knees, he wrote a prescription for an herbal compound.

It was night by then, someone turned on a lamp. We were slightly soused on the cognac, which, papal though it might be, was also a high-quality product of the well-known Stock company. We heard many curious and striking things about life and ourselves, making special note of the clairvoyant's brief psychoanalysis of Irek, which is probably better forgotten. After that strange séance, which I'll dream of for the rest of my life; after that metaphysical session, which no doubt has had some influence on the course of our lives; after that eerie psychodrama steeped in brandy, we set off on foot for the hotel to sleep, that is, to collect our thoughts and doze off with the help of some domestic liquor. Irek had begun to flag and now his curses sounded like the usual moans and groans of a poet getting on in years, a man of a once-rebellious generation.

The next day we drove back to Warsaw with a fourth passenger, Father Klimuszko, or Father Andrzej, whom we treated with all due reverence. The priest, at a slight loss because of the daylight and vague memories of the night before, admired the view through the window. Each time the priest pronounced a suitable dictum, Irek would reach for the flask of vodka inside his shirt and say, to justify his actions: "The priest spoke so beautifully you have to drink to it."

Naturally, Irek did not go in for the operation. In two weeks' time Father Klimuszko's herbs had eliminated the dangerous inflammation and Irek soon forgot what had brought him to Elblag in the first place.

And here I am, blabbing endlessly on about every last detail of that unimportant incident, but I am relating it in all its particulars and savoring its memory because I want to say something here that I have never told anyone before.

On a few earlier occasions I had tried to induce Father Klimuszko to say what the future held for Poland, for all us peasants and workers along the banks of the Vistula. The priest had recoiled as from a sacrilege, pleading the professional ethics of the clairvoyant, categorically refusing, but we intuited, no, not intuited, we could almost tangibly feel that the priest knew something but did not wish to tell what he knew.

On that evening in Elblag, over cognac and memories, in the intimacy of evening, I quietly but decisively assailed that somewhat frail clairvoyant. He defended himself, dodging, sidestepping me, until finally, in a conspiratorial whisper, he said more or less the following to us: "Boys, things are going to be fine. Poland has fifty good years coming—he held his thumb up— Poland's time is coming and so is her enemies' decline. I see clear sailing for Poland. Things will be very good, just keep it quiet, shh."

That prophecy would have been laughable if in a few years, out of nowhere, a Pole had not become Pope, if Polish lobbies had not gained some power in one country or another, if a Pole had not been awarded a Nobel Prize. I will not be mentioning August 1980 here and what is dawning before our eyes and in which I firmly believe as I bow deeply to the spirit of Father Andrzej, Father Klimuszko, that marvelous saint from Grodno, who brought solace to so many suffering people, who lent heart to so many, and who helped so many to understand the incomprehensible meaning of our hopeless existence.

A success can't be repeated. There's no way of taking the prize twice for the same idea. A book cannot be written a second time and be a success.

That's how it is. That unfortunate book *The Calendar and the Hourglass* hangs over my head like a storm cloud full of thunder and lightning. It brought me no success; actually it afforded me a quarter of a success, while at the same time forever barring me from that trough again, that formal framework able to generate a bit of frothy prose.

I recently signed a contract for a reissue of *Calendar*. At some other point I might have hesitated, but now I have no doubts. That little piece of shameless prose deserves a prize. An award for record obsolescence, for the fantastic speed at which it became ready for pulping.

Like ants, writers circle the pots where they brew their literary broths and concoctions. But each one takes care that his product achieves longevity and has a chance to take its measure against inexorable time. And so they choose solid, long-lasting ingredients, sprinkle in various stylistic condiments that act as preservatives, and mix them, blow on them, and praise them steadfastly to produce an ambrosia that will not lose its flavor in five years, ten, or perhaps even seventy.

Meanwhile, I had recklessly whipped up some preserves that went bad after seven years. Not one prediction came true, not one diagnosis withstood the short test of time, not one judgment held up after a few springs and falls. That's hardly a record for me. And that is the reason I have allowed the good old *Calendar* to see the light of day again and be made a laughingstock.

Yes, but that poor book used up all my gas for the future, wiped me clean of tasty stories, and actually even killed my interest in the form and the formula. Now I'm throwing whatever's around into the pot, but it's coming out thin and causing me doubt and sudden dread. What have I gotten myself into?

Back then, seven years ago, I sailed off toward the irrational, in a metaphysical direction, even heading slightly toward the dark light of mysticism. Now I find both metaphysics and the irrational a bit on the repulsive side. Suddenly I am once again attracted to common sense, which I had so mocked.

How to write? Why write? For whom am I writing? To remain active, to be with people who I wish meant nothing to me but who somehow hopelessly do. To deceive myself. To delude my smart self with my stupid one.

Brrr. Eeee. Ho-ho-ho. Clank. Clink. Quack, quack. Zounds. Attaboy. Bum-bum-bum-BUM. I can't take it anymore. And so forth and so on, et cetera. Have another. Allonzenfande. Up yaws with gauze. Splat.

10

My favorite jaunt is the one from Wilno to the Wilno Colony, sometimes even to Nowa Wilejka. Often those are business trips, meaning I make them when writing a book or repeating myself in my latest novel. All of them, or nearly all, take place in the small area between Wilno and the Wilno Colony; it is rarer that I go to Nowa Wilejka, where I was born.

But I often indulge in those trips even when I'm not on business, with no ulterior motive, just to afford myself some pleasure, to dispel depression, to shorten a long night of insomnia. Hunched over, I creep into some chance atom of memory and, riding the current of time and logic, it's on to Wilno and environs, so far away, so close, brushing the darkness of the night outside the walls of my beloved faithful little den.

A split second later and I'm in Wilno, traveling faster than a spaceship, and it is only in front of the railroad station that I slow down and begin purposefully selecting an itinerary with its own particular charms. Then, leisurely, I set off on foot toward Subocz Street, paying my respects to houses, huts, roadside crosses, and treacherous alder blackthorn bushes, once all so familiar.

I know that these are my own private expeditions to Mars or some other planet which is of no concern to anyone and which has already lost its transient allure. The last of my generation will be dying off soon, taking with them to nonbeing flickering images of mornings over the Wilenka, dates by the church steps in the Upper Colony, the skating rink in Markucie, the brawls in Podjelniaki. But I mention those barbarous names with a queasy delight and enjoy saying them over and over, breaking them into syllables, accenting the words in our special way, chuckling to myself, even though they don't matter to anyone else and the less patient reader will speed with a furious eye over these provincial knickknacks, so parochial you could scream.

But I'm giving myself pleasure, me alone in all the world. You will find no traces of magic in these landscapes. Neither Heine nor Shelley ever strolled there, Montaigne never walked there with Julius Caesar, or Xerxes with Mark Twain. I'm not even sure if Adam Mickiewicz ever traveled to that backwoods by the Wilenka. At most, Jerzy Putrament, also a writer, also from Wilno, stayed there a few times. But that does not confer any distinction on the Wilno Colony.

A curious thing—literacy was not particularly high in our part of Europe, and for that reason many terms and even people's last names lived on in speech without ever, or hardly ever, having been written down. That's why there are so many variants on the words I, we, use and even on people's last names. The ear is unreliable, aural memory is imprecise. My beloved river, which, at a wide point, would be no more than ten meters across, is to this day called the Wilejka by some and the Wilenka by others. So many supposedly literate people, some who even became prominent in Poland, immersed their sinful bodies in that river, but somehow or other no one could ever quite agree which river it was, the Wilejka or the Wilenka.

The maps ended up calling it the Wilenka, and that's the name we used in the Colony. But not everyone. There were those out-of-date people who insisted on calling it the Wilejka. My point is that while living in so defined a manner, one so abrupt and so beautiful, meaning surreal, we at times also inhabit a geography that is incompletely defined, expanses that are undelineated, ocean depths that are unnamed. That fact can be a source of shame or pride. I take pride in it, even though I do repeat by ear many words, songs, and sayings which would sound entirely different on other lips.

But I'm straying, as I'm fond of doing, instead of turning left by Pushkin Hill (where's that name from?) and heading for Markucie, my Markucie, because there may well be others, then on through Markucie to the Wilno Colony, Jesus, Mary, and Joseph, the Colony which doesn't matter to anyone, which at best might matter to a few of my peers who have not yet died of heart failure.

I have a complex, a neurosis, and something else too about boring you, because boredom can't be avoided in a description of completely unknown, basically banal footpaths, meadows, rivers, woods, backwaters, farms, steep vertical skies, and clouds that send down rain sweet as maple syrup.

Obviously I was laying it on there at the end with those steep vertical skies and sweet rain, but it was all to keep your attention. I swear by everything I hold dearest that, concealed in these outwardly sterile and colorless descriptive passages, is some uncommonly important esoteric knowledge, an entire system of information which you will agree is a great treasure if you succeed in uncovering it.

Yes, I was seldom in Nowa Wilejka, even though it was my hometown. A town, I wish to emphasize, and not a burg, as the envious would have it. A railroad junction town with large troop garrisons. One branch of the railway went north to Dynaburg and most likely continued on to Latvia. The other went to Molodeczno and then, after crossing the border, to Moscow, and perhaps even to Leningrad. I never forget anything as fast as I forget the maps in an atlas, I who boast of perfect visual recall.

And so, I don't remember much of that Nowa Wilejka of mine, so very much mine. I do know that you came to Castle Mountain before you reached Nowa Wilejka coming from the Wilno Colony. Yet another mountain castle, there was no end to them in our parts. Probably because Lithuanian and Byelorussian princes and the Polish lords were always ready to build them, as were the bishops and archpriests, and perhaps even some audacious tsaddiks, for we truly had endless tsaddiks, wonder-workers, splendid Hasids, Talmudic scholars, and learned Judaists in our parts. In time our Jewish scholars emigrated to the West to prop up the collapsing temples of Talmudic philosophy and learning there.

What I remember best about Nowa Wilejka is the enormous slope of the hill outside the town, always in sight, always flooded with sunlight. At the peak of that hill, at the peak of its far-flung slopes, where the blue of the sky was at its brightest, was a small cemetery crinkled like a coarse shawl. My father was buried there. I don't remember his grave, even though I must have been taken there and told to pray. I only know that my unknown father has been lying in that hillside for a very long time now; he lies on his side, looks at the sun, and thinks to himself: I wonder what my little Tadeusz is doing. Did he grow up to be a decent person, does he act properly and not guzzle vodka, smoke cigarettes, read impious books and see immoral films?

I was three years old when my father died. And it was then that my wanderings began—I stayed with aunts, grandparents, cousins. I was given out to be raised. Only my great-uncle and -aunt, very distant relations, took me to be theirs forever, a short forever there in the Wilno Colony.

I spent most of the war in Nowa Wilejka. But I think I've already written about that: that first I worked on the railroad, then in a German military hospital for volunteers, meaning German units composed of Soviet POWs who had volunteered to fight. Anyway, I spent only the days in Nowa Wilejka; toward evening time I'd return home, to the Wilno Colony. And so Nowa Wilejka really didn't count and all I can remember now is the Oberzahlmeister's fit of fury in the field hospital when I asked him to sign a paper transferring me from the capricious Arbeitsamt, which wanted to send me to the Reich to perform manual labor.

That typical German military official, a tall, tolerably well-fed, petty squire with a round, flushed kisser (attention, experts—I know you're not supposed to write things like "flushed kisser"), in any case, that official with a ruddy kisser, wearing a gold pince-nez, leaped up from his desk and began to roar so ferociously, to stamp his feet so vehemently, to threaten me so with his Pelikan fountain pen, and to sputter with so much ersatz froth that my heart froze and my only desire was to escape as quickly as possible. And that Oberzahlmeister ranted about the Eastern Front, young Germans dying, his own son, saying what a son of a bitch I was. And so, he shouted the way all Germans shouted during those days at the beginning of 1944.

My poor head also contains some vague memory of being slapped in the face by a German on patrol in the woods between the Lower and Upper Colonies. But I'm not certain of that. Maybe I made that up along the way to use as part of a book which I ultimately abandoned for some other work and which to this day is pigeonholed somewhere and thus over time became a historical document, just as the feature films of Eisenstein, Pudovkin, and Chiaureli are turned into historical documents by the Soviet propaganda machine. At one time to be struck in the face was a fact of enormous significance in a person's life, a type of suffering difficult to measure by today's standards. Perhaps the tragedy of Gierek's fall, perhaps his subjective tragedy, can bear comparison with the moral disaster that a slap in the face constituted in the old days. Nowadays there would seem to be no difference between a slap in the face and an hour-long massage, but before the war, a slap in the face would make people blow out their brains, or someone else's.

Let's move on, because I keep getting sucked into longueurs of memory which are pointless for the reader. Damnit, it's just that I'm drawn to the Wilno Colony. I want to roam its little streets, which were actually country roads. To peek in on those elegant villas and those cottages, almost like peasant huts, to see what the neighbors are doing, or rather the ghosts of my neighbors, my schoolmates, the girls whose looks once sent thrills through me.

But meanwhile, Mr. Mikhail Suslov, the number-two man in the Kremlin, has arrived here in Warsaw. An expert on ideological purity. He arrived without notice, immediately after our poor Party announced the conclusion of its latest desperate plenum, our poor Party, which is in flight now, but perhaps prematurely so. Anyway, Suslov has come to put the Poles' little house in order. The same Suslov who served under Stalin, a Politburo veteran since the mid-thirties.

There's a freeze in the air. Spring had seemed just around the corner, no one was talking about Soviet tanks concealed in the forests, an exhausted Europe had already begun breathing a little easier, and then, before you knew it, a new contredanse seemed to have begun.

Luckily, no sooner had Suslov arrived than he was on his way back. No doubt he just shook a finger in warning, bestowed the rank of Motherfucker on a few Polish leaders, and then reboarded his plane.

Had he stayed the night and, before bed, turned on the state-owned television in his hotel and seen the late news, he would surely have gone white and suffered a heart attack. Solidarity was in charge of the late news on TV. And those union leaders had something to say about everything: political prisoners and censorship and abuses by the authorities charged with keeping order—the police and the Security Police. Just as if this were America or Great Britain. But after all, fifty million Soviet citizens watch Polish television on the sly. And their hearts pound as they watch insolent little Poles ridiculing authority which derives from the tsars and, before that, from Byzantium. What they see are "rebels" who disregard the police, Security, and Soviet agents, flouting Soviet tanks, missiles, divisions.

A plague is coming down on the great Empire of Ice. A plague from aristocratic Poland, the land of the Pope of Rome. Brrr. Brrr in Russian.

Now I'm writing with some gusto in my quiet, but not too quiet, little den. But what will happen when they come to search my place? When I hear the old familiar bang at the door and a

Russian voice shouting melodiously, "Open up!" What will happen to this manuscript then? I won't be able to swallow it, because it has grown too swollen over the last four months.

And who will publish this *Last Page of the Calendar*? To whom should I submit this acrimonious text? Whatever happens, happens. It's not worth worrying about in advance.

I don't know whether I bring people happiness or unhappiness. But I do know that there are certain mysterious or occult forces bubbling around me. I have no influence on them, neither do they have the final say on my fate. All the same, people coming into contact with me should watch their step.

Here is just one striking example, an incident which took place at the end of last year. As I've already mentioned, in the fall of 1980 I visited America—I should say Marysia, my daughter, who lives in New York City. I flew there with my wife and we spent five wonderful weeks in the heart of Manhattan.

But the Americans I knew, moved by extravagant ambition on my behalf, decided that I must meet Zbigniew Brzezinski, the Great Zbig, President Carter's advisor.

And so, I was dragged to Washington, where I waited two days for that meeting, as if it were Halley's comet. I had no specific business with Mr. Brzezinski and could brave those two days of anticipation. I walked around that lovely, majestic city, thinking of other places I had visited before, alone or with my wife and daughter. Washington was chilly at the time, almost bitter cold, but sunny and still green, or rather, black-green and purple, though I'm not so sure that it was all that purple, but purple sounds better than red.

And so, I waited, not really awaiting that audience. Meanwhile, my sponsors were bustling about, mopping sweat from their brows. This evening, tomorrow morning, before noon, in two hours, in fifteen minutes. He stepped out, he'll be back in a minute, he's away, he'll be flying in this afternoon, he's here but he's busy, important business, he can't now, please wait, please have a seat, would you care for a coffee.

It didn't bother me. I went to a map store. The largest map store in the world. But they didn't have my Wilno Colony. So, off to the Kennedy Center. A biting wind, red leaves in the air, no one around. Arlington Cemetery on the far side of the Potomac, and on top of that gigantic hillside, at the edge of that green infinity, was the white manor house of General Lee. Straight from the Wilno Colony. Something not unlike Puszkarnia.

And so we went about the American capital, shielding ourselves against the wind. I was constantly glancing, forever peeking across the river at Virginia, that state which reminded me so much of the Wilno area. I kept my eyes open, feeling both bored and not bored, but at bottom I was actually waiting to learn if the President's advisor could find three minutes to see me, possibly confusing me with Adam Michnik, to encourage me, bolster my spirits with a good word.

But we kept coming up empty-handed. The election. The presidential election was a few days away. Zbig had no time. He was busy day and night. So maybe it wasn't worth waiting. By then my patrons had also lost hope. Fate insulted Mr. Brzezinski on my behalf. Providence took vengeance on the Great Zbig for the wrong done to me. It's been like this for years now—destiny gives me nothing substantial, no prizes, but it keeps watch over my prestige and severely punishes the mighty of both hemispheres who are frivolous and careless with me.

Innocent as a newborn babe, America sailed past the window. Ugly little towns, pretty ones, overpasses, enormous bridges, glimpses of a bay, Philadelphia. The train wheels clacked evenly along as they do in every hackneyed novel, but I was worried sick that Mr. Brzezinski would soon have to endure his punishment. What should I do? How to warn him, save him?

It was too late, too late. And he could have avoided trouble so easily. Just three minutes. Hello, hello. What's happening in Poland, are you here for long, good luck. And then everything would have assumed a different form and American history would have taken a different direction. Had he only known. But how could he have? I had no chance to tell him. Fatum. Moira. Or the usual Nemesis.

One of my daughter's neighbors in New York is Ela Czyzewska, the famous actress, whom you've no doubt forgotten a little by now but who still remembers you. Ela called as soon as I returned, asking me for advice—who should she vote for, Carter or Reagan? She has faith in my political wisdom and waited to hear my instructions.

And so, I instructed her to vote for Carter. Out of consideration for the Polish lobby. Carter was surrounded by Poles and was on good terms with Poland and things Polish. Carter was better for us. Ela obediently agreed to carry out my bardic instructions the following day in the voting booth.

All progressive America would be voting for Carter. The Poles and the Jews and the blacks and the Puerto Ricans. The intellectuals and the homosexuals, the students and the Eskimos. Carter would win a sweeping victory, Carter was out in front, Carter was in no danger.

I watched it on television, despondently digesting the terrible calamity which you know by now. Carter would lose, Carter had to lose because his advisor had rashly chosen not to see Tadeusz Konwicki from the Wilno Colony. The shoo-in, the favorite, would tomorrow lose by a mile, despite the obvious expectations and the facts, because Zbig had begrudged an audience to a certain bard from Eastern Europe or, to be more precise, from the Wilno area.

The next afternoon I felt a sudden, inexplicable sense of crisis. As if the chemical composition of the air had altered, as if the earth had begun to revolve in the opposite direction, as if our solar system had slipped its trajectory and gone sailing blindly off into the depths of the galaxy. In a word, I felt a sudden and uncanny change, and I had a violent urge to vote for Reagan, even though I found him utterly alien spiritually and physically and even though I had no right to vote.

Ela called later on, ashamed of herself. "You know what," she said, "I went to vote for Carter as you told me to, but I voted for

Reagan, I don't know why." "No harm in that," I said, "that's the way it had to be. The way it has to be. You're not to blame."

That evening we went to friends' to watch the election results on television. Supper was ready and waiting, three color TVs tuned to three different channels, and the sweet, elegant lady of the house. We would sit there till morning. The results would be announced only the next morning. The furious battle would last through the night. Who'd be on top? Carter or Reagan? But it had to be Carter. The only question was by how large a majority.

But I was on edge. It's really a terrible thing to possess the sort of passive power I possess. A power which brings me no benefits but harms people who come my way, or who refuse to come my way out of rash arrogance.

We sat in deep armchairs, drinks in hand. Plenty of time. All night, all election night. The famous American election night. I had extended my stay especially for this. It was to be a historic show. Worth seeing and worth telling my grandchildren about in later years. That genuine miracle of crazy America. Attention, the show is about to begin.

And then—bip bip, and it was all over. Carter was down for the count at ten o'clock. The favorite was down. He was trying to get back on his feet, but he wouldn't make it. A knockout. Astounding. Stunning. Something like that.

It had happened before anyone knew it. Carter swept from the ring. By some force. Some fatal force. Mine. My passive force, over which I have no influence. Mr. Brzezinski, what have you gone and done?

Milosz was in similar danger when he didn't want to see me in Berkeley when I was dragging myself through there on my way across America. Dark clouds were already massing over him. But, after all, Milosz is a fellow Lithuanian, he could smell trouble, he was alerted to the danger by Lithuanian spirits, and so he patched things up and came to an agreement with the forces that accompany me.

And look—at once a prize comes his way in this chain of luck and prescribed prayer. A prize. And not the worst of them either. The Nobel Prize.

I've already spoken of my admirers or, rather, of my women admirers. When I pick up the phone and hear a woman's sensual whisper pulsing with sexuality, I take the safety off my pistol. An admirer. Mysterious, erotically languorous, seductive, intellectual, enchanting. But I'm an old bird. I've been around. It's hard to take me in.

Had I allowed myself to be talked into a meeting for a literary chat in a café where office workers slurp brandy with coffee or coffee with brandy, had I allowed myself to be tempted, I would, after waiting fifteen minutes, have seen an old and infirm person of the opposite sex in the doorway. Yes, my dears, my women admirers, the ardent lovers of my coarse Byelorussian-Wilno prose are old women whose husbands left them forty years ago, widows in the midst of nervous breakdowns, category-three invalids, ghastly hybrids thirsting for love and affection. And I blunder straight through that hobbling, cough-ridden, moaning crew. I'm working my way toward the shores of the Styx, my head held high, surrounded by a traveling infirmary, like a pilgrim bound for Lourdes.

Stash Dygat. He had women admirers too. His clientele were young ladies in high school or the first or second year of university. Nothing like mine with their eyeglasses, leprous foreheads, their stockings rolled. His girls were movie stars. From good prewar films or today's Hollywood.

Stash liked it when I visited him and found him with some elegant graduate student who was writing her master's on him. Stash loved it when I found him with a romantic high-school student from a good family who'd been madly in love with him since the first grade. And those were all tall, long-legged girls with lovely faces. Girls who were well-cared-for, fashionably dressed, redolent of Dior or something even better. Girls well versed in *Winnie the Pooh, Peter Pan*, and of course in Dygat as well.

Stash, that lowlife, liked to watch as those young ladies regarded me with horror, their eyes seeming to say, "So that's Konwicki," before shifting with pleasure back to the immense and sometimes potbellied figure of their idol, their guide to imaginary Elysian Fields, Munich Train Stations, Disneylands.

I accepted those trying moments with dignity, the only trying moments he ever caused me. Apart from that, he was an affectionate and faithful friend. On one condition, of course—that I wasn't working on my next book. If Dygat read in an interview that I was writing again, all manner of restrictions would begin to be imposed.

Besides, he had once forced me to promise that I would never write again. I swore solemnly not to and Stash was pacified. Until I discovered that when we had been on vacation together he had tortured my wife with allusions, malicious remarks, launching rumors among the other vacationers to the effect that "Tadzio has betrayed the cause." This made my wife, Danka, feel bad and put her on edge. Finally, she drove the slanderer into a corner with the words: "But Tadzio has just written a new novel without letting anyone know."

I've just remembered another Danka. Danka from the Wilno Colony, whom I loved wildly when we were in an underground study group together. That was forty years ago and so I can no longer recall exactly what I mean by "wildly." But I do know that it was a mad and probably unrequited love.

To me Danka was gloriously beautiful. She had a thick—how to put it—wheat-colored braid, a complexion like peaches and cream, as people used to say, and all in all was simply extraordinary.

She carried herself with dignity, for she was certainly aware of how gloriously beautiful she was. No silly kittenish ways, no giggles, no rolling the eyes. Danka was probably even haughty and it was her haughtiness that pained me the most. But no doubt that haughtiness was not deliberate, not directed at me in particular. It was the usual, normal haughtiness of a gloriously beautiful young lady from Wilno.

My love, being true love, was undoubtedly composed of millions of flickers of longing, joy, dolor, delight, and despair; billions of elusive premonitions, the seeds of bitterness and the seeds of hope, an entire Milky Way of them. That's why it all has vanished into oblivion and been blurred by the ever-quickening tempo of days and years. I don't remember anything, I don't remember a thing, all that I remember is that it was sweet and sublime.

But one detail stands out. One incident has lodged in my enfeebled mind. While suffering the agonies of unrequited love, I was also tortured because of my wretched appearance. By an exceptional turn of misfortune, there was an enormous, impressive, dark-brown freckle located at the very tip of my nose. On the whole I was unpleasantly freckly, and in those days freckles were thought quite unsightly. And so, in the midst of all those hateful freckles, a giant had appeared, a titan, the god of Wilno freckles. I tugged at the tip of my nose, but nothing could dislodge that freckle. I rubbed away at it with my finger, I smeared it with the juices of various herbs, even the cuckooflower, whose juice can burn through ox hide. I sandpapered that freckle. Nothing helped. The freckle blossomed and grew, assuming its freckle shape and horrid color.

Every morning I would run with pounding heart to the mirror, hoping that the Good Lord had caused that eyesore to disappear under cover of night. No such luck. The bastard would be even bigger as it peered mockingly back at me.

And so, one day I took a needle you could sew horsehide with; I took that huge, thick needle and began digging the freckle out from the tip of my nose.

The blood flowed and my nose nearly fell off; I came down with a fever, and the wound festered for two weeks. In the end, my nose recovered, and then out from under the scab there emerged a vigorous healthy freckle, twice the size of the previous one. What lousy luck.

Danka left the country after the war. She and her husband moved to another continent. She moved to another world. But still, a little of her has remained here. A single, gloriously beautiful specimen, beneath the lids of my eyes, a bit bleary now.

To please the reader. To please the cavemen, the middle class, the philistines, the pretentious intellectuals, colleagues, rivals. To know how to endear oneself, to be winning.

That's the temptation. An irresistible temptation. To be the darling, the favorite, the pet. But at what price? The price of obedience, flattery, the price of playing the game?

To communicate with the reader or with God? Dostoevsky dealt with God. He forgot about his readers' good graces. Dostoevsky, that's the first time I've mentioned him. And all the bores of literature have been walking around with copies of Dostoevsky in hand for quite a while now. They go for literary strolls with him, colleagues in art. They value Dostoevsky because he would value them too were he to rise from the dead.

But that's not the point. The point is that Dostoevsky did not chase after his readers' coattails and offer them fake friendship. I would like to imitate Mr. Dostoevsky in that respect, even though my soul lusts for adulation from the faceless crowd. Cheers, big and little, and kisses are sweeter than furious boos and anonymous kicks in the butt.

This is a constant and eternally relevant dilemma. To write what has to be written, to do the writing that is necessary, unavoidable, or to write so that people line up for you at the library, read your books until they're dog-eared, slobber over you, tear you apart out of love, fellow feeling, and the sense you're already pals who've been through a lot together.

And that's the truth, my dears. All those types whom you admire and of whom you say: He writes with such ease, ah, the grace in him, oh, is he intelligent, let me just jot down those brilliant thoughts of his—all those types ingratiate themselves with you out of cunning, savage egotism, a terrible urge to be assistant gods. Nothing else matters to them. They are interested in your admiration only as a statistic, a figure they can use to crush a literary rival.

They see right through you, dear readers, they know your pitiful tastes, your fondness for pornographic murmurs, for any sort of fast action, shallow insipid philosophy, and snobbery, no matter what its basis may be. For you they pretend to be stupid; that is, they pretend to be you. Because they despise you. And, despising you, they flatter you. Sucking up to you, they despise you. Bowing down to you, they despise you with everything they've got.

A kilo of chicken costs four hundred zlotys. Turkey is two thousand a kilo. The prophecies I made in A *Minor Apocalypse* have long since come true. Reality is now outdistancing me at great speed. A rapist has been apprehended because of his sugar ration card, which his victim found after the rape. There are lines in front of newspaper kiosks which have no newspapers. A few thousand letters from the West were found in a garbage dump in Ursus. All the letters had been opened, by persons unknown. A ton of bacon is rotting in another garbage dump. The post office still has not delivered the packages which arrived from abroad last August. Local Party and state dignitaries pack their bags at night and flee to remote provinces. With the money a peasant gets for a liter of milk at a state purchase center, he can buy three and a half liters of milk at the store next door.

My dear, beloved country, you seem like a quote from the poet Galczynski.

No one reads anything these days.

If they do read, they don't understand.

If they read and understand, they forget it all immediately.

This was said by Stanislaw Lem in a television interview and it made me fall off my chair with delight.

Yes, I used to be in touch with Lem often. At one time, as a member of the contemporary Polish literature board at the Spark publishing house, I used to read every new book by Lem. I remember those typescripts—I don't know what to call them, Lem the pro's typescripts—and those amusing, lengthy letters he would send. Lem might say that he had grown so feeble from his straitened circumstances that he no longer had the strength to walk and therefore had to purchase a car, which was why he was requesting he be sent an advance as quickly as possible. I may be confusing things here, perhaps my version is not exact, but I clearly remember those letters, which were little literary gems of their own.

I simply am very fond of Lem, even though that author infuriates many of my colleagues. Perhaps I shouldn't have even mentioned that, because those were off-the-record pouts, made in confidence. But they stem from normal, healthy, positive envy. Lem has had the world-class career typical of the popular author. No one hypes Lem, no mafias inflate his reputation, no political or social machines are hoisting Lem up to the Parnassus of Europe and America. Lem has mentioned two or three times in the Polish press that he is no longer able to deal with galley proofs in dozens of languages, with all the bank checks, the letters from readers on six continents. Sometimes when I consider Lem's actual success, one genuine and deserved, my heart does bleed a little. Sometimes I too feel the pinch of envy and the bile begins to gurgle in my booze-stunted liver. But what can I do? You can groan inwardly, but you've got to go on living somehow or other.

Fortunately, I'm fond of Lem, meaning I admire his turn of mind and his sense of humor. His philosophy and his distance on things on which I have no distance. His skepticism and the gentle friendship, free of any insolence, he bestows on those he loves.

But even with my lousy memory, I do remember Lem from 1945–46. In those days he wore a Jagiellonian University medical-school cap and, if I'm not mistaken, knickers. Those slightly old-fashioned trousers were engraved in my enfeebled memory cells because they were a certain sign of his provincialism. From those knickers I guessed that Lem came from the borderlands, probably Lvov.

At that time I was working for *Rebirth*, and with my fresh Wilno eye was observing the people who came to our editorial offices, and at the same time I was nosing about the new, young, intriguing, fascinating literature of postwar Poland.

I can clearly recall Rozewicz's poetry and, though it's shameful to admit, Zukrowski's early short stories. But I also remember Lem's poetry and his first attempts at prose. Yes, Lem began as the usual hermetic poet and rebellious prose writer dealing with contemporary issues.

Lem used to come to our editorial offices on Basztowa Street. But his business was mostly with the journal *Creative Work*, which shared office space with us. Most likely wearing that cherry-red medical-school cap of his, he would step into Kazimierz Wyka's office. But it's from *Tygodnik Powszechny* that I remember Lem's poetry. Hence it follows that Lem's reticence bore on political life as well. He kept apart. He sided with the apolitical *Creative Work* and the oppositionist *Tygodnik Powszechny*. But I may be confused here. At that time Lem may have been in charge of censorship and a member of the Krakow Party committee.

Later on he married a Scandinavian-type beauty with an air of Scandinavian mystery about her, after which there was no word at all of Lem. Once in a while I would hear something in passing about him, that he was skiing in Zakopane, building a home, acquiring fame as a gourmet and an expert on cuisine.

But none of that is important. What is important, mysterious, and astounding is the literary volte-face Lem executed in the fifties. Suddenly that uncommonly talented prose writer with a bent for the lyrical, that poet of a prose that attempted to settle moral accounts with the era of the gas chamber, our feverish, tragic, fascinating modern era, suddenly Lem, a fellow alumnus of Jagiellonian University, slightly older than I, began to write science fiction.

Obviously I can easily assume that he did so in order not to write as I did. Not to sink into the swamp of socialist realism, not to poison himself with self-deceit, not to stew in treason to literature and philosophy. Yes, Lem was able to walk off, into the cool shadows of asylum. There he would wait out the worst years in our literature, our country's worst years. In the asylum of fantasy, the lair of the imagination.

But why did he stay on there permanently? Why did he submit unresistingly to the rigors of literature and philosophy at their most severe? Why wasn't he tempted to return to the easy life of the present day, so propitious to literature, to its intellectual and emotional rebellions, even to the technology of literature, even to the means of creating it? Lem continued to operate in the closed world of science fiction, rivaling the masters of the genre, the sly old literary foxes of the great metropolises, the mighty sharks of the international publishing market.

I've been waiting years for Lem to come back. With a certain inward trembling, I await the day when Lem returns and speaks our language, the language of contemporary authors, whether they be political, social, pornographic, psychological, accusatory, or anarchistic. I am waiting for Lem to return and take a piece of the cloth of our times from us, the cloth from which each day we cut our greatness and our pettiness.

But Lem is not coming back. He has cut his way through the Himalayas of the literary genre of science fiction. The mountains and the valleys. The sun and the cold. Vegetation and eternal death. Hope and despair. He walked the path of faith in the future and went flying down the stony slope of pessimism. He took consolation in the omnipotence of futurology and battled breezy prognoses. Lem had a hand in building the magnificent edifice of science fiction, and now he is setting explosives around that edifice. Now a slightly tuckered-out terrorist, Lem is detonating that palace of human pride.

A lovely avenue that proved a dead end. I mean that Lem has seen it as a dead end. Other literary ants will continue working that dead quarry for centuries to come. But Lem will not be coming back. He's staying there atop the ruins created by his own uprising, his own philosophical and literary uprising. Lem has destroyed his own empire and stayed on in the eye of the disaster like the captain of a sinking ship.

Stanislaw, you should shake a leg. You should beat it while

there's still time. You should escape to our side before it's too
late. But I know that you'll stay there amid the rubble, which
will again be joined to build a castle a hundred times more
imposing and which will crumble into dust a hundred times
again. You created that Golem and you kill him every day of
the week. This is the purest creation possible on this earth. Birth
and death. Creation and destruction. What do those heights have
to do with us, we, who like broken liquor bottles reflect bits of
sky, dust particles, scraps of an Indian summer.

Lem is a high court unto himself. He sentenced himself to a
greatness that did not reach high, and to a low fall. Lem the
pessimist, whose own writings authorize me to take these liberties.
Lem the optimist, whose skeptical thought discouraged me from
friendship with him. Lem my friend, whom I never met and
probably never will.

As befits a real writer in his old age, I should make mention
of my illness. That I'm lying here in my den, knocked out of
commission by an inflammation in the throat. And my throat is
a sore spot for me. At any rate, that's one way of putting it.

And so, the day before yesterday, early on a nice morning, I
went posthaste to the assistant professor who operated on me
twice last year. He examined my throat and praised it to the skies.
It's perfect, the scar has assumed the function of a vocal cord,
and it's difficult to detect any sign of an operation. Speaking
softly, I said: "I'm running a temperature, I'm trembling, I don't
feel good." And my good doctor replied: "Well, in fact, you have
a viral infection at the top of your throat. And so what do you
hear, what do you think?" I replied: "Are you talking about my
throat?" The doctor: "No, the situation the country's in." And I
said: "My good man, I have the shakes and rheumatism."

But all the same I'm satisfied. Even a bit pleased. It's nice to
see a first-rate physician downplay your inflammations, your
swellings, your foolish indispositions. The most important thing
is that everything is all right in there. Cancer-shmancer, we
should all be so healthy.

And so, with prescriptions for vitamins, lime, and gargle, I rushed to the drugstore, then home, where I hopped back into my little den.

And so, ladies and gentlemen, I am a sick man. I suffer bouts of mild depression, I find myself grimacing, and feeling generally out of sorts. Please lower your voice, walk on tiptoe, and keep your philosophizing to yourself. A writer is indisposed. A prose writer is in ill health. A novelist is grappling with his own frailty. Present arms. Ladies and gentlemen, the National Anthem.

11

A very odd business, suspicious even. I was summoned by the chairman of my former university's philology department. Summoned may not be the word, but rather, politely invited with no reason mentioned. At one point I did, in fact, spend some time at that worthy institution. Many, many years ago, when today's professors were still in grade school. But then I stopped attending because I was bored, and from then on, I would walk past the university's venerable buildings with absolute indifference, as if they were the municipal slaughterhouse or a museum. Once in a while I might by chance glance over at the clock in the library portal, but later on, like everything else in this increasingly lousy world, that clock went awry, and so I stopped glancing into the university courtyard altogether.

I tapped my cane on the sidewalk, partly from a sense of good cheer, for which I had no particular cause, and partly to alert the other pedestrians. My son-in-law had painted the cane white over my objections—my sight is still decent, even though I cannot make out the faces of the people I pass. But he painted it just to be on the safe side, with the aim of winning me respect. A white cane is the royal scepter of old age.

A lovely early fall was everywhere—in the streets, the squares, the little lanes. The newspapers were saying there hadn't been a fall like this in memory. But that wasn't true. I can remember many similar ones. I just can't recall what was happening to me, my friends, or my family during those lovely early falls.

My memory puts up resistance; sweet, good-natured resistance. I banter with my memory, and sometimes, as if to reward me, it lifts one end of its colorless curtain and shows me some moment long past full of stunning colors and exciting aromas.

Tangles of caterpillar filaments float upward like the strings of invisible balloons. At times they catch on chimneys or television antennas and wave in the warm air like white seaweed soaring to the sky. The girls are dressed in their spring clothes, wearing everything they had no chance to display earlier. I still like the girls, even though I now look on them as nicely shaped clouds or pretty stalks of wild herbs. But I must admit that I've grown more particular. My eye is no longer tempted by just anything that walks by.

I was tapping my cane merrily, because I had made it to the fall, one more fall. Now if I could just skip those dark days full of mist and ice storms, and just set eyes on January and February, when the days begin to grow longer and the sun stands higher in a sky fresh and renewed . . .

Wait a minute, hold on, where was I headed again? I stopped in an arcade and began collecting my unruly thoughts. It's nice to lean against a mossy column; the pain in my left leg subsided at once, a long moment of blessed relief. Where was I going? What had my daughter sent me out to pick up, what errand was I running for my nervous son-in-law? Now I know, I remember, because I always remember everything. I was on my way to the university, to see the chairman. Maybe they're in the market for a sagacious rector.

A lovely day and I was looking pretty lovely myself. I was wearing a nice suit, one that I'd had for years and which had outlasted many changes of style and would soon be in fashion again. I had gathered my hair, of which there is not a great deal, into a rakish, greenish-gray wave. I had also splashed on some eau de cologne from the old days, of a sort not manufactured today.

An older man carrying a net shopping bag was approaching me on the sidewalk. He greeted me by raising his hand to his forehead. He must have been in the military, or maybe he'd been a railroad man. We exchanged salutes like two old ocean liners, even though we didn't know each other.

I was about to cross the street when a young man with a noble look in his eye scurried over to me.

"I'll help you," he said.

"God bless you, but it's all right. I can manage."

I pushed his helping hand gently away, raised my cane in warning, and set briskly off for the gate to the university. I still had no idea what it was all about, not even an inkling. Scandal, crime, folly lay in store for me. A final flight. The loveliest of madnesses.

The secretary looked up only when I spoke and at once indicated a chair.

"Please have a seat. I'll inform the chairman you're here right away."

A vigorous fellow with a disheveled head of hair, his eyeglasses held discreetly together with adhesive tape, the chairman came out to greet me.

"Please come in. I've been looking forward to this." He took me by the elbow and escorted me to his office, which had an air of great age about it.

"How are you feeling? You're clearly in the pink."

"Yes, I can't complain. When a man takes a nice stroll during the day, he forgets entirely how old he is."

"Marvelous, marvelous," said the chairman. "So let's sit down and talk shop."

We took stock of each other, friendly smiles on our faces. He made a casual note on a piece of paper lying on his large desk.

"You were a student here, isn't that so?"

"Ohoho, that was years ago. No one remembers that."

"Not so. We do. Wasn't your major Polish studies?"

"Yes, it was, Mr. Chairman, but I'm ashamed to say that I really didn't apply myself."

"Well, let's not overstate the case either," protested the chairman, removing his glasses and picking a paper up from his desk. "There were some C-pluses, a number of B's, and even an A, I see."

"That must have been for conduct."

The chairman laughed and wagged a finger at me. Just then someone poked his head through the half-open office door.

"Not now!" barked the chairman. "I have some urgent business, couldn't be more urgent," he said, winking at me with a vile eye red from too little sleep or too much to drink. I'd heard that nowadays professors like to hit the bottle.

"You see, Mr. Chairman," I said with some embarrassment, "I dropped out of Polish studies in my final year. Back then it was fashionable not to graduate. A postwar fad."

"That's just my point. There was so little left to go."

"That's for sure."

"But I'm looking ahead here. Just a few more lectures, classes, seminars, then the exams on world history and literature and a thesis, minor details."

"I'll say."

"That's just my point. So as not to take up your valuable time, I propose that you complete the work for your degree."

I was speechless. The chairman was quick to hand me a glass of water, a glass that had clearly been used before, for I could detect red traces of lipstick on the rim. A woman had been in to see him before me.

"But I never had any more to do with Polish studies after that."

"Doesn't matter, doesn't matter. We'll refresh your memory, fill you in. What seminar were you in when you quit?"

"A seminar on Kochanowski's songs, if Kochanowski ever wrote any."

"Marvelous, marvelous!" exclaimed the chairman. "Tomorrow's the first day of the seminar I'm giving on Kochanowski's songs. What a coincidence! It's absolutely symbolic!"

"Wouldn't the university be wasting its money on me?"

The chairman smiled enigmatically and bent close to my ear, but I couldn't hear what he was saying.

"Could you speak louder, please, Mr. Chairman. My right ear's been stopped up for ten years now."

"Television!" cried the chairman. "Television's going to pay for it."

"Why television? Why me?"

"Don't ask. It'll all be clear soon enough! It's a social and educational experiment! My initiative! My brilliant idea!"

He was shouting so loudly that a fly which was about to dart through the window into the office suddenly changed its mind and flew off among the yellowing chestnut trees. I had no chance to point out to him that overall my hearing was fairly good.

"And what will it cost me?" I asked, choking on the water.

"One television appearance. A gala event. That's all. Is it a deal?" He extended his hand, the thumb bandaged. The chairman was clearly not only a drinker but also a bit of a barroom brawler. I remember seeing a newspaper print an apology from an assistant professor who had assaulted the staff in a fashionable restaurant.

"But what will my children say, my grandchildren?" I whispered in horror.

"Marvelous, marvelous!" cried the chairman. "Your children and grandchildren, that's precisely the point. You'll be the most famous grandfather in the country. Perhaps we should wet our whistle." Carried away, he reached between the volumes of a commemorative edition of Adam Mickiewicz's works for a gleaming bottle of vodka flavored with rowanberries.

"But what if I die while I'm in school?"

"We'll bury you with full university honors."

By then he had taken my glass, emptied the water into a vase, and poured me a stiff drink of rowanberry vodka. "Down the hatch!" I don't know how it happened, but I gulped down half that drink, which at one time had often diverted me in my hours of doubt. Some lovely music began to play above my head; I could hear trumpets, bells, and women's voices too, I think. Suddenly I felt just like bursting into tears.

"I'm not as strong as I once was."

"College hasn't killed anybody yet, my friend. Let's shake on it." Once again he extended his mangled hand.

"But what if I can't make the grade?"

"Your comrades will give you a hand."

"I'd prefer a firmer guarantee."

"Television will help you out."

"Shall we knock down another one, old buddy?"

Afterward, I sat for a long time on a bench in front of the library. The sun was friendly in its warmth, a breeze brought me fresh oxygen, and a sparrow's chirping brought me back to my senses. Now all I wanted was to appear dignified, as befits a man my age. But, weary of life, my eyes flitted off in every direction, my work-weary head fell back to rest against the bench, and there was an ominous rumbling in my stomach. Young people were wandering back and forth, casting shrewd, unfriendly glances at me. They had no idea that inside my summer coat, which I had bought during a trip abroad, that inside that coat my sweaty hand was clutching my student ID.

Boy Scouts brought me home. Their enterprising leader rang our bell and my daughter Marysia opened the door.

"God, you look awful," she said, clutching her head.

"Well, we'll be going now," said the leader on behalf of the other Scouts. Chilled to the marrow by the way I looked, Marysia forgot to thank them for their kindness.

"Where have you been? Stefan, for God's sake, give me a hand."

Still in his pajama tops as usual, my son-in-law emerged from the depths of the apartment. But I was smiling serenely, as I have been for quite a few years now. Taking me by the arms, they led me into the living room, where the television stood careful watch on a low table. I sank into an armchair.

Stefan nodded with pity. "Well?" he asked. "What has my reckless father-in-law been up to this time?"

"Everything's under control."

"But where have you been, Dad?"

"At the university."

"Aha," said Stefan, feigning surprise. "Interesting. And what were you doing there?"

"Enrolling."

Marysia and Stefan exchanged meaningful glances. Rock 'n' roll was blasting in the next apartment. The window was filled with sky and intense sunlight.

"We should put him to bed," decided Marysia.

They carried me, dragged me to my little den, which at one time, many, many years ago, was a lion's den and is now a doddering hermit's cell. They laid me down on a couch short and narrow as one you'd find in a doctor's waiting room.

"Loosen his tie," said Marysia, whom I playfully used to call by the English name Mary many years ago.

Stefan leaned over me and undid the collar button of my unfashionable shirt.

"He smells of schnapps," he announced with a certain satisfaction, since he too had been known to be unable to return home under his own power. I had loosened his tie and pulled off his pants many a time.

"And in the middle of the day," said Marysia with a sigh. "Who talked you into it?"

"The chairman," I groaned.

"What chairman?"

"The chairman of the philology department."

Once again they exchanged glances.

"First let him get some sleep," said Stefan. "Later on I'll give him a Vichy tablet."

"Yes, you're an expert on hangovers," said Marysia ironically. "It's your influence. He never came home tipsy in his life."

But that wasn't true. Once, I was even late for Christmas Eve, I knocked over the Christmas tree and sat down on the presents from St. Nicholas. Marysia had lied for instructional purposes.

"You know that if I take a drink, it's only from nervous tension," snarled Stefan. "I think I have the right to relax once a month, or don't I?"

"You might try relaxing at home with your wife. But vodka's the only thing that relaxes you now."

Stefan was about to play out a grandiloquent scene of anger and offense and had even raised his hand, intending to smash some small and worthless object, when I came to his aid.

"Let me rest," I whispered. "I have a tough seminar tomorrow."

Stefan lowered his hand and began nervously chewing at his fingernails. "Listen, something's the matter with him," he said softly.

"We'll see what you're like at his age."

"Fine. As you please. It's not my business. It's your father, your headache."

They did, however, walk in harmony to the middle of the room, where they observed me with shared concern.

"What do you think?" whispered Marysia. "What's this business about the university?"

"One time I thought I was at a banquet at the Royal Castle," said my son-in-law in a trifling tone of voice. "The janitor must have treated him to a drink. That bum does nothing but sit by the window and corrupt the tenants."

"We should let him sleep," said Marysia with a sigh.

"It's the best medicine," added Stefan.

They stood for a moment observing the deceased, then left the room to go about their own business. I stretched out my aged limbs, which the alcohol had caused to stop paining me, the first time in I couldn't remember when. I felt blissful and a little ill. Leaving a snowy trail, a jet plane flew across the high ceiling of the sky. A wasp had strayed onto the window and sat looking at me or into the gloomy cavern of my room. Anyway, it may not have been a wasp but an air bubble in the glass. Still, I'd have preferred it to have been a wasp. A furious, hostile wasp from my childhood which was seeking revenge for its sack-like nest, which had been smashed in an attic full of dead spiders and withered leaves.

And so, I lay there fighting the tide of unconsciousness, but every so often my old heart would accelerate its rhythm, the way it used to speed up at the onset of an adventure. I knew with remarkable clarity that some improbable folly still awaited me in the twilight of my life.

"Are you drunk, Grandpa?" I heard a hoarse voice say.

With some effort I turned myself from the blackened wall that had been drinking in my failing breath for ages now. My grandson was standing by the couch, little Pawel, six or maybe seven.

"Don't you believe that empty talk, Pawel. I met a wizard who treated me to a mysterious elixir."

"Daddy says you're always making up stories," said little Pawel skeptically.

"I couldn't care less if you believe me or not." I was about to turn back onto my other side.

Little Pawel grabbed my cheeks with his paws and tried to peer into my weary eyes.

"Wait, Grandpa, don't turn your head away. Where did you meet the wizard?"

"That I can't tell you."

"At least tell me what he looked like."

"He pretended to be a regular person, of course. But I'm a hard one to trick, because I've seen a lot of wizards."

"How can you tell them?"

"By their eyes. There's something unusual about their eyes, a strange brilliance, a glow, a mysterious light, like rays."

Little Pawel sat down at the edge of the couch, seeking my inert hand.

"Did you really meet him?"

"I really did. But don't tell anyone. Especially your mother and father. Because some extraordinary things are going to be happening here."

"You have to tell me, Grandpa, please, please."

"I'll tell you a little bit every day, all right?"

"All right, but you haven't told me enough for today."

"That's all I can do."

"Then tell it again."

"I met a wizard and he put me under a spell."

"Are you under a spell now?"

"Yes, I am."

"What did he turn you into?"

"I still don't know. It'll show tomorrow."

"You won't fly away from us in your sleep, will you?"

"I will, but I'll come back."

"Promise?"

"Promise."

"All right, go to sleep, but don't go too far."

He stroked the wave in my hair, then began to tiptoe away as if I were already in an enchanted sleep. I closed my eyes, and the dome of my eyelids immediately began to dance with black dots like mice in the evening and some sort of black coils like spores from trees shedding their blossoms. I knew I would not be falling asleep in any hurry.

When I can't fall asleep, I like to think about my funeral. My upcoming funeral is the only event that can still stir my juices. I imagine it as if I were directing a scene in an upbeat film on local customs. And so, the first thing I do is retrieve from memory the great wilderness of the Northern Cemetery, which came into being, or rather, nonbeing, a few years ago. That new cemetery reveals a shocking and macabre side of modern civilization and progress. A modernistic castle with structural allusions to the sacral, it was erected on sandy soil on the outskirts of the city. On the left-hand side—a bit reminiscent of a train-station interior or a pretentious self-service lunchroom—atheists pay tribute to the deceased, while in the right-hand section, also reminiscent of a lunchroom but one in a bishops' curia, Catholics pray beside catafalques. The dead of both sorts are conveyed to their distant accommodations by the same type of electric-powered carts. And those carts, which elsewhere are used to transport golfers, here are followed at a quick pace by the mourners. They trot because the cemetery is enormous and the gravediggers are on a tight production schedule. Those without the strength for trotting are not, however, forgotten. A limited number of children and old people can be accommodated on the small seat behind the grave-digger-driver. And so, those black catafalque-chariots speed about that colossal, oval-shaped cemetery as if along the horizon, trailing black trains of funeral processions.

And this is my future fatherland, a hopelessly bare wasteland devoid of bushes and trees but strewn with weathered wreaths and crumpled sashes, and plowed everywhere into grave mounds lashed mercilessly by rain and the godless winds.

I imagine myself slipping surreptitiously into the cemetery. I dig a hole wet with groundwater, I place my pine coffin beside the grave, and then I assemble the remainder of my acquaintances and distant relatives. I try out various eulogies and mood music; I order one person to sob and another to stand modestly to one side, holding a small bouquet of field flowers. I instruct the priest to recite the prayers. I command Marysia to faint, and I impose a violent repentance on all those pigs who made my life miserable. Sometimes, on a whim, I switch to the old Catholic Cemetery and hold my funeral there, in the Path of the Just. For some reason that location makes me particularly ingenious. Perhaps because there are no places left in that cemetery and only the most venerable of the dead are buried there. My moments of greatest delight occur when I pace with dignity behind my own coffin, down narrow paths lined with old chestnut trees, lindens, maples, and perhaps even oaks. History peers from every grave-stone at me and my coffin; the majestic, beautiful history of this pitiful, ugly country.

Sometimes, when I'm in a hurry and not being careful, I end up with my remains in the Municipal Cemetery, where high state officials are buried. There I arrange a funeral for myself that would befit a head of state or a president. I line up the honor guard, listen to the military band and speeches magnified by loudspeakers; I order cannon fired in salute and drums to roll. I do not stint on wreath-bearing delegations, nor do I refuse myself large numbers of schoolchildren among the mourners. I honestly must admit that for some reason none of this brings me any pleasure. Still, my thoughts keep returning to that steppe of a cemetery on the outskirts of the city, that terrible field—flat and fallow—that covering, shallow as fieldstones, over the disintegrating remains of all those who guzzled vodka with me, who loved various ladies and young women, and who waited their whole lives for something and did not live to see anything come to pass.

"Would you take Pawel to school, Father?" asked my daughter, Marysia, in an imperious tone of voice.

"I can't. I'm going to school myself."

Stefan stopped tapping away at his typewriter. Marysia opened her mouth and looked, dumbfounded, in my direction. Oblivious to it all, little Pawel grumbled while jamming his feet into his shoes, which were a bit on the tight side. Stefan rose slowly from his chair and came closer to me.

"But you've sobered up now, haven't you?"

"Yes, I've sobered up."

"So then what school are you talking about?"

"This one." I handed him my student ID and my course list.

He took a while to read them, arduously. Marysia peeked over his shoulder.

"I can't make head or tail of it. Who's paying for this nonsense?" said my son-in-law.

"Television."

The two of them shared a glance of concern.

"I hope you won't bring any shame on us, Father." Like a policeman, Stefan returned my documents with a sigh. "My position is shaky enough as it is."

"Are you unhappy here at home?" asked Marysia. "Why tempt fate?"

"I'll be the most famous grandfather in the country."

"Who told you that?"

"The chairman."

Once again they exchanged glances, each seeming to ask the other for help. Stefan smiled understandingly, but with a certain air of disdain as well.

"So, fine. You're an adult. You know what you're doing. Just as long as it doesn't make any trouble for me. My situation is terribly complicated. Please don't count on me."

"It remains to be seen who'll be counting on whom," I replied haughtily.

12

I can allow myself a certain frankness here. I can afford to be shameless. Instead of making up stories and attempting to charm. Instead of putting on the airs of a refined writer with an intellectual style.

You will excuse me, ladies and gentlemen, but the above section is a fragment of a novel, the beginning of a romance, a book which I will never finish. I'll never even get to the middle of it. I'm inserting it into this prose diary the way you slice a little stale kielbasa into a soup. I'm using those dozen or so pages in order to pad my book. I'm very tight about ink and the old manuscript, on whose reverse side I usually scribble out my modest prose in longhand.

A few years ago I began writing a book to amuse old people. Young people have their own literature, there are books just for children, and so why not provide old people with fiction suitable to their age?

It was to be the first love story about old people written for old people.

The hero of the novel, an old man returning to the university to finish a degree he had begun as a young man, attends lectures and seminars, where he runs into the woman he had loved in his youth; she is now old, but still pleasant and appealing. The old feelings are reawakened. The grandfather falls in love again.

In fact, he is seized by a mad passion that proves the death of him.

Ambitiously, I wished to capture all of old age's beauty, all the charm of its doddering body, and all the eroticism in the last of its biological reflexes. I intended to devote lengthy paragraphs to describing the beauty of old withering skin mottled with liver spots. Or to delight in the aesthetics of a face framed in gray; the charm of the slightly sagging breasts of the woman who was in love with my grandfather-hero.

I wanted him to stand for hours outside her window, to be chased away by her daughters and granddaughters; I wanted him to be driven wild by love, to pursue the woman by night, to hunt the poor woman down stealthily in a park, or to throw her onto a furrowed field on the outskirts of town. I wanted that grandfather, who could be me in five or ten years, to get pneumonia, a stroke, a heart attack from that blindness, that love, that erotic strain, that madness. So that, to the outrage of his family, he would die shamelessly of love like a youngster.

My intention was to plot the novel so that the children of both the lovers were against the affair, which they found ridiculous. The children would plague them, persecute them, forbid them to continue. The old people would be forced to hide from the young, the way young people hide from their elders. I dreamed of a great rehabilitation of love among the old. My dream was to write a sneering piece of trash, a romance that would make fun of all love's customs and taboos, all the lies connected with that foggy subject. I dreamed of basting my prose in a rich sauce of poetry, grace, and humor. To rivet the reader to this novel about old people, to compel the reader to participate in that erotic escapade, to bind him with sympathy and compassion to that pair of old people dying of love and the hardship of life.

That was my ambitious plan. Had I carried it out a few years ago, I'd be a self-indulgent millionaire today, flying in my own plane back and forth from the Canary Islands to California. Today I'd be read with a blush by all the old people of Europe, America North and South, and Asia. My readership would have been unequaled in size. I would have been the discoverer of a new literary genre: the old people's novel.

But life shoved me away from the money, success. There began to be unrest in my native land, I became furious about the lousy, stupid life we live under this idiotic system, and as usual, I was carried away in the wrong direction. And so I set aside that novel, barely begun. I'll never go back to it. But I can put it out of my mind forever by inserting it here among these anemic, sickly pages, which remind me of the days when I was younger and better-looking myself.

I am making a long and romantic voyage. I have traveled to Konstancin, fifteen kilometers from the center of Warsaw. I set about preparing for it as if I were traveling to Australia. A sleepless night, three hours to pack my bag, my nerves on edge. I had to devote an additional two morning hours to servicing my flagging organism. I've sprained my foot for the fourth time this year, I caught a virus somewhere that's inflamed my throat, something's the matter with my eyes that makes me look like a rabbit, plus there is a toothache, a little kidney failure, and some signs of hyperacidity. I won't mention the rest of my ailments, because even I find them boring.

And this is how an old man, though one still in his prime, behaves during an epoch of great national upheaval. It's raining here in Konstancin, actually it's been pouring from morning till night, the old villas of Warsaw's patricians are swollen with water like puffballs, which they even resemble. Gray, cracked, grotesque. A resort on its last legs. Put to death by socialism. Rotting woodwork in the Russian-Polish style, disintegrating plaster, musty turrets, fallen fences, gardens gone to seed. Only the small palace used by the Soviet embassy shines with a fresh coat of paint. This is the Soviet system to a T: not to restore but every so often to give a corpse a new coat of paint. Like poor old Lenin in his mausoleum on Red Square.

I'm hiding out in Konstancin, while in Warsaw good people are doing the pre-production for *The Issa Valley*. But they're not working at top speed. Someone's always leaving. They may all be sincere, well-wishing, and devoted to Milosz and me, but life has its own rules. Life in a country reverting to the wild. In this melancholy empire, where there are lines for everything, even in front of stores whose shelves are bare. In this spectral land of drunkards who are vaguely purple, shriveled from drinking denatured alcohol and hair tonic, in this jungle teeming with the wild beasts of Soviet agents. Thus, on account of that life, everyone seems to have lost his sense of proportion, his perspective, and his instincts. People hustle to make it through to the fall or even the end of the summer. Plans, ideas, initiatives. Who's in the mood for making a film about people who lived by the Niewiaza River at the end of the First World War?

For me this film is a vacation, something on the order of a paid leave at Milosz's expense. For the others it's endless commotion. A mixture of art and literary self-indulgence, a little sentiment and a lot of anachronism, a bit of money and unused ration cards for meat and kasha. What times these are. What a world.

I'm surrounded by old people here. Horrible old people who should have died before the last war or right after it. Old people who don't close the doors to their rooms at night because they're afraid of dying all alone. Old people who when they go out leave cards on their door telling who should be notified in case they die suddenly. I hobble among these mastodons wasted by life, who tremble, convulse, grab on to walls, gurgle and belch, who fall backward and who want to live, to exist if only for the week, the day, or the hour made of sixty long minutes.

I used to come here at one time. Thirty years ago. On a slow narrow-gauge train. You could jump off the train while it was moving, pick marigolds for a girl in a meadow, catch up to the train, and jump back on. But that wasn't me. That was somebody else using my ID. A young man with a great head of wavy hair and a romantic, somewhat foolish heart. He fancied himself a colleague of God, and in his free time he corrected some of the universe's more minor flaws. The universe of the postwar years, galaxy-like in their vastness. But I've already forgotten those years now. I no longer recall them.

And so that twenty-year-old guy would go out to Konstancin on Sundays in spring and summer, along with a whole mass of Varsovians, festive families bearing cold chicken, home brew, and accordions, good-humored, burned red as raspberries, wearing as little as possible, tipsy, free with their hands, very Varsovian Varsovians. But what do I care about that young man?

Near Konstancin, near the Vistula's old, original bed, lies Obory, formerly the estate of the Potulickis and today a state farm belonging to the Main School of Farming, as well as to the writers of Warsaw; property which includes an old palace and an equally old park, whose trees are monuments in themselves. The entire source of the Pravistula near Obory was once an almost African-like sanctuary; nature there was ageless, marshy, wild, a paradise with an enormous number of species of birds which were born and died there. Over the years, along with Adas Bahdaj, my friend from forest, water, sky, I discovered that unknown continent rife with unbridled vegetation, old trees, bushes suffering from elephantiasis, tremendously tall grass like upended scythes, and flowers that could have been brought there from the Amazon.

You could lie down amid wild sorrel tall as Italian cypress and listen to the stillness; that is, listen to that audible stillness made up of the chirping of crickets and various beetles, the rustle of lizards and grass snakes, the drone of bumblebees and savage wasps, the chatter of storks, the imitations done by talented mockingbirds that counterfeit every sound they hear, the cries of somewhat hysterical golden orioles, and sometimes an echo of industry, but one beautifully integrated into nature, an echo of the paper mill in Jeziornia, a famous factory whose soccer team once did me the honor of contacting me.

Among those marshes, those secluded, mysterious spots, those pits, a man, a young man was saturated with visions, strange hallucinations, naïve fancies: to shift back ten centuries and run along the banks of the virgin Vistula in the place where in time

Warsaw would arise. And so, lying by a wind-fallen tree prickly as a giant hedgehog, I would imagine that valley and myself in prehistoric times and picture my solitary life, my encounters with bisons, spending the autumn sick in a lean-to, recovering my health on a carpet of sun-warmed berries, my search for another human being, my longing for God, or perhaps only for the infinite. I would light a fire with the aid of a flint and kindling, I would catch fish by hand under river stones, I would shake with fever and fear at a summer storm, and covered with a mound of dry leaves, I would await the return of spring.

Then suddenly I would awake and go back to Obory, where typewriters would be rapping out poems and novels long since moribund. Then I would enter the shady, tree-lined paths in the park, those allees (as in books of old) where my colleagues strolled or sat at the edge of lawns, my colleagues who have died long ago or who to this day are still industriously climbing their way up an Olympus which after all no longer exists, dismantled by someone at some point. Perhaps by the Germans, perhaps by the Party, but most likely by those hippie terrorists who demolished Christian civilization in the second half of the twentieth century.

One day, dirty, slovenly machines drove into the meadows around Obory. They began digging up the ground, laying sections of pipe, clearing away the trees. In a word, that island of wild birds was invaded by professors and assistant professors. Soviet science had decided to utilize those meadows that were being frittered away. Now they were to yield thousands of tons of hay or fodder. They were to become the agricultural pride and joy of Warsaw's outskirts. But the professors and assistant professors had made an error. Instead of meadows and gardens, the first signs of desertification had appeared. Suddenly the Sahara's rotten teeth were bared at the gates of Warsaw.

The trees, bushes, swamps, and wild grasses all disappeared. The birds flew off, the roe deer and foxes ran away, the frogs and blindworms died in stinking ditches. A free wind from the steppes began to howl, the shifting sand making a chirping sound as it formed far-flung dunes. But what's the point? Things are the same everywhere. What was I driving at? I've had an oppressive feeling today. A sort of longing, mild and slightly painful, like a dead tooth. A longing for the past, or for what is yet to be?

Two years ago I was in Obory at the end of May and the beginning of June. Adam and I went for a walk to see the roe deer on the meadows by the Vistula and a certain dignified and beautiful sea gull which hatched its eggs in the middle of a huge beach, more than a kilometer long. Adam said that those roe deer were now field deer or, rather, field-and-meadow deer, and that, in connection with the general ecology movement or, rather, with the ecological disaster, they were being transformed before our very eyes into a new species of roe deer that had adapted to people and took advantage of their protection, meaning of course people who were human beings and not those homunculi who throw children out windows and dig up corpses in cemeteries to feed the nutrias they raise for their fur.

And so, suddenly one day at the beginning of June, when spring was at its very height, a wild Vistula spring, maybe the last of its sort—and so, suddenly one morning military helicopters with Soviet insignia began flying over Obory. Needless to say, we are a colony and our masters are free to fly over us, but in general the Russians observe a bit of form and do not fling things Soviet in the face of the capital of a state which passes for independent. The helicopters flew back and forth, aggressive, making a racket, very irritated about something. Little by little their passes overhead gave rise to anxiety, something like the hysteria I remember from '39.

Later, someone came back from Konstancin and said that he had bumped into a Soviet patrol headed somewhere through the fields and furrows. Afterward it became known that they'd been looking for a deserter. A soldier had run away from a Soviet troop transport in the town of Calvary Hill. Calvary Hill is on a line of communication linking the Soviet occupation forces in East Germany with the mother country. And so a soldier had deserted.

As in the eighteenth century or during World War I. A vengeful country pursues its unknown soldier through fields belonging to others.

The day was beautiful, sunny, green, colorful, joyful. The peasants were scything the fields, houses were being built in the little towns, young people were sunning themselves by the Vistula, a few couples from town were copulating in the bushes, the writers were working on high-minded books, while in Calvary Hill a hunt was on for a person wearing an army uniform. A pack of foot soldiers, aided by others in vehicles and planes, was hunting a comrade-in-arms.

I don't know why, but all day I had the feeling that they were after me. That, panting, sweaty, goggle-eyed, I was hiding in the corn and lying in the cornflowers and thinking about my situation, which looked lousy, to say the least, and once again I started running, looking for another place to hide, crawling into bushes of alder blackthorn or wild lilac, startling the beautiful birds. Suppressing my breath, I could see that this spot was even worse than the last one, and I started running again, dashing at an angle toward the haven of the forest, followed by the hostile eyes of alien people working alien and unfriendly fields.

Yes, I could have run away and circled Slomczyno until nightfall, or actually until early evening, when I would have been spotted by a helicopter carrying soldiers my age and who, like me, were fed up with an army and discipline foreign to them, and with foreign countries, languages, and cruelties. Yes, it could have been me running away, or my son, a deserter.

If those Girl Scouts had not pulled me and my colleagues out of the Rudnicka Wilderness in the spring of '45, if they hadn't shoved us on a train for those being repatriated, if we hadn't made it successfully across the border . . . Yes, if it weren't for those seven thousand ifs, it would be me who that patrol caught today, half dead from exertion, brute-like in fear, and then put on a prison train to spend the rest of my life in the cool and shadowy fjords on the banks of the Arctic Ocean or in the misty mountain passes of the Pamirs.

It was my brother or my son who was picked up at dusk. My brother from Lithuania or Byelorussia, my son from the Tatar Republic or Armenia.

I somehow seem to remember that at one time the environs of Konstancin were a wild sex preserve. I may be mistaken, my memory may deceive me, but at one time men came here in spring, summer, and fall with young women, widows, other men's wives. Not me of course, I was always a venerable and stately man of letters, who quarrels with God and history, who goes out strolling wearing a straw hat, and who later holds forth resoundingly on poetry while sprawling in an armchair. The very idea of me out roving the banks of the Vistula or the Kabacki Woods. It's ridiculous to think that I might have been caught with some blonde or brunette in the willow bushes or under a weeping willow.

Here I'm speaking of my colleagues, acquaintances, and friends, those Warsaw Romeos who were so industrious in flattening meadow grass on both sides of the Vistula, around Konstancin, and near Otwock.

And so, there were all sorts of little corners, hiding places, safe spots, byways, recesses, thickets. On the beaches, spurs, sandbanks, islands. By the river's rapid current and the rotting branches left from the spring flood. In the juicy sour grass and on beaches of the purest siliceous sand. Those were our, I mean my colleagues', preserves, so to speak. Some were up for it only on the sand, others only among the flowers. Some would run into the willows, while others would be shameless about their nakedness on a deserted sandbar seen only by the excited terns. They all pretended not to know one another. Those hundreds of thousands of sex maniacs, male and female, passed one another in the bushes and silvery aspens, walking by village fishermen and shepherds, making believe they did not see, know, or esteem one another.

Romantic walks in the springtime. Smelling the flowers, sighing, observing nature. In the summer there were games played in the water, suntanning, a pretense of sport. But in the fall, with its heavy, clumsy clothing, there was mournful, passionate, furious copulation on the dry leaves, beneath a frost-withered rowan bush, or in the back seat of a car obtained with coupons from a friend in government.

Who of us, I mean of you, did not walk, drive, or drag himself with the last of his strength to the Vistula for erotic purposes? This was done by manly men and by effete auntie types trying hard to pass as men. Even back then, there were various hybrids who tried to pass themselves off as men. Crippled men, men injured in war, men handicapped by nature slipped down to the Vistula. Types with faces like Quasimodo and elegant fops who styled themselves on Gérard Philipe made their way to the river. That was Warsaw's isle of Lesbos, its Sodom. A Place Pigalle, a proto-Slavic Copulatorium. A brothel for poor artists, and heaven for the Marquis de Sade.

But meanwhile, there have been disturbances in Otwock, of which I have spoken so idyllically. An enraged crowd first demolished, then burned down a police outpost on the railroad. And that's not the half of it. Young people hammered the remaining rubble into dust. Solidarity intervened, but people wouldn't listen. And so they brought in Adam Michnik, the entrepreneur who ordered the piece on the Wilno Uprising from me. Adam stood before a lynch-hungry mob and, stammering, said: "I am Adam Michnik. An anti-socialist element. An American agent. Please disperse."

And suddenly the mob calmed down. It dispersed obediently without grumbling. Here we see the power of the Party press, *Trybuna Ludu*. In introducing himself, Adam quoted the same invectives which the Party press lavishes on him.

In *The Calendar and the Hourglass* I complained a little about the humiliating fact that this poor contemporary literature of ours is labeled by rash intermediaries—translators, philologists—as incomprehensible, hermetic, and indigestible for the foreign reader. But those Western protectors of ours were quick to compliment me on *Calendar* and, taking me by the elbow, to begin winking at me with a knowing eye: you see, the thing is, our readers won't be able to understand *Calendar*. That's history, local events; our readers won't be caught up by them, won't be interested.

This they said with a certain offensive compassion and an unconscious, unwitting sense of superiority, but after all, they meant well, they were friendly, except that my, our, provincialism and inferiority would seem to have been imposed *a priori* by me, by us, on that foreign individual; as if we were, objectively speaking, snarled, obscure, lacking contour, inarticulate, a subspecies, on a different wavelength, with a different biology, a different brain. As if God had condemned me, us, to be secondary, incommunicado, and banished eternally from the European intellectual community.

That incomprehensibility of mine, of ours, is a thick rope woven of a variety of motifs. A strong rope you could use to hang yourself, though why bother. I will skip a great number of the factors involved here, except for those resulting from the power of journalism. Publicity can make any book popular, with both young ladies and old dodderers going wild over it. A lot of money can turn a little scribbler into a genius.

I will also skip the natural law that a mighty civilization produces better artistic works than a poor civilization, one that is barely alive, primitive. That in the end a great empire must create great art, while a little country can only come upon such art the way a blind chicken comes on seed.

But I wish to concern myself with other circumstances that shape provincial art's lack of power and ability to communicate— provincial art meaning the cultural output of little countries grappling with fate, in a bloody struggle for life, for existence.

Near Marysia's house in New York I saw lines a kilometer long for weekend showings of some trashy French film. American philistines and the middle class made a point of flaunting their presence in that line, so that everyone could see that they were not philistine or middle class and that a life of dignity requires the deeper spiritual content of French art, that marvelous, intellectual, sparkling, inspired, philosophical, and poetic spiritual substance concocted on the banks of the Seine, where a few small rocky islands jut from the water.

Why do talented Americans who themselves produce art that is brilliant at times stand in line like sheep to see films that are sham, tawdry, foolish, trite, and smug? Why does our poor sister France, who has long since grown old, ugly, foolish, and commonplace, why, I repeat, is that coquettish slut still able to excite handsome, young, competent American men?

Oh, to tell the truth, my own grumpiness bores me. What's my point here? Order? Logic? Criteria? An ordered world would be boring. A life based on iron logic would not be interesting. Art created according to immutable criteria would be unbearable. It is probably to the good that we are not ruled by philosophers. Our fate is probably more attractive when guided by brainless chance devoid of all sentiment.

In general it would probably be better not to be too intimate with that mess of ours, the incomprehensibility, that uncommunicativeness, that lack of allure. Actually, to be blunt, my own personal imperfections. I would like to please, but I please no one; I would like to be nonchalant, someone to whom nothing matters and who attracts success, money, and the fair sex; I would like to be a charismatic rogue, a delightful scamp, a dissolute artist, but I am only a grumpy old geezer, an envious provincial genius, embittered by my paltry talent celebrated throughout all Mazovia.

But how not to grow slightly furious when the time is coming when the output of individual societies and individual languages will be filtered into a general world language, like animals entering Noah's ark. And after all, they can take only ten, fifteen, maybe twenty items from this poor literature of ours. What will be among those twenty, what will qualify them for the next heat in the race for the infinite? What circumstances, situations, and chance events will determine one choice over another? And will those that are rejected be smelted down, used for manure, phosphorus, nitrogen? Will there remain some spider's thread of contingency in case someone at some point glances into old scraps written in forgotten languages and suddenly finds a pearl or diamond of human art overlooked centuries ago by the writer's distracted contemporaries driven blindly on by fears, poverty of mind, herd fashions, snobbish complexes, the aberrations committed by molecules of protein in an enormous, unfathomable universe full of eternal ice and nearly eternal fire?

I will tell you the truth. I'll tell you the ins and outs and back-ins of it. You have to cheat a little from time to time to get anywhere. Slip an extra ace out of your sleeve or peek adroitly at your opponents' cards. There's no chance of winning otherwise. No one has ever won without some of that. But I am determined not to cheat in this game. I will stick to the rules. That's how honorable I am. How Wilno I am. Actually, how Wilno Colony I am. And so I'm out of luck and resentful of everyone, because I am not cheating at cards, though I could cheat as easily as anyone. Feh, there's something unpleasant about this. I've gotten sidetracked again. Stop being so boring, brothers. Switch the jack for the king and don't try to turn the other players' heads.

I started on the incomprehensibility of minor literatures. I sat down to do a literary essay. I wanted to embrace us, the Hungarians, the Czechs. But the Czechs and Hungarians are doing just fine. So then it must be all to the good that I veered off into the ditch of the personal and am now groaning in the nettles. But that was just for show. I wanted you to have a close look at a writer suffering agonies of ambition.

It's a fierce summer outside. Day after day. Like a spring storm. There's no more openwork. The foreground, mid-ground, and background all the way to the horizon are filled to overflowing with a bright, joyful green. The fruit trees are in blossom. All at the same time. Paying off their arrears. A hornet fights a windowpane. It's trying to pierce it and shoot out into the microcosm of the garden.

Meanwhile, my colleagues are doing business. You can make a little change off a country levitating in revolution. Now they're in the front lines, though a couple of years ago they were in the dumps. They shed some blood for the fatherland and immediately portray themselves with that wound for the fatherland. They feign death for the fatherland, in order immediately to rise from the dead with laurel wreaths on hair gone gray with cunning.

What now, do I envy their cunning? After all, I'm doing a little business off the Nobel laureate myself. Some make theirs off the Pope, others off Walesa; I make mine off Milosz. Even though the most foolproof thing might be to make it off God. Someone's seized on that and I even know who.

Yesterday at 5:17 p.m. a Turk made an attempt on the life of Pope John Paul II. All evening and all night there was a constant stream of reports, one often contradicting the other, or at least at variance with it. Now, meaning the day after, it appears that after a several-hours-long operation, the Holy Father, who is gifted with an exceptionally hardy body, will slowly recover his health.

I'm curious as to what thoughts are now occurring to the Polish hacks who have been zealously justifying terrorism in the newspapers and weeklies, who warmly termed the sly Iranian bandits "boys" or "students." Those clients paid by our neighbor's paymaster who have given mass murderers the romantic tag of "desperadoes."

Lord, Lord, it must be fifteen years now that bestial individuals have been murdering the defenseless and the innocent, shooting at women and children, blowing up chance collections of people, stuffing bombs in churches and hospitals, while, its mind elsewhere, the wonderful poetically inclined left in the West gives progressive terrorism a kiss on the lips. Where do all the kibitzers come from? What is the origin of all that sentiment for mass murderers who are forever mouthing whatever demagoguery suits them best at the moment? Where does all the money come from, all the organizational networks, all the means to commit shameless crimes?

Why didn't those Western shills say anything, and why don't

they say anything when the unfortunate countries of Central Europe have been fighting for a scrap of freedom and human dignity for centuries now? Why hasn't anyone hijacked a plane to protest the Byelorussians' being wiped off the face of the earth, why have there been no processions filling the entire width of the Champs-Elysées in defense of Lithuania, why has no Bavarian gone on a hunger strike to the death on behalf of Czechoslovakia?

My dear crafty progressives, who live high off progress and leftism, who make a business out of being progressive, I know and you know who created terrorism, who instructs and educates the terrorists, who arms them and then later protects them from punishment. We know that the terrorists have a great patron and protector who arches the great rainbow of moral and political apology over them.

A new fashion has developed in diplomacy today. Criminal empires are not mentioned by name. Small states and nations can be freely reviled, they can be treated like dirt and profaned without even a pretense of maintaining the forms of discretion. The Latvians can be insulted, the Slovaks mocked, the Ukrainians abused. But the refined genocide of totalitarian empires is to be borne in tight-lipped, humble silence.

And so I too, in order to honor that slavish custom, will not mention who has sired terrorism in our time. You can guess it without my help. You do the work.

The water gurgled lazily among the pine-log rafts anchored by the shore. Some of the bark had been stripped off those pine logs, making for slippery spots, while others were suddenly sticky with the resin oozing from the maimed tree's wounds. Where the bark had been left on, invisible miniature knots pricked at your bare feet. The path through that dike made of rafts was forever tempting me that summer. It was nice to jump from one log to another, catching my balance on their wet, round surfaces, to hear the river babble in a world that was fainting from the heat.

Later, I would stand at one end of a raft and, reflected in the water, would fill my lungs with air and jump into the river, cool, but also warmed by the July sun and smelling of silt and a bit like honey, algae, and the morning glories that grew along the shore. I would swim under water like a young turtle. Squadrons of little fish would dart by in depths the color of a beer bottle amid shafts of wavering sunlight. A mossy stone crouched on the bottom. And so I'd swim, parting the water in front of me with my arms, peering at that mysterious world, a mighty roaring in my temples like that of distant waterfalls or an approaching earthquake.

And then one day, with the air I had left in my lungs, I turned a somersault and headed straight back up to the surface of the water. I was just opening my mouth for air, just raising my eyelids for a wet-eyed look at the sun, just about to shout in triumph to my friends, when all of a sudden my head struck something hard as a ceiling; reaching out for dear life, my hand encountered the rough surface of an enormous coffin lid. I struggled in the water, which had been warmed to some depth, dashing in one direction, then another. A firm dome. An unyielding vault with terribly bright chinks in it. A heavy pine-slat tomb submerged by the river.

I was under a raft. The current had swept me under that trail of water-logged logs. I realized that I was dying. That the end had come. But no grandiose thoughts came to mind. I was too young to have brilliant ideas in the final moments of my life.

And so I began thrashing about in a desperate frenzy, like a chicken with its head cut off. I don't know how long it was before my battered, bloody head chanced on that small stretch of clear space where one of the shorter logs ended and I shot up like a stopper, emitting a sound like a bottle being uncorked, choking on my first gulp of life-giving oxygen.

My friends were lying on the hot sand. They had followed my acrobatics drowsily, certain those were the frolics of a mid-afternoon swim. That was my first brush with death.

That river was the Wilia. And the place where the rafts paused on their journey to the Niemen was called Bujwidze. My hand hesitated here, because I was not sure about the name of the place. That was because Bujwidze existed in three forms. There was the landed estate of Bujwidze belonging to Makowski, the speaker of Parliament (or the Senate) before the war, an estate that was directly on the Wilia. There was the little town of Bujwidze connected to the estate by a miserable road, a little town which consisted of five or six homes and a church with a presbytery and a cemetery. The church and cemetery were set on a gentle hill, behind which lay the village of Bujwidze, but I have absolutely no memory of that village, even though I must have been there two or three times. That village holds no interest for me and it's no problem for me to empty it from my memory into the black abyss of nonbeing.

My thoughts constantly returned to Bujwidze, which I have already described in one place or another. I know that this little town could not matter less to you and that you'd prefer I picked up some of the more interesting threads of my life, even those erotic motifs that caused so much scandal in the capital city of Warsaw, in various vacation spots, and even abroad. The sex will come later, my dear little blindworms, now I have to enter Bujwidze. I have dreamed of that strange little town so many times, so many times has a sudden stillness reminded me of that place at the bend of the Wilia, so often has a paroxysm of metaphysical dread summoned up from dark oblivion those dozen or so months I spent in that little town not so far from Wilno, where there were three Catholic homes, a presbytery, a police station, my Grandmother Helena's inn, as well as three or four Jewish homes, a little store, a blacksmith's shop, and probably a bakery that made challah.

And my Grandmother Helena, who was actually my great-aunt, took me in to raise me right after my father died, when I was three or four. I spent eight months growing up there, or maybe it was two years, I don't remember now, I don't remember anything at all. But that's not true, I do remember some things, entire dreamlike sequences, micro-stories and allegories like scenes from a traveling theater. Or maybe it's actually my childhood dreams I'm remembering, the dreams which became the story of my life.

But still I can always see, against the background of the western sky, an old church in a tangle of trees and the stone wall which surrounded the churchyard and little cemetery. What I could see facing the church as I looked from the porch on Grandmother's inn was a not very steep stretch of the town square overgrown with succulent green turf. The little town's few little houses stood around that square, some of them actually village huts pressed to the ground, thronged by trees, orchards. And a few times a year "festas" took place on that square, great fairs on the days of the patron saints, great gatherings of merchants, tradesmen, cheats, swindlers, thieves, the sick and the lame. There was nothing that didn't happen on that sloping little square brimming with stalls, stands, shooting galleries, and perhaps even merry-go-rounds. Even Manhattan has not eclipsed those fairs for me.

But here, before I forget, I should be quick to mention Yom Kippur. The other children my age and my only friends were the Jewish children, who probably didn't speak Polish. And so I lived their lives, their religion, their customs. And for pious Jews Yom Kippur was truly apocalyptic. I don't remember much of the ritual, but I will never forget the terrible fear, the piercing dread during that long night when the devils snatch godless Jews off to hell. I swear to you by everything that one night my Orthodox Jewish friends and I saw the devils carry off a godless Jew known as Pluska, saw them drag him across a dark and cloudy sky at an angle to the horizon, tormenting him out beyond the church steeple somewhere above the village of Bujwidze, which I probably never did actually visit.

Pluska the Jew was a red-haired, furious type of man who didn't like children; we ran down the road after him so many times, taunting him, calling him names. And so, that terrible, nasty, godless Pluska tore free from the hands of those invisible devils. He must have hidden behind a cloud, but then they dragged him back out into the open sky. He was heavy for them, and so they fell nearly to the horizon, then soared up to the zenith again, where the entrance to hell must have been located right beside the entrance to heaven.

In my film *So Far and Yet So Near*, the Jew levitating above the earth is no echo of Chagall but is Pluska, the actual ill-tempered blacksmith from Bujwidze who once pulled me by my ears and who, pulled by his own red ears, was dragged by devils into hell, thanks to which he was delivered from the gas chambers, which began to be constructed ten years later.

I'm well aware that all this Bujwidze bores you, but I couldn't care less about that. You're going to have to spend another quarter of an hour in that small town, that very small-town small town in Wilno's borderlands. That was one small town in an enormous archipelago of other such small towns which produced the founders of Metro-Goldwyn-Mayer and Jozef Pilsudski; illustrious wonder-working rabbis, as well as the super-traitor and tsarist spy Balaszewicz; the leader of the Warsaw Ghetto Uprising, Wilner; and me, a cynical old scribe. All that was best in Europe and America came from there, everything that pushed old Europe and young America to the forefront. And sometimes things that are not overly successful come from there as well, but we will not be mentioning them here for lack of time.

I'm starting to remember Bujwidze clearer and clearer. I dream of Bujwidze all the time. That microscopic town was tremendously typical and it formed types like myself, Romain Gary, Soutine, David Halberstam, and three-quarters of America's film directors, writers, actors, and politicians. I close my eyes and I can see the sloping square where church fairs were held on various saints' days, and, coming from the church gate, the local mad inventor, who had built a bicycle out of wood and was now performing experiments like those of the Wright Brothers, racing at breakneck speed toward the sandy road and being sent sprawling immediately, head over heels, by a fresh rut in the road. I can also see myself in winter, wrapped in shawls on a sled by the church on the road that led to the village of Bujwidze. I would go speeding downhill past the firehouse, or maybe the community center, and come to a stop by Grandmother's inn. What community center and firehouse? Maybe Bujwidze was larger, maybe it was only my memory that surrounded it with boundless forests where agarics and boletus were gathered twenty kilos at a time.

I was fond of drowning in the Wilia. The second time I nearly drowned was also near the Bujwidze estate; this time I had some help from a ferry. I was walking through the warm brown water late in the afternoon when suddenly I lost my footing and began gabbling like a drake before I went under. But I'm alive and writing these words; and so someone must have pulled me out, or else I came on some shallow spot myself.

The man who ran the ferry lived by the dock in a hut overgrown with flowers, bushes, orchards. You would never guess there was a human habitation within that beast of greenery.

But if someone pulled up on the far shore of the Wilia, arriving from the depths of the boundless forest, where we sometimes went with our hearts in our throats to gather mushrooms, so, if someone drove up from there in the heat of noon and halted his horse, calling, Whoa, whoa, as it neighed and shook its rump a few times to shoo away the gadflies and bullfinches, the fishermen would tear themselves away from the sandbars to run over for a look at what was happening, until the new arrival tired of waiting and began shouting to our side of the river. He shouted what he felt like shouting, or what people in his parts did, some long calling vowels, because we still hadn't discovered the American "hello." He could have shouted like that for an hour, two, even till nightfall, because none of us there ever hurried and the man who ran the ferry might have been off transporting some rye or gone to town. But later the ferry would always push off from our dock, the passenger using a wooden handle to pull the ferry over on a line; no, no, no, I saw that sort of setup somewhere else, our ferry had a different system—a line went between two vertical wooden cylinders and you made the mechanism turn with a wheel like the one in a chaff cutter. I don't remember the details of its construction, but I always remember the way the ferryman and the passenger would peacefully chat, a slow and easy conversation that carried over the peaceful waters of the Wilia right before sunset.

Then evening came with a terrible stillness in which you could hear your heart pounding and the roar of your blood. Even the bats darted under the trees in perfect silence. A soundless night approached in that seclusion of forests, marshes, and sacred groves. Somewhere close by was an evil god who did not like children. Trembling in fright, I learned a fear that would later accompany me out into the world, disappear somewhere along the line, but has now come back to me from its distant voyage and is with me again, older, weak, not as ambitious as it once was, and not as *bojki*, as we used to say in those parts. *Bojki* described a person who was vigorous, resourceful, quick, and brave; that is, the sort of individual you could not find today no matter how hard you looked and who could have been, and who should be, the positive hero of the dead art of our times. So long for now.

Today, stealthily, cautiously, uncertainly, I set out for Obory, poor Polish literature's phalanstery. Hideous allotments of garden plots at an ancient bend in the Vistula, in the midst of an ancient landscape with age-old trees and an old-fashioned road paved with fieldstone. Neglected gardens, crooked paths lined with chestnut trees, and a park in terrible condition. But erupting from those ruins is this year's vegetation, swollen with the warmth of May and the copious rains at the beginning of May.

I've remembered everything. Thirty years of this place, part prison, part hospice, part bordello for Warsaw's writers. I've spent so many months there. I've drunk so much vodka there. Been through so much there. The only problem was the writing. I killed myself working there in the snowy, icy winter of 1954. The book *From a City under Siege* put a hex on Obory for me. I never tried to write there again after that.

Then suddenly, in the middle of the park, I thought of my fellow writer and filmmaker Janusz Nasfeter. One time at Obory I nicked myself shaving and had nothing to disinfect the cut with. Someone advised me to go see Nasfeter for some eau de cologne.

And so I went and knocked on his door. Nasfeter opened the door and invited me in. I asked him for some eau de cologne, and he was glad to oblige. He headed for the washstand, where he kept his toiletries on a small shelf under the mirror. As he was walking toward the washstand, he suddenly caught sight of his reflection in the mirror. And right before my eyes he fell in love with himself. He forgot all about me while gazing at himself, his handsome face, his great blond mane, his chest in an open pastel-colored shirt. He began fixing and smoothing his hair, then tousling it again, started walking toward the mirror as if he were stealing up on it, then withdrew from it again to be able to see more of himself; he would check his reflection, encouraging it with his eyes, and appear satisfied. Still, a moment later he seemed to grow critical and said something to me, but I too had lost track of reality and was speechlessly observing this event, the complex process of falling in love, which had begun to affect me as well; against my own will I smoothed the hair at my temples and sat down, puckering up my lips.

It's not nice to pick a colleague apart like that. After all, I did finally get the eau de cologne, disinfected my mug, and it all ended well. I like Nasfeter so much that I must have some right to joke at his expense, even if it has a little bite. And so while I'm on the subject of Nasfeter, I'll tell another story.

It happened in Jablonna, in the Potocki Palace, where a conference of filmmakers was taking place. Tadeusz Galinski, the minister at the time, was the lead speaker. At one point he began to name films which, in the opinion of government people, were ideologically out of line, bereft of laudable aspirations, devoid of humanistic values, and unreflective of the romanticism of the age. Among the films named by the minister was Nasfeter's *Colored Stockings*. Unaware of what he had done, the likable official went on declaiming, parceling out praise and reprimand, making one stipulation or another, providing instruction in this field and that; in a word, floundering toward trouble with all the self-satisfied confidence of a pompous potentate of the Polish People's Republic. Staggered, Nasfeter was in a fury at one side of the hall. He wanted to jump from his seat, but his colleagues held him back by his jacket; he raised both hands but, absorbed in professing his faith, the minister failed to notice; Nasfeter was nearly shouting now, but the minister did not hear him. There was a hubbub around Nasfeter, movement, a tussle. Everyone was trying to calm him down, comfort him, but the proud director tore free of their hands and was just about to defy the minister. Fortunately, Galinski had finished his speech, when, his mane as wild as Paderewski's, Nasfeter began shouting in a very excited voice about his family's progressive traditions, about the enlightened ideals that had guided him through life, the humanism which was his daily spiritual bread. But then I saw that, the louder Nasfeter shouted, the more menacing his tearful eyes became, the higher he levitated on his holy wrath, the more anxiously and nervously the minister whispered with the others at the speaker's table, the more keenly he inquired about something. And suddenly, just as Nasfeter was achieving an ecstasy of ideology and humanism, Galinski interrupted that hymn in a breathless voice to say: "Comrade Nasfeter, I'm very sorry, I confused you with Passendorfer, the director."

Nasfeter seemed struck by lightning. He had set so many progressive and humanistic forces into motion, called upon so many holy of holies, made so many beautiful and sublime declarations, and there it was—a mistake. And so, from sheer momentum, he attempted another bombastic platitude or two, but in a quieter voice now, the desire and intention still there, but the momentum was waning now, his knees beginning to bend. Then he suddenly fell silent and sat down. And that was how Janusz Nasfeter's would-be downfall came to its end.

At this point devils are tempting me to recall a certain dinner that took place in Nieborow years and years ago. Polish film people were entertaining the Soviet director Grigory Alexandrov and his wife, the actress Lyubov Orlova. The poet Arnold Slucki was sitting beside me, and every so often he tried to speak, burning with a desire to give a toast. Sensing there'd be trouble, Krzystof Gruszczynski and I used every ounce of our strength to hold

Arnold back by his pants leg, trying to persuade him to spare us the toast.

But Arnold wouldn't give up. Suddenly, after diverting our attention, he banged loudly on his glass. The room went still and everyone's eyes were on us. And the Soviet film star Lyubov Orlova, ethereal, still youthful, springlike, lovely, also glanced toward us. Furrowing his brow severely, Arnold began to deliver a drawn-out toast in what was not the best Russian. Delicately and poetically he said that when he was a little boy he had loved the films in which Lyubov Orlova had played the heroine. Those films had taught him his commitment to ideology, roused his progressive feelings, and encouraged him to fight for socialism.

The dining room was seized with horror. Pale with confusion, the entire table stared goggle-eyed at that bald old Jew who had dubbed himself the spiritual and artistic son of that Soviet pinup girl.

13

Lyonka P. gave the impression of being calibrated. Everything about him seemed to expand from the smaller to the larger. He had a large head, large hands, enormous feet, distended ears; even his freckles were of a supernatural magnitude and strangely dark, almost black. I mention Lyonka without using his last name, concealing him behind the letter "P," and for good reason, one which I shall bring up in a moment. And so, Lyonka lived near us in the Wilno Colony, on a slope by a forest that reached as far as the Upper Colony. When I glanced down at our valley during that operation in Wilno in July '44, I could see our house, that is, the Blinstrubs', my grandparents' house, and, a bit higher up, the old villa where Lyonka P. lived with his parents. I mean where he lived before the war, because I lost contact with Lyonka during the war. Lyonka vanished and his parents disappeared; I forgot about Lyonka, who flew out of my mind and my life. Then suddenly, out of the blue, it must have been in '43, I ran into him on Dolna Street, not far from the train station. Lyonka was on his way somewhere but did not tell me what had brought him back to the Colony. I asked him no questions either, since Lyonka was wearing a German Wehrmacht uniform with some insignia indicating that he was serving in the Vlasov division or the Russian Liberation Army. We greeted each other coolly and without curiosity, since I was in the underground scouts, which he could have guessed. We had a look at each other—good luck, good-bye—and then went our separate ways. I don't know if Lyonka survived or where he is these days. But, if he is alive, he can't have heard about me in Canada, New Zealand, Australia, wherever he chose. If he got off cheaply during the war, he would have had to make tracks in '45.

But before the war Lyonka and I had been pals for quite a few years. We'd gone to the same elementary school, and being neighbors made us close, even though we were never actually close. It was, however, through Lyonka that I slowly, gradually, step by step entered the dark and mysterious Continent of Things Russian. We sang Russian tunes, obscene, hoodlum songs; we cultivated a beautiful vocabulary of curses from Odessa, Ryazan, and Moscow, observed the Russian Orthodox holidays, and followed Russian customs. There may even have been a dozen or so Russian families in the Colony. Old Believers, White émigrés, or people who back in the nineteenth century had settled in Wilno or nearby. And so, a piece of true, genuine Russia was always right there beside me; it overgrew our life, even entwining itself in it, a morning glory wrangling with our dense Jewish jungle. I brushed up against things Russian from morning till night, just as I hobnobbed with the Byelorussian, Tatar, and even the Karaite elements. I recall Lyonka P. without any special fondness. He was not my best friend; there was nothing particularly attractive about him, no charming sensitivity. Lyonka was a crude part of my childhood and that is why I will remember him as long as I live.

A classmate of mine in our famous high school, the Zygmunt August High School, was a boy named Sazonov. He was thin, his hair fair to the point of transparency, his manners impeccable. A true Russian aristocrat. We never became close, because Sazonov was killed by a German bomb in September 1939. But for some reason I remember him to this day out of all my many other Russian schoolmates, whose Russianness by and large was never obtrusive. They were what they were. The Russian Orthodox religion was also part of daily life. I don't know how many

Russian churches there were in Wilno, but probably no less than the number of Catholic churches in the Warsaw of today. I may be exaggerating, but the Russian element really did stand out in our town, because for a century and a half the Tsars had been doing everything in their power to Russify those Western provinces which the empire found embarrassing; to wit, the former Grand Duchy of Lithuania, once a part of the Polish-Lithuanian Republic. To us, Russian Orthodoxy was a little worse than Catholicism, less serious, wilder, sloppier. Russian took third place among languages, with Polish first and Byelorussian second. Russian was the language for bon mots and many-tiered curses, a tongue for provincial obscenities, backwater pornography.

For that reason, when I encountered Russian literature later on, I entered that edifice as if it were a vast and marvelous winter garden which I'd known since childhood, if not, as it were, even earlier. I immediately felt that literature to be mine. Its pathos and its mockery, its vulgarity and incredible refinement, its saintliness and blasphemous cynicism, its godliness and boorish anarchism, its lyricism and burlap coarseness, its shameless falseness and its profound veracity, its dreadful didacticism and uncanny ambiguity, its hypocritical messianism and humor unmatched in the world; all this—the contradictions, the follies, the sins against good taste, beauty, reason—all this, I repeat, found in my anemic inner life a ready matrix, some negative waiting to be developed, some cursed predisposition to accept that damned legacy not a legacy, that bribe not a bribe, that hemlock not hemlock.

I am a hideous hybrid formed at the boundary of two worlds. The boundary of Polish life and Russian life. The mind of the Roman Pole chatters in me, making judicious calculations, and the wide-open steppe of Russian Orthodoxy howls in me. In the morning I run my fingers down Johann Sebastian Bach's harpsichord, but by evening time I'm dead drunk in the gutter. Yesterday I was toying with syllabo-tonic verse, tomorrow I'll rip out your guts and use them to trim the statue of Kosciuszko. I am a changeling at the junction of two galaxies, this border star which burns blood-red and white and any moment now will erupt in great flame, fusing the edges of the galaxies into one. Into one community.

Yes, we think about Russia often. As it had before, Russia now occupies a large place in our life; meaning in our hearts, minds, and livers as well. But Russia seldom thinks of us. It does not often think of us, a red flash of anger in the limpid eye of an old woman Chekist. Russia has forty-four nations by the throat. Russia can't be bothered to think about each one of them individually.

Yes, I love what is deceitfully Asiatic in Russia, but I long with all my might for what is rational and European in it. I worship the ground Dostoevsky walked on, but I dream of a new Chaadaev or Amalrik. I bow down to Solzhenitsyn in his shirt and pants of peasant linen, but my heart beats for the Mandelstams, though they are foreign to me. I prostrate myself before the God-bearing Russian peasant, but when out for a walk I'd prefer to run into Mikhail Lunin, the Decembrist, so Russian and yet so un-Russian.

Yes, every day I read everything that speaks of Russia and tells of Poland, tells of my Russia and speaks of my Poland. Grandiose, soaring Russia proves mean and low compared to Poland; mean, low Poland appears grandiose and soaring compared to Russia. There is some string, some cord of fate or noose linking the Warta and the Volga. Hanging over the head of Byelorussia, over the skull of the Ukraine. Sometimes we do it to them, other times they do it to us. With the help of Byelorussia, with Ukrainian aid. We Polonize Byelorussia. They Russianize the Ukraine. Why? Why?

One December nearly thirty years ago, we traveled to Moscow. Naturally via the "snowy deserts" of Byelorussia. Snow and sky; actually, no sky but a monotonous gray above the brighter gray of the snow. Ours was a decent group of Polish writers, the first official delegation, headed by Putrament, that strange person for whom I've always had a certain weakness. But even though he is from Nowa Wilejka, the heart of the Polish military garrisons in the borderlands, he always—judging by his reminiscences in *Half a Century*—wanted to be, always dreamed of being a Russian; his whole life he was drawn to Russia, and with inexplicable persistence Russia rebuffed Putrament for half a century. In my opinion, Putrament joined the Communist Party before the war out of a hatred for things Polish, because that Party promised to abolish the Polish state and deprive the Polish people of their sovereignty. If anyone thinks I'm exaggerating, he should read the scene in *Half a Century* where Putrament describes his encounter with Poland after returning from Soviet Minsk. Little Putrament was walking with his mother down a sandy road on a sweltering summer day. An army wagon drove up carrying two Polish soldiers, who are described in the manner Polish literature reserves for German soldiers. Putrament's mother asked the soldiers if they would give her a lift along with her child and bundles. The soldiers nodded their consent, but when Putrament's mother reached to grab hold of the side of the wagon, the soldiers lashed the horses and drove away, laughing at the woman they had tricked. And haven't we seen such little scenes elsewhere as well?

I've made a digression, but one which did add something to our theme of Poland and Russia. And so, we were traveling through the snows toward the heart of the empire, toward the depths of Russia, the very heart of old Muscovy. Our leader was Putrament, who is what he is and for whom I cherish some irrational fondness, as he may for me, who knows. Along with the older writers like Morcinek and Fiedler, there were younger people making the pilgrimage: Broszkiewicz, Mach, Kijowski, Scibor-Rylski, and me. Everyone was keyed up, nervous, excited by curiosity. Many of them had involved themselves blindly, without knowing what they were getting into. But I know Russia, I know it like my own cradle. I know everything. The only thing I don't know is at what point ordinary daily human civilization came to a stop in Russia. At what moment the October Revolution froze it for years to come. Then, at last, Moscow. Old houses corroded by the poverty of socialism and ancient temples which proved to be modern skyscrapers. And a certain smell, a terrible sad odor, the air stuffy with despair. And that all-pervasive stink, the reek of poverty. I'm an expert on that. I could do a Ph.D. on the subject. The same stink that comes from fabric— cotton, denim, or wool—that has lain for decades in a chest, has moldered with age, has been sprinkled time and again with naph- thalene, safeguarded from thieves in cellars, in the ground. That fabric was the rain-damp Ukraine, the ice-slashed Kamchatka, or the Pamirs wrapped in gales. There hadn't been time to bring those pants, pelisses, and mantelets to the dry cleaner's, to have them turned and pressed. And so, all the sheepskin coats, quilted jackets, uniforms, and Russian shirts give off a near-imperceptible scent of poverty, age, and neglect, but in a huge city those ephem- eral smells unite to become a single tragic hymn of aroma, one great odorific oratorio.

I speak of this because I was horrified by that closeness in the air, which deterred me from journeying there again, until finally in the sixties it was dispersed over Russia, blowing somewhere far away, perhaps to the North Pole, where it waits to return to some country fallen on evil days.

But at that time we were kept carefully isolated from the specters of poverty that hung over Moscow like barrage balloons during the war. We stayed at the Savoy, an old merchants' hotel, and when we came downstairs to take our meals in the Secession- period dining room, we were invariably greeted by the twenties- style band and its stout woman singer doing their rendition of "The Little Town of Belz," which they clearly took to be a Polish partisan song. We sat at tables with old porcelain and lovely crystal. On the porcelain were sturgeon, salmon, every variety of caviar, various types of game; and the crystal held cognac gleaming with a discreet glow, Georgian wines, and well-chilled champagne. We were discreetly served by gray-haired waiters who could still recall the days of the Counts Sheremetev, the Princes Gagarin. I am purposely using names which you know as that of an airport and a cosmonaut. I do so to make things more accessible. And at the same time more complicated.

Russia was what I had always known it to be. But poorer.

Poorer even than those frightened, emaciated soldiers who appeared in the Wilno Colony right after September 17, 1939.

We were to spend New Year's Eve at the Soviet Writers' Union restaurant. Once again we were escorted into an interior that was somehow merchantesque. A band in tuxedoes was playing on the balcony. People went up and down the staircase near our table. Some of them were dressed wonderfully, even fashionably, while others had worn whatever was at hand and looked almost as if they were at the front lines. The band was playing some song, the tables were as sumptuous as in tsarist times, but now some guy with furious hatred in his eyes had attached himself to us. Actually, not to us, but to Putrament. Things were looking dangerous, for this man was sincere about wishing to beat up our leader, an intention to which he kept returning. Pulling him to one side, diverting his attention, pouring champagne—nothing helped. Every so often, he would come staggering in our direction and shower us with horrendous abuse; his anger had now begun to extend even to us ordinary little Poles and we had to make our escape through the cellar, the boiler room. The entire august delegation, illustrious authors and ladies from a neighboring country, had to hightail it, fleeing from the holy wrath of the Soviet combat veteran whose wife Putrament had slept with while the husband was busy driving the Nazi vermin westward.

Later we emerged somewhere in the vicinity of Red Square, where amid ruby-colored lights Stalin was standing watch; Stalin, whom we were vainly trying to love with all our heart. Nearby was Dzerzhinsky Square and the famous Lubyanka, the most famous building in the world, asylum for all the people of this earth, tomb of all contemporary mankind, a beautiful monument to twentieth-century civilization. And then, in the pale glimmer of the moon—for it was indeed a moonlit night, you can check that—and so, in that cadaverous light, someone suddenly began screaming from within the depths of those walls. It was not the cry of a person being tortured or suffering pain or taking fright in the middle of the night. This was a howling that made the flesh creep on your back and your hair turn gray on your head.

This was the roar of some animahumanoghost. This was a terrifying sound from a human larynx, a sound that contained a longing for crime and a disgust for the holy, relief at liberation from humanity and a dread of the cosmic void, a delight in the meaningless and a licentious pleasure in its own agony.

But that's not what I meant to say. For two weeks I was forced to use ball-point pens. Today, home again, I can go back to the fountain pen I once received as a present from Kurt Weber. I don't know if it has brought me luck, but it has served me faithfully for fifteen years, luring me to blank paper, jumping up like a cat when I open my desk drawer, and at night I can hear the reedy voice of that aging Waterman, which, urging me on to my next experiment, promises me perfect success, this time for sure, word of honor.

And so, since the writing's coming easier now, I will mention my last trip to Moscow, where I took part in a screenwriters' symposium. My film *So Far and Yet So Near* served as my pass, my safe conduct. On account of that film I was given a polite but cool reception. My work was screened at eight o'clock in the morning for a select audience of twenty. In a corner, off to one side, a young man approached me and invited me to a meeting at his factory's film club.

I allowed myself to be tempted. We took a cab to the factory. A large auditorium, packed. An unofficial film club. An illegal association of devotees of the cinema. Old people, young people, workers, university lecturers, good-looking women, men with swagger. What sort of posture to assume? The viewer's humble servant or a haughty intellectual from the magnificent West? To flaunt my modesty or strut my creative freedom and some prize or other that I'd snatched in Pernambuco? Should I speak to them on an equal footing, or do some backslapping?

"What are we going to talk about," I asked my guide softly. "About your films," said the young man in the colorful shirt. "But you haven't seen my latest film." "Yes, we have, I've seen it four times." "That's impossible," I said, "the film was only in the embassy for four hours. The ambassador, Comrade Nowak, saw the film and immediately ordered it taken to the airport." "Yes, but on the way to the airport, we arranged a screening for ourselves," said my patron with a smile.

Well, then the talk started, and I began sweating with emotion. Because that was the most interesting discussion on contemporary cinematography in which I have ever taken part. The audience was completely different from those that had at one time broken down the doors of movie theaters to see crappy Polish films, just as long as they were Polish. These were brilliant, educated, witty, demanding moviegoers, versed in art, part of the European elite. They no longer had any intention of worshipping a film simply because it was Polish. They held some of our classic films in contempt and had no difficulty in spotting humbug, easy shots, cheap tricks, opportunism, and ruthless greed for success. I'm not saying I was sad to hear Polish cinema vivisected. I did, however, dread when it would be my turn to be ground into Wilno snuff, but I also felt a strange and bracing joy that there were still people in this world whose brains hadn't gone soft, whose opinions hadn't gone stale, whose tastes weren't washed out, and who had maintained some sort of standards. I mean that, while fearing for my own head, I was filled with the delight of communicating with people who emanated something superior—in Gombrowicz's sense—which in my old age I have begun to bow down to even as I drown in a sea of the inferior. My bows are, of course, the best a drowning man can manage. By and large, you should forget about my approach to style, because it's the style of the functional, the logical, the emotionally expressive. That's what's in today, that's what the masses demand. The masses of my creaking admirers.

And so, at the time, I hoped that evening, a reckless one on my part, would be over as quickly as possible. But it went on and on, longer and longer, running past midnight. They performed what amounted to an autopsy on me. Every bone, each tendon. They brought up everything I had ever said and written about film as an art form. Dark clouds gathered over me a few times and it looked as if I was in for a good drubbing, but all that apparent, somewhat negative tension was discharged in the simplest of catharses, when I realized that in fact their only concerns were for film as art, for humanistic values approached as matters of principle, and for the ordinary joy of being in touch with film that was alive, individualized, intelligent.

I suddenly realized that the people in that rather dingy auditorium were my brothers and sisters. That it was thanks to such people that I had not as yet hanged myself while vacationing by the sea or during some vile winter, that thanks to them, those Russians, and perhaps those Georgians and Uzbeks as well, I still write books and from time to time slip behind a camera. God only knows why.

During the sixties I was again in Moscow with a film of mine. It too was given an acerbic reception by the officials. Then one drunken night we ended up at the apartment of some furious artist, maybe a sculptor or maybe a painter, I can't remember now; all I remember is that it was hot.

We were sitting in a room full of modern furniture, and the artist's friends kept winking at us, pointing to the lamps and tables—they're Polish, Polish. It's not clear whether they wanted to flatter us or, rather, make fun of their host. Sitting beside me taking hits of vodka was an old filmmaker who had worked with Kuleshov and Eisenstein. He wheezed, groaned, and hissed in my ear: "The Poles are a two-faced bunch . . ."

Meanwhile, the host, who apparently had just woken up, deftly downed a flask of cognac and began shouting out compliments to Poland and the Poles: Poles are all right. I love Poland. Oh, are Poles good guys!

And so, on one side I felt a cold, icy compress from the old filmmaker, who had been one of the creators of Soviet cinematography, and on the other, my drunken host's warm and generous shower. But that painter or sculptor's compliments, vocal and demonstrative, were not to the taste of those present, and all of a sudden some strapping gentlemen put the artist in a full nelson and dragged him off to the bathroom.

I don't know what happened there; in any case, my host returned to the living room fifteen minutes later under his own power and immediately began heaping intense abuse on Poland and the Poles, becoming quite heated and flushed as he bristled, foamed at the mouth, grabbing his flask by the neck, preparing to do battle with us insolent, feckless Polaks.

There was a reception held at the end of that other visit to Moscow. I can't remember now where, or who gave it. Two older men, Russian filmmakers, came over to me sometime near the end of the banquet. They told me about themselves in a whisper, uncertain, seeming fearful, saying they had spent many years in a camp. As colleagues, they wished to do me some honor for my film, which, incidentally, had once again not been to the liking of Comrade Nowak. And so they asked if I would accept as a keepsake a brass Russian Orthodox scapular which had been with them through all their years of exile.

I went rigid and suddenly began collecting my thoughts. I had been around, spent a little time in France, a little in America, done a little auteur cinema, a little shrewd experimenting, kept my wits about me, and seen the great continent of Europe, even the Bay of Biscay. And they'd spent twenty years in the camps. And now they were off the field of play, beyond life and art. An old brass scapular. A souvenir of human life, terrible and cruel. What did it mean to them, what to me?

The next day, suffering from a merciless hangover, I packed my bag for the plane. Where should I put that scapular? Better to keep it on me so they wouldn't take it away at customs. But I'm so weak. I couldn't carry that weight. Off it went to my suitcase.

There were some petty formalities with our woman interpreter at the airport. She wanted to pay our airport tax. I was against it. I still had some rubles left. I thrust a wad of bills at her. Poles are always chivalrous with ladies, as the artist who'd been put in the full nelson might have said.

The two young customs officials allowed our bags through but stopped us. We stood waiting and waiting. The passengers were all on board, the stewardesses were calling to us. We were being held by one of the customs officials, a young man with a shaved head who went by the book. The other one came running over carrying what could have been an enormous bassoon case. You come with us, they ordered. They brought us to a room without even a single window, and with a solitary table in the center of the floor. They ordered us to empty out everything we had onto the table. We pulled out our apartment keys, passports, handkerchiefs. Where's your money? they asked. You, they said to me, you gave the interpreter money. I could have said that I gave her a million rubles and they knew where they could kiss me, those underage Chekists. But I didn't want to drag things out and explained that I had given her money to pay the airport tax. No, we saw it was a lot of money. You saw wrong, I replied frostily. They opened the case, removed a metered instrument of some sort which they ran over our clothes like an iron. The meter maintained a disconcerting silence. The customs officials, Komsomol members who had grown up on *How the Steel Was Tempered*, had tears in their eyes. Here they had nearly trapped an imperialist spy. Admit it, they whimpered plaintively, show us what you've got hidden, be human about it. But I am cool and haughty. A venomous Pole. A proud little Polak.

They let us go, making no secret of their despair. Had they only known, the poor men, that the camp prisoners' scapular was already safely aboard the plane in the cargo hold of the flight to Warsaw.

When I finish this section, I will have a look at that relic darkened by human sweat and perhaps by human blood. I had accepted that gift lightly at the banquet. But now, over the years, it has taken on weight, that small brass rectangle that is also made of the metal of human trust, faith in man, and the hope of a better future for the human race.

・ ・ ・

The curtain rises and one actor says to another: "It's a dreary life, Igor Ivanovich." A chill immediately runs up my spine. No line in English or French, no Italian or German bon mot, no other phrase could move me on so many different levels, could stir so many layers of passion, mood, intuition, and longing, psychological and intellectual, as that Russian statement, vulgar and majestic, plain but profound.

Needless to say, I concocted the opening of that play for purposes of stylistic convenience. But, after all, it's enough just to recall the scene in Gorky's play *Summer People* when the old orderly reminisces about the sergeant in his regiment. "Oh, what a villain he was," he says with a sigh. "What a mean man, and could he make your life miserable. But when he'd drunk some vodka, he'd rip open his shirt and say with tears in his eyes: 'People, spit in my face.' And some people did."

Yes, it's time to admit that, of all literatures, Russian is the closest to me. Apart from Polish, of course. That I am permeated with it from my heels to the hair my head keeps shedding. That it resounds and murmurs in me, roars like coal down a wooden train chute. I can sit without discomfort for two hours watching some sorry little Soviet television production, but a refined French film full of Diors, stripteases, and Sartrean melancholy bores and wearies me after fifteen minutes.

Russia occupies at least half of the time I spend reading. It is not circumstance which imposed these interests on me, although circumstance has played its role. What lures me to Russia is the attractive power contained between its extremes of great evil and enormous good. Russia is nearly a world unto itself. A world of human pain, sin, and suffering. A world of human kindness, heartfelt kinship, and mournful hope.

A gray-haired Polish woman, who was born in Petersburg and spent her childhood and early youth there, said with a species of pride when speaking of the social relations between the two groups at the time: "The only Russian to set foot in our house was the mailman." And Antoni Slonimski told me that when his uncle, a colonel in the Tsar's army, wished to visit his sister-in-law, Antoni's mother, he would go to the doorkeeper to be certain that Dr. Slonimski was not at home, and only then would he dash up the backstairs.

The Russians loathed the Polish element as well. It's enough to read a little Dostoevsky, whose anti-Polishness may have been intensified by his own supposed Polish origins. A Pole who renounces his own nation is a horrible thing. A more splendid renegade is nowhere to be found.

But let's get back to the subject. The Russians could not abide Poles in the nineteenth century. Our history, traditions, religion, mentality, and psychology aroused genuine abomination in Russians. There was always something un-kosher about the Poles. Poland was seen from afar, from miles away, through seven walls and seven fences.

Finally, in the second half of the twentieth century, the wise Soviets have found a solution for things Polish. Instead of disdaining and isolating what is Polish, it's better to annex it, incorporate it into the flesh of Russia, more expedient to change Polishness into a regional manifestation of Russianness. Byelorussia and the Ukraine serve as the canal locks in this process of displacement. In the decompression chamber of Byelorussia and the Ukraine, Polishness goes stale, loses its Latin culture, its occidentalism fades, it becomes un-Polish. It slowly assumes Byelorussian forms, Russian Orthodox colors, and begins emitting Muscovite sounds. Now, completely Byelorussian, or actually half-Russian, it can be thrown into the crucible of true Russianness, the handmill of All Russia, that baptismal font of a new Israel.

The name Stanislaw has, imperceptibly, become a favorite first name in Moscow. Sierakowski, Siemiradzki, Mineyko—my favorite—Tomasz Zan, Apolinary Katski, and even Melchior Wankowicz have without any to-do entered the Russian Pantheon, the Byelorussian wing. All of a sudden the Uprising of 1831 has become a revolt of the enlightened Russian states, while the

January Uprising of 1863 is now a bourgeois revolution of the Russian liberal intelligentsia, with centers in Moscow and Petersburg, as well as in the western provinces; there were also revolutionary centers—adds the scrupulous Soviet historian—even in "ethnic Poland." The Polish dance, the *krakowiak*, has suddenly turned out to be a provincial form of an old Cossack dance.

The more intelligent Soviet journalists take particular pleasure pointing out whenever appropriate that the head of the KGB in Leningrad is General Kosciuszko. They are much amused by the fact that the leader of the Lenin Komsomol in Ryazan is a certain Comrade Pilsudski, and that a man named Sienkiewicz sailed with Heyerdahl on his raft. They are also diverted by the coincidence of an embezzler in the fish-processing industry proving to be named Mickiewicz.

I am unshakable in my conviction that somewhere out in the Urals there is a Mordovian writer, Tadeusz Konwicki, who is laboring over a work which he has already entitled *The Last Page of the Calendar*. And suddenly one day he will relieve me at my post as a Polish writer, like taxi drivers changing shifts. Perhaps an intelligent Russia, albeit one diminished a bit by Bolshevism, will out of the blue suddenly exchange this exhausted, spongy, moldy Poland for a fresh, new, vigorous Poland, one that was carefully made ready over the years somewhere in the depths of that uncanny continent which is the homeland of real sin and false sanctity.

I have no Russian friends, but I don't have many Polish friends either. And so I won't be writing any rhymed apostrophes to either my friends the Rooskies or my friends the Polaks. But would I like to become a Russian like P.? That would have been easier for me than for him. If I had not left Wilno. If I had stayed there and gone through the Purgatory of Byelorussia to Russian Heaven. If I were now writing in the language of Pushkin and Gogol about the charms of life on the collective farm.

That was a cruel journey we made back then in '52, '53. Through the snows, through the still un-Europeanized Soviet world, with Stalinism at its height, on the eve of the "Doctors' Plot." We traveled from north to south, or south to north, in a literary kibitka carefully watched over by guards wearing literary uniforms of various ranks. But we were led by Putrament, whose first book in Russian must have already been suspended in a drop of ink at the tip of his gold Parker pen. All right, that's enough of that, I keep picking on Putrament, I can't leave him alone, even though he has a certain irrational weakness for me or perhaps rather a leaning toward me (he'd gladly flay my hide), and in my own way I like him too, which is why I bring him up here. But enough of that, not another word. Silence, hands at your sides.

Before then I had known Russia from the far shore, the side, the edge. But then I saw it spread before me like infinity itself. And I was taken by its dimension, its scale, its capacity. The people, their fate, their splendid poverty, their shabby greatness. No, that isn't true, their throttled greatness and their truly gigantic pettiness. It made me feel bad that we are so practical, provident, judicious, logical, so well educated, European. I envied them their madness, their cruel God, their camps.

But still we're a little on the mad side too. Being neighbors for centuries hasn't left us unscathed. The European Poland of the Piasts, which certainly differed little from Saxony or Moravia, no longer exists. Today's Poland is a Poland of defects, faults, and imperfections acquired from our brothers in the Grand Duchy of Lithuania and Little Russia. Today's Poland is a pyramid of sins and frivolities from the aristocracy and nobility of the borderlands. Today's Poland is not Poland. It's something completely different, with the name of Poland. But whatever it is, we love it, are attached to it, and will fight for it, whatever it is, to the end.

I have lost my Russia once again. That was a good choice of words—my Russia. I have the right to say that, because I've invested a great deal in Russia. I will always have people I love and love very much there. There meaning the whole world.

Wherever there are Russians with their samovars and flagons of aqua vitae.

I recently got drunk with a great Russian poet in a huge Western metropolis. And out of drunkenness I attacked him all night long for the wrongs done to Poland, and for the wrongs done to the Czechs, the Lithuanians, Ukrainians, and Tatars. He fought me hard, defended himself, using superhuman effort to repel my charges heavy as lead, until he finally breathed a sigh, fell back on a middle-class couch, and began groaning: "It's impossible to be Russian."

14

I am about to embark on a daring enterprise. I've already passed
Chapter 13 without a scrape and now can afford to take a little
risk. So, let's take the plunge, go out on a limb.

What I intend to do here is deliver a thin-voiced apology for
a man whom the healthy, moral, progressive, and noble segment
of society has permanently excommunicated, making him into
a symbol of modern treachery, treason, reaction, Fascist leanings,
the Targowica of the Polish People's Republic.

Our progressive, noble-minded elite is a problem in itself, one
to which I shall address myself at some later point. And when I
do, woe to those self-appointed fathers of their country, those
moral leaders, "King-Spirits,"* the white-handed, as they're called,
meaning that their hands are clean.

I made his acquaintance late; actually, it was a year or two
before his death. We took careful stock of each other, but out of
the corner of our eye, making no big deal of it. Like two boxers
in the first round. I knew that he didn't like me. It could even
be said he had a special dislike of me. I had no liking for him
either, and that too got across to him. And so, we conducted our
business as if there were no bad blood between us and we were
meeting for the first time in our lives. It began in that fortress of

* "King-Spirit," a poem by Juliusz Slowacki (1809–49), a major Romantic poet.

a television station on Woronicz Street, in the principality of that notorious wretch, Maciej Szczepanski, who caroused and caroused until, as in a nineteenth-century novel, he ended up in prison.

I mention Chairman Szczepanski because he was in our corner at the time. Impolitely extending the finger he used to threaten bureaucrats rooted in terror, he flaunted his power, his personality, and his biceps. Later I described our meeting in *The Calendar and the Hourglass* (and so I must have met the chairman and his assistant a few years earlier), and I predicted the downfall of that vigorous chairman with the manners of an American boxing manager from the first quarter of this century.

But let's return to my hero, tall, slender, his coloring darkish. He struck Mephistophelean poses, played the villain, gave himself diabolical airs. But this he did carefully and with an eye to its effect. I took the part of the grateful spectator. I was not cool to him, offered no sudden objections, treated him to no sudden mockery, and I did not start out with a grimace on my face.

He could feel my encouragement. We had had an "incident," as the bureaucrats say, but it had been put aside for the indefinite future. Covered by a quiet moratorium never openly declared. So, we were starting our game at a clean, freshly covered table.

Why should I hide it, his twisted but naïve mentality was very much to my liking. I found it more attractive than the venerable, noble-minded, and religious traits of my friends in Poland's martyrish opposition. He was willing to reveal his tastes to me, naïve camouflage for his actual passions. He regaled me with provocative paradoxes while, like an old swine, I pretended to believe him in order to egg him on to further displays. It was an ideal arrangement. He did not recognize or respect me as a prose writer and filmmaker, while I despised him as a false critic, a pipsqueak, an armchair Machiavelli. At the same time, he seemed a hair's breadth from liking my prose, and I from beginning to admire his political principia.

What am I doing, what am I doing, why am I writing this? Who needs to hear my confidences about a few nondescript meetings with a person who is no longer alive and has turned to dust in a grave whose location I don't even know, a man whose remaining memory has been besmirched and besmeared with libel, lampoon, and ignominious invective? But I feel like speaking of this person who, simply because he was hated so terribly, deserves my warm response, my reflection, my epitaph composed of words that do not drip lather, bile, and excrement.

Because deep down I am grateful to him for a great many things; I mean a few moments of pleasure bordering on delight. In those terrible times of total despair at the end of the Gierek era, in those hopeless months of apathy, in those days of utter disbelief, he, my negative hero in the world of culture, or actually the demimonde of a subculture, provided me with a bit of diversion, a few niggardly mood-elevators, lighting the darkness of my life with his black humor.

To torment flunkies, brownnosers, and collaborators had become his passion, a bizarre predilection, a vital imperative. Walking the fine line of good Party manners over the abyss of the Security Police and the hell of *raison d'état*, Janusz allowed himself to play a risky game with people who were the favorites of the Central Committee's secret departments, the darlings of our neighboring countries' embassies, the stool pigeons of Rakowiecka Street. Out of the blue, Janusz would rap the knuckles of some zealot ready, for a few thousand zlotys, to refashion the history of his own country and the story of his own father's life. Without provocation, he would show some solemn moralist the servants' exit, reminding him that he too was a lackey. Or all of a sudden he would kick the fox in the teeth, the fox who had changed its color, bringing the remnants of its honor and that of its loved ones to market, dangling under its snout.

Groaning with pleasure, I heard accounts of how this person, Comrade Janusz W., had treated the co-creators of a film about Felix Dzerzhinsky. They had come to him with a shooting script for Part Two of that film. His reply: Who's going to go see it? The Minister of Internal Affairs and a few policemen? There's no need for a Part Two. The filmmakers were dumbfounded.

After all, zeal like theirs deserved a medal. What did it all mean? We'll have to consult with the embassy, they said in consternation. Aha, so you take your instructions from the embassy, said Janusz W. in an icy tone of voice. But it's the embassy of the most wonderful country in the world, mumbled the filmmakers. And I advise you to stay away from there, replied Janusz.

Why had he climbed so high, strenuously kicking the teeth of everyone who held the ladder of his career? Why did he take such risks in building an edifice whose foundations he destroyed every day of the week? Why did he go so far into that alien and barbaric universe, whose natural laws and moral injunctions he evidently held in contempt?

I think it was because he was a modern Count of Monte Cristo. He acquired and amassed his capital, political capital of course, so that, rich and powerful, in the political sense of course, he could inflict a cruel vengeance on all those villains who daily sell a piece of the fatherland to a foreign power. I timorously suggest that this Party Count of Monte Cristo intended to return stealthily one day from the fortress of the Politburo or the stronghold of the Central Committee Secretariat and settle scores with all those whose flunkeyism, servility, and whorish underhanded dealings were corrupting society. But cruel death cut the life thread of the avenger who had made his way to Warsaw from distant lands, having perhaps resolved to declare a battle to the death on everything that was propelling fair-haired, tormented Poland into her grave.

Perhaps he dreamed of a fate like that of Konrad Wallenrod. Perhaps he had climbed the steep slope of power to take possession of the thunderbolts and then use them to strike a blow at a loathsome system. Perhaps he had forced his way into the cave of the most trusted cells of the Party in order to blow them up along with himself. Or perhaps he had entered the highest levels of the administration in order to poison the others there with his own breath, to corrupt them, to demoralize them with his way of life, to deprave them with one of my books or a film by Wajda or Zanussi.

That is how you should preserve him in memory—Janusz W.,
scourge of the servile.

Ludwik Hager, an old friend of mine who emigrated in 1968,
had been one of the heads of film production here. He began
producing back before the war, quite a few years before September
1939. I use the word "producing" with special relish, because in
that strange profession one cannot work, be employed; one cannot
practice that profession. In film, and this goes for the prewar
period too, one can only "produce," and that, ladies and gentlemen, is the proper word for it.

So, Ludwik knew all the ins and outs of the little world of the
prewar film business. He rubbed shoulders with the directors and
cameramen of the time, but first and foremost with the people
who had the cash or, rather, the people with the bills of exchange.
I'm thinking here of those splendid people who owned the movie
theaters and the halls for hire, owners of small film studios, the
producers, without a penny to their name, who made memorable
lighthearted comedies.

It was Ludwik who in the new era reintroduced the favorite
saying of the Selznicks and De Laurentiises of prewar Poland: If
I say I won't, I won't, and if I say I will, I might.

Ludwik had a style and a sense of honor of his own which, in
my opinion, were unsuited to his trade and were redolent of a
slightly old-fashioned gentry attitude. Ludwik had a philosopher's
eye and could make total sense out of what seemed to him the
mist and magma of incomprehensible metaphysics. That anachronistic sense of honor cost Ludwik the remainder of his hair
after his emigration, which he bore with restraint and with dignity. I would like to describe my visit to Ludwik and those ten
days of the Munich Olympics, but perhaps I'll deal with that
incident elsewhere, the next chance I have.

Here I prefer to speak of Ludwik's uncle, an important prewar
businessman, an Orthodox Jew. His uncle, being a thrifty man,
would buy his family a year's worth of apples to last them till the
next harvest. The fine-looking apples would be spread on straw

in a spare room, and a careful eye was kept on them through the long winter months. Frugal and parsimonious, the uncle would choose for eating only those apples which had already begun to rot. And so Ludwik's uncle's family ate nothing their whole lives but rotten apples.

At first glance a simple and obvious story, but what an instructive one.

That story about Ludwik's uncle didn't come out right. It should have been a smashing story, a great philosophical anecdote about the wisdom of the Jews of Warsaw province and environs. But there's some worm eating away at me, maybe not a worm, that's disgusting, but some ant or, rather, a termite. Yes, the termite of fear. Or, rather, the termite of unpleasant anxiety.

Because Janusz W. is no longer alive. But those flunkies whom he terrified, humiliated, or exposed have survived and are prosperous. And they're not sparing me any blows. They've long since forgotten those vile peccadillos of theirs; they've long since been living the good life and accepting the homage of their contemporaries as something self-evident, natural, and deserved. Because the types whom he stung, throwing their shabby corruption in their faces, are today the fathers of their nation, modern Skargas, legislators of Poland's morality.

Well, we'll see what comes of it.

I love Gombrowicz and every so often I am seized by a brief paroxysm of hatred for that cavalier idol of mine. I think of him now because I recently happened on a letter he wrote to someone who offered him his services as an agent.

In love with himself, cackling to himself, endlessly embittered by himself. From his diaries I recall Gombrowicz's astonishing resolve when setting out on his great journey to Europe, setting forth to conquer France. He had a complex about France, which for my generation was a boring, meddlesome, old bourgeois woman. So, when embarking on his ship or boarding his plane—I can't remember which it was now—Gombrowicz kept repeating stubbornly, doggedly, and at the same time triumphantly: "I'll be a bone in their throat. France won't swallow me. It'll choke on me."

Why did my god need to stick in that old woman's throat? Where does that doleful, not to say pitiful, egocentrism come from? It's egocentrism, egotism, and egoism that stick in my throat.

Here, out of anger, I could bring a few reproaches against the master who wrote the *Diaries*, yes, and *Ferdydurke*, yes; but his other works require my indulgence, if the reader will permit my saying so. O master, there is no greatness in and of itself. Greatness is only a matter of context. The context has to approve. Has to affix its seal.

Yes, but it was Gombrowicz who created the doctrine of superiority and inferiority. There's nothing you can do. You have to abase yourself, fall on your knees before superiority. Whatever sort it may be. Tough luck. I prostrate myself and grit my teeth.

I flew through eastern Poland. Almost birdlike. In two weeks' time I had traveled by car from Sejny in the north to Siedlce in the south. Almost birdlike. Without touching the ground. Through meadows, streams, shrubs, towns, villages. Half a meter or so above the grass, an entire ell above the treetops. First in the sun, swelter, and sweat of a premature summer; then in gray autumn, my teeth chattering from the cold.

We were scouting locations and what are called structural sites for filming *The Issa Valley*. What we needed was the Issa, the Niewiaza, a few bogs and forest clearings, and we also had to find the proper sort of gentry manor house, a suitable farm, the right sort of Lithuanian church. Spitting blood, panting and wheezing with the last of our breath, we found something on that order, but it was spiked with concrete utility poles, brutally cleft by the horrible buildings of today's Soviet Poles, gray air brick roofed with ash-colored asbestos tile. We pulled out a decent wooden church like a mushroom from moss, and in a thicket we came across an old farmstead that with some work could pass as the farm. One can travel for hundreds of kilometers in gentry Poland without finding a single manor house that has been pre- served and maintained. Those Polish manor houses were a thorn in the side of everyone who has frolicked on our lands. The Russians started destroying them in 1940 or when they were routed in '41. And the Russians had made a point of this up until the beginning of the fifties. A civilization leveled to the ground. A culture drowned in the ocean of oblivion. A world Mediterranean in spirit turned into nothing.

Some smart guy will say that this is the natural course of history. That's how it's always been and how it'll always be. The infrastructure of the departing classes crumbles to dust. But I've had it with those smart guys. I've had it with everything.

I was first in those lands where the Wilno area begins, in January 1945. In seven sleighs we sped though the snowdrift-covered reaches beginning in the Niemen River area, past Wilno and some little backwater which may have been near Sejny or Suwalki or Augustow. We dashed over the border at night, taking a giant step into that strange new Poland, or perhaps three baby steps, and there were overtaken by a leisurely winter day. We spent the day at some farm; I don't remember a thing about it, not a single person, no old man or romantic girl, none of the people who lived on that farm grooved the plasticine of my mind or lodged in my integrated memory circuits. But we were keeping a low profile ourselves, acting very conspiratorial, posing as some Soviet pacification unit. Later we returned to a point outside Wilno to report on our reconnaissance of that route, which could be used as a path of retreat for the Wilno Home Army, but by then all our commanders and colleagues were gone, resting in peace under the deep snows in a long sleep until the Day of Judgment.

All I remember from that expedition, which was almost like a school field trip for thirty boys, or maybe twenty, some in underground high schools, some already graduates—all I remember are the terribly clear moonlit nights, bright as day, the snow creaking under the runners, the horses farting, momentary skirmishes at guarded railway crossings, the bitter cold, the heavy frost, and the horrible canopy of stillness above us, an ice-covered coffin lid that began at the Dvina and ended by the Narva.

This time I was enjoying myself in a summer setting, the landscape juicy, bursting with vitality, rare luxuriance. It was another country, even though it was the same on the map. A country of air bricks, asphalt, and concrete poles. Socialist civilization, Soviet city-planning, Mongolian aesthetics. The car radio played unending funeral music for Cardinal Wyszynski, then suddenly someone began talking about Milosz and the Issa Valley. In the great lake of rain between Grajewo and Lomza, someone was saying that he had sent Milosz a record of the Old Theater of Krakow performance of Mickiewicz's *Forefathers' Eve*. And Milosz, who found Mickiewicz dished up in that style not in the least to his taste, replied that his Mickiewicz and he himself lived in a land that is called the land of nowhere. I may have twisted things, but it seemed to me that here Milosz was proclaiming his allegiance to the land of nowhere. That world of the new, ballyhooed values was not his.

But, accompanied by my childhood and my youth, I too had emigrated to the land of nowhere. There, stored in wretched trunks, my fancies, my vitality and rigor, my artistic loves, and my paltry, anachronistic morality had all gone their way. That land of nowhere is my body, which functions lazily, haphazardly; it is that dull pain in my skull above which there sprout a few graying hairs, an object of daily concern for my old cat Ivan, yes, old now, Ivan who had scarcely begun his life with me and was now ending it in a hopeless apathy that drives me to despair.

Requesting your discretion, I will here confide that now I am visited at times by a new kind of fear, one I had not known before. My friends are dying one after the other, my acquaintances, my enemies, my old bosses, teachers, and students, my neighbors and janitors, doctors and priests, even some of my former young ladies have moved on to the next world. And I remain alone in this same old, terribly crumpled, and shabby world, lonelier every day, solitary, isolated. Then suddenly in the morning, or the evening, a violent, oppressive, hysterical dread swoops down on me like a bat. What am I doing here? Where can I run away to? Whom can I open my asthmatic heart to?

I am alone. I am a foreigner. I am a sort of *Gastarbeiter*. No one needs me, no one understands my language, no one will help me if suddenly I collapse backward in the middle of the street.

At one time I loved to keep track of all my new experiences in life. Whatever they were, and if only to claim them as my own. I was a collector of impressions, experiences, psychological adventures. Why am I not happy with my new experience? Why aren't I in ecstasy over this new psychological adventure—my proud solitude in the very epicenter of a thickening crowd of carnivorous bipeds evolved from some idiotic amino acids?

In Konstancin a nice older woman once read my palm and predicted a very long life for me. I may have already mentioned that, but maybe I forgot to. Anyway, the prediction was for an unnecessarily long life. What does a merchant need health for, asked Benya Krik. What does a romantic writer need a long life for, I ask, I who invented myself.

We were on our way back from Suwalki and Augustow, where I used to go for vacation at the end of the fifties; we were on our way back from scouting locations on a rainy day, and not far from Warsaw we intersected a long column of Soviet military vehicles. They may have been mobile radio stations or radio-location devices, or perhaps some small rocket launchers; in any case, those hi-tech vehicles were adorned front and back with Polish driving-school plates. It was quite bizarre—ominous vehicles, ready to annihilate any supposed future rebellion, and those foolish license plates for automotive kindergartens.

But there, near Sejny and Sokolka, one could feel a foreign power without seeing foreign vehicles or foreign uniforms. That power smoked and steamed like hot air out past the horizon in a sun-drenched eastern sky. That presence, or rather that omnipresence, could be felt in those ruined manor houses, in those faded, ravaged propaganda slogans, and in the minds of the people there.

It's true but it's banal. There's nothing to say. How could this concern a left-wing Frenchman or a German who leans toward Communism? Given that, let's cast our mind back to those vacations in Augustow by Lake Necko, when those sentimental tangos about Augustow's lakes were composed, when we danced a bit erotically to the rhythm of those tangos on that open-air dance floor in that little town right by the canal.

What do I remember of Augustow a quarter of a century later? I remember that I was tormented by a constant inflammation of the ear, that I could hear practically nothing except for the pain, and since I couldn't hear anything, I smiled foolishly and apologetically at those around me. Worn out by suffering, I went to the local hospital, where a middle-aged doctor with a Wilno accent told me to stuff the ear with cotton batting before swimming in the lake or taking a bath. Seeing no other solution, I followed those idiotic instructions, and as if by magic, from then on to this day—knock on wood—I've never had another ache in that ear.

What do I remember? I remember the cemetery in Augustow and the enormous number of graves of young people who had drowned in the nearby lakes; I also remember that the cemetery's nooks and corners contained the tombstones of tsarist officers who had been buried there before World War I, when innumerable Russian garrisons had been stationed in Augustow and Suwalki. Weeds had grown over officers who had died from wounds in a duel or from homesickness, who had died from disease or perhaps even ordinary old age. Those awful graves, barely visible in the rampant greenery, graves that had collapsed with their twisted, rusted Orthodox crosses, graves that tugged at my heart, rousing a vague regret for something, something I did not know from my own experience but which I had dreamed of in childhood or had experienced in some other life.

I remember the year 1956 and the sky slowly cracking open

above me. I was kayaking on Lake Bialy—dread, uncertainty about the future, shame, fury, and persistence in sin, crime, and despair.

And now there were storks, actually stork nests, on top of the high-tension concrete utility poles. How can they live there amid those wires whose shock could kill an elephant? Air bricks, asbestos, and concrete. To whom can I cry out in the dimly lit darkness of the Milky Way? Of those who have already lived and those who will yet live, whom can I call upon? The hell with everything.

I know everything. I know the writing's going poorly, that I'm spinning cotton candy on a stick, of the sort children used to eat, great clumps melting down in their mouths to a small tasteless blob. I know that I'm writing a lot, but that it has no aroma, no seasoning, no vitamins. *The Calendar* taught me caution. I have a dread of using people's names, I'm afraid of juicy stories, I'm wary of revealing my tastes. It's no pleasure to receive anonymous letters chewing you out. In any case, I now regret that I threw those letters away in a fit of disgust. I could have encrusted these pages with them like medieval illuminations.

I'll be taking a break soon. For a few weeks I'll put aside this crumpled, tattered cardboard binder where I keep my manuscript written on the back of Nalkowska's diaries prepared for print by Professor Kirchner. That good woman has supplied the diaries with such excellent footnotes that my own education has risen a few levels, and now on the field of intellect I could rival the ruling team overthrown a year ago.

Anyway, I'll be taking a break soon, but before I do, I'll sigh softly about something I think about often: In thirty or forty years will someone reading my writing feel a sudden closeness to a person who lived so long ago, who had his own twisted life, who was almost persistent in his pursuit of something or other, and who in the end achieved nothing? Will that future reader perceive a sort of spiritual and intellectual affinity—if only in the sense of humor—with some man by the name of Konwicki, an ex-socialist realist, ex-conformist, ex-oppositionist, ex-pen pusher, envier, and sex maniac? When I read an old author, I sometimes suddenly long to be with him and would be glad to go out for a walk with him or drink a glass of booze and have a little talk about this shitty life which isn't worth a damn.

My business. We've started hiring actors for the film *The Issa Valley*. Every two seconds there's a categorical refusal. I'm on my knees, I coax and I flatter. But those theatrical clowns with their arrogance, their superiority, their disdain. That's how it is, my dear ladies and gentlemen. A bookstore where volumes of Milosz's poetry were on sale has been demolished. People stood in line for twenty-four hours in the freezing cold in front of another bookstore where Milosz might be available. A certain illustrious virgin exchanged her innocence for a time-worn volume of the Nobel laureate's work.

But there's no one to play in a film based on Milosz's novel. Everyone wants to play in films based on Kekusia's or Krupczalowski's books (I made up their names). But for some reason they won't go out of their way for Milosz.

What matters are those people crowding in line for Milosz. What matters are those refusals to act in Milosz's film (which is mine too, a little). Nothing matters, nothing means anything. It's all just the steppe. And the winds of Asia. It's all the same. Everything's the same height. The grass and the bushes and the trees.

15

A journalist from the *Guardian* asked me why I was writing this new book, and who was going to publish it. I answered truthfully that I had no idea who would publish it. What the journalist meant was: Did I intend to give the book to a state publisher or to an unofficial one like Nowa, which had published both *The Polish Complex* and *A Minor Apocalypse*? I was about to tell that nice journalist that I did not foresee any publisher for this book. The official publishers won't do it because of reasons of state, and the unofficial ones will probably cease to exist when Parliament passes the law on censorship. Renewal has brought a renewal of everything but me. Renewal gives everyone liberty and freedom, everyone but me. Renewal rewards everyone for the past, but totally passes me by.

Needless to say, I've started grumbling now for the sake of grumbling. The newspapers are full of complaints of every sort by the regime's ex-sweethearts, who tattle about their persecution at the hands of Gierek's now-devastated crew. And so I am groaning here for the sake of symmetry. But I did all right under the previous Party mafia. They harassed me a little, ignored me a bit, and from time to time inflicted a glancing blow on me, but always with respect and deference. Deep down, those apparatchiks considered me a gifted writer, and for that reason I seemed to pose a danger to the system. I was someone to them. I could feel their watchful eyes on me. Eyes that seemed hostile but were also friendly. That seemed disapproving but at the same time were encouraging. That blasted regime did not do me in as cruelly as it did my colleagues, who are now pushing and shoving to fatten themselves at the trough of Renewal.

Wait a minute, why am I writing this? What am I giving myself airs for again? Am I a moralist, a bore who makes life miserable for those around him as he murmurs, creaks, and rustles in the folds of a penitent's robes?

I picked up Radio Free Europe today. They were doing a reading of some novel. I listened closely, cocked my ear, switched on my comparative-literature machine. But the novel was a mish-mash, unwieldy, lumpy, artless prose. A half-baked, haphazard mixture of journalism and what was supposed to be psychology, but full of completely unverifiable assertions; it did not take the imagination by storm. This epic had an astounding air of anachronism about it, as if its author had never read three pages of contemporary prose. As if he had not only not read Heller or García Márquez but not even Dobraczynski or Zukrowski. I kept listening to that presumptuous text and then it suddenly occurred to me that Stefan Kisielewski was capable of writing that sort of thing. And so I waited curiously to see if it would lead to anything of interest. It did. At the conclusion the announcer said that they had just read the latest in a series of selections from Stefan Ki-sielewski's novel *The View from the Top.*

I had already heard a lot of nice things said about that novel. Professors and philosophers of every stripe had expressed their admiration and profound pleasure. Applause, cries of Author! Author! Children, it's a classic of Polish literature. But unlucky old craftsman that I am, I have been carpentering realistic prose half my life, prose with political, ideological, and moral errors, and I, a Warsaw plumber from some other provincial epic, I know that right opinions don't make good prose, I know that proper attitudes do not lend a sentence wings, and that political and moral infallibility provide no oxygen for those who are suffocated by airless chapters. It's a very sad thing. You can know best about everything and still not be capable of much.

I have taken the liberty of writing this section with my crooked, sinful pen, since I assume that his novel is of the least importance to Kisielewski the journalist, Kisielewski the critic, Kisielewski the composer.

How can I free myself from the label of controversial writer if I go ahead and put such frivolous generalizations to paper, such irresponsible literary opinions? What good does it do me? The hell with that sorry mess! In that regard I request the reader to consider the preceding section null and void. Let us move on.

I do not have the chronicler's Benedictine patience and cannot do a day-by-day description of the great and bloody uprising launched by the Poles, or by the Pope who comes from Poland, this perhaps the greatest of all our uprisings and certainly the most arduous and the one played for the greatest stakes, an uprising without bombs or bullets or wounded flesh, but one somehow exhausting for both sides and mortally dangerous to each opponent. Because this is the final battle for Poland, but also for that dread empire concealed behind those innocent letters from the end of the alphabet—U.S.S.R.

I am aware of the gravity of the times in which I live, but I can't overcome a certain mixture of laziness, fear, and superstitious premonition—to make a long story short, I just can't kiss everything goodbye and sit down each evening with a thick book of cross-ruled paper and write down what happened at home, in Poland, and throughout the world: who died, who's still alive, what went up in price and what went off the market, who said what where, and who conjured up what when. But no doubt other people are doing that for me; with photographic accuracy nameless chroniclers are recording these exciting and at the same time ordinary days in the history of a small planet in a microscopic solar system.

All the same, I am witness to some astounding revelations. In a state with a scientific social doctrine, in a country that is part of the world's most progressive system, in the camp of eternal happiness created by mankind and for mankind, in a country untroubled by war or natural disaster, a country rich in natural resources, an industrialized area, in this unlucky Poland sold down the river to Russia forty years ago, you can't buy cigarettes or matches at the newsstands, there're starting to be shortages of milk, soap, gas, electricity, bread, toilet paper, kasha, books, even vinegar, the very same vinegar that not so long ago was used to stock the empty shelves in food stores. The ruling party is fighting the ruling party, that is, it's fighting with itself; the ministers are nowhere to be found, one factory after another comes to a standstill, the police are on strike, the prisoners in prisons declare hunger strikes, the nation's leaders are embracing people on the left and the right: Sheremetev (who may be the owner of three airports outside Moscow), Ivanov, Volchev.

We're in a nose dive. Picking up speed, we are falling toward the very bottom of human existence, dragging the enormous body of the Soviet empire with us like a heavy millstone. But when our feet touch that slimy bottom, we will have a split second to disengage from the monster and surge back to the surface in a single burst of energy and gasp a mouthful of life-giving air.

And here I am droning away at this un-kosher book, which is no sooner born than it dies. If we win our freedom, no one will want to return in memory to these vile days, these lousy years. And if we remain unfree, pages and paragraphs like these will cost a person his head.

I went to a cocktail party in honor of Czeslaw Milosz's arrival in Poland, and the first person I ran into at Lazienki Palace on the water was, needless to say, Stefan Kisielewski. I hadn't seen him for quite a few years and all I had to do was tweak him in these pages for that novel of his and there we were face to face. Stefan was feeling frailish after an operation, avoiding liquor and jokes. I felt dismay, regretting that little section on him which I could no longer cross out, simply for reasons of honor. That's how it came out when I was writing about Kisielewski's prose, and now it's come what may.

Warsaw's little world is ruled by cliques. Zbigniew Cybulski used to call the little world of the elite "the Duchy of Warsaw." That definition, "the Duchy of Warsaw," contains all the destitution of Warsaw's dazzling life. Its constraint and its fragmentedness, its collaboration cloaked in old Polish garb, and its venality, its provincialism, its inauthenticity, and something else as well, which is both paltry and aggressively pretentious. Unfortunately, in some way we still resemble the Duchy of Warsaw, but perhaps we're even more reminiscent of the Congress Kingdom.

For several years Stefan was one of the fathers of the nation. A favorite of the émigrés, a star of the Polish radio stations in the West, the idol of the little papers and magazines published by Poles abroad. Now he has been outdistanced by those who gathered strength during the dark days of the Gierek era, who assiduously focused their powers without wasting their vigor on the opposition. Anyway, he has suddenly been outstripped by the brand-new, spick-and-span favorites, fathers of the nation who show no signs of wear and tear. But Stefan continues to shine though his glow is fading; he still keeps near the epicenter of Poland's horizon.

But I don't like his prose. It might be easier to take if it wasn't held up as an example. I have no taste for literature sealed with the stamp of a clique's charisma. And, dear readers, an important and insoluble problem is coming into being right before your very eyes. I won't yield. I can't yield, because I am unable to swallow those stories with their pretensions to erudition and psychology. I cannot give in because that epic of Stefan's offends me. It strikes at my intellectual capital, my tastes, my vital professional interests.

My conflict centers on the facts that Kisielewski's novels have a good-size readership and a certain group of people consider his prose to be elegant, intellectual, beautifully written, radical, avant-garde, and of the highest quality. My conflict is heightened by the fact that an enormous number of readers are incapable of reading even seven pages of my prose; my prose infuriates many people, it causes eyes to wander and sudden foaming at the mouth, my poor prose which, at the very least, bores, irritates, and hastens the coming of sleep.

I am against his prose apart from any question of cliques. I mean, I of course also belong to a little clique, an extemporaneous clique, created of the moment and for the moment, a clique more like a coincidence than anything else. But I never succeeded in joining any of the important cliques which decide the nation's fate and the hierarchies of our culture. What I mean is: I could have joined at one time but I didn't. For reasons of honor. For reasons of pride.

And so I'm a little bit like a sprinter who begins the race in a standing position while the competition is crouched at the starting blocks. I don't have to do what they do. I do things my way.

Years and years ago, sometime in the thirties, Jan Sieniuc drove a wagon for my grandfather. It is with pleasure that I write his name, which has stayed in my memory through so many wars and disasters. Jan was a man of honor. Honor was the only fortune he possessed, a true and noble gem. Thin, gaunt with illness, weathered, he had a flashing gold tooth, and that gold tooth, which I have never forgotten, that marvelous tooth personified Jan for me; enormous, preternaturally distended and rampant like the nerve in a tooth, his honor was the terror of everyone else's. Mr. Jan Sieniuc was an honorable man.

My Grandfather Blinstrub had great need of his help, and my grandmother was constantly calling respectful attention to the honor which resided in the fragile body of that man, who was somewhere between forty and fifty, because, where we lived, the years after forty had no meaning and went uncounted. Jan labored from sunrise to sunset, surrounded by that aura of honor which terrorized us. Weak, thin, constantly sick (I remember one terrible spell of pleurisy), he would hitch the horse to the wagon, drive off somewhere, then come back, unhitch the horse, feed it, tether it, bring something in, take something out. And then, at the proper time, wearing a snow-white shirt, he would sit down on the front porch and enjoy a cigarette, his gold tooth flashing, what must probably be called the smiling tooth of honor.

I will add only that it was solely for his own pleasure that Jan, at the urging of my grandparents, married Miss Emilia, a young lady who was no longer young or, rather, who was a youngish widow. I don't believe they had any children and so this will be the only epitaph of their life, but, above all, the epitaph of a man who was the embodiment of honor, the quintessence of honor, a Sèvres model of honor.

Yes, but now having offended Kisielewski, I cannot extricate myself. I really had no wish to hurt that demonic older man whom—why beat around the bush—I truly like and gladly read, the novels aside. I see so many types who deserve a good flogging and I pick on Kisielewski, whom I should respect and honor. The whole fandango would have never occurred if I hadn't woken up too early and felt a need to listen to Radio Free Europe, which is quite monotonous in its sympathies and antipathies.

Czeslaw Milosz has come to Poland. He has come to Poland after thirty years and after a deluge of accusations, curses, slander, aspersion, threats, insults, and affronts. He descended from the heavens above Okecie Airport, another saint in our brief moment of national ecstasy. Until recently he was a mysterious Lithuanian sorcerer borne by evil forces all the way to San Francisco Bay. His invisible, magical presence had kept us from sleep, but now suddenly he was here, physically present, and every waiter and every female men's-room attendant can demand his autograph, a fellow Pole on whom fortune has smiled.

Czeslaw Milosz is not much taken with this new incarnation, and has no taste for hysterical honors and ambiguous tribute which conceal a threat at their center. A furious, menacing Samogitian, a real devil from the banks of the Niewiaza, he casts a disapproving eye on the insolent.

He doesn't know what a terrible devaluation of success, fame, and renown he has caused in this poor and until recently agricultural country, what a drastic drop in the price of admiration, adoration, and homage. After he goes, it won't be worth it for us local yeomen to scramble for the home audience's scraps of attention, crumbs of approval, its thimbleful of love. We will never outstrip the laureate, whose victory chariot has cruelly trampled our modest dreams, yearnings, aspirations. We will never surpass this new god of the Western Slavs, who accepts the love potion of his adoring countrymen so sourly.

I've stolen into his retinue a few times. My ill-starred position as director of *The Issa Valley* served as my passport. I joined the throng of romantics and businessmen, the latter predominating. Today everyone's trafficking in national devotional articles. Even I, a man of honor from the banks of the Wilenka, which, it would seem, is a lovelier little river than the Niewiaza. I've seized on Milosz because that's how the cards fell. No one any worthier showed up. Perhaps that absolves me. God grant that it absolves me.

Anyway, I was in his entourage a few times. I could see how weary he was. A year before, he could have traveled through our devastated land in peace and quiet; two or three decently attended readings and a stream of aggressive questions from a nonchalant audience. Now, bearing the cross of fame on his back, he staggers from one Polish Station of the Cross to the next; his feet are pierced by the rose thorns of his homeland's Golgotha.

Czeslaw, what do you need all that for? So many of your colleagues here would be glad to replace you in that mission. How elegantly they would bear the halo of the Nobel, with what dignity would we celebrate our own utmost superiority, with what grandeur and zest would we permit our own apotheosis and bring our nation's saints to Calvary.

I am also an infantile type. I seem to be talking nonsense here, criticizing, degrading one thing or another, deriding this or that, ridiculing one person and instructing another from on high, I am so mature, adult, experienced; but enough of that. In a word, appearances are deceiving. Yet another childish creature is beating his breast here before you.

And my childishness, dirty old dog that I am, stems from a shameful separation from life's realities. I lie around in my little den and sulk at the world for not having enough happy endings, like the ones in the old Hollywood films. No event in my life and that of my friends and enemies ever ends like those American films of the thirties, or maybe even the forties. In my naïveté I am furious that good cannot conquer evil, that the villain can taunt the positive hero. It sets my teeth on edge that truth is trampled in the mud while the lie is carried about like a magical portable altar. It infuriates me that both white people and black run to the movies to see shameless trash, while true masterpieces are mocked by humorists in satirical rags.

This is my weakness, because I was brought up on Hollywood. I have been pitifully crippled by the old dream factories. I want to wake from that idiotic dream full of crazy anachronisms, and I cannot wake from it. I strain to rouse myself but no longer can. An old boy, an eternal child, a moral drooler. Yes.

Once again quick, cold flashes of hatred have come to me. They came flickering at me from behind, from the side. I could not catch a glimpse of them, though sometimes by chance I did. What can I say—they grieved me. Because my determination and hardiness are only a front. In reality I worry like any other quasi-public person. With a certain pride I add that, were I humbler, were I to go hat in hand to the reader, were I to suck up to those oafs and flatter them, then I might be forgiven for my mistakes, distortions, and the insolence which I maintain only for your own good, my dear pink-eyed little rabbits, dashing about in your no-exit cages. In your cells of the impossible. Your hermitages of despair.

My insolence humanizes you. It forces you to make a minimal

mental effort. Spurs you on to make a choice. Offers you a catharsis of emotional and moral fulfillment.

But I'm sad. Actually, I've been sad all my life. And that's why I'll tell you a happy story. In the past I would usually reel off the story of competing for my wife's hand. How after the war I would travel to Poznan, how I hid the holes in my socks, how I went off to the wedding having invited the janitor at city hall to be our witness, and how my father-in-law, Fredzio, whom I love and hold dear, returned from abroad to learn in a café that his daughter had married a young Warsaw writer. Naturally, that monologue had its witty moments, someone would burst out laughing every so often, and when I finally came to the conclusion of my tale I would meet with fulsome praise.

Then, over the years, I struck on a new theme. I'd tell a tale of being mistaken for someone else. This was a more demanding intellectual pastime. Some people laughed, but not wholeheartedly, maintaining a certain reserve, while others accused me of playing for attention. Still, all in all, the story was a hit.

Now it couldn't be worse. No sooner do I open my mouth and cackle out two words with my one vocal cord when something occurs to someone who begins his own disquisition in a stentorian voice. And so today, in these difficult times, I have become something of a starting gun. I can't tell any stories of my own, but I start ten others in on theirs.

And so here I am opening my mouth again. Maybe you too will be reminded of something interesting.

At the beginning of this summer, famous Poles from all continents began converging on Poland. The only one missing was the Pope, who is recuperating after the attempt on his life. Some of these people seemed to have already forgotten their original homeland and to have lost their old nationality completely; then all of a sudden there's a flash of magic, some fluid shifts, some mysterious shudder, and our celebrated countrymen come flying to the land of their fathers on a variety of airlines.

Among others, Jan K., that is, Professor K. from Stony Brook, suddenly turned up. To get to see K. in America is a great achievement, and by all accounts, he is the toast of New York. But in Warsaw Professor K. is just Jan K., someone you can go right out for a vodka with.

And I went out for one with him. We ended up in the journalists' restaurant, which had undergone its own renewal and where I had last reveled at some point before March 1968. Now things were different. Now that interior served for feverish meetings of those supporting Renewal; a breeze of patriotism delicately ruffled hair damp with sweat; something luminous was afoot in that bar, which had the dignity of a holy place.

Jan and I, I mean Professor K. from Stony Brook, took a table on the veranda. The menu was brought by a blond child with the mighty breasts of Mother Poland. The professor fixed a kindly stare on that splendid work of nature. We ordered something, we ate something as we had in the good old days, but that didn't matter, that wasn't why the professor had flown eight thousand kilometers here. And so I promised to take him to the Quarry, and I kept my word. The Quarry is the nightclub at the Hotel Europejski.

A flock of porters and bouncers looked us over with impassive gravity as we emerged from a car on Ossolinski Street. We went into the bar, purchased the so-called prix-fixe coupons, and took a booth. Three Arabs were sitting near us, and there were a few old men there too. The band was playing some tune, a songstress of dubious sex was singing some song. Janek, that is, Professor K., shook his head in dissatisfaction. He did so unconsciously, automatically, perhaps even in a sleep state, for when awake he would never do anything to annoy me. A huge stone men's room with a deranged street band blaring away. The chill of the void. The Arabs left, making no secret of their disappointment.

Hey, let's go to the Kongresowa, someone suggests, there's more life there. I ridicule the idea. The Kongresowa is a bar for paupers, members of delegations. There cannot be anything more provincial than the Kongresowa.

But the professor is hot on the idea. The professor wants to go to the Kongresowa. He says that he's writing a scholarly book on night life in some of the world's capital cities. What can you do—we go to the Kongresowa in the Palace of Culture.

There's my favorite, the Palace of Culture, which I dream of at night and which dreams of me at night. The entrance bright, red stairs that seem to lead to hell, a toothless woman with a little metal cash box.

"Wait a couple of minutes, boys, it'll be cheaper in a minute."

"What do you mean?" asked the ill-mannered professor.

"The show's almost over," said the woman who sold the coupons, adding "Eight hundred" in something like English. The latter piece of information concerned the Arabs. The Arabs pay eight hundred zlotys and enter the murky rotunda, where music no one seems to have any use for is blaring away. The toothless woman smiles patriotically at us.

"Let the Arabs pay. But I won't take money from my own people. I'll let you in for two packs of cigarettes."

And then we entered something which I had conceived of long ago but had never gotten around to describing. A murky oval pergola with a mass of empty tables. On one side, a dark, seated group of athletic waiters; on the other, a flock of whores, but whores that would make even Fellini proud. Past the pergola a bright oval dance floor with an enormous fountain operating at full force despite the country's water shortage. Around the fountain and on the dance floor, women, dressed to look like God knows what, were lifting their legs while men sang and gestured. I swear, you never see people like this during the day. Something about their bearing, their makeup, their degeneration is reminiscent of phantoms in dreams, apparitions at dawn, the vampires of a malignant fever. It was just ending, the finale. Fortissimo, kettle drums; come on, girls, do your splits and then exit into the damp darkness of caverns hewn out by Stalin's oprichniks.

By then three prostitutes sitting by the entrance had caught sight of us johns and were calling us over. One madonna, one middle-class-looking, one absolute dog. A stylized, dynamic combination. Sex and syph. Eros and herpes. Arabic.

"Hi, boys, made a date yet?"

"Of course not. We're just here for a minute."

"So have a seat."

"No, later. We're going to have a look at the cocktail bar right now."

We walked through the pergola between the empty tables to the bar gleaming in the distance. Three Arabs were discussing something with the manager. The manager called over a waiter, who was told what the guests from the East desired, and a moment later he parted the curtain that led backstage. Something large and lumpish flashed by, maybe a cow. Those were sodomites from the Levant. But the cow was clearly ugly. The Arabs grimaced while the waiter haughtily drew the curtain made of something that had once been plush. No means no.

There was a little group of prostitutes at the bar. We stood modestly by a column. A few pimps, tall and beefy, craned their necks, keeping an eye on their girls.

"Jan," I said, "you can get killed here."

"I know. And I have a lot of cash with me too."

"So, let's go back."

The girls seemed to be from some cosmopolitan paradise where the Communists had been in power for a week. So they had a certain elegance, but also a certain obscenity, about them. They seemed extravagant beauties, but they also had their dermatological shortcomings. They had a species of innocence, but the name of the male member was on their bright-red lips.

A cool and haughty lady in a dress the color of wild strawberries walked by. Subtle makeup, a Parisian coif, an intellectual melancholy in her eyes. I knew her from somewhere. We'd rubbed shoulders one night. Could it have been in an embassy? Or at the opening of an exhibit of Aztec gold sculpture? Or at the name-day party of one of the fathers of our country?

"Why so shy?" asked a girl who resembled a rhinoceros with a broken horn.

"We're bashful."

"All right, so come closer. Let's see what you look like. I've never seen you here before."

"We're just in for a minute."

Then her pimp began jacking up the price.

"The ass on her," he shouted to her and to us. "She's got everything you could want. And I've got good stuff too."

He began elbowing his way toward us, pulling money out of all his pockets. He was tipsy but pretending to be drunk.

"Here you go, kid, take it." He thrust the money at her. "Let's go party."

We withdrew to a nearby partition made by the columns, which had once been polished by Stakhanovites at the foot of the Caucasus or the Urals.

For a moment we hesitated. Fear and delight. Danger and pleasure. The professor had started to come to life, and I had too. Word was out that we were oddballs. The whores had even told the band, which stopped playing. A hustler who was at the electric organ was standing in front of us, batting his eyelashes. All ready for the taking. A musical type.

"Let's come back another time," whispered the professor.

"Let's come back next week," I answered in a whisper.

And off we went. It was a beautiful night on the square, where a hundred taxis with rigged meters stood waiting. Two cab-drivers began pulling toward us. Fags were fares too. They didn't discriminate against anyone.

"Where can we get a regular cab?" I asked.

"By Central Station," muttered one of the crooked drivers.

We headed humbly toward the black ruins of the station. Just then a cab came flying from a side ramp, made a quick turn, and braked near us. The door opened. Two jolly, smiling girls.

"Get in, boys."

We squeezed ourselves in. The professor pressed his precious wallet to his heart. The woman driving was tall and thin. Her friend was even taller, at least two meters, and beefy as a sumo wrestler. The driver's gorilla, her bodyguard. They gave us friendly smiles.

"Where can we drop you?" asked the thin one.

"Mokotow," said the professor.

"But I'll get out on Krucza Street," I was quick to add. They didn't even so much as glance at me. They liked the professor. The professor was a real man. They would take him where he was going.

I hopped out on Krucza. The Fiat bearing the professor darted away down the dark tunnel of the street. We'll see what happens to that Shakespeare specialist. Yet another experiment. "A Warsaw day dawns over the Vistula"—I was mumbling the words of a popular song. Let's see who survives it.

The harvest of the century. They're predicting an extraordinary harvest. The grain is as tall as the corn. The mowers shown on television were chest-deep in weeds, herbs, and succulent aftergrasses. I had played in aftergrass like that in the dark. A glimmer from my childhood—people going out to cut those aftergrasses. But what they look like, and what they're good for, I really don't recall.

And so there's an abundance of vegetation, flowers, the first fruit. This harvest will also turn into a disaster. Everything will rot because of a lack of transportation, storage, and willing workers. A summer of harvest and disaster. We'll die of hunger on heaps of rotting potatoes, fermented apples, and vegetables pecked by vermin.

Once again the worm of uncertainty is gnawing at me. What am I writing and why am I writing it? I had a little pleasure at times when working on *Calendar*. Not this time. Nothing but despair. Not enough jokes, too few details, not enough pure prose. But after all, I can't do a repeat of *Calendar*; I shouldn't try to make it stretch like forty zlotys' worth of kielbasa in a dishonest butcher shop. To plagiarize oneself is quite unseemly. And so this lush and wholesome summer I'm winging it. Later on, we'll see.

．　．　．

I'm looking through *Trybuna Ludu* and suddenly my bloodshot eye snags on an article whose title reminds me of something: REQUEST TO BUY BACK FORMER GERMAN TERRITORY. I begin reading this report from Bonn and come across the following: "The request to buy back Germany's former eastern borderlands, transferred to Poland as part of the Potsdam Agreement, has become a key conceptual component in national organizational plans since the beginning of the social and economic crisis in which our country has found itself."

And thus my final mocking prophecy in *A Minor Apocalypse* has come true. Wandering in search of a bathroom during an illegal Central Committee banquet, Dr. Hans Jürgen Gonsiorek (I think that's what I called him) can now calmly place a call to Bonn and request another sackful of marks to purchase one of our western provinces.

Everything's collapsing. The earth is quaking. The sky is rent with lightning. The water has gone bad. The air is poisoned. The last taboos have fallen. Wrapped in its winding sheet, Poland stands beside its own grave.

People await an invasion, a coup d'état, Russian tanks and Russian kibitkas. And now our Slav-Tatar brothers have come up with something new, a fresh economic/psychological concept. Now they're encumbering us with debts to the East, to the applause of Party conservatives. Tomorrow they'll announce that we owe the Soviet Union 50 million dollars, and in three years they'll say that now we've borrowed 120 million, maybe even a billion. No one will ever be able to check those figures; our Party will endorse every note with alacrity. We'll be in the Russians' pocket until the end of time. Insolvent, bankrupt, we'll be stripped of our factories, railroads, and the uneaten grain from the fields. The Party will help load the trains and send it all off to the east. And in the end, the Party will turn off the lights and leave for Siberia too.

But the strategists in the Kremlin and Lubyanka were too clever.

The Soviet Union is an anachronism in this day and age. The Soviet Union is not up-to-date.

Everything is collapsing, but it won't fall apart. The earth is quaking, but it'll be calm again the day after tomorrow. The sky is rent by lightning, but it won't be torn to shreds. Poland will spend a while in its winding sheet, then switch back to its everyday clothes and finally get down to work.

And me? I'll go looking for a country with censorship, where I can write modern allusive prose for the rest of my days.

I'm constantly reading articles, reminiscences, and epitaphs for Jaroslaw Iwaszkiewicz, who died more than a year ago. Some laud him, some find fault. The former love him, the latter hate him. I myself think Iwaszkiewicz filled a very important gap in nineteenth-century Polish literature.

16

I'm not clapping my hands for joy and not whacking my thigh in delight because the totalitarian Communism practiced in our poor land will fizzle out in the end, because this so-called socialism which we all curse, this enormous labor camp, is coming apart at the seams, unsteady on its feet. It gives me no great satisfaction to see that we're returning to the old motivations which compel my fellow bipeds to make some moderate progress. I shall not gag with vengeful Schadenfreude because selfishness and the rapacious instinct for possessions are once again becoming man's main drives.

It pains me that yet again human reason has proved a hundred times weaker than the stupidest urge. It saddens me that my actions cannot have sufficient premise in honor, a sense of dignity, common human decency, or an understanding of social duty, or respect for the autonomous existence of others.

You'll pardon me, but that's how it is. The ideas of socialism, the doctrines of Communism, have been compromised right before our very eyes. At last we have some peace. We can slam the door to our own little philistine houses with relief and, with no pangs of conscience, feed our rapacious, blustering selfishness, which is hostile to everything that is not ours and which becomes more gigantic from one day to the next.

We never used to close the door to the staircase during freezing weather, but now we will take great care that every last keyhole in our own homes is in good repair. We threw tons of bread out with the garbage, but that was free bread, from society; now we pick up every crumb that belongs to us from the ground and kiss it with religious reverence. In the co-op store we always had a headache and our nerves were on edge, but there's no illness in our private shop and we can do business for eight long hours, from dawn to dark.

When visiting foreign cities I experience an unhealthy interest in phone books and cemeteries. Lists of subscribers and grave-stones are life stories condensed in the extreme, extracts from the drama of earthly existence. I derive a slightly painful and senti-mental pleasure from using my imagination to add water to those freeze-dried fates. I look at some strange-sounding name, an impassive set of numbers encoded with a modest sum of years, meaning of earth's revolutions around the sun; I look at those letters and numbers and suddenly I see a person's life filled with desires which fate did not allow to come to fruition, or I catch a glimpse of a person's gray, prosaic stagnation, completely empty, terrifying in its futility, or perhaps suffused with a great secret which neither I nor anyone else will ever divine.

One time in Moscow I made a trip to a cemetery—it must have been Novodevichy—and when walking down its tree-lined paths, I experienced many strange emotions. I remember, I think I remember, Chekhov's tomb, or Gogol's, the grave of Alliluyeva, Stalin's wife, monuments to Soviet pilots of the thirties. I re-member that many gravestones were shielded by plastic casings, transparent sheaths or hoods, to protect the precious stones from the effects of the weather.

But I was most impressed by the red brick wall with marble slabs, which I believe contained the ashes of people buried there during the twenties and the beginning of the thirties, before Stalin began to bury Bolsheviks and non-Bolsheviks in the ice of Ar-khangelsk or the eternal frost of Kolyma.

Each of those slabs had been inscribed with a non-Russian

name: German names, Spanish, French, Italian. The ashes of representatives of all the nations of Europe reposed behind those slabs, and all those people had willed that beneath their names be engraved the highest title of nobility in those times, the greatest merit, beautiful sobriquet of a forgotten epoch, a single word which must have meant a great deal at the time: Communist.

Somewhere out past that cemetery wall was Butyrki prison and, a bit farther on, the legendary Lubyanka, and then, extending all the way to the shores of the Pacific, the prisons and camps built by the hands of Communists for Communists, built by the people's hands for all the people of this world.

Sparrows chirped as I read some of those names: Erich Krauss, Communist. Giovanni Dorazzi, Communist. Willy Smith, Communist. Jean Pierre Dupont, Communist. All Europe had flocked to this the fatherland of the world proletariat and had left their bones to molder here.

Were they apparatchiks in pursuit of a brilliant career? Were they sadists persecuting innocent victims? Were they psychopaths craving cruelty and crime?

Who were those Krausses and Smiths who, at the beginning of the twentieth century, made their way to remote, impoverished, freezing-cold Russia to build misshapen factories, wasteful power plants, and clumsy tractors? Were they angels or butchers? Prospectors for gold or romantic missionaries of a new religion?

A wailing wall. A wall of unintended mockery. A wall of desperate men. A wall of melancholy. A wall of vain vanity.

I am not especially happy that the experiment begun by two German scholars has ended in fiasco. I find it no occasion for joy that suddenly newly victorious Private Initiative has been resurrected from its shallow grave along with its progeny. Selfishness and Greed. How good that Communism will lose. What a shame that Communism will lose.

The French Mill. A white-and-yellow cube with a gray roof. Maybe a tin roof, maybe tar paper. Roaring like a church organ, the building was bounded on the north and east by a high, steep precipice, a reddish wall of dry clay. A glittering die lost in a jungle of forests, copses, hills, and jolly clouds sailing north, to the ice and wind.

The French Mill is Wilno's St. Tropez, Palm Beach, Easter Island. A person might forget his own name, but everyone remembers the French Mill until the end of his days. Even Milosz, whom I asked about the French Mill, replied without thinking twice: We used to go to a different place. To Werek, the Trockie lakes. But I remember the French Mill. Isn't it out past the Wilno Colony?

Of course the Mill which I dream of to this day was out past the Wilno Colony; it was on the way to Nowa Wilejka, where I was born. No, not really on the way, a little to one side, at the bend of the Wilenka, dammed at that point by the Mill's floodgates until it was the size of a good-size pond, and naturally shielded by green slopes that were sharply reflected in that vast pond. The elegant part of our spa was in front of the floodgates, which made for one wall of the bridge that ran to the mill. There the shores had been timbered at one time; on the meadows on either side, vacationing families would spread out their liter bottles of juice, their little baskets of hard-boiled eggs, their accordions or playing cards. We'd wander around, prepubescent, skinny, suntanned dark as Arabs, lusting for the opposite sex. A little excited by the relative nakedness of the women and girls, every so often we would run into the cold water to allay that unhealthy excitation. Wilno's high-school and university students and its street kids lurked a bit above us, a level above us. They already had their own girls, their own blankets, and their own business in the bushes at sunset. But all that wasn't enough for them, and they'd come wandering aggressively along the timbered shore, along the bridge, the boards slippery and plastered with algae, bristling with rusty bolts, down the steep boards that dropped from the floodgates to the emaciated, evaporating Wilenka, which was cut in two like an earthworm by those floodgates and that dust-covered bridge. When a section of the floodgates was suddenly opened to allow excess water to pass, the current would seize some incautious swimmer and we would dash to the other side of the bridge to see the water fling the poor man against the pilings, to see him spun downstream by the foaming waterfall, to see his shorts catch on a screw and be torn off him, until finally he vanished in the rainbow-haloed surge where our beloved river the Wilenka's new life began.

I took that walk in my imagination today. I strayed to the sun-golden, grass-green, and sky-blue French Mill, because I had met with trouble, terrible trouble, simply horrible, viler than anything I'd experienced in years. And so, overcoming that inward trembling that arises from seeing no salvation for myself, overcoming the shakes, I went to the French Mill, which I spotted from a distance, hearing it drone like telegraph poles auguring bad weather; and I kept on walking, hearing the voices of my friends, since in that melodious roar it was easy to recognize my friends' nervy cries and the bottle-like voice of the water as it received the body of a valiant leaper.

We jumped off whatever we could. Off the concrete spurs that broke up the ice in spring, off electric-light poles, off the dike bridge made of railroad ties. Some daredevils—and in my childhood and youth I never saw more than three or four, people who would suddenly appear one Sunday out of nowhere, mysterious people—had the courage to leap into that surging water from the ends of the boards over which water from the opened floodgates fell. You were supposed to jump from the edge of a ten-meter-high concrete wall into seething water a meter deep at its deepest, bubbling furiously along the stony bed, splashing foam and drops of a friendly rainbow.

I stood at the edge of that abyss for many hours. I stared at that monotonous surge of water until my eyes hurt. I would gather my courage, I would scrape the courage out of every cell of my thirteen-year-old body, but I couldn't gather enough to tense my muscles, break free of the rough concrete, and fly headfirst to my fate.

At those moments I would remember all the crap I'd heard

about daredevils breaking their backs. By then I was perfectly well aware how the jump had to be made; we had long since worked out the technique in theory. We helped one another practice how to extend the arms, how to fly for those ten meters, how to enter the water as shallowly as possible, so that the water itself would eject the diver from the surge and keep him from being smashed to pieces on the multicolored rocks.

I stood on that wall for a few seasons. And one day I jumped. Feet first. But that didn't count. It was as if I hadn't jumped at all. And so, in fact, I never did jump. One of those things that never got done in life and now never will, because how can I go to the Wilno Colony in my old age and dive headfirst into a pile of river stones.

But I'm babbling about all this in order not to remember, to drown out the misadventure I encountered today, one which I have been encountering in installments for some time now, and which I will encounter tomorrow, the day after tomorrow, and in a month's time.

The French Mill can help dispel my black thoughts. But why was that mill called the French Mill? Perhaps because, during the time of the Tsars, French engineers engaged in construction in that neck of the woods. Or perhaps the locals associated all technological civilization with the French and France. The railroad repair shops in Wilno were called the depot, and when my Grandfather Lisowski, a metal worker, went to work, people would say that he'd gone to the depot.

The French Mill, a complex of dark water, dark greenery, dark precipices, dark oaks, and dark nights, during which both drowned men and drowned women would wander along the shores and over the moonlit surface of the water, coming every year, every scorching summer, of which there were many then and of which there are none whatsoever today.

One time, I no longer remember when it was, one July or August, I was there sunbathing by the bushes with a bunch of high-spirited friends, and one of those young people, a handsome kid, a hit with the girls, athletic, well built, an eye-catcher—anyway, suddenly this good-looking guy strips naked and walks across the grassy beach among those people on their Sunday outing. And the sight of his shocking, shameless nakedness has also stayed with me all my life and never fails to rearouse my dread; and as in a painting by Gainsborough, against a background of splendid green, I can still see that naked young man with the dark lower belly, his awesomely white pecker dangling forlornly, like some alien creature which that poor fellow was taking around to show everyone he knew.

But I was also drawn to the French Mill by my eyes, my speculations, and my fierce desire for girls a bit older than I, especially for one who already had everything where it belonged, though still on a junior scale, not quite full grown yet.

I can still see her walking down to the water where the shore was not supported by timbers, slowly, carefully submerging in the warm, dark water smelling of mint or nettles; the water embraced her, though I would have embraced her better; I watched the water touch her light-blue bathing suit of fine wool, which was what they wore then; the water's lips touched her hips, her delicate, schoolgirl breasts, her white, slender neck, until finally they touched the lips of my girl. I would be watching from the shore, trembling all over like a Wilno aspic while my girl opened her lips to the edge of that greenish water redolent of sun-warmed weeds, while, in the distance, cows lowed as they were driven from pasture before nightfall and flocks of wild birds flew south across a rose-colored sky, which heralded the approach of an early autumn from somewhere in the north.

Yes, yes, but the French Mill and my late childhood or early youth cannot deflect today's events, cannot undo the terrible incident which so innocently befell me at the beginning of the strange summer of 1981, a summer of terrible tension and heavy languor, a summer of the worst premonitions and the most joyful hopes, an especially onerous summer for me, a summer I will curse for a long time, if I am able to go on cursing for long.

Here I had intended to quote my letter to the administration of the film group Perspektywa in which I requested that they accept my resignation as director of the film *The Issa Valley*. The administration consists of my old colleague Kuba Morgenstern, who is horror-struck by my determination, and the group's literary director, Mr. Juliusz Burski, who has been friendly to me from the start and very helpful in the pre-production for the cinematic butchering of that ill-starred *Issa Valley*.

So what happened? Nothing happened. Like a boxer, I never lowered my guard, never let my eyes off the Party, the government, even the Soviet Union, when all of a sudden I received a murderous blow to the jaw from the Church. I was down for the count, seeing stars. KO'ed.

Our filming required the Church's permission; actually, that of the bishops' curia, to enter certain Church property—for example, the church courtyard or presbytery that would serve as a manor. I was turned down. The clergy does not support the film.

Just yesterday Czeslaw Milosz was shown through chapels and cathedrals, just yesterday he was at the Catholic University of Lublin; the Primate's speech was read posthumously, and Milosz was appointed a Catholic writer—while today making a film from his novel is out of the question.

I fell over backward, moaned softly all night and the better part of the morning, and then, at midday, high noon, I set off with my retinue to see the priest who held my fate in his hands, my swain glory, my cachectic health.

The priest was likable, intelligent, wise, but also polite, restrained, and icy. Sagacity, flare, an iridescent gleam, concrete, stone, 270 degrees below zero. The Church does not prohibit the making of the film, but neither will it have any hand in it. Grave reservations of a liturgical or moral sort, as well as mistrust of me—would I take advantage of their goodwill and cheat them as other film riffraff have? No, no, please take your screenplay, and may God be with you.

But I explained myself. Church properties were not what mattered to me, I could get by without them. What mattered was the Church's approval, spiritual support. I did not want to be in conflict with the Church; given the times and my own situation, I had no need of a run-in with this unexpected new power, this new censor. I said that I had allowed myself to be manipulated into making this film, other people had thought me the right person to do it, that the film was not my own personal work. Given that, I had imagined I'd be filming under entirely different circumstances, that for the first time in my life I'd be working in peace and quiet, surrounded by the benevolence of all around me, granted assistance and rewarded with applause. For refusals, harassment, nagging, and censorship I had the Party, which might even secretly like me a little.

The priest seemed to be both looking at me and not looking at me, but in the end he changed his tone a bit. I was supported by my colleagues—Mr. Burski, and even my producer, Ryszard Chutkowski. We made a dignified showing, but in the end I said that I would withdraw from the entire enterprise.

We fought for another two rounds in a lighter mood. Now the priest had warmed to us, he understood artists, he wished us luck, but still he refrained from granting us approval. And he never gave it, even though my eyes were filled with affliction and I concluded that audience by acting like a ripe old elf.

We forced a draw. Or perhaps it was forced on us. Yielding a little ground, and a bit more benevolent, the priest expressed a positive opinion concerning the purity of my intentions, but did not conceal his reservations about certain scenes in my screenplay and, I guess, certain episodes in the novel by the laureate, the darling of the cardinals. A qualified bishop would make the decision. I resigned myself to a vote of confidence in regard to my miserable person. I had been thrown into the water. If I sank to the bottom, I lost. If chance kept me on the surface, I won.

For the first time in my life I had warm thoughts for Martin Luther.

· · ·

O Mother of God, it's night already. My neighbors are stirring. They're turning on their radios, rearranging their furniture, starting up their power saws. And I'm still here going round in circles. Good Christ, when I think of the day just passed, I get chills up my spine. That high-minded priest placed me somewhere between Poreba and Krolikiewicz as an artist. The priest kept harping on their supposedly having disappointed his expectations. And I was one of them. An interloper, an insolent hustler.

Night outside the open balcony doors. A short summer's night. But not as short now as they were a few weeks ago. We're already moving toward fall. What could have saved me from that film? Only an illness. A serious, respectable disorder.

Night. I'll start waking up just before morning, at daybreak, at first light, sunrise. Yesterday a married couple returned from a banquet. Dressed neatly and prosperously, like respectable middle-class people. Nicely plump, large-breasted, she held herself well as she heaped abuse on the man with her, reviled him in a tearful voice, reproaching him for making her into a woman of loose morals, as people used to say. But there was an air of untruth about her insinuations. Gasping with fury, a man shouted from his balcony for them to shut up, they had woken the whole street. And then the milk truck drove by, an enormous vehicle with a trailer. I knew that once again the driver would not make the turn and would come barreling into our courtyard and drive his truck and trailer over every flower bed, flower pot, and bench, tear down the clotheslines, flagstone bases and all, and then someone else would start yelling from his window and the driver would yell back from the cab of his truck in a vengeful tone of voice: "You want your milk or not?"

Night. If my mind was more at peace, I'd be able to count all the nights of my life. Perhaps it would come to some magical number, perhaps some important clue to the future would be revealed, maybe something would happen. I've worked myself into a no-exit situation. In an interview Czeslaw Milosz said that he had granted me permission to adapt *The Issa Valley* because I had gone to the same high school he had graduated from. And so I too must take this opportunity to mention that I undertook making a filmed version of that novel because its author had graduated from my high school ahead of me.

Night. The French Mill's floodgates have certainly been lowered to let the water back up for the night's grinding. But does that mill, that vestige of my youth, still exist? No, I will travel in my dreams tonight to the Wilno Colony, through which many famous people have passed, even though it is a small settlement, a bit of a village, a bit of a resort, a bit suburban, a bit elegant. I will groan in humiliation, I will groan, and maybe fall asleep.

Is that fact worthy of being noted in this grotesque journal? Is it worth the effort to search my mind for the right nouns, adjectives, and verbs to record on paper such historical, quasi-historical, and garbage-dump-historical events? Isn't it a waste of time and trouble?

In a few days there will be a special congress of our ruling monopoly Party, which at one time was called the Polish United Workers' Party. Of course, like everything east of the Elbe, this name too is a pure abstraction; the concept has no connection with reality. That Party formed two other parties: the Democratic Party, for the tradesmen, and the United Peasants' Party, for the peasants. In exchange for bed and board or, to be blunt, for money, both those small parties pretend to be independent party coalitions, for the sake of decoration, Byzantine ritual, the Russian cult of the word's domination of fact.

Our beloved Party is assembling for a historic congress, one on which, as they say, our fate hinges. Either the dawn of freedom, or the final stage in slavery and vassalage to Moscow. People should be extremely keyed up, but meanwhile, things are rather restrained. Everyone's standing in line. Those lines are a form of occupation. And Poles don't work during an occupation.

I belonged to that Party for almost fifteen years. My friends dragged me into it, as if it were a beer house or a brothel. I had fallen into bad company, and they had convinced me, a good boy from outside Wilno, to join the Party; they got me addicted.

I fell into bad company—comrades from the Party basic organization—and my family, my relatives, and my mother were all worried sick that I'd gone to the dogs.

I stuck in the Party's throat like a chestnut still in its greenish, spiky shell. Prickly, aggressive, outwardly unswallowable. But inwardly, in my unhusked center, I was a super zealot, super engagé. Soft soap on the inside, sandpaper on the outside. Exactly the opposite of what should have been, according to the technical prescription for corrupting a person's morality and world view.

The poets and the younger prose writers mock me. They shake their fingers at me, tap their foreheads, they spit copiously. The young poets, the young writers of epics, the young venomous critics. You still have your whole life ahead of you. The fate and life of the Kosciuszkos, the Lukasinskis, and the Grotow-Roweckis still await you. The destiny and life of the Ksawery Branickis, the Azefs, and Kalksteins still await you.

For two hundred years now, every generation of Poles has had the commandment to save the fatherland encoded in its genes. But to save the fatherland is much more difficult than making shoes or writing novels or conducting policy.

Western Europe, England, France, Switzerland aren't familiar with the concept of "saving the fatherland" and can't understand it. But they will know it, will understand it. Because the world is on the way down.

I seem to be writing out of spite. To spite myself, to spite my friends, to spite my countrymen. But I was born to write ingratiatingly. The ingratiating, the warm, those are my innate specialties. If I had not fashioned a set of opposition reflexes for myself, at the cost of great labor, there would have been lucre waiting for me; I would have stirred people's hearts, squeezed fat tears from my dear reader's eyes. To be frank, it was I who chose my own hideous biography on purpose, in order to make my own artistic career more difficult, to complicate the task of historians of literature, to make a tragedy of my bardic ethos.

And that must have been the true basis of my exploits during the Stalinist period, my literary crimes, my genocide in the world of the heroes of socialist-realist novels.

But then how did I end up thinking of nothing but priests and *The Issa Valley*?

Outbreaks of war. The outbreaks of war in my life. The first in September 1939. A sweltering morning after a hot vacation. The first day of school. I was on my way from the Colony to Wilno, to Zygmunt August High School, where I would be a sophomore. I was thirteen years old, a high-school student who'd passed his baptism of fire. The first year, the worst year, was already behind me. The most horrible time in my life until then. A rural shepherd starting out in a European metropolis. A piece of cake. By then there were 160,000 people in Wilno. It could make your head spin. The city had bus service. We called the buses "arbons" because that sounded French. We liked everything French. That's how we are.

And so, a sweltering morning and wonderful news. Classes had been cancelled due to the outbreak of war. We high-school students weren't particularly disturbed by the outbreak of war. I belonged to the Anti-Aircraft Defense League (I think I'm remembering the name right), I had a yellow-and-green armband, and a bottle containing some solution, and a strip of gauze that was to serve as a gas mask. And, most important of all, my pocket sagged with a blank pistol whose barrel had been bored out and now contained a cartridge from a fowling piece. We had tried many times to shoot a hole through a board with such cartridges. Now I was a grown-up and there was a real, grown-up war on around me. There was something mosquito-like flying across the sky and cotton puffs of artillery, explosions reverberating like groaning giants. People said that the Germans were bombing Wilno. I was sitting by the Wilenka and gazing into the gully of the valley which surrounds the misty rubble of the city to the south. I had been swimming in the river fifteen times and had turned blue, looking as helpless as a plucked goose. I was shaking and trembling from the cold, waiting for evening to come, for then I could don my armband. I would put the strip of gauze in my bag, put the blank six-shooter in my pocket, and go on patrol along the railroad tracks, which we had been assigned to protect from saboteurs.

And so, for me, the outbreak of that most horrible war was a sweltering day, a terribly blue sky, adventure-story emotions, the joy of playing hooky with permission, the sudden revelation that I was grown-up, that my friends and I had grown up.

The brief, barely perceptible, strange outbreak of the Soviet-Polish war on September 17, 1939. I recall the sound of gunfire, explosions, not very loud, commotion, flurries of action, all for a day or maybe two. Rumors, feverish news: the Boy Scouts were defending their position on Castle Mountain, or maybe Three-Cross Mountain; an army division was doing battle with Soviet soldiers; and as is always the case in Poland on such occasions, an officer had been seen to shoot himself so as not to be taken prisoner.

But I remember the dawn when I ran toward Wilno with my schoolmates through fields, bushes, and groves. We crept stealthily along, driven by some uncanny curiosity; we trembled, our teeth chattered, we couldn't get a word out. Then, suddenly, at the top of a hill where we'd stopped for a breath of air, we spotted them and they saw us too. In the heavy light of a reluctantly rising sun, by then an autumn sun wearied by the heat-wave summer, we could suddenly see the huge gully down below, its road white with dust, and a dark-green serpent of soldiers with sunburned faces winding its way toward us through the steep hills. The serpent slowly wound and unwound with magical, somnambulist movements which seemed to remind me of some other life, some previous incarnation; there was something majestic and even a bit ritual-like about that sight, something dream-like, something from a votive procession, something other-worldly, something from the Valley of Jehoshaphat; in a word, I had suddenly seen a stunning and dread-inspiring symbol of human existence, or a sign of its extinction, and I was overcome by a strange, sudden fear which also seized the boys with me and the railroad workers who were on their way to work in Wilno, carrying their little wooden boxes, and preceded by frightened rabbits, foxes, and badgers, we all began running away as fast as our legs would carry us, and we ran with piercing pains until we had to rest by the tracks, on the embankment, a steep embankment covered with sunburned grass, whose silvery tracks were as taut as guitar strings.

But scarcely had we begun to get our breath there by the tracks when we were overtaken by men on horseback, wearing dark-green uniforms and round, not very clean caps, Nagan revolvers in their hands. They surrounded us and began charging us on their horses, whose hooves ground against the sharp, oil-streaked gravel. The riders shouted, their voices wild with restraint; the railroad workers put their hands up, and for the first time in my life I saw people surrender. The horses snorted, a yellow-white foam splashing from either side of their bits. The railroad workers sounded plaintive as they answered questions, and we went whirling down the middle of the tracks, pressed on every side by Asiatic invaders. I could see their faces every so often, ordinary male faces, except a little frightened, hysterical, red from the sun and their exertions. Then all of a sudden they began to twist and turn, reining their horses, then dashed through the clefts, gullies, and hills to rejoin the others, that army from Asia lazily, sleepily inundating this poor Europe of ours.

Then came a few weeks of Soviet occupation. Encampments of soldiers, tents, campfires, the watering of the horses, wheezing accordions, gray people seeming oddly old. And the ever-present smell of canvas, tar, and poverty. Patrols walking down the middle of the street out of fear of the capitalist natives and White Poles. The wives of the occupation officers dressing for the theater in the nightgowns they'd just purchased here.

Another earthquake, like another war. The Russians were giving Wilno to Lithuania, still independent, still democratic. That turning point in history took place on the sly, out of sight, at night. At first there was a lot of talk about it, guesses, assumptions, rumors, and then suddenly one morning enormous Lithuanian policemen began appearing all over the city wearing dark-blue coats and uniforms with red lapels, and high blue-and-red caps on their heads. The street immediately nicknamed them *kalakutasy*, from the Lithuanian word for turkeys. Along with the police, a Lithuanian bureaucracy began to penetrate the city. There were a good number of well-fed men of peasant appearance wearing herringbone topcoats with a special weave, so that you could always tell a Lithuanian immediately by his coat. They also wore jodhpurs that were none too elegant and soft boots rolled at the ankles, which were called loose stockings. They all looked like well-to-do peasants from the provinces, or once-wealthy farmers from the backwaters.

But even more clearly than that Lithuanian incursion into Wilno, I remember the Lithuanian currency, the *lit*, silver money with stupendous buying power. Money that was like diamonds, the pot of gold at the end of the rainbow. Under the Russians our poor city had long since forgotten what money with buying power meant. For that reason those silver *lits* were awe-inspiring, breathtaking. You probably could have bought a horse for a silver *lit*. I remember only that a railroad ticket good for a month between the Colony and Wilno cost around two *lits*. That was a fortune, an expense my grandparents could not afford. That being so, for the entire school year under the Lithuanians, I would walk to high school, coming to know all the beauties of the village roads, the roads on the outskirts of the city, the high roads, and the streets in every season.

Of that Polish-Lithuanian war—because there was such a war, though one rather reminiscent of quarrels between neighboring villages—anyway, of that war I remember only the excellent Lithuanian butter, our oppressors' excellent hams, and the Palm Beach cigarettes, which I sold for a while and also smoked on the sly, enjoying their exotic, heavenly flavor, which seemed to contain some promise, some prophecy, some proposal, to us fourteen-year-olds, serious and exhausted with the charisma of history, sprinkled with the holy water of patriotic mission.

And then came the Soviet-Lithuanian war, imperceptible, unnoticed, and unrecorded by any scholarly apparatus. I've completely forgotten the outbreak of that war. I have some confused memory of Lithuanians taking flight, desperate acts, mad assassination attempts. But I am unable to put any of that into specific form and recall only that one day the farcical police and the peasant bureaucrats vanished, that the symbol of Lithuania went underground, and the Jagiellonian columns—the other seal, sign, and symbol of the Lithuanian state—were carefully hidden away somewhere. And once again there were encampments of Soviet soldiers, campfires, wheezing accordions, and gray people who seemed oddly old. And the ever-present smell of canvas, tar, and poverty.

But now the Soviet state loomed up in all its imperial enormity out of the chaos of that provincial war. A great many Soviet bureaucratic institutions began popping up like mushrooms after war's rain of suffering. And collaboration began to occur as well, timid at first, but bolder and more self-confident all the time. Everything was covered with a Lithuanian-Russian veneer and seemed to take on the luster of a Soviet Lithuanian republic, but beneath the surface, Polish, Jewish, Byelorussian life was crackling, impudent, rebellious, independent, even though by then everyone was being dragged to meetings, marches, and reading rooms full of Communist propaganda. But here and there a few grown-ups recalled their prewar leftist genealogy and began approaching the Soviet authorities on familiar terms. Day and night the theaters ran films about the revolution and the nightmares of life in gentry Poland.

A great change took place in my life—after years of mental anguish and wounded self-esteem, I had at last begun to grow. Quite out of the blue I shot up in height, now taller than the girl I loved, and taller than a few of my schoolmates, who every so often would pound me with impunity, and almost as tall as those shady types, those swindlers, crooks who governed, abused, and despised the Wilno Colony.

June 22, 1941. My birthday. I began my sixteenth lap around the sun. But planes had been zooming over Wilno since the morning, the sky clear and sunny, as it usually is in the summertime there. Only a few of the planes were zooming—the ones with the slender shapes, quick, agile, their markings black crosses. But those poor planes with the red stars, heavy and graceless as hens, flew headlong toward the ground and smashed to smithereens in clouds of black smoke on the hills outside Wilno. A new war had begun, the German-Soviet war.

We slept lightly that night, half sitting up, our eyes not fully closed. Our bags were right at hand, packed for a long journey, an uncertain fate, a terrible deportation to Siberia. The NKVD had been deporting Poles, and not only Poles, at a rapid clip for a few weeks now. People were plucked like crabs from the entire Wilno area, from the Dzwina to Nowogrodek, and then packed in cattle cars and shipped east, into the depths of Asia. Half awake, half asleep, we waited for our turn every night. I lay by an open window, one jump away from the thick lilac, currant, and raspberry bushes, and I could run through those bushes, fences, and forests all the way to the North Pole. Trouble usually happened at night and was preceded by the throaty drone of Soviet trucks, old-fashioned, unwieldy, always breaking down and always being fixed; trucks which were diligent in transporting people to the railway platforms, where they were awaited by wire-enclosed cattle cars, old hands that had already seen legendary Siberia a number of times.

And so, that new war erupted when deportation was at its height, at the most trying moment for Wilno's Poles, and that war too broke out at dawn, bringing sudden relief like a July downpour. The battle in the scorching sky was going poorly for the Russians, while the entire Soviet bureaucracy that had invaded Lithuania and the Wilno area was now in flight on the roads and footpaths, taking shortcuts across the fields. The officers' wives and children, the political instructors, and the commissars who had already managed to bleed goodly amounts from the Lithuanians, the White Poles, the Jews, and whoever else was at hand were now fleeing eastward in panic. And so those riffraff hightailed it, pushing handcarts, dragging sacks, collapsing under the weight of meaningless furniture; watched closely, with pleasure and applause, by a crowd of locals whom they hadn't had time to deport to Vorkuta, Kolyma, and Magadan. That crowd was glad to applaud their oppressors' haste even as Hitler's tanks could be heard somewhere on the far side of Wilno.

I remember the last train which, stopping and starting, blundered through the Wilno Colony to the east, to "Rashya," their salvation. A black antlike mass of people clung to the train. Commissars, political instructors, secretaries, teachers of atheism, policemen, sweat-covered women, a whole mass of them on the roofs, hanging from the steps, clutching the handrails and window frames. And we, who had not yet been deported and who might never have to undergo deportation, stood dressed in our Sunday best on the platform and gazed upon the humiliation and ruination of the occupier, and we smiled festively, because in the Upper Colony the bell in our church was ringing, calling us to High Mass. We were carefree as we watched our recent persecutors suffer, fall, and meet with a sudden and terrible punishment. We followed that train with tranquil, tearless eyes, and then, on the bottom step of the last car, we spotted a commissar wearing a leather cap and a leather jacket despite the heat, because that was how a real commissar dressed. And that one-hundred-percent-pure commissar, slowly receding with that final train, hung from the handrail with one hand while raising the other to point a fist in our direction. We could see his eyes burning with hatred and his clenched fist aimed at us White Poles.

"Just you wait till you get a taste of Nazi occupation!"

That's what he yelled, or else that's what I to this day think he should have yelled. But what he probably really yelled, outshouting the clattering wheels, was:

"Just you wait, you motherfuckers! We'll be back!"

. . .

Next, the Polish-German, actually, the Wilno-German, war
broke out. I was already a grown-up, because adulthood begins
at sixteen for the Germans, but no one was splitting any hairs at
that time and so you could be cannon fodder even if you were
younger. And thus, as a grown-up, I suffered all the harassments
and restrictions of a twofold occupation, that of the German
military and that of the Lithuanian administration.

What was it like? It was good. Jolly, romantic, a waterfall of
attractions. A few months of working on the railroad, then a short
spell in a labor camp, escape, hiding from the police, a job in
a military hospital in Nowa Wilejka, and constant caution despite
my good *Ausweis* because the Lithuanian police still had their
eye on me. And so, a little bit of the underground, a good dollop
of patriotism, a lot of cramming in the secret study groups, frequent little banquets, a raucous gramophone, girls from the Upper and Lower Colonies, love affairs, passionate loves, delirious
glimpses of a marvelous future, a terribly aggressive talent somewhere within, under the heart or the spleen, but a talent for
what? Bitter winters, hot summers, a little fear and a lot of excitement, a weapon, the Boy Scouts—modest and grandiloquent,
cosines and tangents, pretty classmates and a terrible, irresistible
desire for those girls, a terrible craving, an awful pressure, a red
mist in my eyes, sweet, fiery dreams, and an enormous, sky-high
hunger for love and sex, love and sex, love and sex.

Yes, the German occupation was beautiful. Beautiful because
it was my youth, my one and only youth, there won't be any
other. I know that people suffered, dropped dead of hunger, were
cut down by bullets. Maybe I went hungry too, maybe I suffered
too, but today all I remember is the sun as it was then, pure and
hot, and the sky so blue it made your eyes ache, and of course the
girls I chased over the mountains, through the forests, and in the
bushes by the river. It was beautiful, the German occupation.

And, finally, the last outbreak of war—so far—that I've been
through in my life. July 1944. The war between the Home Army

and the NKVD. It broke out unexpectedly, on the qt, and went unnoticed by many. The French, the English, and the Americans haven't heard of it to this day, even though it was over almost forty years ago. But I've already described the beginning of that war earlier, when I gave my account of Operation Wilno, so-called, the Home Army's attempt to rise up against the Germans in Wilno.

You remember that scorching afternoon of July 6 or 7, 1944, but it must have been the sixth, that wooded hillside near the Wilno Colony, and the silhouettes, not quite peasants, not quite soldiers, emerging one by one from the shady edge of the forest, all of them flooded in the heavy, hot light of a setting July sun.

That was how it began, and for me it lasted until May 1945. Dreary, dangerous, the atmosphere going from bad to worse. There was one roundup of partisans after the other, lines of KGB combing the Wilno area from one shore to the other, through the meadows, streams, forests, villages, and backwaters. Every last little bush run through by bayonets, every well sounded with a grappling hook, every haystack poked with sharp rifle brushes. The only place to hide was in heaven or in hell. And there were new deportations too. After a three-year interruption. Stash D., my friend and schoolmate in the underground study class, was sent to Vorkuta for belonging to the Home Army during the German occupation. In the eyes of the Wilno KGB, the Home Army were collaborators.

But even amid that violence, those desperate attempts to hide, escapes, gunshot after gunshot, killings and self-inflicted wounds, atrocities and spectral poverty, animal fear and human despair— even among those images I see myself in a truly golden field of rye stubble as my schoolmates, the village girls, and I threshed the grain in the farm's threshing machine, and, while threshing and choking on the asphalt-black dust, we stole feels of those blond-haired girls and made dates to spend the night with them in the hay in the big barn, where we'd get drunk on strong home brew. I can see the ground frozen in the early winter of '44–'45, I can hear the ice, thin as glass, crackling underfoot; a manor house, its bright window, women's heads, an oil lamp, a fire warbling in the stove, a child carried in arms, and someone humming softly. Something from Grottger, a little bit of Miss Maria Rodziewicz, and a lot of Mickiewicz. The golden thread of Polish dreams, Polish memory, Polish phantasms.

No, no sweetness, charms, and lovely sighs can be wrung from this material. Those were eight months of partisan life with death right by your side. A death that was drunken, wild, and blind.

And then the leap to pacifism. A very deep immersion in the pacifist ocean of inward numbness and moral hysteria. Could that have been the reason behind the reasons for all my deviations during my own personal five-year plan at the beginning of the fifties?

I've been reading the diary entries for September 1939 written by a twenty-year-old soldier who was later interned in a camp in Lithuania and then of course deported to Russia in 1940, when the Red Army took Lithuania. In June of the following year, Polish soldiers found themselves in a camp near Murmansk, and one entry by the author, Officer Cadet J. K. Umiastowski (killed a few years later at Monte Cassino), ran as follows:

One night we saw a sorry spectacle. We were woken by a great noise and we ran out of the barracks to see what was happening. Some sort of chase was under way on the hills above our camp. The Muscovites were half undressed, as if they'd jumped out of bed, and were running along the crest of the hill. They shouted and pointed, evidently chasing someone. But then, why weren't they shooting? The night was clear and we soon caught sight of the fugitive. It was an awkward young reindeer. It was running down toward the valley and trying to make its way to the opposite slope, but its path had already been cut off. It was about to turn back, but there was another group of pursuers behind it by then. It leapt into the lake and swam, snorting loudly, out to the middle. Its small head could be seen above the surface of the water. Unfortunately, it swam slowly and the pursuers had already managed to run around to the other side of the small lake, where they waited self-confidently, having brought a dog along. The reindeer came out of the water and looked helplessly around. It was staggering on its feet and no longer had the strength to run away. But it did not get much time to rest, for its pursuers began approaching and it had to go back into the water. It began returning to the shore it had just left, even though there were Muscovites waiting there as well, but clearly the reindeer was more afraid of the dog; it was primarily the dog it was fleeing. This time it swam very slowly, the water splashing into its nostrils. It reached the shore and was on the ground by the time the Muscovites had raced up to it. This made us very sad. There was nothing else to see, we went back into the barracks. Here, in the north of Russia, where one camp can be seen from the guard towers of its neighbor, and where people come only as prisoners, everyone is a prisoner. There was one free creature and they had to grab it, as if out of envy that it was free. Does a man who is not free really have to hate and destroy even the slightest sign of freedom? [*Through the Land of Bondage*]

17

Breakdown, collapse, annihilation. I haven't been doing anything for the last few weeks. I walk around, I look on the world with a bleary eye, and I listen. I hear my own words, ideas, aphorisms everywhere. But those are not echoes of me, no one repeats my bon mots, no one is staging my concepts. Everyone keeps repeating the same thing, we are all repeating ourselves. We are reminiscent of cats, all those roof cats, lap cats, cellar cats, brown, black, spotted cats, cats which seem to differ a bit but which essentially are all the same, identical, cut from the same cloth. They resemble one another in looks and habits, in tameness and wildness, in the rhythm of their movements and in the dictates of their souls.

Biological magma. An immense mass of living cells. An ocean of flesh and bone. When did it seem to me that I was one of a kind? Unique in the universe. From heaven to hell. Why wasn't I warned? I would have made efforts not to be born.

Breakdown, collapse, annihilation. I've been the cause of my own breakdown, collapse, and annihilation many times. But that wasn't the same thing. Those other acts turned out to be romantic gestures, attitudinal buffoonery, shows of festive emotion. Now a real breakdown has come out of nowhere. Unfeigned collapse. Genuine annihilation.

I am in no condition to record everything that is happening around me. I don't have the patience, I don't have the desire, I don't have the faith. Something's been happening here in my country for a year now. Something hideous or splendid. Childbirth or death throes. The coming of God or the opening of the gates of hell.

Breakdown, collapse, annihilation. I cannot write prose, I don't feel like writing prose, I don't believe in prose. My only reason for living is to satisfy myself that what I have written was written by others before me or is being written at this moment, this passing moment, or will be written in a month or thirty years. Uproar. Turmoil. A blizzard of words. A flood of discoveries discovered monotonously and already discovered many times over since the world began.

And I'm dragging this book around by the hair like a corpse. These pages, this humiliating repeat of a repeat, these yellow pages embroidered with my handwriting, I hate them with all my might. I try to push forward this weight of words worn smooth by use. They rustle, stir, rasp, clink, and clank. To jam myself. To bury myself. To close the lid. A lid of words, the embryos of nouns. The carcasses of adjectives.

The city hove into view around a bend; distant but clearly visible through patches of alder. Adam stopped chewing for a moment, and with his kielbasa in his outstretched hand, he stared vacantly ahead, then quickly swallowed his saliva and shouted into the back of the train car: "I swear to God it's Lublin!"

"Why bother me about it, I couldn't care less," said Labusiewicz with a grimace, wiping his greasy fingers on a crumpled newspaper.

"God's name shouldn't be used in vain," said Miss Sobolewska from her throne in the corner. "My cousin of sacred memory, Ksawus Pociejko, was married in that city."

As the train pulled into the station, its brakes squealing, the passengers clustered by the doors. Only Miss Sobolewska remained among the rubber plants, her restraint underscoring her intellectual independence.

Teodor and Adam threw their knapsacks made from real sacks over their shoulders, slung their coats over their arms, and moved toward the door. Seated, his thumbs in his suspenders, Labusiewicz shook his head and said: "Pretty town."

"You could at least put on your jacket," muttered Korejwow, who was still sulking.

Labusiewicz's brows went up vehemently and he cast Korejwow a withering glance.

The train came to a halt.

Men in civilian dress with rifles on their backs were walking back and forth along the platform.

"Look, look," shouted Adam. "Do you see, that one's wearing a red-and-white armband."

"Big deal, there's the officer," said the know-it-all Labusiewicz, pointing a finger.

And, indeed, a captain in an unbuttoned uniform stood beneath the clock, smoking a cigarette and running his weary eyes along the train that had just arrived.

"There's a Polish eagle on his cap," said Adam in surprise.

Teodor tapped Adam on the shoulder. "All right, old man, let's get off."

"What? What?" said Labusiewicz, astounded. "Are you running away?"

"We'll be traveling on alone," shouted Teodor from the platform. "We have some business of our own."

"Stay with us. It's always more fun together. Nobody knows what's going to come of this, maybe we'll be going back home soon; after all, the war isn't over yet," said Labusiewicz heatedly, but then immediately thought better of it and cast a suspicious eye about him. The officer by the clock had finished his cigarette and ground it out with his heel.

"Goodbye, goodbye," said Adam with a bow from the platform. "Happy holidays . . ."

"What holidays, what nonsense is that." Remaining in the

shade of the wilting rubber plants, Miss Sobolewska had taken offense.

The street smelled of fresh vegetation and feather quilts, both warmed by the sun. The crooked signs, the red bedding hung out the window to air, and the mustached men busy with their brooms in front of the houses all reminded Teodor of his native city. A flock of blue pigeons whirred above the street.

They walked at a slow and leisurely pace. They could feel a soft dampness under the sacks on their backs, where their shirts had been sweated through.

"Do you remember the address?" asked Teodor.

"What a question," snorted Adam.

All the same, at the intersection of two narrow lanes, Adam walked over to a mustached man wearing an apron of coarse gray material. Adam saluted nonchalantly, bringing two fingers to the grease-stained brim of his forage cap, and inquired about the store they were seeking. The mustached man leaned heavily on his broom and regarded them for a moment with indifferent curiosity.

"Where you here from?"

"Pinsk," said Adam casually, like a man back from distant Africa.

"Ho ho," said the man with the mustache, shaking his head in respect, and then he began providing complicated directions.

It was a small store, squeezed between two old houses.

Bored flies slithered across stacks of cheese in the store window.

A woman wearing an enormous brooch stood behind the counter.

"We'd like to speak with Mr. Sobiszczak," said Adam without removing his cap.

"He's not home, he's at work," said the woman sleepily, wiping beads of sweat from her broad forehead with the palm of her hand.

"We're friends," continued Adam undeterred. "We have instructions from Pinsk. We arrived from Pinsk today."

The woman looked at them closely for a moment, then again lowered her eyelids and with a sleepy, automatic gesture raised the countertop. They went behind the counter and up a small set of stairs to a room surprisingly large and bright.

"Wiktor," said the woman softly.

A barefoot man rose from bed, his mouth wide open in a yawn.

"They're here from Pinsk," she added, indicating Teodor and Adam with her eyes; then she quietly withdrew and returned to the store.

The man sat at a table and stared expectantly at his bare feet extended before him. Adam took off his cap and removed a small scroll of paper from inside the leather lining. He unscrolled it and handed it to the barefoot man, who read it once, then once again, checked the signature, then looked up at Adam.

"So, let's introduce ourselves," he said with a faint smile. "I'm Sobiszczak." They all shook hands and then sat down on stools Sobiszczak drew over.

"What can I do for you gentlemen?" asked Sobiszczak, rubbing a large puddle of milk on the table with his finger.

"Put us in contact with a detachment," said Teodor quickly. "That's all we're asking."

Adam nodded in approval.

"Ooh, that's not so easy," said Sobiszczak, raising his brows and tilting his head. "The boys are all hiding out now, there's no regular detachments. We're in hot water here. This isn't Pinsk. Things are tough. We have to rebuild our network in the field."

"The only reason we came here was to keep on fighting!" hissed Teodor, flushed with anger.

"Easy does it, you could have fought in Pinsk too. Things aren't that easy here. I can direct you to where they're hiding. They're doing some work there too."

"What kind?"

"Curious, aren't you?" said Sobiszczak with a smile. "You know—passing sentences, a couple of assassinations, and anyone who falls into their hands gets it bang in the head."

"That's not for us," said Teodor. "We want to join a regular detachment, not some network."

Adam cleared his throat, squirming on his stool.

"So what are you going to do, then?" asked Sobiszczak, rubbing the instep of his right foot with his left.

"We have another contact in Warsaw."

"Thank God for that," said Sobiszczak, his head beginning to sway.

The park was quiet. They lay down on the luxuriant grass beneath an old spreading chestnut tree beside a crudely painted sign: KEEP OFF THE GRASS. A couple of shirtless workers were setting up a platform on the small, gravelly square by the fountain. Divisions of starlings were squalling in the treetops. Girls and boys wearing knapsacks strolled down the tree-lined paths. Car motors barked impatiently out past the far side of the park.

Teodor untied his sack and pulled out his immortal kielbasa. He gnawed it in silence, chewing the stringy meat slowly. The workers muttered complaints as they hammered strong five-inch nails into the thick boards. It was pleasant in the shade. Squat horseflies buzzed above their heads, the large tops of the yellow sow thistle tossed slightly in the faint breeze.

"Why go to Warsaw?" said Adam all of a sudden. "Let's go into hiding here and take our time about picking them off one by one."

"You can stay, I'm moving on. Assassinating people's not what I had in mind."

"What do you mean, assassinating people? It's practically the same as in a regular detachment."

"No. In a detachment you don't shoot people from around the corner."

"Come on," said Adam, bridling.

"If only they hadn't ordered us to set up a network in the field and form a detachment from it. That's no job for us," said Teodor, thinking aloud. "They have plenty of half-dead old majors for that."

"But listen," said Adam modestly, playing with a thistle he'd picked, "we could have started a detachment of our own by now.

We've had some experience," he drawled modestly. "A little more than the guys here. It wouldn't be so bad to do a little marching without being watched over by a bunch of lousy colonels. A small detachment, a hundred men or so, what do you think?" he said, blinking his eyes.

"Could be," said Teodor reticently, not wishing to betray that he too had been nourishing a similar plan. "In the end we did do something and we can prove it too. We've been out with a detachment in difficult terrain."

"Anyway, as long as they don't park us behind some desk," said Adam with a sigh. "They might do that because they're short on specialists."

Teodor did not reply, but there was a nearly imperceptible assent in his silence. Done nailing the platform together, the workers gathered up their tools and set off down the tree-lined path toward the exit, dragging their feet. A gang of kids immediately took possession of the deserted platform, the boards rumbling hollowly beneath their little shoes.

Teodor closed his eyes. Still, he could feel a stray beam of sunlight tickling his sore red eyelids. From time to time a strong gust of wind would sweep past overhead, rustling the treetops like a mountain stream.

The hours dragged by as if asphyxiated by the sweltering heat. Only when the afternoon was over did the military band arrive and take seats in front of the platform. The first waltz attracted the little children, the first girls appeared during the polka, and when the first tango got going (the girls were already leaping about with each other on the platform), crowds of people began pouring into the park. The first to jump up onto the platform was a young lieutenant with a mass of curly hair tumbling out from his cap. He marked time with his feet, clapped his hands, and asked the girl closest to him to dance. Soon the boards were bending under the weight of about thirty couples, each passionately dancing their own version of a new tango which the military band had brought with them from some faraway place.

A thin railroad worker in a grimy four-cornered cap was the

first to start dancing on the gravel paths. In the orange light of the setting sun the park and the throng of dancers were reminiscent of a crowd scene in a trashy opera.

Teodor grimaced as he pulled on his boots, exhaling loudly each time, though the boots went on easily enough. With some interest Adam's eyes followed a slender girl in a light-blue dress who was nearly being swung up into the air by an unshaven soldier with a slanting eagle on his cap.

Every so often the musicians would break, and holding the damp buckets in both hands, they'd take long, greedy drinks of the water someone had brought them. At the far end of the park the first fireworks were set off. They exploded in red against the blue sky and red tears fell slowly to the ground.

A cry of "Aaaah!" ran through the crowd. The dancing ceased for a moment and all eyes were on the sky.

When the rocket died out among the now darkening chestnut trees, the band struck up a *kujawiak*. The self-possessed young lieutenant with the tumbling hair began his own version of a squatting Ukrainian dance around his partner, to the hearty applause of the spectators crowding around the platform.

"To victory!" roared a Polish platoon leader in Russian. He was standing in a group of Soviet soldiers and struggling with his mighty pistol. Finally, he got it to work and fired its entire magazine up at the empty sky, seconded by a soldier in a fur cap who fired a long burst at the tops of the chestnut trees.

The curly-haired lieutenant rose from his squat and, waving a sweaty hand, shouted in Russian from the platform: "What are you shooting for? It's better over here. There's girls here." He pointed to a wreath of girls behind the band.

The planks on the platform were soon cracking and people began moving to the gravel paths and the lush, thistle-laced grass. To the accompaniment of the band, people began singing, some in Polish, some in Russian. The ground groaned under the hundreds of feet.

"The war's over!" shouted someone in joy from the crowd,

suddenly recalling that strangely joyful and nearly unbelievable news.

"Over, over!" cried the lieutenant, and slapped his boot tops with such gusto that the people dancing near him covered their ears.

They had a second contact in Marynina. It cost them time and trouble to find the little house whose address they had been given. The house was more like a storehouse of boards, plywood, cardboard, and pieces of sheet metal thrown together. A very substantial-looking and disproportionately large chimney jutted from the roof. A microscopic garden was drowned in vegetables. Anemic that year, the tomato plants drooped dolefully on the yellow ribbons which fastened them to the carefully carved stakes.

They spent a while making a show of grappling with the lopsided front gate, but no one came out to meet them. It was only inside the cramped quarters that they found a half-undressed man with a child in his arms. Another child was in the corner sucking on an enormous carrot.

"Are you Mr. Lokuciewski?" asked Teodor.

"I am," said the man, wiping some drool from the child's chin with a dark finger.

As he had in Lublin, Adam removed their letter of recommendation from his cap. Lokuciewski barely glanced at it.

"Sit down, please," he said, with a look toward some rickety stools.

When they had sat down, laying their coats on the ground beside them, Lokuciewski helped the child from his lap and asked: "Do you have any news?"

Teodor swallowed his saliva (his throat was dry in the sweltering heat). "We need your help in making contact with a detachment."

Lokuciewski smiled. "You seem in a hurry."

"That's what we came here for."

"Straight to me?"

"No, first we went to Sobiszczak in Lublin."

"Aah, Sobiszczak," said Lokuciewski with a dismissive wave of the hand.

"What about him?" asked Teodor.

"Nothing. He's a crook and a swindler."

"What does that mean?"

"He pretends to be a big shot, but he's full of it. He's out for money—"

"But back to us," interrupted Teodor impatiently. "We'd like to join up with a regular detachment as quickly as possible."

"But where do you start looking?" said Lokuciewski, raising his thinning eyebrows.

"What do you mean?" said Teodor with excitement. "What's your assignment here?"

Rolling himself a cigarette, Lokuciewski made no reply. In the corner the children were fighting over the half-gnawed carrot. A fly buzzed industriously beneath the oil lamp on the wall.

"I can only put you in contact with my former commanding officer," Lokuciewski said finally, licking the cigarette paper with his whitish tongue.

"Where is he?"

"He lives in Konstancin. He bought himself a nice villa during the war."

For a long time they did not say a single word to each other as they walked down the empty sandy lane hemmed in by dilapidated fences. Adam plucked a heavy spray of blossoms from a lilac bush hanging over a fence and stuck it in the lapel of what had been his army jacket. A dry cloud of dust rose heavily from their feet. They went past a wide curving pond that was drying up, where muddy ducks swam. The green of the grass was especially intense by the water. There was a whiff of what seemed a distant chill in the air.

"A fine kettle of fish, hey, buddy," said Teodor, shaking his head.

"Bah!" was Adam's laconic summation.

It was long past noon when they slogged into Warsaw. Adam removed his boots on a pontoon by the bridge and lowered his feet into the Vistula. Teodor followed his example. The sun made them squint. On the other side of the river they saw the corpses of buildings with dirty smoke floating above them, as if the dead were still dying. The sand haulers were ferrying people across the river in heavy boats, pushing against their long poles. By Saxon Hill the surface of the water was still and gleamed dully like a sheet of platinum.

Intently hitching up his pants, Adam asked casually, as if it were a mere detail: "So, should we keep going? I have relatives in Krakow."

It was already very dark and cold when they clambered onto the roof of the train departing at midnight for Krakow. There were a few workers and a boy wearing a high-school cap on the roof with them. Adam displayed great resourcefulness, tying himself to an air pipe on the roof. The high-school student was fidgeting recklessly right by the edge of the roof.

Dimly lit, the station buzzed with hundreds of voices. Up ahead, locomotives bellowed.

At midnight on the dot the train pulled out, heading south.

They fell fast asleep, even though the sharp wind went right through their coats. Only the next morning did one of the workers notice that the high-school student was missing. It was obvious that he'd fallen off while asleep. The workers cursed the world and the war while tying themselves tighter to the air pipes.

Heavy with sleep and thus ill-tempered, Adam gagged on the wind and muttered: "Anyway, bread'll be cheaper there."

One of the workers heard what Adam had muttered. "And who might you be, sonny?" the worker asked, getting up onto his hands and knees, holding his cap on tightly against the wind with one hand.

"Back to sleep, buddy," replied Adam. "Better watch out you don't get knocked off too."

The workers spat over the side for a while and then, hunched over, they pressed themselves to the roof of the train. The stars were fading.

In the morning the train came to a stop in front of a tunnel. That was as far as it was going. They would have to walk a good mile over the mountain above the ruined tunnel to the next train, which was supposed to be waiting for the passengers at the exit of the tunnel.

Frozen, they climbed down from the roof and stumbled stiff-legged along the railroad ties. The workers, who had clearly been that way before, plunged ahead at full speed, wanting to secure good places on the train. The one who had accosted Adam was capless. The wind must have blown his hat off as the train took a sharp corner.

A long line of passengers streamed through a sparse copse. The men were sweating as they carried their heavy suitcases tied with cord, while the women, antlike, industrious, dragged their bundles along in their checkered shawls.

Teodor and Adam straggled slowly along, tearing off resinous shoots of young pine. The sun was growing scorching hot. They passed two well-dressed men bent to the ground beneath the weight of their suitcases.

"My brother-in-law brought three typewriters in from Opole, nice new ones. Valuable things are just lying around for the taking," said the smaller of the two, who was wearing tight, checkered pants. He had to trot to keep up with the taller one.

A flock of crows rose cawing somewhere behind them and went fluttering over the heads of the bent-backed crowd. A thick, heavy dust entered their mouths and stopped up their noses.

They must have covered three-quarters of the way when there was some jam-up and confusion at the head of the line. Women screamed, a shot rang out, a capless soldier ran toward the back of the line, the rifle on its burlap strap knocking wildly against his back. A couple of men were thrust aside, the weight of their bodies breaking branches. The young pines began rippling as if a herd of boar were blindly running away from the path.

Adam squinted anxiously once, twice to the side, then glanced over at Teodor, who was clutching his coat under his arm as he walked at an even pace toward a knot of people surrounded by men in semi-military dress, their weapons at the ready.

"We're on your side," groaned the small man in the checkered pants.

The assailants segregated the people they were detaining. A man in a military trenchcoat wearing a religious medal on his chest herded the women with the bundles to one side of the road. With trembling hands the men extracted their papers from their pockets. After being disarmed, two officers were escorted off into the dry pine woods.

Teodor and Adam stood in the group of groaning men. A kid wearing a German field cap adorned with a Polish eagle nudged Teodor in the back with the barrel of his Russian Pepesha submachine gun.

"You, let's see your papers," he said.

Teodor turned around slowly, his eyes seemingly vacant as he spoke, each word costing him effort: "You should be a little more careful, you shitass, or I'll show you what's what."

"What the hell is that son of a bitch talking about," bellowed the man with the medal, running over to Teodor. In dismay the boy with the Pepesha was inanely marking time with his feet.

"Easy does it, friend, easy with the rough talk," drawled Teodor, squinting at the man with the medal.

"Shut up, you motherfucker, I'll teach you respect for partisans."

"You asshole, you were still selling bacon when I was in the forest," said Teodor, enraged now.

But by then the man with the medal had sprung over to him and punched him with all his might between the eyes. Teodor went sprawling full-length on the trampled moss. Adam humbly pulled his repatriation certificate from his pocket.

"Are you Party?" asked the man with the medal.

"Come on," said Adam, riled.

Smearing the blood from his broken nose over his face, Teodor rose from the ground. His legs were shaky as he picked up his sack and coat, which had tumbled from his hands.

"Ha ha ha," brayed the man with the medal, looking at Teodor. "Was that what you were looking for?" Then, turning to Adam, he asked: "Was he repatriated too?"

"Yes, yes, he's with me," said Adam with restraint.

Meanwhile, the rest of the soldiers were working over the two officers and a few members of the Polish Socialist Party. At first they gave heartrending howls as they were beaten, but then they fell silent.

A dark-haired man holding a bamboo stick walked back and forth in front of the peasant women and (the apolitical) men herded together on the right side of the road. An enormous pistol made his gleaming belt sag. Tapping his forehead as he thought, he gave instructions to the detainees: "We're fighting Communism. We are your friends and defenders. We won't rest until the last Communist is hanging from a branch. Is that clear?"

"Yes, sir!" cried the man in the tight pants, from the heart of the crowd. "My brother-in-law's in the underground too, Major."

"I'm not a major, not a major," demurred the officer modestly. "I'm only a lieutenant."

"You'll make major!" shouted the man in the tight, checkered pants with sudden audacity.

The crowd stayed silent. Teodor stood to one side, holding his nose. The blood trickled down his hand and into his sleeve, forming a sticky mass on his elbow. Adam's jaw was working hard, his teeth chattering. The reddish tops of the young pines swayed slightly in the light breeze.

The officers were eating the ribbons from their medals, and the socialists, their faces mangled, were chewing their Party cards. They were all squatting by a dry pine tree, guarded by six men with English tommy guns.

The man in the trenchcoat ran over to the commanding officer to report.

"Everything's under control, sir."

"Did you check everyone out?"

"Yes, sir."

"Then give the order to march."

With quick, efficient kicks the partisans brought the prisoners to their feet and herded them off into the forest. The rest of the detachment marched off the remaining prisoners, leaving only the commanding officer and the man in the trenchcoat.

"Tell everyone you meet what you saw here," said the commanding officer to the crowd. "You've seen how we punish the people who sold Poland out. We'll see you in Warsaw when it's free."

"God be with you!" cried the man in the tight pants. When the officer and his aide had disappeared in the thicket of pine, the man glanced uncertainly at the silent crowd and muttered: "It's better to be polite with them. Did you see what they did to those other people?"

"They'll shoot them," groaned a woman carrying milk jugs.

They all were still standing in place, uncertain, helpless. Teodor was the first to regain his wits.

"Why stand around here after all that," he shouted, and began walking, still holding his nose. Passing a railroad worker, Teodor and Adam heard him say to a terrified old man: "You see, you see the beating they gave that one."

The more distance the travelers put between themselves and the scene of the trouble, the higher their spirits rose. They discussed the entire event in vocal detail. A bird dazed by the heat screeched in the bushes.

A gray-haired man in a long, homemade jacket slashed down the back sighed with relief: "Well, we came out of it all right."

The man in the tight pants was walking beside him. He and his tall friend were once again bent under the weight of their suitcases. He wiped the sweat from his brow and muttered: "What do you mean we came out all right? They're on our side, those people."

The train was waiting at the other end of the tunnel. Enveloped in steam, the locomotive puffed as it made ready to leave. Boys with bags bursting with bottles walked along the train hollering: "Lemonade, cold lemonade . . ."

The crowd stormed the train's narrow doors, but somehow without any great enthusiasm. The hot air shimmered above the sizzling tracks. Half-undressed people lay in the shade of sickly bushes by the embankment of the track, waiting for something, though it wasn't clear what.

"What fun, huh," said Adam when they had finally made their way into the airless train. Teodor sniffed through his swollen nose.

The fat owner, in his shirt-sleeves, held the glasses carefully up to the light. A slightly cross-eyed girl, clearly his daughter, sat behind the small counter where she worked as a cashier. She yawned as she read a book. The four men in the corner were already half drunk and spilling their beer on the table's paper covering. "What can I serve you?" asked the owner grandly from behind the bar.

"Two quarter liters of raw alcohol and something to nibble on," said Adam elegantly. Teodor said not a word, as if his vocal cords had been paralyzed.

They drank quickly, carelessly, and in fifteen minutes Teodor's feelings were stirred and he began to open his heart.

"Adam, the fucking thing is we've got to wait a little and get our bearings on everything. That Lokuciewski, he's a cunning one, isn't he? He says he's in touch with the Communist partisans and the Peasant Battalions. Who the hell knows who they all are. If I'd had my pistol with me, they'd already be saying a Mass for that guy in the trenchcoat. We've hit bottom, brother, what can you say." Teodor let his disheveled head hang morosely.

"I'm always saying we should bide our time," replied Adam, glad to pick up that subject. "We're in no hurry. We did our bit, and better than those little shits at the tunnel. We can take a little rest, travel west a ways," he said, thinking of the small man in the tight pants. "At least we can get ourselves some equipment, one way or the other."

Teodor made a gesture of resignation. "We'll probably go," he said, and spat with distaste, then took a swallow from his glass. Teodor began choking loudly, his eyes bulging, until Adam had to intervene, whacking him skillfully on the back of the neck with his open palm.

"Brrr . . . I haven't had a drink for a very long time," apologized Teodor, wiping his tearing eyes.

"And it might be easier to make a dash across the border in the west," whispered Adam.

Teodor's face hovered above the table. "My old friends will probably be coming to Poland soon too," he said, as if to himself. "Elka too."

"Elka too?" said Adam with interest. "Are you still going with her?"

Teodor hiccupped with emotion. "Going around her little finger."

Adam cast a caustic glance at Teodor's swollen nose and stubbly cheeks.

"You said she's got you around her little finger?"

"Uh-huh," confirmed Teodor, nodding sleepily. Then he straightened up and, swallowing heavily, continued his confidences.

"It's a rotten world, Adam. We've been fighting in the forest since we were eighteen. We risk our lives, and then some cunt leads you around by the nose. Sometimes, when they opened fire with machine guns, I'd think to myself: Now you'll catch one and it'll be all over. All over, you get me, all over. Then you want to jump up and run away because it's springtime, you know what I mean, springtime, and there's skylarks, and hepatica so damn blue with its floppy leaves. We risked our necks for the cause, for the cause, that's what they said everywhere, at home, in church, in the line, under fire. But now it turns out there's more than one cause. There's a lot of fucking causes," he said in a fury, hammering his fist against the fragile tabletop.

"Easy, easy," said Adam reassuringly. "People are looking."

"People, you say," said Teodor emotionally; "that means I can't cry? You know how old I am. You don't. I'm twenty-one," whimpered Teodor.

They were pretty well drunk when they scrambled onto the empty freight train passing slowly through the station. They chanced onto a car strewn with wood shavings in an advanced state of decay. A few weeks before, some clever guys had used those shavings to ease their journey, and since then that rotting luxury had made traveling more pleasant for hundreds of people.

With a drunkard's obstinacy, Teodor pushed through the shavings in pursuit of something known to him alone. When the train switched tracks, the car jerked so sharply that Teodor crashed inertly into a bony person sprawled in sleep.

"Who's that?" asked a voice, deep with sleep and slightly hoarse, from under a coat.

"I'm sorry," said Teodor, retreating, with his wretched sack dragging behind him.

A dry, bony head emerged from under the coat. Without rising (his blond hair glimmered distinctly in the clear moonlight), he spent a moment regarding the intruder closely; then, with sudden impatience, he burrowed back into his coat.

"There's another passenger on board," muttered Teodor, returning to Adam.

"It'll make the trip more lively. I heard the Bolsheviks have been raiding this line."

"No one's giving them any food here," said Teodor, laughing with a crooked grin and crumpling his sack into the most pillowlike shape possible.

They lay as close together as they could. The scorching days were followed by cold nights. The scenery outside was always the same: a pretzel moon at the top of a greenish sky, meager handfuls of stars at the far ends of the night. A plume of red sparks rippled over the roofs of the cars.

When the train was stopped by a semaphore at a station, they were woken by the clatter of feet by the side of their car. They rubbed their eyes sleepily. A narrow bayonet appeared in the doorway, followed by a head in a Soviet field cap.

Their minds cleared at once.

"Now we've had it," whispered Adam.

Two Soviet soldiers with bayonets fixed on their rifles had now clambered up into the car. They looked around and went like a shot to the men lying on the floor.

"Get up!" The command, in terse Russian, came from the one who had entered first.

They rose awkwardly from the shavings, with a dismal feeling of powerlessness. The first soldier issued another terse command in Russian, this one easier to understand: "Your watches!"

"We don't have any," said Teodor with a shrug.

Undeterred by that flat denial, the soldier carefully squeezed both of Teodor's and Adam's wrists, then reached automatically for their sacks. Adam tried to protest, but the soldier jabbed him efficiently in the chest with the butt end of his rifle, making Adam groan. Teodor made a gesture of surrender. The two soldiers began gutting the sacks with zest. Unwilling to watch, Teodor turned his head away and caught sight of the stranger's blond head jutting from the coat, clearly visible in the sickly light. Motionless, the man was watching the robbery.

The soldiers were clearly displeased by their search of the sacks, because the first one stood up straight and grabbed Teodor by the collar, clutching it in his powerful fist.

"Money?" asked the soldier laconically. Easy to tell he was a Kalmuck.

At that moment Teodor noticed that the blond man was slowly removing his coat, rising, and stretching.

The blond man's presence came as a surprise to the soldier, who seemed pleased by it. With a practiced gesture, he reached for the blond man's wrist. Freed from the soldier's hearty stranglehold, Teodor sighed with relief.

The blond man, however, began moving his shoulders up and down as if he was testing the stretch of his jacket, and then with a sudden punch to the teeth he knocked the unsuspecting soldier off his feet. The soldier somersaulted backward, his feet flailing desperately in the air for a moment as he went head over heels out the train door. The other soldier did not waste a moment. He leaped away from the sacks and dove into the darkness as if into water. The hem of his overcoat caught on a hook protruding from off the side of the car, leaving a ragged scrap of cloth fluttering in the air. His coat ripped to the collar, he scampered away under the cars.

The ruins were still fresh, untouched by any reconstruction, unlike those in Warsaw only in seeming less archaic. Newspapers with Goebbels's last speeches were strewn like autumn leaves along streets that were no more than mounds of rubble.

They stepped on shirts still in good condition, military jackets, family photographs, canned food less than half eaten, upside-down bowls, and puddle after identical puddle made by the spring rain. First Adam picked up a gleaming inlaid ceremonial sword, the blade of Damascene steel flashing blue. He tossed it away at the next corner, his interest caught by a broken typewriter, an interest that did not last for very long, for he was distracted by a pair of high SS boots that had miraculously survived intact.

The streets were empty. The grass had not yet had time to grow over the ruins. The air whirled with the stink of burning.

Finally they made their way to a small square. A building that had survived had been draped with bright banners and a strangely cheerful inscription in Russian: WE WON. Teodor came to a halt and stared at the words while trying to roll a cigarette. The soldier standing guard in front of the building kept rising comically on tiptoe while attempting to slice off an absurdly violet spray of lilac with his bayonet.

"Hey, guard, where's the Polish government around here?" shouted Adam in Russian.

The soldier calmly decorated his round full-dress cap with the violet spray and with a wave of his hand said: "Straight ahead!"

They followed his directions and continued straight ahead until they reached a building whose front had been sheared off. They spotted a few people inside, like bees in cells of wax, looting the litter-strewn cages of the rooms. Someone dashed nimbly past them with a battered bicycle frame over his shoulder. On one corner, as on dozens of others they had passed, they saw a gray-haired man wearing a red-and-white armband. This one was rummaging through a pile of rags with the barrel of a musket-like rifle.

"Are there any government offices around here?" asked Teodor.

"Government offices?" said the man pensively. "Government offices, you say?" he repeated, as if not trusting his otherwise excellent hearing. "Nothing like that around here."

"But there must be somebody allocating living quarters," snapped Teodor.

"You should have said so right off," replied the man with the rifle. "The housing office is on the first street on the left."

And, indeed, on the first street on the left they found the housing office, adorned with a mighty eagle, whose crown was as large as a pot, and some modest lettering beneath it. An unshaven man was sitting at a carved desk sorting socks that had rotted slightly. In one corner of the room was a light-blue safe, whose door was open a crack. The man at the desk looked intently at Adam and Teodor.

"Yeah?"

"We'd like a room."

After resting for an hour, they set off in search of Bahnhof-strasse. The district where the street was located had suffered relatively little destruction and was composed of identical row houses without a sliver of space going to waste between them. The district had been nearly entirely German and the apartments now bore outward decoration which reflected their inhabitants' enthusiasm. Those with middling enthusiasm had hung white sheets out the window, those with more enthusiasm had hastily stitched red-and-white flags from bedding, while the most enthusiastic had draped gigantic sheets of red cloth out their windows. The few empty windows indicated that their inhabitants were Poles or Soviet officers.

They rang the apartment doorbell briefly, politely. When the person inside had overcome his mental resistance, slid the peephole covering aside, and unbarricaded the door, they affected an air of weary, unassuming tourists.

"Was?" asked a middle-aged German woman with smoothly combed hair through the half-open door.

"Wohnung," explained Adam haughtily, with a Polish accent, thrusting the allocation order through the door.

Someone was coming up the stairs with a heavy tread.

The German woman began weeping bitterly, sprinkling the official document with tears. Adam, however, kept his foot unflinchingly in the door, not yielding an inch.

The blond man from the train appeared on the stairs. He held on to the banister with one hand, clutching the canvas strap of a field bag with the other. He paused impassively by the two men battling to enter the apartment, read the name cards on the door, then continued slowly up the stairs.

Finally they forced the door. Sobbing, the German woman showed them to a room with old-fashioned furniture—two beds covered with eiderdowns against a wall with hideous wallpaper.

"Haben sie Tochter?" asked Adam rakishly as the woman withdrew from the room. She rolled her eyes with indignation, looking upward at the sky, which did, after all, exist, a few stories above.

"Leave her alone, Adam," muttered Teodor, who did not wish to make a bad impression on their landlady.

The German woman disappeared into the depths of her cellarlike apartment, leaving behind only the fusty aroma of the sandsoap popular during the occupation.

Adam examined the old-fashioned room with pedantic thoroughness. He peeked behind the curtains, pulled the empty drawers from the bureau, then discovered a minute balcony lined with sickly nasturtiums.

They used a basin decorated with a few little painted flowers to wash up, then spent a long time drying themselves in front of a large mirror. Adam examined his profile with pleasure, first one side, then the other, smoothed the skin of his cheeks with his index finger, and again thrust his lower lip forward, thus enhancing his face with yet another noble feature. Finally, he scratched his ribs and glanced over at Teodor.

"Hey, you're a handsome guy," Teodor muttered, poised between malice and admiration.

Teodor bent closer to the mirror, though with a certain reluctance. A long, dry nose, pitch-black brows, large eyes, nondescript mouth. His scrupulously shaven cheeks glowed with a light-blue shadow. He turned reluctantly around.

Half undressed, they dragged chairs out onto the balcony and found comfortable spots facing the sun, which had just emerged from heavy cloud. There was a spreading linden surrounded by industrious humming beetles beneath their balcony. A German woman was pushing a baby carriage down the sidewalk, the child wailing.

Somewhere up above them someone was choking on quiet giggles. Slowly they raised their heads. One floor above and a little to one side, two adolescent girls were tittering in a window. Poking each other, they couldn't contain their laughter. Teodor was examining his clothes for anything that might be offensive, but everything was in order. Meanwhile, Adam was already making eyes at the girls, who accepted that small token of appreciation with uproarious delight. Adam blew them a kiss and the two of them blew a kiss back at once. Unable to believe his luck, he lowered his eyes and slapped his knee. The girls were still giggling.

"Some girls," he said with admiration.

At first Teodor seemed to be bristling with male readiness, but then, suddenly recalling the disaster on the train, he became somewhat crestfallen, stuck his nose into a nasturtium, and lost interest in all the enticements of that window.

But Adam didn't waste a minute. Assuming an aggressive posture in his chair, he asked the girls their names. Trudchen and

Greta, they were quick to reply. A limping dog ran dolefully across the street.

"Look at the breasts on the one on the left," whispered Adam, sighing deeply.

Teodor's head swayed in deprecation as he continued to stare dully at the cracked slabs of the sidewalk. A just-plucked geranium fluttered down from above. Adam made a courtly bow and raised the flower to his lips. The girls *ooh'd* and *aah'd* with admiration and pleasure. Keeping the flower by his nose, Adam began humming a sentimental tune, which he seemed to be making up as he went along. One of the girls was now sitting on the windowsill, her flowered silk skirt spilling softly onto the rough-textured wall.

"They'll be ready to go after five minutes of talk," whispered Adam with confidential braggadocio, indicating the laughing girl on the sill with his eyes.

Steering clear of the clouds, the sun slipped lower over the roofs of the buildings. Teodor was gnawing mechanically on a bitter nasturtium leaf. Down bedding was being aired on the balcony in the building across from them.

Unable to contain himself, Adam asked "*Kommen?*" pointing to the girls in the window.

The girls' heads bobbed in assent.

Adam brought his chair back to the room and rummaged through his overcoat pocket for the last of his zlotys. The faces in the window had disappeared at once, like the sun covered by clouds. From the balcony Teodor watched Adam getting ready.

"I'll just pop over for a minute. A little talk, a little fun can't hurt. And maybe they know something, they just might be useful," said Adam, justifying himself to Teodor.

"Why all the gab?" asked Teodor in a sleepy voice.

Adam slipped from the room a moment later. From the height of the balcony, Teodor had a clear view of him trotting to the stands where food was on sale. He walked away slowly, shame-facedly straightening his bulging jacket and not looking up at the balcony.

Teodor went back into the room and lay down on the bed,

which smelled of laundry starch. A ray of light slid along the mirror. He began thinking about their long journey and the mysterious man with the blond hair, who apparently lived in the same building they did. In the slow progress of his thoughts he was careful to bypass the stage of their journey between Lublin and Warsaw, where his tender heart had experienced new disenchantment. He felt a sudden loneliness in this strange and alien city. He had left his parents far behind and now he longed to be with his father, a gruff man of few words who had a passion for building radio sets. His eyes closed, Teodor could see his father hunched over a radio receiver that he had partially dismantled, a radio that brought voices of encouragement from London and America to distant Polesie. He could see his mother wearing spectacles, an aristocratic pretension (her eyesight was excellent), as she read a thick, dog-eared book. And he could see Elka. He had kissed Elka for the first time two years ago in a damp woods outside of town (while the Germans were pacifying Soviet partisans in the nearby marshes). They were supposedly out gathering acorns. She did not try to fight him off, and he kissed her carefully, as if she were an ikon. Half closing her eyes, she listened carefully, as if hearing a new song. He pressed her to him, then kissed her again, afraid to seek out the charms of which he was so licentiously aware. Surrendering, her interest roused, she settled herself on his legs (she sat on his lap because she did not want her skirt to get wet). The moss beside them gleamed with fresh moisture, wet ants were building a scaffolding of needles around a dessicated pine cone. She did not return his kisses. At one point he realized that this was not enough for him, but he did not dare reach out for more. He freed himself from her weight and rose laboriously from the ground, his entire left leg asleep. He began hopping comically in a circle, shaking the afflicted leg like a crippled rooster. Elka laughed, tears in her eyes. Then they set off for home, their arms draped lightly around each other. He entered his house whistling casually, as if he were just back from a boring film. His mother would not tolerate youthful romance. It had been established in advance that Teodor would marry at the age of thirty-four, just as his father had. His father had no definite opinion on the subject and Teodor suspected that the old man had never really noticed that he was married. He taught tow-haired Polesian children Polish grammar and then tinkered with his radios, dozens of which stood on the shelf, covered with dust, victims of developments in technology. Teodor was eighteen years old at the time but, unfortunately, his emotions were quite immature.

Late that evening Teodor was awakened by his friend's return. While the light was on, he dragged himself out of his rumpled bed and began to undress. Adam was dreamy, happy, and smacked his lips with pleasure as he pulled off his pants.

"Oh, what girls, what figures, I'm telling you. I took care of them both, just to be on the safe side." Sighing, he stretched until something cracked in his back. "Delicate little flowers, I'm telling you."

"What are they, Germans?" asked Teodor, matter-of-factly crawling under the eiderdown.

"Hm, let me see," said Adam, at a loss for a moment. "Actually, they're Volksdeutsch."

"Aha."

Adam crawled into bed and sighed as he turned off the light. "They could do things you never dreamed of."

They woke up rather late the next morning and were supposed to go out looking for work. Adam stormed the German woman's door and shoved his way to the bathroom, from which he returned pale and confused. As he pulled on his jacket, he lost his self-control and launched into a long litany of curses.

"What happened?" asked Teodor, concerned.

"Goddamn those lousy fucking Volksdeutsch whores," he snarled, passionately seeking more inventive curses.

"Yeah and so?" said Teodor impatiently.

"They gave me the clap," said Adam mournfully.

"Hm," responded Teodor philosophically.

. . .

Carrying a thin pad of forms in a looted briefcase, Teodor set off at once for the address he had been given. He knocked at a door on the third floor of a shell-pocked apartment house. The door was opened by a spectral man wearing a hat and a trenchcoat, an apparition reminiscent of a cheap detective novel.

"The office sent you. My name is Wierzchniak," he said happily. "Please come in."

Though the rooms were in a state of disarray, Teodor quickly realized that the apartment was quite opulent and well furnished.

With an official air, he sat down at a table, frowning as he searched his pockets for a pencil that would work on carbon paper (a copy to be made of each form). Then he gave a bureaucratic glance about the room and said: "All right, let's get it listed."

Wierzchniak removed his detective-novel hat, and obviously excited, he ran from one piece of furniture to the next, pointing out its uselessness or poor condition. Teodor impassively noted down all Wierzchniak's well-rehearsed words. A green necktie was hanging on a yellowing cactus.

"Two reproductions of paintings, a damaged table, a coffee service . . ." mumbled Teodor, filling in the blanks with his spit-moistened pencil. "And now the contents of the safe."

Wierzchniak opened the safe door with an expressive gesture to reveal a series of men's suits nicely arranged by color.

"Whew." Teodor whistled in admiration. "This is a good place you found."

"Well, I've had my eye on it for a long time," said Wierzchniak, lowering his head modestly.

"How many suits are in there?" asked Teodor, pencil in hand.

Wierzchniak ran lightly over to the table and bent confidentially close to Teodor. After clearing his throat, Wierzchniak said: "Listen, you're not going to get anything for yourself by listing things that way. I know a better way." Now his voice became ever so slightly patronizing. "There's eight suits. Four for you, the rest for me. Why list them at all? I'm being honest about all the rest, but there's no sense in listing the suits," he said, looking for his hat on the table and then placing it back on his head.

Teodor was confused; he felt as if someone were trying to convince him to fool around with one of his father's radios. He gnawed at his pencil, unsure what to do.

"What's there to think about. Let's get on with it," said Wierzchniak in an encouragingly sprightly voice.

Teodor clucked in dismay. "It's not that easy, you know . . ."

"It's easy as pie, my good man. I have a barbershop on Freedom Square. You can always get your hair cut free of charge there, a shave, a facial plus aftershave lotion," he said, waving his arms like a swimmer at the finish line.

Teodor slackened, wearied by the prolonged discussion and encouraged by the prospect of free barbering.

"The thing is," he said timidly, "I don't need the suits. But I won't list them, I'll leave them for you."

This gladdened Wierzchniak, but not overly much either. He lost the servility he had displayed until then and his eyes were not without contempt as they ran over Teodor's ragged jacket.

It was an odd goodbye. Teodor was respectful and Wierzchniak openly dismissive. Teodor sighed when he was out on the street.

Soviet soldiers, convalescing at the numerous military hospitals in the city, were out strolling the streets. They were not embarrassed by their incomplete clothing—the white legs of their long johns, taped pragmatically to their ankles, showed below their cotton dressing gowns.

People with things to sell sat on stacked bricks in burned-out gates, their shabby suitcases full of bacon, butter, and cigarettes beside them. The powerful aroma of flowering jasmine wafted from the nearby park.

As she did each day, Mrs. Fürter opened the door partway and smiled timidly. He noticed that she had put on a little weight. The first signs of ruddiness had appeared on her greenish face beneath the corners of her eyes. He had nothing for her today and so gave her an unfriendly greeting and slid his gaze along the stairs, which had been sprinkled with sand.

Adam was already waiting for him in the room and had placed

the day's loot on the table: a few bicycle parts and a gleaming new microscope.

"What did you get?" he asked Teodor, who was still at the door.

"Nothing," said Teodor with a shrug.

"As usual," said Adam, and returned to what he had been doing. He pulled a typewriter out from under the bed, and took a piece of leather and a dozen sporty neckties out of the bureau. Then he put all these items into his sack and tied it carefully.

"I'm going to Katowice," he said, looking at the mirror.

"What?" said Teodor in surprise.

"To see my cousin, that scum. He knows someone who can move this junk," he said, pointing at his sack.

Teodor pulled on his boots in silence.

"He promised to come see us with a truck sometime next week," said Adam, as if talking to himself. "We've got to have something substantial for him. You might give up your grand ways and act a little more intelligently. Everybody's stealing left and right, why should we be any different?"

Teodor scratched his chin while watching a ray of light frolic on the wall.

"You could at least say something," said Adam impatiently.

"Nothing to say," mumbled Teodor, and pouring some stagnant, lukewarm water into the flowered basin, he began lazily washing himself. Adam took his sack from the table and slammed the door without saying goodbye.

On a corner of a street a short distance from their apartment building, there was a small, solitary structure whose windows had been broken and whose doors had been ripped out. The yellow lettering above the windows read: ERICH WISYOREK, KOLONIAL-WAREN. The empty windows revealed a stretch of floor covered with wet paper, blackened pieces of straw, and small coils of excrement left by people who had lost their way on that street. The thought of that small structure had often caused Adam to sigh. "Naturally, all you have to do is put in the windows and doors and you're in business. We'd find enough things to sell. You'd have a store and the money would come flowing in," he would say with a sigh, half closing his eyes in reverie. "And what about our plan to flee the country?" Teodor would ask. That would anger Adam. "There's always time for that. You can't leave with empty hands."

Several buildings away there was a long blast on a factory whistle. Teodor was surprised, for he had not imagined there were any working factories in that half-dead city. He shook his head and walked up two more flights to an empty apartment full of broken furniture and stacks of dusty books. This was a recent discovery. The lock had not proved complicated; all it took was an ordinary nail to open it.

He did not close the door behind him. His feet rummaged mechanically through collapsed piles of books; then he walked over to the piano, whose keys had turned yellow. He tapped a few soundlessly so as not to disturb the man next door, an ex-Nazi, one of the first who had been given—for a modest sum, paid in dollars—a beautifully sealed certificate of full Polish citizenship by the municipal government.

A moment later Teodor began grappling with the wardrobe, trying to move it out of the way for better access to the tallest stack of books. Then, taking a seat on the formidable volumes of the Gutenberg Encyclopedia, he began leafing through the books. He had been doing this for a few days now during the sweltering afternoons, which outraged Adam, who would pop in only briefly to hunt for bone buttons, which, according to him, were in fantastic demand in Katowice.

Teodor looked lazily through the damp and yellowed volumes of third-rate maudlin novels, with their pitiful illustrations. He would perk up from time to time seeing the name of an author he recognized. The owner had been a man of odd tastes: Goethe, Heine, Remarque, Romain Rolland, *Mein Kampf*, Courths-Mahler, Elinor Glyn, and hundreds of trashy novels. From the multitude of volumes Teodor extricated the old classics bound in imitation leather. He rubbed their covers done in the style of

the Viennese Secession, grimaced at the old-fashioned Schwabacher type, and set them aside to bring down to his own room
later on.

In the heat of discovery, he knocked over stacks of musical
scores in hardcover bindings. Making a terrible racket, they fell
onto panes of glass in the doors torn off the wardrobe. He looked
around with anxiety, the sudden racket having made him conscious of his solitude in the deathly hush of the now darkening
apartment.

He heard the stairs creaking as someone mounted them with
a heavy tread. His heart beat wildly as he waited. He was afraid;
even though he knew it was a living man drawing near him now,
he was still afraid. It was quiet. A sparrow was chirping loudly
outside the window and his heart was pounding inside his jacket.

The door gave a long groan, revealing the blond man standing
in a dark rectangle. They looked at each for a moment, neither
speaking a word. To his own surprise, Teodor began to justify
himself: "I'm just looking through the books. I come here sometimes. It's mostly junk, but you can always find something," he
said with a smile.

"What kind of books are those?" The blond man's eyes nar-
rowed into an inscrutable smile. Teodor felt ashamed of himself
as he realized that he was sitting awkwardly on top of a pile of
books.

"Just some novels. And a few translations, nothing else." Teodor rose and stood straight and tall. It gave him satisfaction to
see that he was a good head taller than the blond man. "My
name is Klimowicz."

"Mine is Stepien," said the blond man, extending his hand
distractedly, as if he had lost the habit of social ceremony.

The room was growing darker all the time. A reddish patch of
sunlight slid with increasing speed toward the corner where the
piano stood.

Stepien bent on one knee and began rummaging through the
books, whistling softly. He paused longer over certain titles than
others, as, moving his lips soundlessly, he spelled out the Schwa-

bacher type. Then evidently taking a dislike to the books, he rose from his knee and walked over to the window. Lost in thought, he drummed his fingers against the glass. Teodor pushed the books against the wall and brushed off his knees.

"Well, that's enough looting for one day," he said with a laugh as he tucked a few volumes under his arm. "Let's go to my place, since we've met. I'm stuck in my room."

Stepien turned around slowly, a faint smile flashing across his dry face. "My place is better; it's a little closer than yours."

Stepien's room was even smaller and more old-fashioned than Teodor's. A narrow bed, the traditional mirror fly-specked along the edges, and a cuckoo clock. A small picture of Dzerzhinsky clipped from a newspaper had been tacked above the bed. Teodor noticed the picture at once but did not let on. He felt a chill go through him, and suddenly vigilant, he began to observe Stepien's slow and heavy movements.

Stepien gathered a thick layer of newspapers from the table (Teodor had not read any press for a week) and pointed to a chair with a weary hand. They sat across from each other, separated by the bare table like two chess masters before a match.

"Are you working?" Stepien asked after a moment of silence.

"Yes. And you?"

Stepien smiled oddly once again. "I took over a little factory. Hardware. But that was a while back. Now it's a pile of rubble."

Teodor made a sound of assent but not sympathy.

"And so do you like your work?"

Teodor raised his eyebrows skeptically and tipped his head back, but at that moment he again caught sight of Dzerzhinsky's picture smeared with printer's ink. He lowered his brows and took a different tack, saying: "It's a job, something to do."

"But are you satisfied?" Now for the first time Stepien smiled openly. His hair tumbled onto his furrowed brow and his skin twitched like a horse's.

"How should I know," said Teodor, choosing his words cautiously. Soon, however, his tongue grew looser and he began telling Stepien about his travels through Poland, careful to avoid mentioning his contact with Sobiszczak and Lokuciewski. Nodding from time to time, but without taking his eyes off Teodor, Stepien turned on the lights at one point; their faint shadows floated up onto the walls. In part from a desire to win the good graces of his likable new friend and in part from spite, Teodor told him the story of the attack by the National Armed Forces men.

"So you say they ate their Party cards?" asked Stepien, shaking his head.

"Yes, of course, I wasn't the only one who saw, my friend . . ."

"Well, it could happen, there are all sorts of comrades."

The word "comrades" immediately chilled Teodor's ardor and he regretted being so open. He looked over at Stepien's furrowed brow with something like hostility. Communist motherfucker.

After a long silence, Stepien began speaking of his factory and the problems he'd had with the Germans. Half-burned machines had to be extricated from the rubble and guarded at night.

"It's my turn as night watchman again today," said Stepien with a smile.

"That's tough work," replied Teodor with an artificial sigh, thinking, Tell me about it, you son of a bitch; you're probably screwing German women all night.

"He has a picture of Dzerzhinsky over his bed," Teodor muttered, pulling on his boots.

His father had known Dzerzhinsky's brother, who had worked for a short time in Wilno. Teodor had seen him only once, when he was still a little boy. And he had been very surprised that he was an ordinary-looking older man perspiring slightly in his woolen railroad uniform. With frightened eyes he had keenly observed Dzerzhinsky's head, looking for traces of horns, since it did not seem likely to him that the brother of Russia's hangman—as his mother used to call him, crossing herself—could be a common mortal. A scrap of his elders' conversation about Dzerzhinsky's

brother—"Dzerzhinsky is going by handcart to Landwarow"—
struck Teodor as being as paradoxical as: "The Antichrist is riding
a bicycle."

After moving to Polesie, he forgot about Dzerzhinsky's brother,
who was a respectable man. But every so often he would recall
the name of Felix Dzerzhinsky with superstitious dread.

The next Sunday Teodor and Adam traveled to Katowice.
Teodor had no great desire to make the trip but allowed himself
to be talked into it. Adam was the very picture of elegance.
Though his new sporty suit was a bit too large, his well-tightened
suspenders kept his pants under control and prevented them from
getting caught under his heels. His navy-blue silk shirt and his
loud tie with its oversized clasp rounded out his stylish outfit.
Teodor was still parading around in his Polesian boots, crumpled
as accordions, and a pair of gray cheviot trousers he'd pulled off
a dead SS man in 1943. During the two weeks he'd been working,
he'd managed to hustle himself a clumsily made brown jacket
with breast pockets.

They left home in the morning. The few people on the street
were hurrying to church. A fat, bald man, who in less than a
week had repaired and furnished a candy store in a half-destroyed
apartment building, was making ice cream in front of his door.
He spit on his hands and churned furiously away at the wooden
tub full of light-blue pieces of ice.

It was a long, hard walk to the trolley, which proved so crowded
that Teodor could not even reach up to take off his sunglasses.
The young woman conductor could barely elbow her way through
the car.

"Damnit, she's pretty," whispered Adam.

When she had reached them, Adam began bantering, haggling
over the price of the ticket. She, however, had a good sense of
humor and did not grow angry, but as she walked away, she
stunned Teodor by pulling off his light-blue glasses and planting
them on her little snub nose. She laughed so innocently that
Teodor did not have the heart to object.

"You're lucky with women," said Adam. "But in everything else you're a losing proposition."

The small café was full. Fidgeting indecisively, Teodor was about to go outside to wait for Adam when, an empty tray in hand, the waiter ran over to him, bent forward, ready to serve.

"You need a table, there's one for you, sir. There's only one person sitting at the table by the window," he said, casting his bleary eyes at a woman hidden by a magazine.

"Would you ask her if I can join her," said Teodor with some trepidation.

The waiter gave him a look of surprise, wiggled one ear in disapproval, but nonetheless muttered: "Of course I will."

Cutting gracefully through the crowd, his tray aslosh with spilled orangeade, the waiter bent to the woman and whispered to her humbly for a moment. The woman nodded. The waiter straightened back up in triumph, his eyes telling Teodor to act at once.

A subdued murmur rose from the sweating crowd. Long streaks of bluish smoke coiled upward into layers like those in halvah. Teodor squeezed his way through the crowd, bowed to the woman hidden by the magazine, and stammered: "May I?"

She nodded, without lowering the magazine. He sat down clumsily, his bony knees jostling the flimsy table, rattling the glasses.

"I'm sorry," he mumbled. The woman turned the page with boredom.

The waiter reappeared, wiped an invisible speck of dust from the table with his napkin, and bent solemnly forward.

"Hm, what shall I order," said Teodor, playing for time, since he had no idea what to order in such an elegant café.

"Coffee, orangeade, ice cream," suggested the waiter.

"Coffee, that's it," said Teodor, desperately seizing upon something he knew.

Still screened by the magazine, the woman was looking out

at the street through the cream-colored curtain. Teodor took out
a cigarette and lit it.

"What's the latest rate?" asked a man with an apoplectic neck
at the next table.

"Six hundred twenty," replied a dreamy-eyed young man mysteriously. They both fell into a businesslike silence.

Teodor squinted over at the magazine as adroitly as he could.
The woman's hair was the color of a sandy country road, her
forehead narrow, her arching eyebrows thick and dark. Stirring
her coffee mechanically, she kept her eyes on the magazine.

At one point she lowered the magazine and Teodor was struck
by her unexpected beauty. A delicate face with elusive features,
the lips full but small. She took a loud sip of her coffee. Without
a glance at him, she shifted her gaze to the wall behind the
modern counter with its enormous coffee machine. He knew
what she was looking for. With desperate haste, he pulled out
his father's antique watch, which ticked so loudly it sounded like
a hammer striking a rail.

"Quarter to twelve."

The woman looked at him for the first time and thanked him,
betraying no surprise. When she took out a cigarette, Teodor
leaped forward with a light, overturning the glasses and the solitary bottle on their table. As she accepted the light from him,
he caught what seemed to be a slight gleam of a smile in the
corners of her eyes. Scared by his success, he fell back onto his
chair and stared down at his coffee. The woman resumed reading
and he immediately regretted not having turned the situation to
any better use. Now all he could see was the King of England,
smiling and kindly, and an old woman in short pants on the
cover of the magazine.

Around noon he glanced up and saw Adam, who had evidently
been standing at the doorway for some time looking for him.
Teodor raised his hand. Adam nodded and began parting the
buzzing crowd like a bull, elbowing slack bodies aside.

Adam arrived at the table so noisily that the woman looked up from her magazine. A brilliant if not original idea flashed through Teodor's mind. He jumped impetuously to his feet, shaking the table for a third time.

"Adam," he said, his eyes indicating Adam as if preparing to introduce him.

Adam immediately extended his rough red hand, and caught by surprise, the woman extracted her narrow white hand from the magazine. Adam shook her hand as if it were a sack of potatoes.

"My name is Adam Porejko," he said loudly, as if announcing the arrival of Alexander the Great.

The woman blinked her eyes uncertainly. Teodor gulped and blundered on: "And now, Adam, since you've been introduced, please be so kind as to introduce me, for I have not met this lady yet."

Adam stood dumbfounded and the woman burst into laughter. Teodor shook her hand hesitantly.

"My name is Klimowicz."

"Eryka . . ." she said, her last name trailing off in a whisper.

Now they settled themselves comfortably at the table. Teodor felt more confident, knowing he had Adam in reserve. Adam, meanwhile, had unexpectedly gone on the offensive, showering Eryka with compliments and witticisms of dubious value. This offended Teodor, who sat up straighter and sipped his coffee until it was finished. Infatuated, Adam told the woman a story he made up as he went along; he presented himself as a prince who was temporarily being persecuted, clasped his hands in a gesture of resignation, then once again burst out in horsy, optimistic laughter. Eryka smiled vaguely, her eyes wandering to the far side of the room. Teodor had not once succeeded in attracting her attention.

At around one o'clock she began preparing to leave. They paid their check and walked out with her. The street was closed to traffic. Boy Scouts in full regalia were marching down the roadway in loose ranks of eight. Their drums rolled fiercely. Taking advantage of Adam's inattention, Teodor bent close to Eryka's ear and whispered: "Can we meet the same time next Sunday in that same café?"

She nodded.

Teodor felt a sudden surge of joy. Now he looked with something like love on the Boy Scouts, who were throwing their hands rhythmically into the air (as if doing gymnastics) and clapping their open palms against their chest as they chanted: "The Warsaw Up-ris-ing, that's us!"

The densely packed crowds along the sidewalks accorded the Boy Scouts heartfelt applause. The three of them turned into a side street and walked in silence to the trolley stop. Eryka extended her hand.

"Thank you for walking me here."

Adam took her hand with alacrity, winking flirtatiously. "When shall we meet again?"

"In two weeks."

"No sooner?"

"No."

"Where?"

"Where we met today."

The trolley was pulling in. Adam clung to her for a long moment, pretending that his eyes were dampening with emotion. She gave Teodor her hand, gazing with indifference at the trolley squealing to a halt. Sadness came over Teodor.

"Goodbye," she said, and with a light, easy trot ran to the trolley.

One morning there was a clamor in their building. Teodor dashed half dressed out to the landing. Stepien came running downstairs coughing.

It turned out that Mrs. Fürter had come home after being out all night. She was lying in bed, pale, heavily bandaged from the waist down. An old woman by the name of Mrs. Weissmühler, the wife of a retired major, who rented a little room from Fürter, was running around the room weeping and cursing. A doctor had to be fetched at once, Fürter had been literally ripped open. Her voice weak, Mrs. Weissmühler explained that Fürter had been coming home late from some friends' place when she encountered some soldiers who raped her.

"The bitch is lying, she was asking for it. I know those sluts," fumed Mrs. Weissmühler. "She'd sleep with anyone for a piece of bread."

In a carriage by the bed a little child was crying. Its eyes were closed as it emitted hoarse little groans from its feverish throat. It must have been crying a long time.

"Leave me alone," said Fürter in a quiet voice.

"Throw her out face-first!" roared Schröder from the doorway, red with rage. He was the ex-Nazi from upstairs who had been the first in the city to receive Polish citizenship.

Mrs. Weissmühler ran to the wardrobe and with trembling hands began tearing the scanty dresses off their hangers. The wind stirred the curtains through the open window.

"Easy does it!" snarled Stepien.

"What do you mean!" said Schröder, flaring up. "Throw her out and be done with the goddamn bitch."

Stepien went very pale, snaky blue veins in clear relief on his forehead. He stomped over to Schröder and grabbed him by the arm. "Get out of here and make it quick!"

Groaning with rage, Schröder quickly withdrew from the room with considerable help from Stepien. Getting its second wind, the child began wailing again, making the carriage rock on its springs.

Her eyes darting, Mrs. Weissmühler sized up the situation and executed a complete about-face. She ran over to the bed and began straightening the pillows, while saying in a conciliatory tone: "It could happen to anybody. The woman needs help. And that Schröder has nothing to sound off about, every officer in the Offizierenheim slept with his daughter. Ho ho, she was a live one, she was."

Stepien squatted down by the carriage and made an inept attempt to distract the child. Fürter closed her eyes. After clucking for a while, Stepien turned and said in a voice of command: "Everybody, *raus*. There's no reason for you to stand around and watch." Then he said politely to Teodor: "Please send your German woman for a doctor."

The door was opened by a tall, good-looking German woman. Having trouble finding the words, Teodor explained in German that she should prepare to move out. The German woman's smooth face went red while she tried to put the latch back on the door, but all three sisters stormed their way through the white varnished door and a moment later Teodor was inside strolling about the huge and comfortable apartment. Military diplomas and short swords hung on the walls.

"*Schnell, schnell*," said Teodor in an urgent voice.

But the German woman was giving no thought to packing. She ran from wardrobe to wardrobe in a fury, and not caring that her dressing gown was coming open at the breast, she carefully locked each of the locks. A gray-haired woman, clearly her mother, was sitting in a deep armchair, calmly reading a book with gilt-edged pages.

"Move it, move it," said Teodor edgily.

The three sisters chased the German woman, trying to grab her keys from her. On a small table by the window there was an enormous Polish radio which had evidently been brought back as booty from Poland by the husband of the good-looking blonde.

"We really have no time, please pack your bags," explained Teodor patiently.

"What kind of official are you! Call a policeman," said the three boisterous sisters, egging him on.

The German woman put on her coat and was gone a moment later. Teodor sat down at the table, spread his index cards out before him, and licked the end of his pencil in preparation for taking inventory. The three sisters had disappeared from view and the gray-haired German woman continued quietly turning the pages of her book. All the life seemed to have gone out of the apartment.

Teodor sat at the table for a good while, twirling his pencil in one hand, until finally he lost patience and was on the verge of going for the police when the front door was struck violently and slammed open against the wall. A sergeant with infantry insignia on his epaulettes appeared in the doorway. His eyes, made smaller by overindulgence in alcohol, darted about the room; an ugly rusted pistol flashed in his hand. Standing behind him, the German woman smiled vengefully.

"That's the one," she said, pointing a finger at Teodor.

The sergeant staggered blustering into the room. "Son of a bitch, who gave you the right to throw people out of their apartment?"

"All right, calm down," said Teodor in an offended tone.

The sergeant aimed a feeble blow at Teodor, who grabbed his fist in midair and squeezed it so hard that the sergeant went blue in his sweaty face.

"I'm a Polish official."

"I know that kind of official. Thieves!" said the sergeant in a rage. "Hands up!"

Teodor stared at the pistol but did not raise his hands.

"Hands up!" shouted the sergeant.

Teodor raised his hands only when he felt the pistol's cool muzzle against his ribs. Humming a tango in a low voice, the German woman was now straightening the napkins in the sideboard. All that remained of the three sisters who had been authorized to occupy the apartment was the smell of their cheap perfume.

The gray-haired German woman lay her book calmly aside and half closed her eyes.

"All right, let's go," said the sergeant ominously.

For a moment Teodor made a bold try at resistance, but the muzzle against his ribs immediately returned his clarity of mind. He was escorted from the apartment by the sergeant, both German women trailing him with derisive glances.

It was an ordinary sunny day. Goods had been placed on display in two new stores; a trolley that had gone back into service a few days before cut down the center of the street. The passersby looked with curiosity at Teodor and the sergeant, but no one rushed to his aid.

Teodor sighed and looked up at the sun. The son of a bitch is drunk and he'll let me have it in some deserted side street, he thought with regret. Suddenly the trees seemed especially green and succulent, the sunlight more golden, the sky cool and near.

I won't let him take me into any side street, resolved Teodor.

All the same, after a brief struggle, Teodor entered a lane shaded by lush chestnut trees. Now the pistol in the drunken sergeant's hand seemed more menacing.

"I'll show you," threatened the sergeant. "You won't give me the slip here. Look at you, you were going to put up a fight. You'll rot in jail for this."

The lane was dark and dismal. Not a soul in sight. He could hear the sergeant behind him puffing with fury.

He prodded Teodor until they reached a house that looked deserted. They went down a flight of stairs to a basement. Two soldiers were sitting on their beds by the wall in a small room. One of them was playing a mournful song on the accordion. Their voices swollen with longing, the soldiers wailed on about the steppe and a solitary well.

They glanced curiously at Teodor.

"A bandit and a nervy one," explained the sergeant.

Teodor was herded into a small cellar room whose door was guarded by a soldier with a bayonet on his rifle.

"Guard him with your life," ordered the sergeant.

Now Teodor was alone. He heard the key turn in the padlock and the sound of the accordion, distant, muffled.

Smoothing his hair with the palm of his hand, he muttered: "It won't be easy getting out of this one."

Sighing heavily, he began to examine the floor with his hand. He was in a small cubicle with a few slightly rotted potatoes on its cement floor. His hand came across a damp mattress in one corner. He sat down with a groan. The little window by the ceiling had been boarded over. One narrow chink gleamed with golden sunlight and sometimes became a vivid green—when the branch of a chestnut tree was blown across it.

Teodor tried not to think about what fate held in store for him. Feverishly he sought to recall the details of his first encounter with Eryka. As he envisioned her charms, her oval face, he was again overcome with serious concern about what awaited him. Well, he thought, the son of a bitch might do me in here, but maybe he'll let me go when he sobers up. No, he won't, he'll do me in without blinking an eye. But he could have done that right off, so why did he lock me up, then?

A damp beetle was marching across his calf. He pulled his leg away in disgust. Gradually he began sinking into a stupor.

That same evening Teodor had gone to see Stepien. It was painful to be cooped up all alone at nightfall. Adam had started making more frequent night trips to Katowice with his loot. That day too he had dragged two heavy suitcases to the streetcar stop. Now Adam had a gilded sword and a heavy copper chain on the wall above his bed, trophies from a secret Masonic lodge he had discovered in an attic. To the dismay of his landlady, he had also placed a black and gruesome skull on his side table.

Lately, Adam and Teodor had not been talking much. Each morning Adam would take malicious satisfaction in the sight of Teodor's disintegrating boots.

Stepien opened the door himself, the grease on his chin gleaming dully in the half-dark room.

"Come in, please, come in," he said, showing Teodor in.

Then, quickly and shamefacedly, he snatched an open can of food from his table and hid it away in his cupboard.

He doesn't eat bread with his food, like a pig, thought Teodor, settling into a chair.

Stepien looked bad. Thick beads of sweat glittered at the roots of his hair. He kept interrupting their conversation to rise and go to the window, where he would spend a long while inhaling the cool evening air.

"How's things at the factory?" asked Teodor, his eyes sliding along the yellowed picture of Dzerzhinsky clipped from the newspaper.

"On the slow side," said Stepien with a sigh. "We're short of people. Nobody wants to get down to work. But we have accomplished something. We're still cleaning house. I went to the city Party committee . . ."

Teodor froze. The son of a bitch doesn't even hide belonging to the Party, he thought with amazement.

A chubby moon freed itself from the rooftops and rose. Stepien turned off the lamp, and in the metallic moonlight, they began doing what everyone does on such occasions, reminiscing about their early years, bygone days.

Teodor arrived at the café at the agreed-on hour. It seemed as if no one had entered or left the café in the course of the week. The same people were at the same tables chatting about the same topics. And the same smoke from American cigarettes floated low over people's heads. In his breast pocket Teodor could feel the pleasant heft of the wad of cash obtained by selling three silk shirts he had liberated.

Eryka was already sitting by the window. He bowed awkwardly, but less timidly than he had the week before. She glanced up at him vacantly and then returned to her newspaper.

"Sweltering," said Teodor gravely.

She nodded.

He ordered coffee. While stirring in the sugar, he let his gaze run over her hair and her smooth, dazzling cheeks. He had never seen a complexion like that before.

Finally, she set her newspaper aside and asked: "And so?"

Teodor laughed with an amiable, studied grin, aware of the skin taut on his cheeks. He had spent a half hour scraping them clean in front of a mirror while Adam looked on suspiciously.

"Sweltering," he repeated. "Is there any place to go swimming around here?"

"There's a pool. We can go this afternoon if you like."

They were both silent for a long moment, then Eryka suggested: "Would you like a look at the paper?"

Teodor seized on the suggestion. With unseeing eyes he scoured the crumpled sheet of newsprint for a topic to begin a conversation. Using a small mirror, Eryka touched up her makeup.

"The war's finally over and they're back making deals again," he said, slamming his hand against the newspaper.

"That's true," agreed Eryka.

It's not going good, thought Teodor with a pang of regret. A distinguished-looking man at the next table was arguing with the waitress, who did not want to accept a torn twenty. The air swirled with fine dust. There were two girls sunning their plump, healthy legs on the balcony of the apartment building across from the café.

"Shall we go for a walk?"

"Good idea, very good," said Teodor, slamming into the flimsy table as he jumped to his feet.

They walked on the shady side of the street, neither of them saying a word. It was only in the park, on a bench under an anemic willow, clearly served poorly by the local climate, that Teodor came to life, settling into a subject he knew well, his own youth. Smiling in distraction and with what appeared to be masked emotion, he began telling her about the marshes of Polesie, sunsets in the country, his longing to see the world. He was well aware that he was hamming it up, but finding the words flowing easily, he began to yield to the charms of his own tale. At first Eryka's bored eyes wandered about the jasmine bushes that were already in bloom, but they began glancing with increasing frequency at Teodor's damp forehead and his shock of black, desperate hair.

Teodor fell silent at one point and absentmindedly rubbed his forehead. "I was talking my head off there."

"That's all right, I'd like to hear more."

"No, no. I get too carried away. Let's go for a swim."

They rose from the bench, the gravel creaking underfoot.

"I have to stop by my place for my bathing suit."

She lived on a quiet street not far from the park. Teodor waited for her downstairs. Two small boys were pushing a handcart loaded with coal along the street. They puffed industriously as they went by, swearing like old front-line soldiers.

Eryka did not keep him waiting long. She came running downstairs with a bulging bag and a bathrobe under one arm. Teodor did not know Katowice well and was curious about what he saw on the way. Heavy clouds of smoke hung over the gray, stoop-shouldered city.

"It looks like the mines are working even on Sunday, doesn't it?"

"That's so more coal can be shipped to Russia."

"Is that true?" he asked in surprise.

"You didn't know? There are shipments day and night, but people are being paid a pittance. That can work now, but not for very long."

They did not speak the rest of the way. Teodor gazed greedily at her bare and already well-tanned shoulders. She really was very nice-looking.

Despite the heat, a few people were sunbathing by the swimming pool. Sitting by the wire-mesh fence, a family was having a jolly time drinking vodka and munching on hard-boiled eggs. The water was clean and reflected the sky-blue sky.

They went to the locker rooms to change. As he removed his clothing, Teodor stared long and hard at his too hairy arms and slightly scrawny rib cage. Finally, with a sigh of resignation, he went back out to the sun.

Eryka was waiting for him by the steps to the pool. She seemed somehow alien, too beautiful, beside his white and haggard body.

"Shall we go in?" she asked.

He nodded.

He was about to help her into the water as an excuse for touching her shoulders, but she moved away easily and, without hesitation, slipped into the water like a well-practiced athlete.

Teodor flailed after her, sending light-blue splashes onto a woman with green glasses who was wearing an old-fashioned bathing suit and sitting at the edge of the pool.

They swam side by side. Teodor quickly realized that his Polesian style of swimming could not come close to Eryka's skill. He looked desperately around the pool, and at once his heart soared with hope: a diving tower.

However, when he looked down at the water from a height of one story, he somehow felt queasy. The few other swimmers craned their heads to see what he would do. He had to make a choice. Even Eryka had stopped swimming and, striking the wrinkled water with the palms of her hands, stood by the steps in anticipation.

His eyes shut, Teodor threw himself desperately into the air. His legs bent backward, sending a pain through the small of his back just before he plunged into the water. He could barely swim to the side of the pool.

"Bravo," said Eryka in a bored voice. "You're an excellent diver."

He pulled himself out of the pool, walking with a limp now, and sat down facing the sun, his hands clasped around his hopelessly thin calves. Eryka lay down beside him, concealing her nose snugly behind a sprig of lilac.

Teodor was angry at himself, at his own ungainliness, and at the circumstances which had brought him and Eryka together. A stray bee buzzed softly over the water. The family by the fence had finished their vodka and were now slowly preparing to leave, cursing as they went.

Out of curiosity he peeked over at Eryka, whose eyes were closed. A faint breeze toyed with her hair; a damp strand slid along her narrow, golden forehead. Factory sirens sounded above the city, and then all was quiet again. The woman in the old-fashioned bathing suit dangled her toes sedately in the water.

When the sun, low above the rooftops, began to turn yellow, Eryka took the sprig from her nose and raised her head. "Shouldn't we be going?"

"Yes, we should," said Teodor.

"My mother would like you to come for tea."

"Thanks very much but . . ."

"Say thank you afterward," said Eryka sleepily, then went to get dressed.

Her mother proved to be an amiable old woman with a vacant smile. She took charge of Teodor at once and showed him to the dining room, where she seated him in an oversized armchair. The apartment was spacious, its furniture modern. On one wall there were two rows of yellowed photographs in fretwork frames. Left alone, Teodor began to contemplate the family photographs—chunky men in high, sharp collars and nondescript women in long dresses with knotted bows along the shoulder line. In a small photograph he recognized Eryka wearing a broad lace collar. A home with an air of sedate affluence about it.

Eryka reappeared wearing a different dress, and Teodor was once again surprised to find her even more beautiful than before. Her father entered the room a short while later, clearing his throat at the sight of Teodor.

"This is a friend of mine, Papa," explained Eryka, examining her fingernails under a light.

Ill at ease, Teodor shuffled his feet, awkward because the situation was ambiguous.

Tea was served with some ceremony. The cook, a deaf-and-dumb woman, waited on the table, silently appearing in the room carrying trays covered with minuscule dishes.

"Are you from Katowice?" asked Eryka's mother.

"No, I was repatriated."

"Repatriated?" she said with shock and surprise.

"Mama, all the people who were repatriated aren't the same," interjected Eryka.

"Yes, that's true, people are different," said the mother with a sigh. "Oh, how this city looks now. It used to be so neat and clean, but it's been filthy ever since those repatriates started arriving here. They're like animals."

"Yes," Teodor agreed courteously, "you're completely right.

But still, what can you expect from people who are traveling with all they have left in the world."

"That's true," said the mother politely.

The father was smacking his lips as he ate. At one point Eryka alluded to his having been a good ophthalmologist before he became senile.

"And are you working here?" asked the mother, keeping the conversation alive.

"Yes, in Bytom."

"The people who were repatriated are taking all the best jobs," she said, shaking her head sadly, and then, seeming inspired by some thought, she bent close to Eryka. "Eri, do you think he could help you?"

"No, absolutely not," protested Eryka vehemently, with an angry glance at her mother.

"Why not?" said Teodor, his interest up. "I know a few people, I could certainly do something."

"You see," the old woman began in a hesitant whisper, "we, I mean, Eri . . ." She paused to crack the joints of her fingers. "Eri is going to be rehabilitated. Because, because we, I mean, she was on the Germans' list of Volksdeutsch during the war. You understand, everyone here had to do that. Otherwise they didn't give you any bread. But Eri even helped the Polish underground in Krakow. If there is anything you could do . . ."

"I'll see, maybe something can be done," said Teodor assuringly, though he was somewhat confounded by this latest piece of information.

Dusk fell. Somewhere a radio was blaring out a waltz. Mosquitoes whined in the curtains.

"Could you play something for us, Eri?" asked the mother.

The father rose with difficulty, knocking against the table a few times, and then, after a hiccup, he went off to his room. Teodor caught a glimpse of the old-fashioned room through the door. A poor reproduction of the Madonna above a yellow bed.

Eryka sat down at the piano. For a moment her fingers wandered along the keyboard as she followed a sleepy mosquito with her eyes, then finally she began to play. Teodor sat straighter in his chair and, resting his head on his hand, covered his eyes with his fingers. He was no expert on music and had little interest in it, but that day he made an effort to give himself to Eryka's playing. Her arms folded across her chest, the mother gazed with affection at her daughter's back.

A clock sounded the hour in the next room. Eryka looked through a stack of sheet music until she found a colored notebook. His eyes closed, Teodor had dozed off.

When the clock struck the next hour, Teodor rose, and after blinking his eyes, which had a vacant look, he attempted to say goodbye.

"There's no hurry, you can spend the night here. Unless there's somebody who would be worried about you," said the mother.

"No, there's no one, I have no one here."

"So, you see, we can make up a bed for you in the parlor. There's plenty of room."

Teodor dozed his way through a few more pieces, then the mother returned to say his bed was ready.

Wishing one another good night, they went off to their rooms. Eryka's little room was across from the parlor. As he undressed, Teodor could hear her splashing water in the bathroom, which was next to his room. Then he heard the rustle of slippers and the sound of a door closing.

Without removing his pants, he sat down on the couch with a worried look and lit a cigarette. The mother and father talked for a short while in their room and then all at once fell silent. A mosquito droned against the window. Teodor jabbed out his cigarette and tiptoed to the door. He opened it a crack. The light was still on in Eryka's room. His courage suddenly left him and he went back to the couch, where he lit another cigarette.

He went to the door twice again and came back each time, unable to bring himself to act. Finally, he felt able to take the chance. Here goes, he thought, gooseflesh on his back as he tiptoed across the hall to her door, which creaked slightly when he pressed the brass latch with his trembling hand. Her room was dark now. He came to a sudden halt, expecting a scream of fear. Eryka stirred in her bed. "So, you finally made up your mind. You thought about it long enough," she whispered, making a place for him beside her.

About fifteen minutes later the door creaked. Teodor plunged wisely under the covers. An electric lantern's thin beam of light passed over the bed.

"Are you asleep, Eri?" asked Eryka's mother from the door, her voice worried and tearful.

"Yes, I am, go to sleep, Mama, and stop walking around or you'll wake up the guest," said Eryka, holding Teodor's trembling hand under the quilt.

Michal Stepien did not feel well, even though the heat wave was over. The sky was heavy with a uniform layer of gray clouds. He was often awakened in the night by rain drumming against his windows. The light from the street lamps recently put back into service fell onto his flowered wallpaper. Michal would then set his pillow on end and recline, half sitting, half lying, until daybreak. He usually took comfort in the thought that the time of chaos was in fact passing, and that, when he had the factory going, he would able to think about medical treatment, if any proved necessary.

When leaving for work in the morning he often ran into Schröder coming home from the night shift. After the run-in at Fürter's, Schröder would whisk off his cap at the bottom of the stairs and bow obsequiously to him.

One day when Michal was washing his hands with gasoline in a rusty basin, a young woman or, rather, a girl, came walking up to the factory. Michal saw her enter the gate, but he did not raise his head and continued carefully scrubbing his hands. For a short time she circled indecisively about the courtyard, then walked over to Michal.

"Excuse me, pop," she said. "I'd like to speak with the director, Mr. Stepien."

"Concerning what?" asked Stepien, without raising his head.

"That's for me to tell him. Just show me the way, would you, pop."

Michal stood up straight and they looked each other in the eye. Her lips are too wide and her legs are too thick, thought Michal, wiping his hands on his overalls. A fine rain rustled on the leaves of a chestnut tree.

"Well, mom, if you want to see Stepien, then I should confess, that's me."

They both broke out laughing.

"Excuse me, comrade," apologized the girl, "you were bent over the basin and I couldn't see your face."

"It's all right, you don't have to explain. If you have some business with me, I'll warn you in advance, you'll come out the loser."

"I'm here from the city committee."

"I see; well, that's something else," said Stepien with a smile.

"You needed someone to help you."

"Do you have someone?" said Stepien happily.

"We do."

"Send him right over."

"I'm already here."

"What's that?" said Stepien in dismay.

"I'll be here with you, comrade, on instructions from the committee."

"Hm, yes, of course but . . ." Stepien wiped his hands, then began nervously buttoning up his overalls. "But I thought I'd be getting a man."

"Grin and bear it, comrade," said the girl with a smile.

"My luck," sighed Michal. "Come with me."

Teodor usually spent the long afternoons thinking of Eryka. Shocked at first by the ease of his conquest, he decided not to visit her house again. However, the more time that elapsed after that memorable Sunday, the more often he envisioned her face. For some reason her delicate profile and her lips, slightly puffy like a child's, had been etched with special clarity in his memory. Often in the evening he would rack his brains for a long time, trying to recall the features he loved. And often he would thrust his head under the pillow, tossing and turning violently, vowing to break with Eryka. But in the morning everything would look rosier, simpler. Then Teodor would usually decide to go to Katowice, but still would postpone going for as long as he could.

In the meantime, the city's increase in population had gone almost unnoticed. Every day carloads of Germans and their belongings were brought to the transports that would take them away to the west. One night a Polish armored division unit stopped in the city on the way back from the front, and the next day the city swarmed with Polish uniforms. Polish soldiers began patrolling the streets. Sometimes the city droned all night with the sound of vehicles—Soviet divisions on their way home. And even though a person might well return from a walk at night minus his watch, his money, and even his clothing, a little dance hall with a good-size band had sprung up on the main street. New cafés, restaurants, and bars kept pace with the multiplying number of managerial types in the city. Still, the majority of the factory chimneys jutting above the rooftops emitted no smoke.

Teodor soon became acquainted with the law and order that had made an uncertain appearance in that territory. He went to work a little late one Saturday, the day before leaving to see Eryka (it was high summer then). Adam was still not back from Katowice. Squeezed into a single small room, his fellow supervisors were talking loud and fast. Four strangers wearing waterproof coats stood in the doorway.

"What's your name?" asked one of them.

"Klimowicz."

"A supervisor?"

"Yes."

"Then please go in that room."

It was only there in that crowd of his co-workers that Teodor learned they were all under arrest. No one knew why. Of course, they all had something on their conscience, but it was difficult to imagine that an entire brigade of supervisors could be arrested for mere trifles. A thick cloud of cigarette smoke swirled above their heads.

"Maybe it was that major, the director, who ordered us locked up," cried someone uncertainly from one corner.

"Impossible. I saw how confused he was by the whole thing. I think he even tried to intervene."

"Maybe it's for parceling out that chapel," suggested a man with white hair.

An hour later the supervisors were escorted by the plainclothesmen to the newly founded municipal court. They spent long hours pacing the waiting room and puffing on cigarettes. Wolkowicz, a small, delicate man wearing wire-rimmed glasses, rubbed his hands nervously. "I'm an Argentine citizen, no one has the right to arrest me."

"You should make a scene, they can't lock you up just like that," said the others in encouragement.

"If I were you, I'd have been bullshitting those plainclothesmen left and right by now," shouted Milewicz, a senior supervisor.

The brim on his cap turned up, a German was scything the grass on the lawn outside. Even though the window was closed, Teodor could still smell fresh, damp grass. Gray-violet clouds were clearing over the buildings, a greenish sky shining through. The sunlight was reflected in the millions of drops suspended from branches.

The room was dark with smoke. In the unhealthy light filtered through the gray windowpane, people's faces looked crumpled and colorless.

"I'm opening a window," shouted the Argentine citizen hysterically.

"It's not allowed," said the Security man curtly from the door.

"Not allowed, not allowed," said Wolkowicz rebelliously. "I'll remember this. How can you lock people up for no reason. I can't breathe, I'm in poor condition, my health is ruined." His yellow fingers raked the damp glass.

It was only in the afternoon that a young prosecutor with the look of a pensive poet arrived. A hush fell over the room. Teodor could hear every tick of his pocket watch.

"Is Mr. Porejko here?" asked the prosecutor.

"Not here," they roared.

"I see," said the prosecutor, pausing to think. Then he shook his fingers and announced in a mournful voice: "You gentlemen are free."

The room began seething with activity. Wolkowicz elbowed his way through the crowd to the prosecutor.

"I'm going to intervene through the embassy. How dare you arrest innocent citizens? I'll deal with this. My health is poor, I'm a very sick man."

"I'm sorry," said the prosecutor, spreading his hands. Thick, light hair fell onto his forehead. "We had to clear something up. And that's why we detained you. I'm very sorry."

Taking the steps two at a time like students after a boring lecture, they all ran outside, where they were enfolded in a warm and steamy afternoon. A broad rainbow was fading in the sky.

"Well, shall we go back to the office?" asked Teodor.

"Are you out of your mind? We're going home," said Wolkowicz, swinging his arms. "We've been through enough."

Back home Teodor found Adam lazing about on the balcony, smeared with oil from the waist up. Whistling softly, he stared longingly at the closed window on the top floor. While taking off his jacket, Teodor said casually, dragging out his words: "We were detained at the courthouse. The prosecutor asked about you."

"You're lying!" said Adam, jumping up from his deck chair.

"I'm not. You can ask tomorrow."

"Not on your life. I can't even spend the night here." He began running fretfully about the room.

"Looks like you overdid things at work," said Teodor, gazing at himself in the mirror with disgust.

"Is that what you think? Ha ha." Adam broke into grandiose laughter. "You're naïve. This is political. I'm going to have to disappear. My turn finally came."

"What do you mean, political? And why didn't they pick me up?"

"Are you stupid," said Adam, laughing like a man encumbered with vast knowledge. "Don't you think I had a reason for going to Katowice?"

"I never doubted it," replied Teodor.

Missing the malice, Adam continued: "I've been working with the underground for a few weeks now, and the only reason I was keeping my lip buttoned about it was . . ." He combed his greasy hair with his fingers and muttered, lost in thought, "I'll spend the night with the girls upstairs."

"Oh, I haven't seen you for a long time; it must be two weeks now, isn't it?" said Eryka's mother in surprise as she opened the door for Teodor. "Please come in. Eryka's not here, but she should be back any moment."

She showed him into the parlor. There was a dark glass vase of light-blue cornflowers on the table.

"So, what's new?"

"Nothing," said Teodor, his eyebrows rising.

"How come you never bring anything with you when you come here? You could make yourself some money. People are paying good money for bone buttons. Everybody brings something, you're the only one who comes empty-handed. You haven't even found yourself a decent pair of boots," she said with a critical glance at Teodor's feet.

"I don't have the time for that," said Teodor in self-justification, then changed the subject. "What's happening with Eryka's rehabilitation?"

"The scum," said the old woman, with loathing in her voice. "We had to give them twenty dollars. But now they leave us in peace. Eryka has even found work."

She thought for a moment and then, covering her yawn, she said nonchalantly: "She joined their Party, the Polish Workers' Party."

Teodor's chair creaked.

"Well, you can't make a move today without them. Can't even get work."

"It's not that bad yet. After all, I don't belong to the Party and I'm working. I don't think anyone in our office is in the Party," said Teodor, watching a thick smoke ring rise.

"Sure, that's in the western part, but here it's a different story. And you'll see, they'll get to you too by and by. Our neighbors who left here before the Bolsheviks arrived wrote us that they'll be coming back soon. The only way they'll be coming back is with the Americans."

"God willing. But I don't see that happening," said Teodor.

"Oh," she sighed, "we're sorry now we didn't leave before the Bolsheviks came. We're old and didn't feel up to traveling, but now we can see how stupid that was."

The deaf-and-dumb servant appeared in the doorway. An inhuman voice came creaking out from somewhere in her stomach and she raised her hands. Excusing herself, Eryka's mother went off to the kitchen.

Left alone, Teodor looked around and saw some magazines lying on a small table. He reached out lazily for a newspaper and picked up a Catholic paper called *Sunday*. His eyes slid down the dark text of the Gospels and that Sunday's sermon, complete with stylistic flourishes. On page 3 he read that prayer had protected Mr. Z.M. from a railroad accident. O.S. had been able to evade military service. He then reached for the *Workers' Tribune*, which the father would later cut into small squares with a knife and a ruler to make toilet paper for his family. A National Armed Forces gang had murdered an entire family near Bialystok, a new engine house had been opened, thirty-seven new co-ops had gone into operation. He replaced the newspaper on the table. All these events seemed as distant to him as if he had read about them in an old, yellowed chronicle. Outside, it was a sleepy summer afternoon.

Eryka returned a short while later. She greeted him with a smacking kiss near his left eye. Jumping up clumsily from his chair, he took her hands and kissed them reverently. While removing her hat in front of a mirror, she asked in a soft, lazy voice: "Why have you stayed away so long?"

"Work, I'm overloaded with work," he lied, touched by her concern.

"No signs of it on you," she said, correcting the design of her mouth with lipstick.

They went for a walk before the midday meal. Neatly dressed children chased hoops down the sidewalks. A couple of dirty-faced boys came clattering down the hill on scooters. Teodor thought of the games he had played in Polesie as a child. They would run outside after their last class to play "five groszy" by a solitary oak tree. It was a game of chance they had made up and played for money. Five-groszy coins were stacked in a small triangle and a line was made in the ground in front of it. Then from a distance of a few yards they would toss a little lead ring, which had been given the exotic name of "the Moor," at the bank. Whoever threw closest to the line had the first chance at breaking the bank. They all waited patiently until the one coin hit by the Moor came up heads, and then the lucky winner would tuck that coin away in his shirt pocket. Teodor was an expert at "five groszy." After the game he would take the five-groszy coin, battered beyond recognition, to Jankiel's store, Under the Yellow Apple, and buy himself some sour drops.

They sat down on a shaded bench in the park. Chestnut blossoms beginning to turn brown lay on the ground at their feet. The sky was the grayish color of well-heated iron in a blacksmith's workshop. The benches stank of blistered paint.

Eryka let her head rest against the back of the bench. She had no need to be ashamed of her face; even in the harsh, naked afternoon light, her skin was pure as cheese. The reflection of the treetops shimmered in the large pupils of her eyes.

Teodor fidgeted, mentally composing accusations against himself: for not having wanted to come see her anymore, for treating their relationship as a lark, for struggling with himself a long time before deciding to see her, for being overcome by longing. What caused him the greatest conflict was his desire to confess that she was his first woman. His misty eyes devouring her elusive, almost evanescent profile, he could not keep still in his seat. Finally, he moved closer to her. The air smelled of sun-warmed puffballs, whole colonies of which were withering on the green cloth of the grass. He put an arm weak with emotion around her.

"Leave me alone," she said, as if startled from sleep. "We can do that at home. So why do it here."

The first movie theater had already opened and was attended by the people convalescing in the military hospitals. The interior looked like an apiary. Canes, sticks broken off in the park, and crutches, the padding sticking out of their torn tops, all jutted above the heads of the audience. A fire department, whose existence no one had suspected, demonstrated its skill at putting out a fire in a deserted apartment. Though it was only a decrepit piano and some ruined curtains that were burning, five people, whimsically arrayed in silvery helmets, took part in the rescue action, and this incident was the subject of long discussion during the boring, empty hours at the office.

Teodor had experienced a new sense of agitation about two days after the memorable fire. As usual they were out on a re-settlement action. That day they were to prepare a few residential blocks on Dworcowa Street for the teachers from the high school which was being set up at the time. Security officials also took part in the action, to make sure that the work went smoothly.

The entire retinue (four supervisors, two Security men, and the teacher's family) mounted the stairs heavily. Wolkowicz stopped on the second floor and carefully read the name card on a door.

"Let's start with this one," he said to the others.

He knocked. No reply. He knocked harder. There was no sound inside the apartment apart from the monotonous hum of the water pipes. Turning red, Wolkowicz began kicking the door with his thin foot sheathed in old-fashioned spats.

"Hold on. I'll show them," said Wilczek, a Security official, in a competent-sounding voice, pushing his way through the dense little crowd. He slammed his shoulder once, then once again against the heavy, ash-wood door. The hinges cracked and the battered door reverberated with a magnified echo on the empty landing.

A woman's voice stammered softly, timidly, on the other side of the door: "Who's there?"

"Open up or we'll smash the door in. We're officials," shouted Wilczek.

A key creaked uncertainly and a fearful eye flashed in the narrow chink between the door and the frame. Wilczek waited until he was inside to make a scene.

"Why didn't you open up? Do you want to be thrown in jail?"

"Sir, we were afraid, there's all sorts of people around these days."

"I'll show you all sorts of people. Whose place is this?"

They had clearly not expected to be resettled. Odds and ends were strewn on the tables and shelves; a watch gleamed on the wall, hung by its wristband. A woman with a sallow face lay in a clean bed. A medal on a multicolored ribbon had been hung on the wall above her, beside a blackened cross.

"Is this your place?" asked Wilczek.

"It is," said the woman in the bed in a weak voice.

"Hurry up and get ready, we're resettling you. You have to pack up right away."

By then, the supervisors had started rummaging through the wardrobes. Teodor stood by the window rubbing the corner of his new briefcase. Outside, heavy clouds were supported by broad columns of smoke. The water pipes gurgled shrilly.

"I'm Polish, sir," moaned the woman in bed.

"Let's see your papers, then," ordered Wolkowicz.

The woman's yellowish hand reached under the pillow. Broken glass could be heard clinking in the other room. A moment later the teacher came running into the room, feverish with excitement, the toe of a woman's new shoe protruding from his coat pocket.

"She won't open the sideboard!" he squealed in despair.

"Who won't? Who?" roared Wilczek, fumbling in his pocket. "This one here," said the teacher, grabbing the shoulder of a tearful girl who had appeared in the doorway. Smearing the tears over her face, she cursed the teacher, her accent Silesian. The teacher's wife attacked her from behind with a rug beater. A struggle began, the girl trying to pluck the shoe from the teacher's pocket. The woman in the bed covered her eyes with her translucent hands and raised a hysterical cry.

Wilczek wrenched his pistol from his pocket and fired twice at the wall. The dry smell of gun smoke filled the air.

"Quiet!" he bellowed, his eyes bulging.

White patches of lime fell slowly from the wall. The woman in the bed was choking on her tears, trying to restrain her spasms. She looked as if she might vomit any second. Teodor caught himself drumming his fingers against the windowpane.

"All right, where's the papers?" asked Wolkowicz sweetly.

The teacher's wife was trying on a summer coat by the wardrobe. The water pipes were still gurgling. Teodor noticed that the nickel-plated watch had disappeared. All that was left was a nail with a large head, solitary against the white wall.

The woman extracted a pack of yellowed papers from under her pillow.

"My husband was in the Silesian uprising," she said, blubbering.

Teodor looked over Wolkowicz's shoulder—an ID card from the former insurgents' association, certificates for decorations, and a rusted Piast eagle.

"But do you have citizenship in the new Poland?" asked Wolkowicz.

"No, sir. I've been too sick to deal with it. People with money have already gotten theirs, but I don't have mine yet. But I am Polish."

"Doesn't mean a thing," said Wolkowicz, tossing the papers onto her quilt.

"Where's your husband?" asked Wilczek.

"He died in a camp."

They exchanged looks of confusion, then turned away from the bed. The supervisors' briefcases were bulging now. The other Security man was in the kitchen solemnly opening tin cans. Swarms of disoriented flies circled beneath the flaking ceiling.

"Well, anyway, mother, you have to get ready. Those documents don't mean a thing. You have to get new citizenship. So crawl out of bed."

"Yes, get new citizenship. Gestapo men can get it because they've got the money to bribe the officials. But me, what was I supposed to give them? Oh, God, oh, God, it's a good thing my husband didn't live to see the liberation," said the woman, weeping bitterly.

"Calm down and get out of bed, please," shouted Wilczek, reaching for his pocket.

Nervously straightening his glasses, the teacher was pillaging a drawer he had pulled out and set on a table. A fine rain hissed on the window.

"Listen, she can't be resettled. She's Polish, her husband fought in the uprising," whispered Teodor.

"Be quiet," said Wilczek in a sullen voice.

Teodor's heart was knocked back and forth like the little metal ball in a child's billiards game. He was aware of his left eyelid trembling.

"I advise you to listen to me," he stammered in fury.

"And who the hell are you?" asked Wilczek, clicking the safety off on the pistol in his pocket.

Licking his dry lips, Teodor slipped out of the apartment. He took the stairs two at a time, unable to control a sudden impotent rage. He stumbled on the landing and fell headfirst down the stairs.

"Easier to do that on your butt," said the gray-haired trolley driver he bumped into at the bottom.

Teodor found Michal installing an electrical machine. Rolling a cigarette, Stepien listened to Teodor's lurching and chaotic story. "All right," said Stepien with a smile. "We'll fight fire with fire. Let's hit them hard."

In the office he pulled a large Austrian Mauser from a drawer and shoved it in his breast pocket.

They took the stairs quietly. Stepien was pale. When Teodor glanced over at him by chance, he was frightened by the sudden coldness in his look. Carelessly tied bundles and loose clothes were tossed on the floor in front of the apartment door. Wilczek's excited voice carried from deep within the apartment.

"Hands up," said Stepien, bursting into the room, his thin hand around the base of the powerful pistol, which, if placed in a stock, could also be fired like a rifle.

Everyone in the room froze. The sallow-skinned woman wearing a hastily donned skirt stood with her mouth open.

"What the hell are you sons of bitches doing," said Stepien, coughing in the doorway. "You're good at scaring women with your pistols. Which one of you is the bravest?" His squinting eyes moved from one of them to the next. Then, with a slow measured step, he walked up to Wolkowicz.

"You're in someone's house, you scum," he said, knocking off Wolkowicz's hat, which had been set rakishly on one ear. "So you're the kind that likes to fight, is that right?" he asked, grabbing the terrified man by the front of his gabardine coat.

Teodor had begun to regret his intervention. He could see the muscles tense on Stepien's jaws and was afraid there'd be shooting.

The teacher's back was pressed against the cold wall. The windowpane was lit by a sudden ray of sun. It was perfectly still. Flies were knocking against the ceiling.

The room seemed somehow more spacious. Both Security men and the other supervisors had slipped away unnoticed.

"So what's it going to be?" Michal shook Wolkowicz like a sack of flour.

"I won't come back here," stuttered Wolkowicz in a childish voice.

"You won't?" said Michal, tormenting him by jabbing the muzzle of the pistol against his trembling chest.

"I'll stop their resettlement," he answered, as if reciting a lesson he'd learned poorly.

"That's good," said Michal in praise. "But just be quick about it or I might lose my patience."

Stepien returned to the factory and Teodor dragged himself to the next round of evictions. The Security men were gone and Wolkowicz pretended not to notice Teodor's presence. It was only when they returned to the office that afternoon to make their reports that Wolkowicz suddenly went on the attack.

"Klimowicz, you're the lowest of the low."

"Why's that?" said Teodor, surprised.

"I'll tell you why," fumed Wolkowicz. "Because you brought in that lowlife with the pistol. And who were you acting against, who I ask you? Against your own people, against people who were in the camps. You see this," he said, impetuously pulling back his sleeve. "You see that number, it was tattooed by an SS man. That's not enough for you? Then look at this." He opened his mouth, pointing to his missing upper teeth. "All kicked out by a boot. I suffered for three years. Do you understand that, three years. And you, you scum, you stand up for an old German woman who grew fat on my blood, mine." He beat his fist against his sunken chest.

"She's not a German. Her husband fought in the Silesian uprising."

"So, what of it? She was here in the rear and calmly eating her margarine while people were being killed in the camps. I don't have anything, I lost everything. All I have is the clothes on my back. I went hungry the whole war, so why shouldn't I grab a few rags from her now? Why not? They never saw the war here and I'm spitting blood . . ."

"Her husband was killed in a camp," said Teodor, preparing to leave.

"Did you see him die? I'll give you some advice, Klimowicz, don't be so merciful, it can lead to a bad end. You're sentimental. But if you'd had your teeth knocked out, you'd sing a different tune. Defender of the oppressed. Millions of people were burned in the crematoriums and you make a stink over a couple of rags." He spat and walked to where a group of other supervisors had been watching with interest. Through the window a sheath of blue electric sparks could be seen flashing from a trolley car's connection rod.

Teodor breathed a sigh of relief when he was back outside. It had cleared up. The light-blue sky was reflected on the wet street. Bells sounded intermittently from a badly bullet-pocked church tower. From time to time Teodor would drop by a church to wander through the empty aisles, and in the dark nooks and corners, he would try to make out the moldering plaques with Polish names written in tight rows of Schwabacher letters.

There was an unusual commotion on Dworcowa Street, near his house. A truck stacked with a modest pile of clothes was pulling away, and on top of that stack was Fürter with her child in her arms. An excited mongrel was snapping at the truck's tires.

"Get out of here, goddamnit," Schröder yelled at the truck, his arms akimbo. "Let the English have a turn with your ass!"

"You just wait, you scum, your time is coming. You bloodsucker, you crook. You sent plenty of workers to their grave," yelled Fürter, red with rage, struggling with her bundles.

Schröder chortled, wiping tears of laughter with the palm of his hand.

"What happened?" asked Teodor.

Schröder turned around, his smile slowly fading. Raising a cloud of dust, the truck disappeared around the corner, its horn honking.

"The last German's been resettled," said Schröder.

Teodor had a hunch trouble was coming. He took the stairs at full speed. There were crumpled rags and scraps of newspapers on the landing in front of his door. Incredulous, he ran his fingers across the seal on the door. His landlady had been resettled. He broke the seal casually, crumpled it into a ball, and tossed it onto the stairs. It rolled down without making a sound. He opened the door and entered the apartment. It had been cleaned out.

The floor was strewn with trash, the open wardrobe doors gaped a cold red. The curtains swayed rhythmically in the windows, which no one had remembered to close. Teodor's room was no different from the others. Even his coat and the sweater he had pulled off a dead German in 1944 were missing from his wardrobe. Of his small personal belongings all that remained was a broken fingernail clipper. A useless necktie was hanging on the back of a chair. He sat down on his stripped bed and unthinkingly began to chew on a straw he found on the table. The hot air quivered above the equally hot metal-covered windowsill. He walked over to the mirror and looked closely at the tired man leaning toward him.

Michal dragged himself to the office. The girl he had saved from resettlement was sitting on a rickety chair beside a rifle rack. Her lips shone with a thick layer of lipstick.

"So, you finally found me?" laughed Michal.

"I had to."

Zoska Wisniewska, who had been delegated there by the Party, lifted her head from a thick account book. Her large, friendly eyes looked long and hard at the girl and then shifted to Michal.

"That's good, good," said Michal with a smile. "Zoska, I'd like you to meet one of our new workers. What's your name?"

"Klejowna."

Biting the end of her penholder, Zoska did not take her eyes off Michal. He thought he saw their huge pupils darken with sorrow.

"All right, let's see," he said, pacing the office. "You should report to the technical section, Klejowna. You'll work with a team of women cleaning bricks. That's where everyone gets started," he said with an apologetic smile.

When he was alone with Zoska in the office, he took hold of the rifle with an air of concern. Looking down the barrel in the light, squinting carefully, he said: "Comrade Wisniewska, don't you have anything to do with your eyes? There's a book in front of you. It's not quitting time yet."

Her pen began squeaking diligently. A thin, scruffy cat ran across the trampled grass. Living in deserted ruins, the cat had clearly gone back to the wild.

"Come on, it's no big deal," replied Alyosha, straightening the bandage over his eye. "I got it from a piece of mine shrapnel. They knew right away they couldn't do anything for the eye."

Teodor was lying on a cot warmed by the sun. Michal was pouring beer from smoke-darkened bottles into tall glasses. The beer was clearly young; its thick yellowish head hissed softly as it poured.

"Listen, Alyosha," Teodor began carefully, "you have someone at home and you'll probably be going back soon; the war is over, after all."

"I know what you're thinking about," said Alyosha with a smile. The steel netting on Teodor's cot squeaked. "My wife's waiting for me, and we'll manage somehow even without the eye. I'm a welder by trade, now at least the acetylene torch won't bother my eye so much."

"Sure, that's right," Teodor was quick to agree. "It would have been worse to lose a leg or an arm."

"They find a place for everyone back home." Alyosha began rolling a cigarette. "It's not that bad. At least we got crippled fighting for our country and not just from screwing around."

Teodor frowned for a moment. He could not bear propaganda. He pulled a cigarette slowly from his pocket and struck a match. A barely visible flame crept lazily along the match stick.

"I had a brother," said Alyosha pensively. "He was a good kid. He was shot and killed by Polish bandits."

"Where?" said Teodor, stirring on his cot.

"It was back in '43, near Lake Narocz. He was the leader of a partisan company."

They all fell silent. Michal examined the bottles under the light.

"All right, you guys, let's do some drinking. The past is the past, no sense dwelling on it."

Teodor dragged himself up off the cot and they clinked glasses. Alyosha wiped his lips and unbuttoned the top of his shirt. A warm ray of light slid across his off-yellow epaulettes.

"Teodor, you've got a record player here, don't you. Let's play something for Alyosha."

They went to the back of the apartment. Thick dust had already settled on the empty shelves. Water dripped slowly from a faucet that had not been turned completely off. The record player, an old and dilapidated gramophone, was on the blink. It would play, but the handle had to be cranked constantly, a defect that made it seem like a hurdy-gurdy.

"Teodor, I think I heard someone come in," said Michal, stubbing out his cigarette.

Teodor's hand stopped in mid-turn, his eyebrows rose. He listened for a moment and then, grimacing, gave the handle a vigorous twist. Footsteps could be heard in the corridor.

"Teodor, go see, there's really someone here."

Teodor released the handle. The machine's diaphragm groaned and the music came to a halt.

Adam was moving calmly about in Teodor's room. Three men stood near the door looking curiously at the walls. One of them was wearing a faded officer's uniform but without any insignia.

"Hello there," said Adam, raising his head.

"How are you, what's been happening?" asked Teodor.

"Things have been happening," answered Adam mysteriously, and clambering up onto the sideboard, he began reaching for the wall clock, which Teodor had not wound in two weeks. He didn't like its insistent ticking and the startling sound of the hour being struck on a quiet afternoon.

"Introduce yourself," said Adam with a wave of his hand. "Captain, this is my friend."

"Very nice to meet you," said the man in the ex-officer's uniform in a condescending tone, extending a bluish hand. The other two men nodded slightly.

Panting with impatience, Adam grappled with the clock until he finally managed to remove its carved casing. Something groaned inside the clock, whose antique mechanism now began slowly sounding the hour.

"The hell with it," muttered Adam, clambering back down to the floor with the clock.

"You exaggerated a little bit about the furniture," said the ex-officer. "It's just junk, not worth the trouble."

"Captain, you'll see—the furniture in the other rooms isn't luxurious, of course, but it's pretty and stylish," said Adam in self-defense.

"Your friend likes to make jokes," said the ex-officer with a smile for Teodor. Now the other two men who had been standing by the door rushed off to inspect the furniture. The shorter of the two, wearing boots that were too high for him, opened an empty wardrobe.

"Excuse me, but I don't understand what's going on here," said Teodor, barely able to get the words out. He could feel a violent anger rising in him.

"I'm taking the furniture," explained Adam, slinging the clock over his shoulder. "It won't be any use to you, because you won't be staying here, and we need money."

"Adam, Adam," said Teodor in a sinister tone, "how can you start cleaning out the whole house without talking to me first? Who's going to answer for it? You've been wallowing in the mud long enough."

"The office is after me for political reasons, you idiot," Adam exploded, his face the color of a ripe tomato.

"Don't try to throw me off the track, I'm not giving you the furniture," said Teodor in a slow and quiet voice, even though his hands had begun to quiver with fury.

"You got nothing to say about it. What do you care anyway, you fool. The Bolshevik upstairs has got you thinking his way," said Adam, bent double by the weight of the clock. He spat on the floor and set off unsteadily toward the door.

"You're not taking it, you son of a bitch," said Teodor, tearing after him, but the ex-officer's fatherly arms were around him before he knew it.

"Easy does it, young man, easy, or you'll get it in the face," said the ex-officer, raising his eyebrows dramatically. Suddenly Teodor freed his right hand and punched the ex-officer's creased forehead with all his might. The ex-officer reeled back, not so much from the force of the blow as from the surprise. Adam was already out of the room. Teodor didn't hesitate. With a vigorous kick he sent the man nearest him flying against the mirrored wardrobe. Glass fell to the floor. His head down like a buffalo's, the ex-officer rushed to the attack. Teodor just managed to leap aside and rabbit-punch him on the back of the neck. Still, the fight would have ended badly for Teodor if Alyosha and Michal hadn't come to his aid. Driven into a corner, Teodor was desperately trying to kick his assailants away when suddenly the door opened and Alyosha was in the doorway, breaking the leg off a chair as he ran in. Michal came crashing in after him, a wooden shoe tree in hand.

The first blow from the chair leg struck the shortest of the uninvited guests. He fell sitting to the floor with a whine but still had enough presence of mind to bite Alyosha's hand. Calmly and methodically, Michal beat the ex-officer, whose head rang quite melodiously.

They drove without their lights, because the red afterglow in the west lit the road well enough. There was very little traffic. People were still afraid of nightfall. On the ground floor of a burned-out building near the square, red light bulbs spelled out the word DANCING. The nightclub had popped up out of nowhere. Adam remembered going inside those blackened walls to relieve himself only two weeks ago. Then they passed a brewery that was being rebuilt and a steelworks that seemed deserted. It was only after looking carefully for a while that Adam could make out the glowing furnace screened from the street by a large empty room. The first stars had appeared in a celadon sky.

Ex-officer Sienkiewicz was holding a handkerchief soaked in water to the back of his head. "That was some mess you got us into there, thanks," he groaned, shaking the lukewarm drops of water off his fingers.

"I would never have expected it. After all, he and I were in the partisans together, we went after the Bolsheviks, and now just look . . . You can't trust your own brother today."

"The hell with him. We'll pay him back when the time comes," moaned Sienkiewicz.

The short one was lying on his back by a bag of clothes. He had been trying to stop the blood spurting from his nose for twenty minutes now. They drove into the suburb of Bytom, where the structures were smaller and had suffered little damage.

In the distance the buildings were few and far between; a path lined with chestnut trees led to one enormous complex with all its windows lit, the former temporary site of a military hospital. The driver shifted into third, the motor groaned, and the truck leaped forward onto the dry asphalt. Two heat lamps banged against the cab and a sewing machine's nickel plating rang softly. The radios had been set beside the sack of clothing and were guarded by a fourth man, since they could be damaged more easily than the typewriters in their black cases. All this was the fruit of two months of effort by Adam. The booty had been kept by people whom Adam had helped obtain apartments and who had helped him lug junk from deserted buildings.

Sienkiewicz took a small mirror from his pocket, and turning his face toward the fading afterglow in the west, he began to smooth down his hair. A flock of crows streamed from the left side of the road over a sparse copse of trees.

Suddenly the truck braked, slamming Adam's forehead against the rough siding.

"What the hell!" Sienkiewicz clambered up off the floor. His broken mirror reflected pieces of the clear sky.

Adam jumped off the back of the truck and began stamping his feet, which had fallen asleep. There were a dozen or so patients in robes and colored pajamas standing in front of the truck. One patient was wearing only a shirt and underpants.

"All right, let's see what you're carrying in there!" shouted a half-naked giant, supporting himself on a pair of rickety crutches. Two young men with eagles on their crumpled field caps stood beside him.

"That's none of your business," Adam barked back, but a few of the invalids had already clambered with the grace of monkeys onto the back of the truck, their crutches knocking against the sides.

"You better beat it or we'll call for a command patrol, you motherfuckers," said Adam in a rage. "Our papers are in order. And we're on official business."

"Hey, Jozef, hit that young man in the head," shouted the giant, who was clearly the ringleader. His shaved head gleamed dully. "I know this kind of official business; you're taking every last pot and pan, you motherfucker."

Having received his instructions, Jozef, a young man in green pajamas, pulled a thick rubber-tipped club out from under their car. Adam retreated cautiously toward the cab of the truck.

"What they got there?" roared the giant to his men, looting the back of the truck.

"Heat lamps and radios!"

"Let's see 'em!"

Sienkiewicz struggled desperately among the sacks, trying to tear the heat lamps from their hands. The other two men lay quietly in the back of the truck.

The heat lamps and radios, passing quickly from hand to hand, were soon in the giant's care. Throwing his crutches aside, he hopped clumsily around the pile of radios. He fiddled with the dials, peered at the lights, then waved to his men: "All right! Let them go!"

Adam climbed furtively onto the back of the truck, where Sienkiewicz, searching for his handkerchief, was cursing the giant in the foulest terms. "I was goin' to go for those sons of bitches, but we wouldn't have gotten out of here alive," hissed Sienkiewicz.

"Did they take everything?"

"They left the clothes and the typewriters."

"Well, thank God for that."

"The less said by you the better," snarled Sienkiewicz.

Adam banged a fist against the cab. "Let's get a move on, you bum, before they start cleaning us out again."

The leaves were slowly turning yellow. The wind had shifted, and blowing from the north more often now, it lashed the broken antenna wires against the building's sheet-metal roof. One day Teodor was forced to bring the faded deck chair, whose canvas seat was always filled with stagnant rainwater, in from the balcony. The grapevine that grew along the wall, lush in the summertime, was increasingly covered with dust, and its blackened stalk had begun to show through its reddish leaves. By the canal a German who was blind in one eye was tending a fat goat. Covering himself with a discolored sack, the man smoked a long clay pipe. One day he had appeared wearing a partially finished sweater with the knitting needles still in it and from then on he wore it all the time, the nickel-plated needles gleaming even in the rain. In good weather, Teodor, Michal, and Alyosha would relax by the canal. Alyosha would bring his accordion trimmed with pseudo-mother-of-pearl, which they would all take turns playing, stretching their tired legs out in the sun, and then would usually pull out a pack of cards. At that point, the goat would stop chewing and look intently, and with what seemed to be mockery, at the seated men. In time, the goat grew accustomed to the intruders' presence, and once in a great while, without raising its head from the dying grass, it would cock a shaggy ear when, after a heated debate, one of the three friends would begin playing the wheezy accordion.

Over the last few months Teodor had not, unfortunately, learned to be any more practical. He had allowed a bald railroad worker to be moved into his apartment. The railroad worker, Zietkowski, was living there alone for the time being, but in the evenings he would think about moving his whole family in. Zietkowski spent only the night there. Teodor would run into him in the kitchen, where they both cooked their dinner over the anemic gas flame. Zietkowski invariably cooked himself an omelette in rancid bacon fat that reeked of hog urine. It was rare for him to bring a piece of dry, salted Russian fish home. He enjoyed discussing prices, while rubbing his elbow against his thin ribs. They often opened the kitchen window to hear the music streaming copiously from Schröder's apartment. Recently a young official from the housing department had begun paying court to Schröder's daughter. The bacon fat sizzled in the frying pan while Zietkowski, standing on tiptoe, craned his thin neck through the none-too-clean collar of his shirt. Then, his curiosity sufficiently satisfied, he came back down on his heels and, frowning, would make his usual remark: "You see, they're playing music . . ."

"So they are," Teodor would reply with his customary astonishment.

Then they would take their dinners to their rooms on small plates that had turned bluish from the dishrag they both shared.

When returning from work, Teodor would try to mount the stairs as quickly as possible so as not to attract the attention of his neighbor, a young man with long hair, whose apartment reeked of melancholy. But each time one step or another would betray Teodor with a startling creak. Then the young man waiting behind the door, whose card read KONSTANTY KUPCZYK—DRAFTS-MAN, would click his latch open and, his sad face emerging from the darkness, would ask in a funereal whisper: "Please come in, just for a minute."

At first Teodor had tried to fend off those invitations, but in the end he had to give in. Kupczyk's character was as persistent as his face was tragic.

Kupczyk's apartment was empty and he used only one room, whose walls were decorated with pictures of film stars posing with their little dogs, clipped from German illustrated magazines. A cherry-wood rosary hung on the wall above his neatly made bed.

Kupczyk did not like talkative people, which was most likely why he pursued the friendship of the taciturn Teodor. On the other hand, Kupczyk could talk for hours about his youth and his numerous emotional and spiritual conflicts. Taking out the butter which he kept between the double windows, he would clumsily slice some bread, his bony hands always filthy at the knuckles, and extract a kielbasa going green on the outside from a piece of grayish cloth. Staring in fright at the rancid butter and half-spoiled kielbasa, Teodor could feel his mouth thicken with the saliva that usually precedes stomach trouble.

Kupczyk moved ineptly about the room, as if tripped up by a body that was too large for his needs. Placing the treat in front of Teodor, he spent a long time urging him to begin eating as quickly as possible—the kielbasa was spoiling by the minute and he had saved this piece especially for Teodor. Kupczyk treated Teodor's refusals as a sign of good taste, a rare quality in those days. Relenting, Teodor took a piece of bread, which expanded as he chewed it, and listened to Kupczyk's tales of woe.

"I think you understand me. I was born a few decades too late. I'm not of these times, I can't elbow my way ahead. I don't have the strength for that, and you know what that means. I was always like this, I suffered a lot even as a child. My schoolmates used to beat me up, I'm ashamed to admit. They dragged me around by the ears. I always had running sores at the base of my ears."

"Uh-huh, uh-huh," muttered Teodor, turning the fibrous bread over on his tongue. An autumn rain lashed against the window.

"Of course I started reading books as a child. The other kids were out breaking their noses and knees and drowning in the river, but I was home reading books. And that's why I'm so hypersensitive now, I'm always just waiting for something to happen. Exactly what is hard to say, but you know what I mean, some unexpected event that will change things. How should I know what it'll be. You know, whenever I hear someone on the stairs, I think he's coming to see me, that there's some news, that something will change, ah . . ."

"You should get married," Teodor would usually say. "Being alone is bad for your nerves."

"Ha ha ha." Kupczyk would laugh with tangible bitterness.

"Me get married, ha ha." Then he would grow serious, and rolling a small piece of bread into a ball, he would explain: "You should understand, I'm telling you my secrets." Then, after a pause filled with menace, he would continue: "You see, I'm afraid of life. You know what that means, to be aware that you have all those years to live. I don't have the strength for it, I'm afraid of the responsibility."

"For what?" Teodor would unfailingly interrupt.

"For life, for everything I do."

"Then go hang yourself," Teodor would advise irritably.

Kupczyk would smile with a look of resignation, taking Teodor's suggestion quite seriously. "That's easy to say. I'm too weak for that, I don't have the strength . . ."

After a few yawns, Teodor would begin checking his watch more and more often. Then Kupczyk would hurry to pack the few minutes remaining before Teodor's departure with as much melancholy as possible.

When Teodor rose, feigning fatigue, Kupczyk would take him beseechingly by the arm and say: "Just a little longer, our conversation was going so well."

Visiting Kupczyk had become a nightmare. Every bit as much as Kupczyk feared life, Teodor feared the creak of Kupczyk's door opening and the visit that inevitably ensued.

One rainy afternoon, overcome by a longing to see Eryka and frightened of being caught by Kupczyk, Teodor turned from the staircase in his building and went back outside. Holding his coat over his head to shield himself from the downpour, he set off for the train station. Traveling to Katowice by streetcar was no longer worth the effort. More trains were running now and they were becoming more comfortable as time went on.

There was an enormous, sprawling newspaper stand in the half-repaired station. Teodor bought a couple of illustrated magazines without giving the choice much thought. The salesgirl took his money, and after nodding to him impassively, she went back to reading her book, an activity that seemed as unreal to Teodor as his distant memories of youth.

He lost a little time at the station in Katowice. All the exits were guarded by soldiers. After showing their identification, the passengers flowed slowly out the numerous doors. A pair of men carrying sacks dashed feverishly around the station, seeking sanctuary which the men's room, the natural choice, could not provide, unfortunately, since it had been maliciously locked. The voice of a person suffering from a head cold announced the departure of a train.

An unshaven platoon leader wearing a brass medal for valor checked Teodor's papers. The puddles on the streets danced with occasional drops of rain.

The deaf-and-dumb servant opened the door. She cackled with what seemed delight, raising her hands. The gestures made by the deaf-and-dumb are never in proportion to the importance of events. Everything was the same as it had been during his last visit there. Eryka was lying on the couch, a brightly colored best seller in hand.

"I didn't think you'd come again," she said, setting the book aside.

Teodor began presenting the excuses he had prepared beforehand but which now, face to face with Eryka, struck him as flimsy and insignificant.

"Save it for my parents," she said, presenting her cheek for a kiss.

He took a seat by the window, clasping his knees with his hands. They couldn't get their conversation off the ground. The rain drummed against the window, a radio whined a floor below.

Looking critically at his clothes, she said: "I can see you haven't straightened out yet."

He shrugged his shoulders.

"And how many times have we said you should always bring us something when you come. We know people, they'd buy things right away."

Eryka's father walked through the parlor carrying a small piece of wood to roll cigarettes on and a plug of tobacco. He smiled foolishly when saying hello. He had become even more childlike;

the opulent, stuffy apartment and the regular meals for which he worked so hard all his life had clearly not been good for his health.

When the old man left the room, Teodor sat down beside Eryka. Outside the window a streetcar flashed a sheaf of sparks.

"How's your work going?" he asked.

"Work? It's all right. I'm at the Coal Association but I've had enough of it. I want to make contact with the English embassy. I worked for them before the war and I've heard the prewar consul is back in Warsaw now."

"Hm, I see. And how are you doing with the Party?"

"Don't remind me of that. I can't take it anymore. I'll probably chuck it all. They can't do anything to me now. I've got my certificate of rehabilitation in my pocket."

Teodor nodded with apparent interest. His eyes ran along the neatly hung photographs on the wall, avoiding Eryka's face, which seemed somehow alien, the face of an obstinate woman.

The rain grew darker. A chilly autumn twilight seeped into the room from behind the furniture and wrapped itself around Eryka's slender legs. Since he was there at night, Teodor felt obliged to put his arms around her. Immersed in her own thoughts, she moved away, displaying some animosity. Taking it philosophically, Teodor crossed his legs. In his room Eryka's father was humming to himself, his soft slippers shuffling on the floor.

After a long silence, the doorbell rang. It was Eryka's mother, who began reviling the servant from the door. Teodor rose and assumed a pleasant expression to greet her.

"Ah, Teodor, we thought you'd grown tired of us."

"How can you say that," he mumbled, shuffling his feet.

"Friends aren't what they used to be. Anyway, Eryka couldn't wait to see you again," she said with a glance at her daughter.

"I've been busy with work," muttered Teodor, looking for somewhere to rest his eyes.

"Yes, yes, it's a fine thing, though. That's how men always are—they seduce a girl, then poof they're gone," she said, her hand making a philosophical spiral.

"Leave him alone, Mamchen," said Eryka warningly.

Coat in hand, Eryka's mother went into the front room. Teodor walked to the door and, frowning, switched on the light.

"You know," said Eryka, squinting at the light, "I had to tell my mother that you asked me to marry you. I had to justify our . . ." She paused, searching for the right words. ". . . our friendship. Naturally, that doesn't obligate you in any way."

A painful silence ensued. Ill at ease, Teodor began to mumble while looking through a pile of illustrated magazines.

"Well, I guess you did the right thing . . . I don't know if I told you that my friend left quite a while ago."

"Is that so?" said Eryka with polite surprise.

Teodor's eyes wandered to the ceiling. There was a damp yellow patch in one corner, the plaster would start falling soon. Whoever designed the wallpaper had lacked imagination. Sallow deer running, all going to the right. The photograph at the top left was crooked and must have been like that for a few months, because the old mark it left on the wall had begun turning red.

In the morning Teodor usually crossed off a square on his wall calendar to signify that another day had passed. He did this out of habit, without giving it a second thought. A few days after he visited Eryka, it was drizzling again and Teodor was staring at the marked-up calendar, whose little squat filled-in squares marked the passage of several months. He sank into a chair and, pencil in hand, amused himself by figuring out how many days had passed since he had left the forest. It was difficult to calculate, difficult to recall the places along the way from Polesie to Silesia. Thus far he had lived as unthinkingly as he had crossed the days off the calendar. He had taken consolation in this being a passing stage, counting on a stable future, for which he was postponing his more ambitious plans. Months had passed, Adam had vanished, the murders and robberies in the city had come to an end, Michal had his factory going full-blast, and a co-op had been set up in the little building where Adam hoped to open a business.

Teodor began to be tormented by a sense of wasted time. Full of vague, rebellious intentions, he kept walking to the closed window to look out at the dark and somnolent autumn day. Children were pushing loads of coal in lopsided wheelbarrows, and suspended by a rope, a worker was slapping light-blue paint on a storefront. Toward evening the miners would return from the day shift bent double by the weight of the coal sacks they'd been carrying on their backs.

The room still had no windows. A wind or the autumn cold passed over the machines covered with boards. Zoska toyed with a monkey wrench.

"What are you doing, Zoska?" he asked in a severe tone.

"I just came here for a little rest," she said, gathering her skirt modestly around her.

"And who's keeping an eye on the boys?"

"Klejowna's there, she can manage."

"Hm," said Michal pensively, looking for a pretext to give Zoska a talking-to.

He sat down beside her on a box, having first brushed off some wood shavings, which rustled like leaves. He took out a cigarette and stuck it in his mouth, but Zoska, pretending to be smoothing his hair, snatched it from his mouth before he knew what was happening.

"What does that mean, what's all this sudden concern?" he said, bristling.

"Nothing, Michal, but you know you're not supposed to smoke. I had a talk with Zakrzewski and I know you're leaving for a few months of medical care. You'll come back in good health and that'll be good."

"And what do you care?" he asked gruffly.

She lowered her head. Through the locks of her hair he caught sight of a swath of cheek flushing a sudden red. He quickly put his arm around her and she raised her head, a look of tender surprise on her face.

"The thing is, you see," he said in confusion, "I don't know if I'll get my health back for sure. I didn't take good care of myself."

"You'll get better, of course you will," she said, as if reassuring a worried child. "There's so much work waiting for you here," she said, confused again.

Michal stroked her cool, smooth arm. A pair of sparrows lighted on the grillwork over the window. They chirped, their heads cocked as if in amazement. A slack banner waved in the air behind them. The acrid smell of lime rose from the boxes by the wall.

For a good fifteen minutes neither of them said a word. The sky was already dotted with stars. A cutting winter wind was blowing from the north. Teodor put his jacket collar up.

"I have a proposition for you," said Michal out of the blue.

"I'm leaving tomorrow," muttered Teodor.

"Where, for how long?" said Michal anxiously.

"To see my parents, I have to see how they're doing."

"And when will you be back?"

"Shouldn't be long, a few days," lied Teodor, to avoid any further questions.

"We can discuss it at length then," said Michal.

They said goodbye on the stairs.

"Remember, come back," said Michal.

"Sure," muttered Teodor without conviction, and tiptoed past Kupczyk the melancholy poet's door.

As he fumbled for the doorknob in the dark, his fingers came upon a small parcel tied to the brass handle. Turning on the light in his room, Teodor unwrapped the package, which contained a pack of American cigarettes and a small sheet of paper. He unfolded the paper and read it under the lamp.

The letter, not free of grammatical errors, informed him that the writer no longer held his well-deserved grudge against him. It was only after reading a few paragraphs that Teodor realized that the note was from Adam.

I took advantage of someone going to Poland to write you a few words. I see now I have no reason to be angry at you. You were always a madman. Things are fine with me, but I miss Poland a little, which is why I'm writing to you. I'm doing very well. It's too bad you're not with me. I'm in England now, in the army. When I told them I was from Polesie and told them what had happened to us, I was promoted to second lieutenant and awarded the cross of valor. You should have got one too. Right now we're living in barracks, but I'm not worried because everybody's looking out for us. We've got plenty of food and money too. I have fun all the time. That captain from Katowice is with me, but he wants to leave for Argentina, he's doing terrific at business. I feel sorry for you stuck in Poland. Don't write to me for the time being because you could get caught and sent to the polar bears. Burn my note right away. Take a good look at the cigarettes I sent you.

Bye for now.

The note concluded with a sprawling signature.

Teodor burned the note and opened the cigarettes. He withdrew one, sniffed it, and put it in his mouth. He struck a match and brought it to the cigarette. The match went out, Teodor inhaling stale air in vain. He took the cigarette from his mouth and glanced at the end of it. Instead of tobacco, the cigarette contained a stiff scroll of paper. He ripped the cigarette open and a rolled-up dollar bill fell onto the table.

A loathsome autumn rain was drumming at the window again. The fly-specked lamp suspended from a cord swung sadly over his head. Teodor glanced over at his unmade bed, his dirty pillow, and carefully inserted the dollar into his watch pocket.

He examined the other cigarettes, but they contained no money. He undressed slowly and turned off the light.

Throughout the entire trip, one and the same landscape could be seen through the windows on both sides of the compartment: blackened fields of uncut grain, shell craters, long lines of rusted artillery and vehicles. Here and there small groups of people were grappling with the wreckage of bridge spans. The car was stuffed with demobilized soldiers and ordinary people keeping a careful eye on their heavy sacks in the overhead racks.

He had to change trains twice before reaching Kolobrzeg, almost the only passenger on the train traveling on a one-track line. For a good two hours he wandered the near-empty streets of that half-deserted city, until he finally found the house where his parents were now living.

His mother opened the door. For a moment she stood with a polite, interrogative grimace on her aging face.

"Don't you recognize your own son?" asked Teodor, removing his knapsack.

"Teodor, Teodor, my son," she said, suddenly bursting into tears. They went into the front room, which had an alien smell, not like the old familiar, half-stone house in Polesie that had an ancient sort of stuffiness about it.

He slowly removed his coat, his mother hovering by him, trying to help. Someone walked the length of the next room, the glass in the door rattled, and then Elka was in the doorway.

He wanted to run to her as he used to, and put his arms around her, but instead he walked slowly and stiff-leggedly over to her and extended his hand. "How are you, Elka? It's been a long time."

Her eyes wide open, she looked at him without saying a word. The electric meter on the wall purred like a cricket.

"So, how are things here, have they been giving you something to eat?" he asked with artificial ease.

His mother fidgeted where she stood, like a person suddenly cured of paralysis. "Come in the next room. All this made me forget that he must be hungry."

New furniture gleaming with lacquer stood beside the old, familiar pieces. A huge Futurist oil painting blazed with color on one wall. Teodor stopped in front of the painting and shook his head. "Where's that from?"

"I don't know," said his mother with a shrug, opening the sideboard, the glass door rattling. "It was here when we moved into the apartment. Your father said it could stay there because pictures like that are in fashion now. It's supposed to be the sea."

Elka had still not said a single word, sitting stiffly at the table

covered with a cotton-thread lace cloth. An old clock from Polesie hung beside the painting, ticking nervously, as if ill at ease in that company.

Teodor ate slowly, chewing each piece a long time. His mother looked closely at him with a kind and tender smile.

"How have you been, Teodor? You never write," she said.

"Fine. All I do is work."

"You couldn't be making much, your jacket's in terrible shape."

Teodor grunted noncommittally.

"Can you stay here with us?"

He stopped eating and looked reflectively out the window. "Maybe."

Through the window he could see a tin tub rusted red fastened to the side of the banister of a half-destroyed staircase. A black, solitary chimney was engraved against the leaden sky.

"Stay," said Elka with what seemed great effort.

He glanced over at her in surprise. Her voice had grown coarser in the last year. Her lips were swollen with blood.

"What are you doing, Elka?" he asked, to have something to say.

She blushed. "I'm taking my certificate in a high school for adults."

"That's wonderful," he said in praise, allowing his eyes to play over her. Now she seemed prettier.

When his mother went off to the kitchen, Teodor moved his chair beside Elka and put his arm around her. Though this surprised her, she did not make the slightest gesture of displeasure. He began speaking without making any special point, surprised by his own words. He wanted to persuade himself that he had finally made his way to a safe haven. Elka cowered beside him, trying to breathe as quietly as possible. His mother's face had told him that, given the new order, Elka would, unfortunately, no longer be a misalliance. Moreover, the fruit of the Klimowiczes' Samaritan inclinations had matured into a beautiful young woman.

The hours dragged. For a time Teodor stretched out on the couch, pretending to have dozed off. His mother and Elka walked on tiptoe, each cautioning the other to be quiet. Teodor's eyes were open and he was aware of the wall's rough surface by his face. Waves of rain and wind splashed against the windowpanes. It was startlingly still. Once again Eryka came to his mind, but he adroitly screened her out with memories of Bytom. He had left all that wasted time behind him. And where was he now? In a moldy museum full of malevolent memories, a living museum that had moved a few hundred kilometers west. His mother dropped a dish; then both she and Elka shushed each other vigilantly.

They ate dinner in silence, a tradition that had been imposed by his father. The father did not like conversation, especially during the second course. That day, however, he made something of an exception and during tea asked Teodor: "Here for long? Staying?"

"I don't know yet."

"He'll probably stay," said Teodor's mother, coming to his aid.

His father carefully rinsed his mouth with tea and then, looking at his glass, said unexpectedly: "Don't go"—he paused and indicated the window with his shoulder—"over there . . ."

Teodor understood the allusion. "I won't," he said, then added a moment later: "Adam's there already."

"What do you mean?" said his mother with excitement. "When did he leave?"

"At the end of the summer."

His father brushed a few drops of tea from his mustache, then said, as if to himself: "I could help get you started here. Why waste time?"

Teodor pretended not to hear his father's suggestion. Silently, he balled up a piece of bread in the palm of his hand. Noticing what Teodor was doing, the father raised his brows.

"Don't play with your bread," said his mother, putting his father's wishes into words.

The days dragged, as time does during a train trip. At first Teodor tried to do some reading. He leafed through the old familiar books from Polesie with their torn covers. He shook the dust off them and then, on those yellowed pages, tried to find traces of the comments he had once penciled in the margins, to his mother's despair. He spent a long time looking through an old-fashioned Polish grammar that belonged to his father. He came on a fragment from a novel by Orzeszkowa in that grammar, and as if reading an old document, he was moved by the story of Jan and Cecylia, who founded the Bohatyrewicz clan on the banks of the Niemen.

He could not find a common language with his parents. Even the most innocent conversation begun by one of them in good faith usually ended in an unpleasant clash of words. The parents could not see who their son had become, and the son did not want to go back to that old constellation of customs and ideas.

His walk by the sea with Elka was not a success. They floundered in silence across the deep, cold sand. Teodor glanced with hostility and irritation at her pretty lips and the little Marist Association pin on the lapel of her coat. A piercing storm wind blew in from the sea, signaling snow.

In the evenings, when his father listened with closed eyes to Madrid, New York, and London, Teodor would pretend to doze off on the couch. When the icy rain lashed the windows with such force it seemed the glass would break any minute, he would think of Adam, who was certainly not wasting his time in England. Many young people were getting the chance to study in the Polish departments of English universities. And Elka, despite his mother's urging, was doing nothing to encourage his interest in her.

For a few days he sat by the window looking vacantly at the viscous, leaden sky. He counted all the chimneys and staircases that had survived intact. On Saturday evening he started looking for his knapsack.

"Going somewhere?" asked his mother, turning from the fat sizzling in the frying pan.

"I'm leaving," he said curtly.

As if not hearing her sobs, he packed slowly and then reached for his coat.

"But come back," she said in capitulation. "You won't make anything of yourself there, with those foreign people."

"I'll see."

Teodor's father did not raise his head from the radio.

He kissed his mother on both cheeks, gave the frightened Elka a kiss on the temple, and then, slinging his knapsack over his shoulder, he moved toward the door. Clearing his throat loudly, his father fiddled with the radio. Despite all his years of listening to the radio clandestinely, he somehow could not get his favorite station clearly that day.

"God be with you," cried his mother, as if having just remembered something.

He closed the door carefully behind him and, holding on to the wall, walked slowly down to the street. The raw wind grabbed him by the legs, pressing his pants tight around his calves.

Yes, yes, my little worms, those are the remains of my novel, the second novel I ever wrote; which I wrote speedily and eagerly in 1948 or 1949, thirty-three years ago, when I was twenty-two years old and mightily ashamed of those sorry twenty-two years. So, this is the corpse of a novel written in my youth. Actually, it's what's left after the autopsy I performed over the last few days. I cut off sections and threw them out. The liver, the intestines, the genitals. I left only the skin and bones, so that you could have a taste of that time, so that you could catch a quick glimpse of me as I slipped stealthily into the future, which has now arrived.

Yes, yes, all of a sudden, from the depths of the cupboard where I keep my dead manuscripts, I'd pulled a dark-blue folder marked in my own hand *The New Days* and annotated by butchers unknown—VERY URGENT, HEAD OFFICE OF PRESS CONTROL, SEND BY MESSENGER—and signed with the name of a certain woman who died long ago but who, before her death, had censored books, shaped authors, coiffed Polish literature; then suddenly she got cancer and departed this world. Everyone has forgotten her and only I have recalled her, so let this be the sole epitaph for that poor victim of the times, wars, ideas.

Yes, yes, from that stillborn novel, for which I never managed to find a good title and which in the spirit of the times I named *The New Days*, I have cut out scenes and snippets which still please me a bit or which contain some genes of truth, authenticity, some photographic fidelity, and then, trying to keep my objectivity about that carcass of my own prose, I, like an old dogcatcher, rounded up three dozen or so sequences and included them in this book concocted in the year of Our Lord 1981, my fifty-fifth ride on the merry-go-round known as the solar system.

Holy Mother of God, look at this archaic typescript. Scribbled on, cut to pieces, marked with someone's black pencil and someone else's red pencil, some stranger's fountain pen and some other stranger's fingerprints. All the censors of the early Stalin era, professional and volunteer, went wild on the pages of this confession of a defeated Home Army soldier, this idiotic profession of faith in the good intentions of the victorious regime. Passages underlined, exclamation marks of indignation, sinister question marks, comments terse as gunshots. Whip marks. On the tattered skin of my retarded child.

But I won't show you this corpse in its entirety. I'd be too ashamed. Tomorrow I'll throw all the rest in the trash, and it'll make a good pile too, and no one will know what I was capable of thirty years ago, how low I had sunk, how untrue I had been to myself. My self which I still had not come to know.

For many years I could not make up my mind whether to

murder that book or to leave it for some future researcher to read with amazement and aversion. Now, in a moment of inspiration, I extricated it from the embrace of the spiderweb, the dead air of oblivion, and cut that petrified mummy into little pieces. And without spilling a single drop of blood.

18

Oh, Mother of God. I'm holding my pen in my hand, surprised myself to have pen in hand. And as I move this pen along paper, I return from a distant journey, a sort of nonbeing, a purgatory, or from what was just a trance of lethargy, that land of marshes and mist where certain types of people sleep off the lethargy assigned them by fate or destiny. I have spent a dozen weeks or so wandering about with Milosz, the people of the Issa Valley, and the ghosts that have been slinking along behind me all my life, following me from Nowa Wilejka all the way to Manhattan. And so, I've been roaming about with them as company near the Lithuanian border, around Wizajny and Szypliski, amid hills packed with iron ore, in valleys strewn with the bones of the Jadzwings, and through forests full of spiderwebs spread by pests bent on sabotage. And there I served out the sentence, no doubt a fair one, that my sinful life had earned me. And what was cooking, boiling, and bubbling close to the exploding point there in that cauldron of nations, far from family, far from the literary and art mafias, and well off the beaten track of politics?

I was just shooting a film. Just shooting myself in the head.

No doubt some scribe is sitting and noting day by day what's happening outside his window, on the street, in the literary salon, and at the bazaar. No doubt, for posterity's sake, many scrupulous people are writing descriptions of these months and hours we have our noses pressed against, understanding very little of it. I am unable to record anything. It all goes right through my fingers like sand.

Yesterday I was by the Cadet Firemen's School, whose students have been on strike for several days now. Dark streetcars cut off access to the gates of the school. All the streets in the area had been blocked off by the police. Stakeouts, dogs, trucks. All the power, all the remnants of the dying authorities' power, has come creeping to this nest of Janissaries to burn it out with this ill-starred shooting party.

It's dark and gloomy; a little flimsy snow, a little freezing rain. Behind the wall of streetcars there is an enormous silent crowd keeping watch, so that no one harms these boys who do not want to be Soviet policemen. The cadets appear in the bright windows, looking out at the city at evening and at the double rows of sopping-wet policemen. A small incident at the end of November 1981. A short strike by a few hundred young people. But everyone feels that history is being made on this street, which bears the name of one of the bards; that Polish history is being made in this place, even though they can be smoked out of there tomorrow and taken to prison or labor camps.

I see all this. The film company driver brought me there. We stopped to listen to the singing. The cadets are singing, their voices strong, but I don't recognize the song. They could be praying for victory or taking heart from old patriotic tunes. We drive around all sides of the area. Checkpoints, barriers, police, men from the Army Security Force. The young men's songs mix with the wind, the snow, and the November dark. The cadets and the end of November. Here, every day is a historical symbol.

But I don't describe any of that. I am unable to sit, look, and describe. I'm an impatient person. Something's always pulling at me, driving me, dragging me off by what's left of my hair. Round and round in circles in the same spot. I rush on ahead, into the distant universe, without stirring from my place. You want an image of the times, pick up a history book. You won't get it here.

An evening in early winter. The electricity has been turned off, lines in front of empty stores, a protest by prisoners who have climbed to the top of a boiler chimney, gray crowds creeping silently to and fro, Poland's debts and my own personal debt rise in the money markets of Wall Street, Frankfurt, Tokyo, infants are dying in large numbers in maternity hospitals, a man had a nervous breakdown and strangled his wife, an unruly wife killed her husband with a knife, but I don't describe anything, all I do is sink deeper into my own paltry pain, my crummy despair, my imaginary failures. Doesn't matter. Vanity of vanities. Yet another incomplete end of the world.

I glued the film together and then watched it carefully, unwillingly. In a cold screening room, whose radiators were being repaired. And still it all went off fairly smoothly, with something like objectivity and professionalism. The lights came on, and concealing my smile of premature satisfaction, I slipped out through a side door. I had time, I could wait to hear the praise from the film's first viewers, my patient co-workers. I took a slow, unhurried walk around the building, went to my office, and there waited for the *oohs* and *aahs* which I had coming, and which are given to every filmmaker, no matter what junk he turns out. And so I threw myself into a chair, assumed an unconcerned air, and strained my ears for the procession bearing me the homage I was due.

They didn't come in any hurry. Dismayed, startled, seized by shame for me and for themselves, for that unhappy film and those many months of exhaustion. They sat embarrassed at the edges of their seats, sat for a while in careful silence, and then disappeared. When they were gone, I was left alone with my producer, loyal, ready for anything, who, when he saw my begging eyes, said with uncertainty: But it's a film, isn't it?

But I'm aware that it's a mishmash, which I'm ashamed to say

I like, though no one else will. Somewhere on the other side of the ocean Czeslaw Milosz waits in ambush to scalp me; Czeslaw Milosz, who, after much resistance, entrusted me with his first-born epic child. And I know that ours is a proud nation that loves its bard and will find a way to avenge this desecration of the Nobel laureate's work. Where can I run to? Where can I emigrate? How can I survive ostracism?

So many of my colleagues are making money off Renewal and I'm the only one showing a loss. I was in my glory when I was not allowed to make films. Universal sorrow. General mourning. The progressive intelligentsia has been deprived of films by T. Konwicki. Then what happens? Renewal opens the door to filmmaking. I make a film, I besmirch the Nobel laureate and reveal my utterly senile artistic impotence.

But enough of these laments, these complaints, these threats hurled at fate. What happened at that old prewar glider school on Lake Szelment at the foot of Mt. Jasienowa, where I spent seven weeks shooting the exteriors for The Issa Valley? What happened inside me, inside my head, and inside my heart during those moonlit nights and those days of haste and labor, packed with surprises? Melancholy demons loitered in the traces of houses long missing, dying orchards, overgrown roads, and blinded wells. A cold and ominous light struck the sky from an earth pregnant with mysterious elements. The forest rang with cries for help that had died out long ago. Nearby, in Olecko, blood flowed from a mission cross by a church. A miracle, one of the many miracles that have visited my country.

Magic. Good magic. Bad magic. The magical. The screenplay, the shooting script, and everyday incidents suddenly took on unexpected significance, subtexts, holiness. An obsession with the magical. The universe of the magical.

I always imagined biological and mental development as resembling a gigantic extended line of soldiers eternally on the march; in a word, I naïvely thought that human evolution took place evenly, uniformly, and that all living beings were equally under its sway.

Now, in my old age, I can see how much faith people place in schoolbooks and popular science, that easy literature on which many a sharp guy has made a killing. Now, in my old age, while moving in Warsaw's dense crowds, I have suddenly perceived that human evolution is more reminiscent of a march in single file, that there is no more or less even, extended line, that all one sees are small groups of loose-linked people as they stumble forward into the unknown. Right now I am being passed on the left by an eggheaded individual who is out ahead of us all in the evolutionary process and who at the very least should be living in the middle of the third millennium. Meanwhile, on the right I am outstripping a fellow creature with a gigantic jaw, no forehead, a sunken nose; a fellow creature who by the caprice of some frolicsome gene has ended up in our times from the Neanderthal period.

That's the way it is. In this herd of five billion, individuals from all *Homo sapiens'* stages of development live cheek by jowl, even including those from eras we have not been able to imagine yet. Man—the word has a proud ring to it. But which sort of man, the Cro-Magnon cannibal or the unnamed man whom chance has not yet selected from a billion variants and possibilities.

Scholars and journalists bemoan the fact that people do not communicate. Quite a number of jerks in literature and art have also made a pretty penny on the subject of our lack of communication. But what kind of communication can exist between a caveman and me, a refined example of what God can do, me, conceived in legendary Nowa Wilejka? What connection is there between one man on the street who exists in pre-Sumerian times and another who has speeded up and put himself five thousand years out ahead? And thus the lack of communication is a correct and natural form of communication. The lack of communication is the ideal form of communication between people. What could be better? That's the way it is and there's a reason for it too.

The first snow. Yet another first snow. I have already written about first snows and the coming of winters. All the scribes have written and are now writing about that nostalgic time between the last rain and the first snow.

But I'm not writing well. The book is wilting and fading in my hands and I hold something almost corpse-like. Time to finish.

At one point I thought that this would not be a wretched repeat of *The Calendar and the Hourglass*. My wit's out of whack. I don't feel like playing the clown. I can't remember any jokes. And I had saved up so many of them to embellish these pages. Not a very merry time. I buried my mother-in-law in the passage between autumn and winter. With great difficulty I found a place for her above my late lamented father-in-law Fredek Lenica's grave, which was covered by a large stone that no craftsman wanted to remove and then replace. But, fortunately, in these chaotic times, in our geographical area there is one hard currency so hard that it does not devaluate. What I'm thinking of is our pure, consoling mother, unrectified spirit, the Polish narcotic which allows us to endure partitions and slavery, hated systems and unwanted friendships. My mother-in-law was buried for half a liter, and then both Danka and I were total orphans. Now it's our turn.

That autumn in the Suwalki region, where witches ride broomsticks and vampires howl in the forests, I was awakened one night by a pain that seemed to be in my stomach or a bit higher. I tuned in to that pain, wondering what it could be. Suddenly I understood. The pain was under my sternum, radiating all the way to my shoulder blades and the small of my back, and that pain throbbed with the sort of powerful spasm that seizes us in a cold brook in the summertime. And I felt a sudden sense of well-being, because that pain was my Curtailer of Torment. That pain presaged a quick and aesthetic death on one day, at one hour that was still ahead of me. I listened to that pain with delight. I already loved it and was grateful to it. My dear friend. My Curtailer of Torment.

All of my life that is now behind me was one great waiting. Waiting for luck, adventure, good fortune, the unknown and the unfamiliar, new love and new landscapes, artificial successes and real defeats, for the good God and for furious demons.

Now I begin the Great Nonwaiting. Though, to tell the truth, I began it on the sly quite a while ago. In my life everything happened too early. And God be praised for that.

What's going on here? This plaintive tone disgusts me. This tearful pathos worthy of a true priest of literature. This sublimity of an old man who wants attention at any price. What's going on here?

Night. I'm by myself. My cat Ivan, who's been called Lech for a while now, comes right over to me. My daughters started calling him Lech and claim that this took a great weight off his chest. Night, whiteness, snow. Not late at night, when my neighbors turn up the volume on their radio all the way and start doing the housework. This is the romantic part of the night. When dogs used to bark in the distance. When the footsteps of people long dead would begin to be heard in the depths of a house. The hour when what used to be our hearts beat violently.

What's going on here? For months I have not set out in memory on any distant journey to Wilno, to the Wilno Colony, to Nowa Wilejka. Once it gave me a painful joy to use my imagination to wander down Subocz Street, then turn near Pushkin Hill toward Markucie. Or to dash headlong down a forest path from the Upper Colony to my house, which fidgeted in the sand of Dolna Street like an old hen.

What's going on here? I've forgotten my youth. I can't remember my childhood. And on sleepless nights I have no desire to run around a dead Wilno, a lifeless Colony, a rotting Nowa Wilejka.

What's going on here? I've started having dreams like I used to fifty years ago, in prehistoric times, when I spent my vacations in Bujwidze. Yesterday I dreamed that I was traveling to Moscow, actually to someplace outside Moscow. I was trying to get there,

I had some vague business to take care of, I had even found a taxi, but someone had greater need of it, so I let him have it and then set off on foot toward the city, a little lost, following the sun because I thought I was on the northwest side of the Soviet metropolis. I walked straight ahead, passing through sunny valleys where shadowy brooks flowed, dammed up in places, and I saw farms, clusters of trees, and everything was to my liking. I went into a house. An older man with a professorial goatee spoke to me politely in Russian when I asked for directions. He came outside with me to show me the way, and then he spoke in Polish, pure Polish, as if emboldened by our intimacy on that empty country road. I wanted to repay the favor and began telling him the news from Poland, various uncensored bits and pieces, but he said that he was well aware of all that and not interested. I lingered there outside Moscow for part of the night or—if the scientists would prefer—for a few instants in the pre-dawn hours and then returned to Poland and my little den on Gorska Street.

What's going on here? This is the first time in my life I have described an actual dream for its own sake. In my novels I have from time to time yielded to such tricks to help me earn my bread. I related fictitious and highly literary hallucinations of the night in order to speed things up and add some mystery to an anemic epic. Now, for the first time in my life, I have acted like a genuine literary old lady who gets pleasure from recording her nightmares on the elegant pages of her diaries, journals, and notebooks. What's going on here?

After all, it is generally known that I am a man distinguished by his innate modesty. For that reason I will allow myself to boast for a passing moment. For a while now I've noticed that whoever associates with me, whoever spends time in my company, whoever gets a place in my court, quickly rises to a higher order of humanity, seems to enter a higher intellectual or artistic level, becomes someone, a VIP in our coarse-cut society. That's my charisma at work; the power of my magical personality is such that I lend luster to common eaters of rationed bread.

In my presence many a scoundrel has taken on the manners of a classical writer, a father of the nation, a demiurge.

I don't know if I've already mentioned this or not: just after *The Calendar and the Hourglass* appeared, Jerzy Putrament was on some television show and, in reference to the stormy book fair that year, was asked what he thought about my new work. Putrament reflected for a moment, then said curtly and irritably: You know, Konwicki pretends to be poorer than he is, *pribednayetsya*, as the Russians say. Peel a few layers off him and then you'll see what he's really about.

There's a dream worthy of a Chekist. To peel some rotten bastard's hide.

A woman called from my publisher and said: "I'm doing a little note on you for a book of yours we're reissuing. I read in a biographical dictionary of writers of the fifties that you come from a working-class background. Have there been any changes since then?"

Nothing's changed was my reply. Even though a few times I had the urge to follow in the footsteps of many people I know and pretend to be an aristocrat, or at least a member of the modest Wilno landed gentry.

I don't know why, but I went through my papers and got out the only photograph of my father that still exists, thanks to my cousin Jadzia. Once again I looked at that person whom I never knew, but I cannot say that with every fiber of my being I feel a kinship with that man along in years who has a firm jaw, a small mustache, and some sort of typical proletarian haircut parted down the middle. That old man died when he was fifty-three, and so I am two years older than he; he's younger than I and would have to show me respect as his elder were he suddenly to be resurrected.

People always used to tell me that he was a good, honest man. That was wonderful to hear, but now it doesn't matter what he was like. A half century has passed since his death. I know that he was once alive. Now no one but me is aware that he ever existed. That he appeared in this vale of tears because of a whim on the part of another man, now entirely forgotten; that he studied the trade of metalworker, worked his whole life in Nowa Wilejka, whose history has been wiped off the face of Central Europe, married Jadwiga Sniezko née Kiezun, had a son by her, and died soon thereafter of tuberculosis. That's all there is.

Or maybe not. He secretly roams the pages of his son's novels, books which are also dying, one after the other, of galloping consumption.

My mother, Jadwiga, also deserves a modest epitaph here. As I remember, my mother never had a house of her own, a permanent residence, a job, a favorite neighborhood, or even a trunk.

My mother was on the road and in poor health all her life. Sick and traveling. Six months with her brother, nine months with her cousin, the summer with her cousin, the winter with her nephews. My mother loved to visit. My mother loved to kibitz. To give advice, to admire, to lend a hand. And, from time to time, actually quite often, to attend banquets. Meaning to sit at the head of the table and cut a brilliant figure.

But that brilliance, that provincial glamour, those backwater aristocratic ways were never directed against the rest of the table, never endangered anyone, and were never used to humiliate even the most abject creature taking part in the conversation. My mother liked to shine just for the sake of shining. She loved the process of shining without any ulterior motives.

She was constantly ill, meaning that she cultivated the life of a person who was ill. She took powders, drank compounds, applied compresses. She moaned, she groaned, she sighed. She talked about her colic, migraines, heartburn, aches, asthma, agues, shortness of breath, blurred vision, and chest pains. And thus she lived to the age of seventy-eight.

In my entire life, not counting my infancy, I spent maybe a year, maybe a year and a half, under the same roof as my mother.

Of all the people I knew, it was my mother I knew least. Even though I have her blood, her hair and eye color, her forehead, her nose, her squat Tatar-Slav build, and her fondness for kibitzing.

After 1956 she came to see me in Warsaw from her kolkhoz outside Nowa Wilejka. She spent some time with me; she flew around the city, visited churches, worried over me a little, then left to see her sister on the Baltic coast. When I sent her some money to pay for her expenses there, she immediately spent it on presents and left for her kolkhoz outside Nowa Wilejka. And when I forwarded my advance on the Russian edition of *A Dreambook for Our Time* to her in Nowa Wilejka, she at once bought presents, got on a train, and before you knew it she was in Warsaw.

My mother loved being the *grande dame*. But not in the social sense, not at anyone's expense, or by hurting anyone. What she loved was being the *grande dame* in terms of psychology. She did not like taking, her desire was to give. Never eager to eat her fill, she liked to feed.

Now I can see that my daughter Marysia walks the same way my mother did, she has the same fine profile, she also likes staying with people and ministering to her unending and complicated illnesses and ailments.

I woke up after eight on Sunday. My wife came in and said that something had happened, because she caught the tail end of Premier Jaruzelski's speech on the radio. He had said some strange things, and then the national anthem was played. He must have proclaimed martial law.

Go on, I said. How could it be martial law? The Parliament hasn't passed the law for that yet. But I reached for the phone to call Andrzej Mandalian, who for a few years now has had to be my replacement for Dygat. But there was no dial tone. Dead. I quickly turned on the television, looking for cosmic order, that's all.

Martial law. Martial law in the middle of a Europe that is

stuffed, satiated, slightly drugged, rampant with unprecedented affluence. Dead telephones, government agencies closed, unions, associations, institutions disbanded, airports shut down, long-distance bus service canceled, leaving the city for the nearby villages and towns prohibited, impossible to move about the streets.

Soldiers everywhere. Frozen stiff, gruff, bottom-of-the-barrel poor. Inert armored trucks. Below zero, newly fallen snow, thin ice underfoot. A rink. The Polish Ice Capades.

In good faith. Someone had put up posters for the Ice Capades during the night. Advertisements for the sole innocent form of entertainment, the only one that creates no associations—the Polish Ice Capades.

The authorities have their hands at the nation's throat. But the people have the authorities by the balls. Both sides are equally strong and equally weak. No one will win. They'll drag each other to the bottom.

Mother of God, how many times does this make? How many times have I seen a rabbit-quick hour of greatness followed by years of weeping, misery, and decline? A moment of peacock splendor for the men rising to do battle, and then decades of hard labor for the women running to prisons, bringing their men packages and warm underwear, caring for sick fugitives, and accompanying those fleeing the country to the border. A beautiful iridescent flare and years of icy Arctic nights. Mother of God.

I took off my clothes to go to bed. Meaning I put on a thick undershirt, flannel pajamas, an enormous peasant-wool sweater, my wool robe, and I hopped into bed.

I covered myself with a quilt and a blanket on top of that, and that's just right. Now I can sleep.

What'll happen in a month when the coal runs out?

Why am I writing this? Where can I stow this decrepit manuscript? Who'll want to retype it? What publisher will bring itself to publish it?

. . .

The words have no meaning, the sentences have no meaning, the gripping, dramatic scenes have no meaning. White pages marred with little black worms of letters. Life has no meaning. Death has no meaning.

It's shameful to write at a time like this. I should stop, but I need a concluding note. All right then, let's end our acquaintance without a concluding note. See you in the next world.

Will I make it to that next and better world? Won't I be outscrambled by my more nimble colleagues, who worked in advance to win God's good opinion? Too many question marks. A manly, dignified style will not tolerate excessive punctuation. Punctuation marks are a sign of lost virility.

Here I am, moaning and groaning, and I haven't said so much as a word about the fact that a few days ago I was at the Mostowski Palace, Warsaw civilian police headquarters. I'd been called in for questioning, and when it was over they proposed I sign a loyalty oath. That would be nothing to write about, it's too run-of-the-mill. But, in the hallway, its stone floor caked with winter mud, on those hospital-like stairs, in those Kafkaesque corridors, I met a person whom in Godlike fashion I had created a few years back.

I was questioned and tenderly probed by Tadzio from A *Minor Apocalypse*, that youthful old man or that old youth who follows the hero and spies on him. That poet, a Security man from a remote province who adores the narrator and quotes from his prose as if it were Mickiewicz's *Forefathers' Eve*. That sleek and painstakingly created literary figure had suddenly sprung to life before my very eyes one December day in martial-law Warsaw.

It almost knocked me off my feet, I almost fell over backward from the shock of it. He could see my astonishment, which gladdened him like a good deed. Shaken and proud, I rubbed my eyes, while he laughed, trying to suppress his roguish, affectionate, intimate laughter.

He showed me to his office, or the room he used for questioning, the way a nephew welcomes an uncle to his home. He calmed and consoled me, amused me, praised me, was concerned about me, and tried to cheer me up.

Then we spent an hour in intimate communion. I was representing the superior—to use Gombrowicz's classification—while he was modest inferiority. I was the father, the uncle, the baronet, while he was the cousin, the illegitimate son, a mere footman. We debated about life, morality, and politics. I instructed him, I preached to him. I spoke to him from on high, and he imbibed my teachings, agreeing to them, praising them. Still, I think he was bored at the end. I'm gnawed by a vague suspicion that I bored Tadzio from *A Minor Apocalypse*. Yes, I'm even certain that he kept glancing desperately at the door, that he was fidgeting in his chair and couldn't wait for my lecture to end. Oh, God, I botched everything. I ruined a lovely metaphor. I was agonizingly boring to a person who was my own creation.

I can give my word of honor on this. That Security officer, or perhaps he was just a noncom, is my work. It was I who invented his every feature in late 1977, early 1978, while lying in my little den, at my wit's end, rotting away, infuriated. I fashioned his fragile body, breathed a complicated soul into it, then added various physical and psychological traits, seasoning him with ambiguity, careful metaphysics, and perhaps with my own affection as well. I pampered him, and now he's working at Warsaw headquarters, another product stamped out by my imagination.

Yes, *A Minor Apocalypse* has come true and will continue to, decade after decade, because its seams, cracks, and fissures still contain enormous reserves of ill omens, prophecies of doom, presentiments of disaster.

No, no, no. We'll be saved by a miracle. The latest real miracle. Poland lives on miracles. To exist, other countries need good borders, sensible alliances, disciplined societies, but a decent miracle will do us just fine. Every half century, a good solid miracle bordering on the unmiraculous. I don't know yet when it will happen, but I do know that it will. An unprecedented coincidence, an astonishing alignment of the planets, or a gust from a gale in the depths of the universe. That miracle will nourish us with divine ectoplasm for the next fifty years. And then we'll see.